Echoes from the Mist

Blayne Cooper

RENAISSANCE ALLIANCE PUBLISHING, INC.
Nederland, Texas

ISBN 1-930928-78-5

First Printing 2002

9 8 7 6 5 4 3 2 1

Cover design by Linda Callaghan

Published by:

Renaissance Alliance Publishing, Inc.
PMB 238, 8691 9th Avenue
Port Arthur, Texas 77642-8025

Find us on the World Wide Web at
http://www.rapbooks.biz

Printed in the United States of America

Acknowledgments:

To Alison Carpenter, Barbara Davies, and Judith Kuwatch—
your assistance was invaluable. To the friends who offered sug-
gestions, opinions, and support—as always, thank you. Bob, I
can always count on you. I love you.

— Blayne Cooper

To the most underrated and awesome holiday of them all: Halloween. The one, lonely day each year when the line between the living and the dead blurs, when ghouls and goblins lurk in shadowy hiding places, just waiting for you to walk by, and when the chill that runs down your spine just might be more than the autumn breeze. God, does it get any better than that?

Chapter
One

Olivia Hazelwood jumped down from the bus steps and was immediately greeted by a blast of cool, fresh air. "At last," she muttered to herself as she drew in a deep, cleansing breath. The air in the double-decker coach had been chilly but stifling, filled with so much cigarette smoke she was sure she'd shortened her life by at least ten years on the all night ride from London to Edinburgh.

Liv stepped away from the parked vehicle to allow the other passengers to move past her. Each one was sticking their hands in their pockets for warmth as they waited for the driver to make his way around to the side of the bus and open the luggage bin. A pair of warm hands landed on her shoulders, and Liv spoke without turning around, identifying their owner through touch alone as her eyes sought out their bags. "Remind me again why we did this." A not-so-subtle twitch of her shoulders earned her a slightly exasperated chuckle and a brief, but satisfying, massage.

"Maybe you're just too old for travel, Liv."

"Very funny, smart-ass."

"Tsk. Such language from one of my elders."

"Hey!" Her green eyes flashed, but in good humor. "I won't be thirty for a few more weeks, and that's only..." She scowled as she calculated. *Five years? Ugh.* "Older, okay? Dougie told you to tease me about that, didn't he?" She'd seen her teenage brother talking to Kayla in the airport before they left Washington, D.C., their heads tilted together in a conspiratorial fashion. "Tell me."

A worried look flickered across Kayla's face. "I would never betray a confidence," she answered seriously.

Kayla's tone instantly stopped Liv's teasing. "I know you wouldn't," she assured, patting the solid body next to her with a

gentle hand. *I keep forgetting she doesn't spend time around people very often. She doesn't always realize when I'm playing...yet.*
Liv glanced at her watch. "Looks like we're going to make our
morning meeting. Though I feel incredibly grungy and disgusting, and might offend your client."

"Our client." Kayla leaned down and whispered in Liv's ear,
"And you always look beautiful."

Liv smiled and reached up to squeeze the long fingers still
resting on her shoulder. "Flattery will get you everywhere, my
dear." She yawned. "I still can't believe all the early morning
flights here were booked, and there were no seats on the train."

Kayla sighed. "The airport construction isn't helping. I tried
to reschedule the meeting for this afternoon, but...um...apparently
our new client is leaving town today and doesn't intend to return
until we're finished looking around and have some answers."

Liv swallowed. "He's leaving because of something in the
house?"

"Maybe," Kayla answered honestly. She was about to say
more, when the driver carelessly tossed their bags on the ground
in front of them. "Hey, watch it! I have a camera in there."

The driver grumbled something obscene about Yank tourists
as he slammed shut the luggage bin and began marching up the
street, intent on having his early morning cup of coffee in peace.

"Who does he think he's calling a Yankee?" Kayla drawled.
She grabbed both bags and handed the smaller one to Liv.

Wordlessly, both women unzipped their bags, pulled out
sweatshirts, and tugged them over their heads.

Liv yawned again. "I bet we get sick." She helped Kayla pull
her long, dark-red hair free of the sweatshirt's collar.

"Why would we go and do something stupid like that?"
Kayla began edging her way towards the sidewalk, a tiny gleam in
her eyes.

Liv shook her head. Despite spending the entire day before
on a plane and all last night on the bus, her companion was in an
excellent mood. *She's so excited,* Liv thought fondly. To anyone
else, Kayla would have appeared her normal, reticent self. But in
a very short time, Liv had grown quite adept at reading her tall
lover. *Oh, yeah. She's ready for another adventure.* "You're so
excited you're about ready to wet your pants, aren't you?"

Kayla's mouth dropped open, and she stopped moving so that
Liv could move back alongside her. "I certainly am not."

"Uh huh." Liv laughed. "I'm excited, too, Kayla."

She gave her partner a dazzling smile. "Really?"

"Yeah. But...um..."

"You're a little nervous?"

Liv bit her lip and nodded. Working with Kayla researching the paranormal had sounded a lot less daunting when she was back home in the States and not about to face ghosts or spooks or whatever it was they could find. Now she wasn't so sure she was up to the task.

Compassionately, Kayla gazed down at her. "It'll be okay. Remember—"

"I know." Despite her underlying nervousness, Liv couldn't suppress a grin. "Mostly good things happen in the dark." She began ticking off her fingers. "And in the morning. And after-' noon. And outside. And in my truck. And on—"

A dark blush crept up Kayla's neck and she glanced around. She lowered her voice. "Liv."

"Yes?" Liv said innocently, batting her eyelashes.

Kayla's mind went blank for a long second before she remembered something Liv had said right after they arrived. "Why are we going to get sick?"

"Oh, yeah, because of the change in climates, of course. That almost always gives me a cold. It's still a gazillion degrees in Virginia; we were only in London for a few hours, but it already felt like fall there; and it's got to be at least fifteen degrees colder here than in London."

Kayla wrapped her arm around Liv's shoulder. "True." She smiled at the fair-haired woman's pink cheeks and nose. "But I'll keep you warm."

"I'm counting on it." Liv hoisted her bag onto her shoulder and pointed toward the crowd who had disembarked from the bus and were all marching up the street. "I take it we're going to make like sheep and head this way?"

"Come on." Kayla gave Liv a gentle push. "We've got time for some breakfast before our meeting. Up ahead is Princess Street, and I think Burger King will be open at this hour." She debated with herself for a moment before adding, "You should eat more, Liv. You didn't eat dinner last night."

Liv's hackles rose slightly, but she knew that Kayla was right. "When I'm nervous, I lose my appetite. I ate two Snickers on the bus at 2:00 a.m."

"That's healthy."

"Just as healthy as that burger you ate in London. Ever hear of mad cow disease?"

"Yes."

"Mooooooo."

"Ha ha." But Kayla smiled inwardly when she felt the muscles under her hand begin to relax. "How about I tell you a little about what usually happens at these meetings, and then you won't be so nervous?"

Liv wrapped her arm around Kayla's waist and matched her stride to her companion's. She could see a busker standing on the street corner far ahead of them, his bagpipes wailing out into the cool morning air. "It's a deal."

"The Witchery, huh? Cool." Liv used the back of her hand to block the early afternoon sun as she glanced up at the beautiful sixteenth century building. They were at the gates of Edinburgh Castle, at the very top of a downward-slanting street called the Royal Mile—home to dozens of pubs, historical buildings, and colorful shops selling tartans, pure butter shortbread, and souvenirs to eager tourists.

Kayla's gaze flicked to the address she had jotted on a piece of scratch paper the day before, then back up at the restaurant. She closed her eyes. "Oh, shit."

Liv stepped closer to Kayla. "What's the matter? Isn't this the place?"

Kayla winced and nodded weakly.

Just then, a woman in a green silk dress and heels walked out of the restaurant on the arm of a man in a tailored blue suit.

Liv's eyes widened. "Oh, shit." She looked down at her own clothes. "'Don't worry,' you told me. 'We don't need to change clothes or take a shower,' you said." She groaned when another immaculately attired woman exited the building.

I hate meetings. But inwardly Kayla was pleased she didn't have to dig out a suit and go to the trouble of pressing it and finding suitable shoes. "I could have sworn this address was for the pub across the street."

"Do we have time to—"

"Nope." On their trek to the restaurant, they'd decided to stow their bags in lockers at Waverly station so they could wander the streets unencumbered. Kayla had sent her equipment and the rest of their luggage on ahead from Virginia, but it wasn't due to arrive until that afternoon. She wrapped her arm around Liv's. "We're next door to the castle, the biggest tourist attraction in the city. I'm sure this restaurant is just filled with slovenly dressed," she sniffed the air, "slightly ripe travelers."

Liv pressed her nose to her sweatshirt. It smelled like stale cigarettes, with the faintest hint of detergent. "Like us."

"Basically. But it'll be okay." *Glen is going to be so pissed.*

"Okay." She nodded a little. Liv was going to have to trust that Kayla knew what was acceptable within her own circles. Especially since she herself had spent the last two years in the Peace Corps in Africa, wearing jeans, t-shirts, and boots nearly every day. "If you say so." But the slight hesitation in her voice gave away her lingering doubt.

Kayla smiled reassuringly, and without hesitation, bent down and kissed Liv gently on the mouth. She turned her head slightly and pressed her cheek against Liv's. "You've already made a permanently good impression on me, Liv. I have one-hundred percent faith in you," she pulled back and Liv caught sight of twinkling eyes, "with or without clothing. So don't worry so much."

Liv's cheeks colored slightly, and her heart beat a little faster at the unexpectedly romantic gesture. For a moment she was tongue-tied, and she simply looked up at Kayla, her emotions showing clearly on her face.

Ooo, I did something right. "C'mon." Kayla grinned, obscenely pleased by Liv's reaction and glad that she hadn't bothered to think about what she was doing before she did it. *Or else I probably would have been too chicken-shit to do it at all.*

Kayla pulled open the massive wooden door and gave her name to a handsome young man dressed in a tuxedo jacket, bow tie, and kilt. The man smiled at Kayla, then his brows drew together when he realized Liv was with her. He looked down at the clipboard he was carrying.

Liv began to fidget as she watched the host and Kayla engage in a quiet discussion about something. After a moment, the man smiled and motioned Liv to join them. They were led through a small hallway to a courtyard that was hidden from the street. A long, steep, stone staircase later, and they were in a large, well-lit room called The Secret Garden.

"Oh, wow," Liv mumbled to Kayla as they followed the host. "I thought you said this job would require roughing it. Please, make me rough it some more. Next you'll be forcing champagne and massages on me, you brute."

Kayla laughed and shook her head, shifting a shock of hair the color of a rich red wine over her shoulder. The room was magnificent, looking like an urn-filled terrace. Flowers were everywhere, their heady scent perfuming the air and mingling with the aroma of fresh-baked bread. The ceiling was painted with images from the tarot, and included a happy, very chubby cherub playing the bagpipes. "Trust me, this has never happened before. The last business meeting I had was held in a Kentucky Fried Chicken in

Mexico City."

They were seated in a corner of the room and given a wine list to examine while they waited for the rest of their party. Kayla looked at the list and frowned. She'd never acquired a taste for the drink. "What do you know about wine, Liv?"

Liv shrugged lightly, relieved that no one seemed to care what they were wearing and pleased that she had a moment alone with Kayla before their meeting began. "One glass makes me chatty, two glasses make me chatty *and* horny, and after three glasses you'll have to carry me out." She smiled charmingly, the gesture wrinkling her nose. "Did you have something in mind?"

"Ale." Kayla grinned and made a mental note to pick up a bottle of whatever wine Liv liked on their way to the bed and breakfast after the meeting. Her attention suddenly drifted from Liv's face towards the stairs and her grin broadened, showing off even white teeth. Her hand shot up and she gave a wave. "There she is."

Liv turned around to see a very striking woman animatedly speaking with a rail-thin man, who was nearly bald except for a longish chunk of silver hair that was combed over the top of his head in a ridiculous attempt to hide its shiny surface. He walked with a cane.

When Kayla looked at her business associate, Glen, her eyes conveyed a warmth that Liv had never seen directed towards anyone but her, or perhaps Marcy, Kayla's younger sister. She felt a pang of jealousy that she knew was irrational. *Not nice,* she chided herself. *You've just never seen her with a friend before.*

The dark-haired woman stood up to greet their tablemates. She towered over both of them. "It's been a while, Glen."

"Hello, Kayla." Glen Fuguchi was at least two inches shy of Liv's five-and-a-half feet. Her hair was long and a glossy black, pulled back in a gold clasp that rested at the base of her neck. Her skin was as flawless as fine porcelain.

Glen raised an inquiring eyebrow at Liv, but quickly dismissed her and focused on Kayla, who she pulled into a quick hug. "What in the hell are you wearing?" she whispered harshly into the ear next to her lips. Kayla's body shook with silent chuckles. "Don't you laugh. You're here to make a good impression." Backing away, she placed a kiss on Kayla's cheek and said brightly, "It's been too long, Kayla." Her voice held the barest hint of a Japanese accent.

"It has," Kayla agreed earnestly, oblivious to Glen's appreciative gaze raking down her body. Baggy sweatshirt or no, Kayla was a beautiful woman.

The hair on the back of Liv's neck stood on end. *You are...okay,* were *a helluva lot more than business associates.* She fought the urge to wrap her arm around Kayla's waist and growl, "Mine." Grudgingly, however, she admitted that that was probably not a very mature response. Maybe later she could just trip her on the way out instead. *God, Kayla, Glen looks twelve friggin' years old! Shouldn't she be in homeroom right now?*

"Kayla Redding, this is Mr. Robert Keith, the client I spoke with you about."

"Mr. Keith," Kayla acknowledged, reaching out and shaking his hand firmly.

The man smiled engagingly as he pumped her hand. His hair shook along with his body, and he reached up and lifted his hair back into place. "I can't tell you how pleased I am to meet you. I wanted the best," he puffed up his narrow chest a little, "and here you are, just as Ms. Fuguchi promised."

He looked at Liv, who was now on her feet alongside Kayla and waiting patiently. "And you are?"

Kayla mentally kicked herself for her lack of manners. *No wonder I pay Glen to take care of this part of the business.* "This is my new business partner, Olivia Hazelwood. She's a linguist from Virginia, and someone who is going to be an invaluable asset to this and all our future projects."

Liv felt a jolt of happiness at Kayla's words. It was *almost* enough to make Liv forgive Kayla for not telling her she and Glen had been involved romantically.

Glen's dark eyes widened almost imperceptibly. "Partner?" she said quietly, hoping she didn't sound as surprised as she felt.

She doesn't know? Liv slowly turned to Kayla and glared. *You are so dead, Ghostbuster.*

Kayla swallowed. "She sure is." The tall woman took Liv's hand and gave it an affectionate squeeze. *Fuck.*

Liv squeezed back. Hard.

Double fuck.

Glen's expression went a little cold. "How nice for you. Shall we sit?" She gestured towards their seats.

Robert Keith immediately slumped into his chair with a sigh of relief. He propped his cane against the wall behind him.

Glen and Kayla remained standing. Their faces were impassive, but Liv could see by the rigid set of her lover's shoulders that something wordless was passing between her and Glen. *Another telepath, perhaps?* she wondered silently, a little surprised by how quickly she was starting to accept certain things that only days before she would have declared impossible.

Kayla's research had begun with the study of her own family's highly evolved set of paranormal gifts. And although the Reddings' phenomenal paranormal attributes had been diluted over the centuries, she herself had considerable telepathic abilities.

It was wholly by accident that the women had discovered that Liv, too, had heightened telepathic skills. Though Liv hadn't even known that about herself. And for whatever reason, each woman brought out these talents in the other. A small part of Liv wondered how much that had to do with the bone-deep, almost innate attraction they had for each other. She regarded Kayla carefully: the sculpted planes of her face, the sensuous curve of red lips, the penetrating intelligence that shone so clearly in those pale blue eyes. *No,* she thought a little dreamily. *She would have had my heart in any case. But I'm still going to kill her.*

A long moment passed while Mr. Keith busied himself with the wine list and menu, then Kayla and Glen took their seats and the Scotsman launched into a detailed diatribe. He ended by saying, "I awoke from a sound sleep wi' chills racin' through my body, and saw blood dripping down the bedroom wall in front of me."

Their first course was nearly over when Kayla quietly put down her fork, looked Mr. Keith in the eye, and asked, "Are you on any medication?"

"Kayla!" Glen cried. "She's joking, Mr. Keith. Truly." Glen's voice was sharp. "Explain that you're just teasing, Kayla." She plastered on a smile as she patted Robert's bony hand. "Americans have such an odd sense of humor, don't you think? Of course, we believe you. Why don't you go over a few more of the specifics?"

Liv went a little pale at the thought of Mr. Keith going into more detail about what had supposedly happened in his house. She subtly pushed away her plate of sweet potato and apple gallette and reached for her water.

Kayla tossed her napkin onto the table. "Glen."

"What happened is clearly not unheard of," Glen said calmly. Her eyes flashed another warning to Kayla, while her voice remained as smooth as silk.

"I know it's hard to believe, Ms. Redding," Robert broke in, willing to do whatever it took to convince her. He paused for a moment while their dishes were cleared and an enormous plate of steak tartare and fried quail's eggs was placed in front of him.

Liv smiled her thanks at the waiter who set down her seafood pie and Kayla's wild mushroom tart.

Glen appeared content to acquire her calories in the form of a very expensive bottle of wine, courtesy of their new client.

Liv's eyes narrowed. *Maybe she's a vampire. They don't eat at all.*

When the wait staff retreated, Mr. Keith leaned towards Kayla and with a deadly serious expression said, "I know what I saw. And now, thanks to my blabbermouth cook, so do the papers. It wasn't a delusion," he said, sounding a little insulted. "I'm sure it was all a hoax." He waved his hand dismissively. "And I don't want all of Edinburgh thinking I'm prone to hallucinations, now do I?" His jaw jutted defiantly, as if he had just made everything clear and it was up to Kayla to draw her own conclusions.

Which were that Mr. Keith was probably drunk at the time.

"Mr. Keith is a very respected member of the community and the City Council," Glen added for Kayla's benefit. Throughout lunch, she had managed to ignore Liv's presence almost entirely. Though, to her annoyance, Mr. Keith seemed intent on addressing both Liv and Kayla when he spoke. "His reputation is above reproach, and he's hired us to confirm that there is nothing haunted about his house."

"This is a matter for the police, Glen, not me. If someone was trying to frighten you—"

Robert shook his head emphatically. "Absolutely not. I intend to open my home as an inn next month. The damage is already done. My housekeeper handed in her notice the very morning she walked into my bedroom and saw me...well, in my state of surprise and fright." He looked a little shamefaced, deciding they didn't need to know about his soiled sheets. "When I told her what I'd seen, she quit on the spot. She wouldn't even collect her parting wages in person. Her daughter, the uppity thing, said for me to post them to her!"

"An article quoting the cook appeared in the next day's papers, claiming Mr. Keith's house was possessed by an evil, potentially deadly spirit," Glen said conversationally, refilling her glass. "I've already interviewed her and her daughter. Besides Mr. Keith, they were the only other people who lived in the house. They don't have anything to add that we can't get straight from the source."

"That's right," Mr. Keith huffed, before taking another bite. "And that's why I hired you and Ms. Fuguchi. I've done my research, and know you are both very well respected within the scientific community. I specifically requested you over several other paranormal researchers with whom Ms. Fuguchi works. People will believe what you say." *And you're young and pretty and would surely make the papers and local news bulletins.*

Kayla's brow furrowed as Mr. Keith's thoughts began roughly taking shape in her head. She didn't have a word for word understanding of his mental musings, but she caught snippets and impressions and a few odd words, processing them all in the blink of an eye. Kayla all but sneered at her new employer. *News bulletins? Like hell. And why was Glen interviewing the residents of Mr. Keith's home? She didn't work in the field. Ever.*

"So you want us to make sure that everyone knows there's nothing spooky or paranormal about your house that would frighten away potential guests?" Liv asked Mr. Keith, unable to sit quietly by for another second.

"Hardly," he snorted, bony fingers smoothing down his wool, regimental necktie. "Specters and spooks are a big part of Edinburgh's history and continued economic success, Ms. Hazelwood. A few of those never hurt any inn's business. And my home has been host to its share of minor hauntings over the years, as is the case with nearly any self-respecting, authentic structure in Old Town." He leaned back in his chair and took a healthy bite of his lunch.

Worried green eyes glanced at her in question, but the look on the younger woman's face reassured her lover. Kayla was happier than ever that she had made arrangements for her and Liv's accommodations away from Old Town.

Liv let out a shaky breath, saying a quick mental thank you. The house on Cobb Island loomed very fresh in her memory, and she wasn't quite sure she wanted to relive that experience so soon. *But that's what Kayla does all the time, right? You don't see her complaining. She loves her job. And you haven't given it a chance. So stop bein' such a baby.*

Mr. Keith tore off a piece of bread from a loaf that sat in the center of the table and used the chunk to sop up the juices and blood from his steak tartare. He popped the sodden treat into his mouth.

Liv looked down at her food to block out the vile image. Kayla's lips formed a thin line, and even Glen began to resettle her napkin in her lap rather than watch Mr. Keith eat.

A forkful of seafood pie was nearly to Liv's lips, when Mr. Keith piped up, "But there's a fine line between healthy fun and having rivers of blood running down the walls, wouldn't you agree, Ms. Hazelwood?"

Liv sighed. Her stomach churned and she nodded her agreement, officially giving up on lunch. "No...er...I'm pretty certain that would not be a good thing."

The man grunted his approval over Liv's answer and turned

to Kayla, who was trying to get a few bites down while he was talking. "I expect that you'll confirm the existence of something otherworldly, preferably having to do with the body snatchers, Burke and Hare, or perhaps medieval witchcraft. But nothing evil, and certainly *nothing* that could be physically dangerous."

Kayla's blood began to boil. Glen had some serious explaining to do. This man didn't want a real scientific explanation, he wanted something to put on his brochures for the tourists. She was about to say as much when Mr. Keith added, "Scary sells. Evil repels. But what I saw was clearly the work of something terribly wicked."

Liv and Kayla sat silently in the back seat of the taxi that sped its way down Portobello High Street. The blonde woman's forehead rested against the window as she watched the houses and shops fly by. Portobello, which was only a few miles from the heart of Edinburgh, dated back to the eighteenth century and was a popular seaside resort. By the early part of the nineteenth century, however, it had been annexed by Edinburgh and was now considered a sleepy hamlet of the city. A bit rundown, it still had its own brand of charm.

Kayla's eyes closed as she contemplated this assignment and Liv. She sighed. Liv hadn't said a single word since they'd left The Witchery. *Not that I have to ask but...* "Are you mad at me?"

Liv reached up with one hand and rubbed her temple, pressing against the throbbing pain that had developed there. "Yes, but I'm mostly tired, Kayla."

Oh, boy. Kayla tapped the driver's shoulder, and he wordlessly pulled over and accepted several crinkled bills from her outstretched hand.

The women collected their bags from the front seat, and began walking downhill along a short road that dead-ended at the beach. The temperature had dropped throughout the day, and a cold wind was blowing in from the gray sea, which was visible several hundred yards away. The sun was gone, and a blanket of heavy, dark clouds had settled so low to the ground that Kayla imagined she could feel their weight on her shoulders.

Liv adjusted her bag over her shoulder and stuffed her hands into her pockets for warmth. She could taste the salt of the ocean on the back of her tongue. "I never realized we were so close to the water," she said absently. "Tomorrow, I think I should buy a jacket. I should have thought to bring one."

"Hold up." Kayla placed her hand on Liv's forearm to stop

her stride.

It didn't work.

"Hey." Kayla took several quick steps and moved directly in front of Liv to block her path. "Liv, please."

Liv let out an explosive breath and reluctantly stopped. A gust of wind sent her shoulder-length hair into disarray, and Kayla found herself wanting to reach out and smooth down fair bangs.

"What?" Liv asked, her frustration from lunch returning with a vengeance.

"I'm sorry."

"Okay." The word was pronounced precisely. She shifted her bag higher on her shoulder and, cocking her head slightly to the side, looked Kayla dead in the eye. "Anything else?"

Kayla blinked a few times. "Uh...I guess not."

"Let's go then."

Kayla visibly relaxed. That was easier than she'd expected. "Great." She scrubbed her face and exhaled a long, deep breath. "That's great. I was afraid you were really—"

Liv silently walked around Kayla and headed down the street, checking the address plates mounted on each of the old Victorian houses as she moved past them.

Two deep red eyebrows disappeared behind equally dark bangs as Kayla eyed Liv's retreating form. *Okay, it's not that easy.* She jogged until she had caught up with Liv and was padding alongside her. "I said I was sorry."

Silence.

Kayla threw her hands in the air, her own frustration boiling over. "But you're still mad?"

"It would seem so." Liv's voice was flat as she continued to hunt for their bed and breakfast, suddenly longing for the tacky but highly effective neon signs that signaled motels back home.

"I don't know what else you want me to say."

Liv came to a sudden halt at the undertone of uncertainty in Kayla's voice. "How about an explanation, Kayla? Why didn't you tell your friend that we were going to work together? That's seems like sort of a big thing to forget about. And it would have been nice to know I was having lunch with one of your old lovers."

Kayla blinked. "How did you—"

"I'm not a moron." Liv could see Kayla was painfully adrift. "That made me feel really lousy. Like some sort of unimportant afterthought." Her voice cracked on the last word, and she knew that her emotions were starting to get a little out of control. Her headache was getting worse, and she was overtired and hungry.

Blue eyes went round with sudden worry. "I...I..."

You're freaking her out. Liv winced. *Just talk about it later, when you're not spoiling for an argument.* "Look, it's not that big of a deal. You apologized. I'll get over it."

Kayla couldn't think of anything to say, so she reached out and slipped Liv's bag off her shoulder, rubbing the spot where the strap had been. She slung it over her own shoulder where her bag was resting, and gestured towards the pale yellow, three-story home just to their right. "This is it," she said softly.

A tiny smile edged its way onto Liv's face despite her foul mood. "It's lovely."

Kayla nodded quickly, eager to grab on to anything positive. "See the little garden." She pointed. "And they have a sunroom around back where they grow herbs and flowers, and a patio right on the sand. The owners are really great, too. I've stayed here several times. It's close to downtown, but..." She looked around, at a loss for words.

"It feels different," Liv finished Kayla's thought seamlessly.

"Yeah." Kayla's face relaxed into a smile. "More cheerful."

"I can see that." *She's really trying. God, I love her.*

Not five minutes later, after a short but warm greeting by the owners, Kayla was turning the key to their room. They were on the second floor, and she had specifically asked for the room whose large window faced the beach. She loved breathing in the crisp ocean air as she slept, and was secretly looking forward to snuggling up with Liv in the room's small, but comfortable, double bed.

"Oh, Kayla." The room was decorated in a delicate floral-pattern of ivory and pink. It was cozy and painfully clean, the large windows and high ceiling giving it an airy quality that most rooms its size couldn't pull off. "It's beautiful." *And not scary and dark in any way.* "I..." Liv's words trailed off when her eyes strayed to the bedside table.

Lying across a box of milk chocolates, Liv's favorites, was a single orchid.

Kayla bit her lip and waited.

You little sneak. Liv sat down on the bed and opened the box of candy, releasing the delightful scent of chocolate into the air. She all but swooned. Then she brought the fragrant bloom to her nose and sniffed appreciatively. "This was the phone call you made at the restaurant, wasn't it?"

Near the end of their meal, Liv had excused herself to go to the ladies room. When she returned to their table, Mr. Keith and Glen were already gone and Kayla was just hanging up her cell

phone. She'd been so angry with her that she hadn't even bothered to ask what the call was about.

"I guess...I mean, yes." Kayla shrugged a little sheepishly.
The look on her face reminded Liv very much of a painfully shy
adolescent.

Kayla slowly removed the flower from Liv's fingers and
brushed its elegant petals softly against her cheek, smiling at the
pink blush it left behind. "You see, I've met this wonderful
woman," she quietly confessed, causing Liv's heart to melt a little
more. "And she's all I can think about."

Liv fondly ran her fingers through Kayla's thick hair. "Even
when she's grumpy and acting like a jealous brat?"

"Even then," Kayla said seriously. "Because she does the
same for me." She ducked her head and chuckled to herself. "I'm
not sure about the scientific reasoning behind it—I suspect an evil
combination of adrenaline, hormones, and endorphins—but being
in love has caused a serious lack of blood flow to my brain." She
looked up, then pressed her forehead against Liv's, bridging the
already small distance between them. "There was no sinister reason why I didn't tell you about Glen or vice versa, Liv. The simple
truth is that she never even crossed my mind. It, along with my
heart, has been otherwise engaged. I'm sorry."

"I'm sorry for not accepting your apology earlier." Liv tilted
her chin up and brushed her lips against Kayla's, humming at the
little thrill the contact stirred in her gut. "Mmm... You're getting
much better at this relationship thingie. You've got the making up
nearly down pat, too. And this is really only our second argument." She thought back to the many cross words they'd
exchanged on Cobb Island, then decided those didn't count. She
hadn't really known Kayla then.

Kayla cupped Liv's cheeks, looking deeply into her eyes.
"Thank God." She laughed weakly and flopped back on the fluffy
comforter, feeling utterly drained. "Are you as tired as I am?"

"Am I still awake? I find that hard to believe, considering
how tired I am." A single pale brow arched over a bleary eye, as
Liv plucked a candy from the box and began to chew it with exaggerated slowness. "Oh, God, this is good."

"Yes, you're still awake," Kayla murmured. She gently took
the box from Liv's hands and put it on the nightstand. "But you
don't have to be."

Wordlessly, the women undressed each other, trading kisses
and tender touches that spoke more of love than passion and
tasted faintly of rich milk chocolate. The covers were pulled
down, and they slid beneath the cool sheets. Bare skin met bare

skin, prompting twin sighs as the women rolled onto their sides and Liv snuggled back into Kayla's warm body.

A peaceful sleep stole over them while *two* mysteries, begging to be explored, waited for them across the misty streets of Edinburgh.

Chapter
Two

Kayla's eyelids fluttered open. Sunlight was streaming through the window, painting yellow-gold stripes across the comforter tucked neatly around her and Liv. *It's tomorrow already? Damn. I guess we were beat.* She didn't move a muscle, though, instead deciding to let Liv dictate when they got going this morning. Kayla was rarely awake before the linguist, and she wasn't about to waste this precious time when she could simply hold her and think.

So much had happened in the past few weeks. She had gotten to know her sister better, and their relationship now seemed like that of true siblings and not girls who just happened to live in the same household as children. With the discovery of the missing family history on Cobb Island, she'd been able to make some remarkable leaps forward with her own telepathic abilities. But as important as those things were, they couldn't even begin to touch what she'd found with Liv.

Kayla Redding, child genius, introvert extraordinaire, lonely adolescent and lonelier still adult, had actually fallen in love. It baffled her logical mind even as it thrilled her heart, and she was torn between jumping up and down like a little kid and weeping. It was wonderful and exhilarating and she'd never been so afraid in her entire life. *I will not blow this*, she swore to herself. *I can't. Yesterday was unacceptable. Well, at least part of it.*

Time, she decided, was what she needed most. Time to learn how to be part of a team and consider Liv's feelings. And that, above everything else, was going to be the hardest thing. In her heart of hearts, she wasn't sure she had what it took to really be part of a couple. She'd spent many an hour wondering what exactly would be expected of her and what Liv needed her to be.

Which was funny in a way, because despite the fact that *she* was the experienced telepath and Liv was only on the very edge of understanding her own abilities, the blonde woman had quite easily read Kayla from the very start. Liv had insisted that all she ever wanted from Kayla was for her to be herself. *But that couldn't be enough. Could it?* The concept alone was so alluring, Kayla had a hard time believing it could be true.

Liv mumbled something in her sleep, pulling Kayla from her thoughts. *You,* Kayla smiled wryly, *think too much for your own good. Don't be stupid. Enjoy what you've got this very second.*

They weren't due at the Keith House until later that afternoon. Glen had talked Mr. Keith into delaying his trip out of town in order to hold a lunchtime press conference. Never one to miss a publicity opportunity, Glen intended to announce Kayla's presence and discuss the work she would be doing. Which is why Kayla intended to stay away until well after the media circus was over.

Liv began to stir, and blonde hair tickled Kayla's face as she moved. Kayla exhaled slowly. Today would be a good day. She had a surprise that Liv, okay, that both of them, were going to love.

"Mmm." Liv yawned, but didn't open her eyes. "I feel too good," she muttered. "It must be morning." She felt Kayla nod against her, then reach up and sweep the fair hair from the back of her neck so she could slowly kiss the sensitive skin there. "Oooo, I think, oooo, " Liv purred like a kitten being scratched, "I'd always like to wake up this way." Kayla's nude, warm body spooned tightly against her back.

Kayla skimmed her palm along Liv's bare hip, and with a slight pull, guided her onto her back. She sank onto Liv, feeling the slight chill of the skin that had been facing away from her before. A loving smile curled her lips, and she brushed a tiny speck of sleep from the corner of Liv's eyes. "Morning," she said huskily, her voice rough from lack of use.

"Morning," Liv greeted happily. Her hands slid up Kayla's sides and found their way into her hair. She threaded her fingers through the heavy locks and gently tugged, bringing Kayla's head closer for a soft, heartfelt, good morning kiss.

"Morning." Kayla used the tip of her tongue to carefully trace Liv's lower lip, listening excitedly for the low growl of desire she knew would follow.

She wasn't disappointed.

Liv's heart began to pound and she instinctively deepened the kiss, swirling her tongue around her partner's. She could feel

Kayla's nipples grow hard against her own chest as their breathing became more ragged with every passing second. They parted briefly, and Kayla looked down at Liv with hooded eyes. "You are so beautiful," she whispered fervently. "I love you."

A warm wave of emotion and desire crashed over Liv. "I love you, too." She surged up and crushed her lips against Kayla's, allowing all the passion and devotion she felt in her heart to bubble to the surface as she kissed Kayla for all she was worth. A deep groan of approval tickled her ears.

Unfortunately, so did the alarm clock.

Kayla didn't break the kiss. Instead, she began ineffectually swatting at the box with one hand.

Liv finally pulled away, laughing. "I don't remember setting that." Her body was still thrumming with excitement and she didn't want to let Kayla go, but the larger woman was on the verge of smashing the clock to bits. She wondered if she should care.

Kayla finally managed to hit the right button, and without blinking an eye, moved her lips to Liv's tender throat where she began a series of slow, steady kisses down her body.

"Ooo." Liv closed her eyes in pure pleasure. "That's a most excellent idea." She was suddenly finding it very hard to concentrate on anything but the mouth that was nibbling its way between her breasts. But she did manage to ask, "Who...who set the..." Liv gasped and arched upward when Kayla's tongue brushed against her nipple, circling it slowly before it was enveloped by a very hot mouth. "Yes... God, that's so good," she moaned.

Kayla propped herself up on one elbow and stroked Liv's thigh with her fingertips, smiling at the state her lover was in and how quickly she was able to get her there. "Oof!" With a quick jerk on Kayla's elbow, Liv sent her sprawling back on top of her.

Both women burst out laughing.

"Demanding little thing, aren't you?" Kayla said, as she nuzzled the underside of the breast she'd just been suckling.

"You started it," Liv snorted. "And if you don't finish it, I'll be forced to kill you and then you can haunt this bed."

"Just the bed?"

"Mmm hmm."

Their mouths came together again in a smoldering kiss that lasted forever. Finally, hungry lips began to drift southward. Kayla spoke against heated flesh. "Mrs. Thicke does it for me."

Liv barely heard the words over the loud rushing of hot blood as it coursed through her veins. Her center was throbbing so painfully that she was sure that its pounding was audible. "Who? What are...you talking about? She turns you on?" *Not another girlfriend!*

Kayla smiled. "The proprietress here." Her hand glided down Liv's body and languidly traced its curves with loving detail. *I could do this all day,* she thought contentedly.

Liv nodded as Kayla's thoughts began to merge with hers. It felt vaguely like being submerged in a warm bath: familiar and more peaceful, the deeper you sank. "Yes," she breathed. *All day.*

Kayla growled loudly at the positive response that rang out clearly in her head, the slickness between her legs a testament to just how good this was. But that didn't keep her from eagerly tormenting Liv by continuing their disjointed conversation. "Mrs. Thicke keeps me from sleeping through breakfast."

Liv groaned in frustration. Her chest was heaving. Using well-developed stomach muscles, she sat up, forcing Kayla up with her. She cupped Kayla's cheeks with slightly shaky hands and demanded eye contact. Swallowing hard at the sight of Kayla's sky-blue eyes gone dark with desire, she said in a husky voice, "I love you with all my heart, Kayla. Don't take this the wrong way, but if you don't finish this right this second, *I* will!"

Kayla's eyes widened along with her smile.

A pale eyebrow arched. "And don't think you're going to watch." Though the mere idea caused a flutter low in her belly.

Kayla's grin vanished so quickly that Liv nearly laughed. "Threats like that will get you everywhere, Liv." Softly but urgently, their lips met again, re-igniting the fire between them. Liv's hands found firm breasts, and this time it was Kayla's turn to moan. "I was just checking...if...um...oh, God...if you were hungry, Liv." Her body shuddered and her eyes slammed shut when Liv rolled her nipples between her fingers and tugged gently. "Jesus...um..."

"Yes?" Liv asked in a voice an octave below normal, drawing out the word. "What was that?" she teased, understanding completely how hard it was to carry on a conversation under these circumstances.

Kayla gritted her teeth, determined not to let Liv win what had turned into a playful game of one-upmanship. "Mrs. Thicke sets... Harder is good, too... Yes!" Her head tilted backwards. "She umm..."

Liv laughed again, finding it much funnier to be on the giving rather than receiving end of such sweet torture. Kayla's exposed throat was too tempting to ignore, so she ducked her head and began to kiss and suck lightly on the delicate flesh.

What was I saying? Trying to regain a modicum of control, Kayla pushed Liv back onto the bed, pinning her wrists with her hands. She began ravishing the older woman's body with a single-minded intensity that might have frightened Liv had she not already been so turned on.

Long moments passed and Liv's hips began pushing upward of their own accord, begging. Kayla had regained some of her focus, feeling as though she'd entered into a zone of pure enjoyment where her only goal was to pleasure her partner. She let go of Liv's wrists, and small hands immediately found purchase in dark tresses, stroking gently, encouragingly. Kayla's breathing slowed as her focus narrowed to the scent, taste, and feel of her lover.

Liv's stomach growled and Kayla kissed the soft skin above it, frowning at the hollowness. "Are you hungry?" she whispered. Her lips circled Liv's perfect navel and she dipped her tongue inside, causing the smaller woman's stomach muscles to contract and release several times in quick succession.

Liv's skin was flushed and damp, every nerve ending responding wildly to the smallest touch or breath or... "Hell, yes, I'm hungry!" She squirmed helplessly under her partner's relentless mouth and hands, her body near the breaking point. Finally, when she was on the verge of pleading or screaming or both, she began pushing Kayla where she needed her most.

"What a coincidence." A determined grin shaped Kayla's mouth, and she slid further down the bed and Liv's lithe body. "So am I." She draped one of Liv's legs over her shoulder and began to nibble the baby-soft, wet skin of her lover's inner thigh, brushing the tip of her nose against the silky surface. Then she turned her head.

Liv cried out. Her hands flew to the sheets, and she gripped them in white-knuckled fists.

They skipped breakfast that morning.

It was past 11:00 a.m., and Liv and Kayla were padding down the beach eating the thick ham, cheese, and cucumber sandwiches that Mrs. Thicke had graciously offered them after they had missed breakfast. They were freshly scrubbed and showered, each wearing clean blue jeans and soft, lightweight, cable knit sweaters that Kayla had purchased at a gift shop in Gatwick Airport. Liv's was a dark charcoal color that contrasted nicely with her fair hair and pink-tinted skin. Kayla's was a classic ivory crew neck.

Liv finished her sandwich first. "Mmm." She wiped the crumbs from her lips with her fingers. Her eyes rolled back in their sockets as she relived each glorious bite. "That was sooo good."

"I could tell." Kayla's eyes twinkled. "You were almost moaning as loudly as this morning."

Liv chuckled in embarrassment. "When I like something, Kayla," she shrugged, "I'm not shy about showing it. I'm sorry if—"

"Don't even go there," Kayla warned semi-seriously. "I love that about you."

Liv beamed at her partner and patted her stomach. "Good. Because at this moment I am supremely sated in every way."

"Me too, sweetheart."

The sun was shining brightly and gulls swooped playfully overhead, flying circles around the woman as they walked, and making frequent detours to the surf to look for fish. The peak of the tourist season had ended a couple of weeks before, and it was just early enough in the day that Kayla and Liv had the beach nearly to themselves.

Liv wrapped her arm around Kayla's waist as they strolled along.

"I have a surprise for you." Kayla wiggled her eyebrows.

"Really? What?"

"Well..."

Liv pinched her partner's hip. "No torturing me this morning. I'm in too good a mood."

Kayla jumped. "Yeow!"

"Spill it," Liv laughed, lightly rubbing the flesh she'd just goosed. She doubted Kayla had felt anything through that thick denim.

Determined to keep her surprise to herself for just a bit longer, Kayla ignored Liv's demand, slowly eating the last bite of her sandwich and brushing non-existent crumbs from her sweater. Finally acknowledging the impatient tapping of Liv's foot with a teasing smile, she asked casually, "Would you have any interest in seeing the Cobb family ancestral home?"

Liv stopped walking. "You mean Faylinn's family home from the history? Wow. That would be great," she said excitedly. "But, Kayla, that wouldn't still be standing."

"It would have to be over three hundred years old, I know. But look around you, Liv." Kayla gestured broadly towards the row of old, but well-maintained homes that lined the beach. "It wouldn't be so unusual here."

She was, Liv admitted, right about that. The "new" buildings in Edinburgh still managed to be one or two hundred years old. Something from the late seventeenth century wouldn't be unheard of. "Can we look in the phone book or—"

"Make an appointment to go over and see the place?" Kayla finished triumphantly. "A taxi should be waiting for us back at the bed and breakfast by the time we get there." She grasped Liv's hand and swung her around in the opposite direction, reversing their course.

The Cobb family estate was about six miles outside Edinburgh proper. And, as in Faylinn's day and age, it was still known for its small but well-respected horse breeding business.

The taxi chugged over a small hill and down the winding dirt road that led to Cobb Manor. They were dropped off at the front gates, where the cabby held out his hand for payment. His fare securely in hand, he smiled and tipped his hat. "Enjoy your day, ladies."

"We will." Kayla took a moment to write down the driver's cell phone number, promising to call him back when they were ready to leave.

Liv had already ventured a few paces forward and was talking to a young man standing in a small wooden booth at the house's gate. As Kayla approached, he stepped out of the booth.

He wore a loose-fitting, homespun shirt, ankle boots, and a pale blue, red and green check tartan kilt. He was half a head taller than Kayla, with full sensual lips that made him look almost feminine despite his well-built frame. His hair was long and shaggy, and tied back with a plain leather strap. In short, he looked like he had just crawled out of the seventeenth century. Only his digital wristwatch gave him away.

Liv turned and grinned at Kayla when she stepped up behind her to peer over her head at the talkative young man.

"You see," he intoned, fully immersed in his role, "the family name Cobb has no tartan of its own—not every name does; but the Cobbs have a strong affiliation with the Lindsay clan, always have had. They, along with a few other families, used to share lands. And it's the ancient Lindsay colors I'm wearin' this lovely September day." He leaned towards Liv and spoke conspiratorially. "I don't care for the modern Lindsay colors." The young man scrunched up his face in distaste. "Too dull." Then he straightened and squared his shoulders, smiling brightly at Kayla. "Hello."

"Hi," she mumbled, a little self-consciously. She hadn't gotten used to Liv starting up conversations with complete strangers.

"This is so cool, Kayla! Did you know the house is a histori-

cal site where everyone is in costume? There's a gift shop, and
horseback riding, and tours, and—"

"Nope." Kayla smiled fondly at her excited friend, amazed
she'd found out so much in what couldn't have been more than
thirty seconds. "I didn't know that." She looked up at the enormous varicolored stone structure, complete with Tudor-style
chimneys and stepped gables. It sat about two hundred feet ahead
of them, and around the side to the left was a walled courtyard.
Kayla guessed it contained the manor's garden. Her eyes flicked
back to the sandy-haired man who appeared barely out of his
teens. "But it looks worth the admission fee."

Liv was digging in her pocket for some bills when the man
gasped, "Are you tryin' to get me killed?" He looked back to the
manor with nervous eyes. "If Mither saw me takin' money from
family, she'd blister my backside." He smiled wryly. "Despite the
fact that she'd have to stand on a chair to do it."

"Family? I'm not—"

"One of you is Kayla Redding, correct?" He looked back and
forth between the women.

Kayla's brows drew together as she realized that they were
indeed relatives, if only by marriage.

The man continued blithely, "Mither, or 'mother' to you
American's, said she and another woman would be stopping by
around lunchtime." He privately hoped that the brunette was
Kayla. Family, no matter how far removed, gave him the willies
and was off-limits romantically. The pretty blonde, however, had
already sparked his interest and libido. *Perhaps she'd be interested in seeing what I wear under my kilt,* he speculated cheerfully.

Liv jerked her thumb over her shoulder. "She's Kayla Redding."

"Splendid!" the young man boomed. "Brody Cobb, at your
service." He flashed Liv another charming smile.

Liv smothered a grin at Brody's eagerness, a little surprised
that anyone would bother to look twice at her when they could be
gazing at her gorgeous lover instead.

Seeing no other customers driving up the road, Brody quickly
locked the door to his booth and pushed open the heavy gate. "If
you'll follow me inside, me mither is waiting for you." He
extended his hand towards the house. "After you, ladies." Liv
walked past him, but when Kayla drew even with him, he stopped
her with a hand on her shoulder. His hopeful gaze darted to Liv.
He lowered his voice. "Is she..."

"Taken?" Kayla arched a menacing eyebrow and spoke in her

most serious voice. "Why, yes. How nice of you to notice." Her tone made it very clear to whom the object of desire was attached.

Brody blushed badly. Even the tips of his ears turned a bright crimson. "Uh...I'm sorry. I uh..."

Kayla glared at him until Liv noticed that she was now walking alone and glanced back at them in question. The dark-haired woman gave her a little wave, and Liv shrugged and kept walking down the path, eager to see the inside of the large house. "No harm done." Kayla assured Brody, relaxing her hard stare only a little. "Yet."

Mumbling a hasty "Sorry," Brody darted past both women and began leading the way to the manor. Family or no, he could tell Kayla Redding wasn't a woman to be trifled with. When he was safely ahead of them both, he launched into his well-practiced spiel about the grounds and the house itself.

"Mother," Brody called as they entered the house. When there was no answer, he raised his voice and tried again. "Mither!"

"Good Lord, boy!" a voice boomed. In walked Sylla Brody Cobb. "Why are you screamin'?" She took one look at Brody, noticed his wristwatch, and smacked him on the back of the head with an open hand. "We're supposed to look authentic, bird brain."

Brody rubbed the head sheepishly, but didn't look surprised or disturbed by his mother's behavior. Apparently, it happened quite often. "Yes, Mither." He slid off his watch, but kept it in his hand.

Liv smiled, thinking that Brody's behavior reminded her of her little brother, Dougie, and that he'd have that watch back on his wrist the second he was out of his mother's sight.

"If you'll excuse me, ladies." He bowed deeply at the waist.

Both Sylla and Kayla rolled their eyes. Liv laughed.

"I need to get back to my post." He nearly winked at Liv, but thought better of it when he noticed Kayla watching him like a hawk. Everyone in the room heard his nervous swallow.

"Let's sit," Sylla invited Kayla and Liv after the women had exchanged greetings.

As Sylla led them towards a set of stairs, Liv wondered if Brody was adopted. A quick look at Kayla, who was studying Sylla carefully, let Liv know she was wondering the same thing. Sylla was a short, stout, big-boned woman with a big head, big butt and...Liv looked down...big feet. Her hair was worn in a tight bun and she had a smile her friends would call infectious.

If she had friends.

Or smiled.

"I was quite surprised to hear from you, Ms. Redding," Sylla remarked as she began leading the women up a large oak staircase whose wooden steps had been stained a shade of brown so dark it was nearly black. They were on their way to a part of the manor that wasn't open to the public.

As they climbed, Liv admired the gleaming, openwork banister that had been cut from solid hardwood and stained to match the steps. The scent of lemon wood polish and dust lingered in the air. The house looked remarkably well preserved, and despite its size, it didn't have that sterile museum-like quality; rather, it looked like a functioning home, minor warts and all.

Kayla cleared her throat and made a valiant attempt at being sociable. "Thank you for agreeing to talk with us." She relaxed a little when Liv took her hand and threaded their fingers together, silently praising her effort. "I was curious after discovering Cyril Redding's marriage to Faylinn Cobb. I'm afraid it wasn't very well-documented in my family."

"That's too bad," Sylla said gravely. "Family heritage is a very valuable commodity to the Cobb family."

Kayla bristled at the implied slight. "I can see that. If I'm not mistaken, the sign out front set the value at four pounds."

Liv gaped at her companion. "Kayla," she chided under her breath.

"What?" Kayla mouthed silently with all the innocence she could muster. "She started it."

But Sylla remained unfazed. "Och! That was not my doin'. We're only open three days a week, and it was my husband's idea that we wear these costumes." She let out a long-suffering sigh. "It was this or plow under the gardens." She shook her head. "Soulless highway robbers is what those gardeners are. Brody is to apprentice with one next summer. Thank the Lord."

Liv had to smother her laughter with her hand. "Are you built on a graveyard?" she asked, remembering the brochure at their bed & breakfast that advertised a pub nearby that was supposedly haunted. "Seems like hauntings of all sorts are big business."

Sylla snorted loudly. "No, dammit. And just our luck, too. Though the tourists do seem to enjoy our home, and we've done quite well this summer." At the top of the stairs the women rounded the corner, and Sylla abruptly stopped and bent over, her new position thrusting her large bottom straight up into the air.

Kayla shivered inwardly and was certain she heard a faint "Be nice" repeated to her silently.

Sylla pulled off her pointy-toed leather shoes and stepped
into an enormous pair of soft, fuzzy, pink slippers. "No wonder
Scotland's population shrank in the sixteenth century," she
huffed, straightening. "I'm convinced the likely cause was suicide
brought on by chronic foot pain." She moaned with pleasure
when she wiggled her toes. "Much better," the matronly woman
announced firmly. She lifted her skirts and began marching purposefully down the red-carpeted hallway.

They passed the library on their way to the drawing room,
Sylla's announced destination, and Kayla had to grab Liv's arm
and pull her the rest of the way down the hall to keep her from
sneaking inside. The tall, book-laden shelves sang out to her lover
with a siren's call. "Okay, okay," Liv whined quietly as Kayla suc-
cessfully directed her course back down the hall.

"You can visit the library anytime you like, Ms. Hazelwood,"
Sylla commented without looking behind her. "I can show it to
you before you leave, if you like."

Liv cheeks flushed as she and Kayla picked up their pace to
catch up with their hefty hostess. Sylla's powerful, rolling gait
had propelled her nearly halfway down the very long hallway.
"Umm... Thank you. That's very kind of you."

"Not really," Sylla answered truthfully. "I'll do nearly anything to be able to keep my slippers on." She stopped. "Here we
are." With an impatient hand, she pushed open the door and ush-
ered Kayla and Liv inside.

The room was fairly small but had ceilings that easily topped
twelve feet. The paneled walls were made of quartered white oak,
and they framed tall, narrow, limestone windows and a large limestone fireplace whose materials had been imported from England
when the house was built in the mid-sixteen hundreds. The fur-
nishings, however, were clearly from the present day, and looked
as though they had been purchased more for comfort than style.

Liv walked to the window and peered down to see Brody
handing out tickets to a young couple with a baby in a stroller.
The early afternoon sky had begun to cloud over again, and she
wondered idly if that was an everyday occurrence in Edinburgh.

"Sit and have a bite. I made these myself," Sylla announced
proudly as she plopped down on the edge of a padded sofa. She
lifted a silver tray from a stand next to the couch and tugged free
the cloth that had been covering the treats.

The room filled with the buttery aroma of shortbread, and
both Liv and Kayla eagerly accepted a golden bar. They were still
warm from the oven. Liv nearly swooned.

Sylla's eyebrows jumped at the sounds of Liv's appreciative

moans.

Kayla found herself growing aroused at the sound. *God, I'm a pervert.* She shook her head to clear it of sensual thoughts and addressed Sylla. She held up a piece of the cookie. "Do you sell these in your gift shop, Mrs. Cobb?"

"By the pound. And please call me Sylla, seein' as how we're family, and all."

"We'll take ten, Sylla," Liv mumbled, her mouth still full.

"Ten?" Sylla and Kayla asked, astonished.

"What?" Liv cried.

Kayla crossed her arms over her chest in disbelief. "Ten pounds?"

"Okay, fifteen, but that's my final offer."

"Liv! This isn't an auction," Kayla complained half-heartedly. Truth be told, all Liv had to do was ask, and Kayla would pull down the stars. Hell, she'd wrap them in bows.

Sylla almost looked as if she was going to smile at the purchase Liv had made, but instead she nodded knowingly. "They are good," she agreed. "Now, I've asked my husband to come up and tell you about Faylinn and her adventures in the American Colonies. He's the real family historian and storyteller. Besides, a Cobb tale is best not told by a Brody."

Liv scooted closer to Kayla. "Sylla, I'm sure you'd do a good job."

"True," Sylla allowed readily, without even a hint of modesty. "But all the same, Mr. Cobb will be up after he finishes showing that group of Japanese tourists our stables. We've several bonnie colts this year. But perhaps a short tale first, eh?" Sylla paused, and Kayla could see the wheels in her head turning as she came to a decision. "Kayla," she began, "you've been to Scotland before?"

"Many times," the tall woman agreed.

"But you haven't, Ms...Liv," she immediately corrected herself, remembering that they were now on a first name basis.

"No. Though what I've seen is beautiful. I should have come sooner," Liv answered.

Sylla grunted her agreement and moved off the sofa to a recliner that faced Liv and Kayla. "Then I've got a story just for you." She lowered her voice, and her accent seemed to increase exponentially. "Have you ever heard of Mary King's Close, child?"

Liv shook her head. "I've seen lots of things with 'close' or 'wynd' in the name, but I—"

Sylla waved a dismissive hand in front of her as though she was shooing a pesky fly. "They're alleyways between buildings.

A 'wynd' is a path with an opening at both ends, while a 'close' only has an opening at one. Some are so narrow, your shoulders scrape the sides as you walk. Now..." She smoothed her dress. "You know that Edinburgh is one of the most haunted cities in the world?"

Liv looked at Kayla in question, but Kayla was forced to nod. That had been her experience.

"Ay, it is," Sylla assured her audience. "Make no mistake about that. And I'm going to tell you one of our most famous tales, and why so many tortured souls haunt our fair city."

Both Liv and Kayla leaned forward, resting their elbows on their knees.

"Before I tell you about Mary King's Close, I need to tell you a little about Edinburgh in the 1660s, the decade before Faylinn Cobb's birth. Edinburgh was a growing city, even then. It was also a walled city; and the large sunken area in front of Waverly Train Station was Nor' Loch, a filthy cesspool," Sylla hissed.

Liv opened her mouth to pose a question.

"Tch." Sylla held up an imperious hand and Liv's mouth snapped shut. "I'm getting to that. Because Edinburgh didn't have much room to expand outward, it expanded upward. We had skyscrapers seven stories high and packed with living bodies even then. It was a time before modern waste disposal, and the streets of the city served as its reeking sewers. People would dump their putrid waste—human and otherwise—out the windows, and let it drain down the buildings and into the street."

Kayla and Liv's expressions turned sour.

Sylla nodded solemnly. "Exactly. Imagine..." her voice dropped again and Kayla and Liv were forced to inch a little closer. "Imagine, if you dare, the vile stench of a hot summer's day. It's enough to turn the strongest of stomachs. Now, most of this foul matter eventually drained down into Nor' Loch, the low point of the city, which also happened to be the water supply that was used for drinking and bathing and so on."

Liv shuddered. "Ewww."

"In the year of our Lord sixteen and forty-five, the plague came to Edinburgh. Rats brought it. Or to be more precise, fleas on rats. Rats became infected when the fleas bit them. The vile little rodents ate garbage and human waste; the streets were teeming with them. Do you know what happens when someone contracts the plague, Liv?"

Liv swallowed. "They die?"

"Oh, yes, they die. But it's *how* they die that makes it so remarkable. At first it seems as though they've caught nothing more than a cold. They get the chills, a fever, and cough a bit, nothing too serious. Until the second day..."

Feeling her partner grow more tense as the tale progressed, Kayla wrapped her arm around Liv's shoulders.

"On the second day, tiny red dots appear all over the poor soul's body. Then they can't hide it. Everyone knows! And they run at the sight of you. 'Plague bearer!' they shout. 'Carrier of the Black Death!' Tumors form in your armpits and your groin, growing by the hour; dark circles ring the victim's eyes." Sylla's hands flew to her chest. "You begin to vomit blood, and your stomach twists with maddening cramps. Enormous, festering boils cover most of your body and fill to the breaking point with hot, thick pus. And break they do, sending more disease-filled fluid over your skin, creating more and more boils." Sylla finally took a breath.

So did Liv.

"Then the boils turn black as death itself, and soon your body is as splotchy as a rotting corpse. That's why it's called the Black Death." Sylla's tone turned more conversational. "You've probably heard that term used before."

Liv nodded dumbly, green eyes wide.

"In that Year of Pestilence, the people of Edinburgh were dying by the thousands, and the dark streets now stank with the foul odor of rotting flesh as well as waste. The City Council tried everything to stem the tide of death. It thought pets might spread the disease, and ordered all the city's cats and dogs killed." Sylla sighed. "Of course, dogs and cats killed rats, and without them the rat population swelled and the disease claimed more and more lives. Why—" She looked up at Kayla, who quirked a slender eyebrow, letting Sylla know it was time to bring her tale to a rousing end.

The older woman cleared her throat. "Back to Mary King's Close. It's a dark, narrow alleyway that still exists to this very day. The plague hit the tenements there especially hard. The City Council was desperate. It had to do *something* or they would all perish. Nearly half the population of Edinburgh had already fallen victim. Mary King's Close was known to harbor a great many sinners, and had been hit especially hard by the disease."

"You mean Catholics," Kayla snorted.

"Ay, they were mostly Catholic." Sylla shot Kayla an annoyed glance for the interruption. "In an effort to stop the spreading doom, the entrance to the close was boarded shut and guards were posted there. No one was to go in or out. *Ever.* All this was done with four *hundred* men, women, and children *still inside*. Their cries for food, water, and mercy rang out for days and days until finally all went silent. And every single wretched, pitiful soul perished in abject misery."

Kayla frowned at Liv's suddenly unhealthy pallor. "Enough," she warned Sylla.

"Fine." Sylla brushed a piece of non-existent lint from her skirts. "I was finished anyway," she said, adding a touch of martyrdom for flair.

Subtly, Liv gave Kayla's hand a reassuring squeeze. "I'm fine, Kayla." Liv turned back to Sylla. "What happened next?"

She smirked at Kayla before continuing. "The plague continued, of course. The City sent two butchers into Mary King's Close, and they dismembered the decaying bodies and removed them from their urban tomb. Slowly, the plague burned itself out and then vanished, disappearing just as mysteriously as it had come." Sylla's voice took on a woeful quality. "But the tortured souls of Mary King's Close haunt Edinburgh to this very day."

"Oh." Liv rubbed her eyes, somewhat dumbfounded. She had no idea how to respond to that story. "That was...an...well, it was interesting, and—"

"Was it really?" Sylla suddenly grinned broadly, and Kayla had to use every ounce of her will power not to recoil at the sight. "Wonderful!" She clapped her hands together gleefully. "Do you think I should spend more time on the pus and blisters?"

Liv stared at Sylla in wonder.

But Kayla thought about the question. "No. I'd say that was just about right. Some do, some don't. But you might mention that when an infected flea bites a human, it regurgitates a speck of adulterated blood into its victim, passing along the disease."

"Regurgitation. Excellent!" Sylla looked directly at Liv. "I'm moonlighting as a guide for one of our city's many 'ghost walks.' We go right past Mary King's Close, and I've been practicing my story. Folks do love to hear about ghosts and pus. But best of all, I can wear my Nikes under my costume. Anyway," she pushed up to her feet, "I'll go and find my husband, Mr. Cobb, and wrap up your twenty-five pounds of shortbread. I can't imagine what's keeping him."

"Fifteen pounds," Kayla clarified.

"Right. That's what I said. Twenty pounds." And with that, Sylla Cobb sauntered out of the room, whistling a happy tune as she mentally calculated the sale.

When she was out of sight, Liv rested her head in her hands and laughed weakly. "Oh, my God, Kayla, that has to be one of the most demented people I have ever met."

Kayla chuckled softly and leaned back. She stretched her arms high over her head. "I'd agree with that assessment. And when she smiled..."

Liv's whole body shook, and she wrapped her arms around herself. "Ugh. I know. It was the most unnatural facial expression I've ever seen on a human." She exhaled a long slow breath and pinned Kayla with an inquiring stare. "You knew what she was going to say, didn't you?"

"I went on one of the ghost walks a few years ago. It was fun, I suppose, but highly unscientific."

"You sound like Spock."

"The baby doctor?"

"The Vulcan."

"Oh." Kayla unconsciously felt her ears to see if they were too pointy. "Are you calling me a geek?"

"Pretty much," Liv said amiably.

"Okay. I was just checking."

"I just thank God Sylla's gross tale was fiction." Liv's face twisted in disgust. "That was horrible."

Fiction? Oh, boy. "Ahh..." Kayla chewed her lip. "Listen, Liv—"

Liv shook her head. "No, no, no. *You* listen." She waggled her finger at her lover. "I don't care about the truth. I just don't want nightmares. I'm very talented when it comes to harnessing the power of denial. Just ask my high school boyfriend. Now, repeat after me: It was just a story..." She smiled impishly. "And I love you more than a pig loves slop, Liv."

Kayla's eyebrows jumped. "Only if you say the same to me— except that you have to love me more than shortbread cookies."

"Don't push your luck."

Kayla burst out laughing. "I'll do my best."

"Thank you," Liv said sassily.

"It was just a story. And I love you *way* more than a pig loves slop."

Liv kissed her friend on the cheek then nuzzled the soft skin there. "Now isn't this nicer than talking about pus?"

Chapter
Three

Liv looked out the window again. She sighed. Brody was still handing out tickets. The blonde woman moved back to the fireplace and examined the large oil painting of a dog.

All the while, Kayla sat quietly.

"I'm bored," Liv said, a little embarrassed by how juvenile the words sounded once she'd said them aloud. Then her face lit up. "Wanna neck while we wait for Mr. Cobb?" she asked hopefully, flopping down on the far end of the sofa then scampering across it to Kayla.

Kayla tapped her index finger against her chin and pretended to seriously consider the question. "What if someone catches us?"

"What if they don't?" Liv countered, her gaze dropping to Kayla's full lips. She inched a little closer to the object of her desire.

"What if they do?"

Liv idly fingered the neck of Kayla's sweater. "They might not," she reminded insistently. One hand slid beneath soft hair, letting the thick strands slide between its fingers before finding its way to the back of Kayla's neck.

Quite without her permission, Kayla's gaze fixed itself on Liv's mouth. And refused to move. She licked her lips and leaned forward. "But—"

"They won't," Liv promised, closing her eyes just as their lips...

"Oh, yes they will," a deep Scottish voice boomed from the doorway.

Kayla flew off the couch, knocking Liv over in the process. "I...I..." Her eyes darted wildly from Liv to the man.

He began to laugh heartily, the movement causing his bulky

form to shake. He held up a placating hand. "No need to get upset, lassies."

Liv scowled at Kayla. "Or dump your girlfriend on her ass," she mumbled.

Aw, shit. Kayla offered Liv a contrite look. "Sorry. I...uh." Her mouth snapped shut. "Just sorry," she finally said, wincing. She extended her hand and hauled Liv to her feet.

The man's eyes shifted back and forth between the women. He smiled indulgently. "Hello, ladies. Welcome to Cobb Manor." Like Brody's, his voice was bright and cheerful, but with an even heavier brogue. "There's no need for introductions," he assured them. "My friends call me Badger. Have done ever since I was a wee bairn. But that's another story." With a confident air, he walked right past them both and sat down in the recliner in front of the sofa. "Sylla explained what you wanted to know. I'm only sorry I kept you waiting."

"Not a problem." Kayla blinked a few times. She hadn't been expecting Sylla's husband to be quite so old. Robust, however, was the word that came to mind when she looked at him. His clear eyes, spry step, and engaging manner indicated he was in good health and better spirits. Not bad for someone who was easily in his middle sixties.

"Did Sylla, The Sullen, scare you?" He laughed again, low and deep. "She's been telling that nasty story to anyone who will listen. I personally think it's more gross than frightening." He put his finger over his lips. "Shhh... But that's my little secret."

Taking their cue from Badger, Liv and Kayla both sat back down.

He looked at them both for a long moment, saying nothing. But Kayla didn't experience the unnerving feeling that often accompanied such scrutiny. It was, she decided, comfortable.

There was a gentleness and intensity in his pale eyes that Liv instantly found appealing, and she found herself relaxing. *Or maybe I just have a thing for blue eyes,* she admitted privately.

Badger's thick hair and full beard stood out against his ruddy skin and were as white as new snow. Even the patch of curly chest hair that showed in the opening of his shirt was white. He wore a kilt and shirt that matched Brody's, and by the way he moved, she could tell he was more comfortable in them than the younger Cobb. A couple of inches shorter than Kayla's five feet eleven, he was sturdily built, with thick forearms and calves and a chest like a tree trunk. When he smiled, Liv couldn't help but smile back. He looked a lot Santa Claus—if Santa were willing to go to a local pub with you and toss a few back.

The man's face suddenly turned a little sheepish. "I'm sorry for startling you. That was a little mean." But there was an undisguised twinkle in his eyes that kept his apology from being *too* sincere.

"Apology accepted," Liv said readily.

Badger nodded approvingly. "Good." Every couple had to have a peacemaker, and in this case it was obviously the pretty, green-eyed lass. "I understand from Sylla that you only have a couple of hours before you need to return to town." He pulled his pipe from the well-worn, badger-pelt sporran at his waist and held it up for their inspection. "Do you mind?"

Kayla shook her head. "Not at all."

He grinned and lit it. A few puffs later and the sweet aroma of pipe tobacco filled the room. "I don't know if I can tell you Faylinn Cobb's whole story in just two hours," he warned, closing his eyes in pleasure as he drew in a deep, smoke-filled breath. "She was an interesting woman, and I don't like stopping a tale too many times once I've started." He pulled the pipe from between his teeth. "Stops the flow of the story."

Kayla worked her jaw. *God, is everyone in this family a wanna-be actor?* "We *could* come back," she supplied somewhat reluctantly. "Later in the week maybe."

"Ay, you could. Tomorrow?"

Blue eyes narrowed. "Maybe."

Liv patted Kayla's knee. She would come back as many times as it took. Assuming she could still walk after consuming all that shortbread. Now that her appetite was back, she felt ravenous.

"Excellent! Tomorrow it is, then. Now, tell me what you already know."

Kayla shifted uncomfortably, feeling a little guilty for even being related to Faylinn's husband. "We know she lived in London for a time, but mostly here. At least, until she married Cyril Redding and moved to the Colonies."

He continued to puff his pipe contentedly. "All true. Go on."

"Cyril...um..." Kayla's gaze flicked to Liv then back, where it stayed. "He died under mysterious circumstances on Cobb Island." She was unwilling to accuse Faylinn of his murder, despite the fact that she believed that's what had happened. "Faylinn, who had recently lost their two-year-old son to a fever, disappeared after that, and was never heard from again." She wondered if her host knew about Cyril's sister, Bridget, and the intimate, if not consummated, relationship she'd had with Faylinn. If he didn't, she certainly wasn't going to tell him.

Mr. Cobb began choking on his own smoke. "Never heard

from again? Och! What crap. Maybe not for a while. But she certainly didn't disappear for good."

"I assumed there was more to the story," Kayla informed him dryly. "Otherwise, you wouldn't have anything to tell us, now would you?"

"No." A tiny smile twitched at his lips. Kayla reminded him of someone he loved very much. "I suppose I wouldn't. All right then, sit back, lassies, and I'll tell you all I know." His face grew serious. "But be warned, this yarn is not some glorified version of the truth, like Sylla spins. This was *real*. Sometimes it's harsh in the tellin'." He stroked his beard thoughtfully. "There are folks who might be more comfortable not knowing exactly what happened on Cobb Island and after..."

Kayla looked him dead in the eye. "But we wouldn't be among them."

Liv nodded firmly. "What she said."

Mr. Cobb chuckled softly. "Why am I not surprised?"

Virginia (Mainland)
November, 1690

The crouched figure worked quietly as she tended the small, smoking fire. The heat wasn't nearly enough, and her fingers felt cold and clumsy. She used a stick to stoke the fragile fire and blew at the fire's base, trying to fan the flames. After several moments of hissing and sputtering, the wet wood began to burn in earnest, filling the room with the sweet smell of hickory and casting it in jagged shadows.

A loud clap of thunder shook the rafters and rattled windows barely covered by slightly warped, wooden shutters. The endless, icy rain that had pelted the Virginia coast all autumn continued to come down in sheets, making everything miserable.

The young, fair-haired woman tossed the stick into the fireplace and put her hand on her thighs to push herself up. Still wearing her damp cloak, she wrapped it tighter around her slender body in mute comfort. A mirthless laugh bubbled up from inside her, and she was powerless to stop it.

She was, she knew, on the verge of sheer hysteria. In shock. How could she not be? She covered her face with shaking hands to avoid the sight of the bloodied rags that lay on the small table by the bed. Her impulse had been to throw them into the burgeoning flame, but she didn't. The cloth might come in handy later. Still, her stomach roiled at the thought of washing it out.

A quiet knock on her door caused her head to snap up. Hesitating for only a moment, she padded slowly to the door, not bothering to lift the skirts dragging across the wooden slats that served as a floor. "Yes?" she called out warily.

"Mrs. Redding, it's only me, Wilfred. I've some fresh linen from my wife." The door creaked open and a man of medium height, who smelled of wood-smoke and livestock, strode into the room. He appeared to be in his late thirties, with pockmarked skin and a large, slightly crooked nose.

"Can I see her—"

He shook his head. "Not yet." Wilfred Beynon's heavy brow furrowed. "Why are you sitting in the dark, Mrs.—"

"Faylinn," she interrupted softly. "My name is Faylinn." His manner was rough and impatient. She hoped she could trust him. *I don't have a choice.*

He nodded once, a little surprised that a woman of her social standing would offer her first name to the likes of him, a pig farmer. The Reddings were a powerful family. Everyone knew that. And though he'd heard talk of Cyril's marriage, and how Mr. Redding came to own Cobb Island, he'd never actually seen Cyril's young wife before today. He studied Faylinn carefully, and wondered how such a miserable man had managed to take such a pretty bride.

"I'm Will, then." He quirked an eyebrow, remembering their mostly unpleasant encounter of a few minutes earlier. "We were never really introduced." He pulled hard and the swollen shutters closed more tightly, stopping the rain from draining down the wall. "Damn things." He pulled a large, cold torch from its holder and lit it in the fireplace before sliding it back into place. "We don't have call for many guests, so I don't come in here often. I didn't know the wood box was bein' rained on. I know it's not what a lady like you is used to—"

Faylinn held up her hand. "Please. It's more than I could have hoped for." Her eyes strayed to the door. "Thank you," she added absently.

He frowned at the slight brogue that peeked out from beneath her upper-class English accent. "Scottish, are ya?"

"Yes." She gave her head a little shake. "Well, no, not technically, I suppose. I was born in London." Faylinn's eyes never left the door.

"Good." He crossed his massive arms over his chest. "They're drunkards and thieves, the lot of them."

Faylinn pushed damp blonde bangs off her forehead. "No they're not," she disagreed gently. "I spent most of my childhood in Edinburgh, and my—" She was about to say "family," but her mind flooded with images of the son she'd recently lost and she felt a stabbing sensation in her guts. *Oh, God.*

Will continued to stare at her, wondering if she was going to continue.

After a full minute, Faylinn swallowed and muttered, "My people are Scots, Mr. Beynon."

"Too bad." He unceremoniously yanked the dusty quilt from the narrow bed and stripped the old linens. "I was born in Radnorshire myself, but have been here in the colonies for nearly twenty years. Virginia for the past five, after I worked off my indenture," he said proudly. He debated his words for a moment, then pointed a thumb at his chest as he worked. "My life is my own now." He finished tugging on the clean sheets. "It's a wonderful thing to be free."

Faylinn turned her head very slowly until her eyes locked with his. In an instant, she knew that he knew, and the blood drained from her face. Her heart began to thump wildly, and she stumbled backwards a step. "I...I..."

He smiled reassuringly. "If you're running away from Cyril Redding, even though he's your lawful husband, you'll get no censure from me. It's God's place to judge, not mine."

Faylinn exhaled shakily. *He doesn't know about Cyril, then.*

Will's face darkened. "But what he did to his own kin, to his own sister." He spat into the fire as though merely talking about Cyril had left a vile taste in his mouth. "The filthy, no good—" He suddenly stopped, realizing who he was talking to. A contrite look transformed his features to those of a child about to be scolded. "If you'll pardon my blunt words, ma'am."

"No need to apologize. It's not as though I haven't thought worse myself," she admitted honestly before her attention turned back to the door.

Will wished that his wife was in the room with this girl instead of him. She would be even worse at this than he was. But, then, that would be his wife's problem, wouldn't it? "I'll be back soon."

He took a step to leave, but feared the girl would drop dead from fretting and holding her breath as she watched the door. Approaching her slowly, he slid the wet cloak from her shoulders and carefully hung it to dry on a hook near the fireplace. "Sit." He pointed to the stool that stood near to the flames. "And dry off, before you catch your death." He softened his normally gruff voice in an attempt to ease the young woman's worries. "I'll come for you as soon as I know anything. It's in God's hands now."

On his way out of the room, Will grabbed the blood-soaked bandages, grunting his approval of the fact that Faylinn hadn't burned them. Cloth could be re-used.

Faylinn's mind was spinning. She barely heard the sound of the closing of the door. She clenched her fists in frustration, digging short nails into her palms. "Send me away like a child," she muttered to herself. "Of all the stupid..."

Ignoring Will's instructions, she stalked past the stool to the bed and stripped off her sodden, torn skirts, blouse, petticoat, and shoes, letting them fall to the floor. She peered down at her sleeveless shift and gave a passing thought to taking it off as well. It was wet and itched, but with a small shake of her head, she decided against it. She didn't know these people. And just because they seemed kind, didn't mean that they were. Her lips formed a thin line. She'd learned that lesson on her wedding night.

Her body trembled when the cool air hit the bare skin of her arms, and she rubbed her hands up and down them briskly, trying to chase away the goose bumps. "I shouldn't be in here." Faylinn's heart felt as though it was trapped in a vise. "I can't help in here," she anguished. She stood there listening to the rain, wind, and the constant hum of muffled the voices. The urge to bolt from the room was nearly overwhelming. But she continued to wait. Numb.

Green eyes flew open and her sagging head snapped up. She was falling asleep standing up. Slightly disoriented, she climbed into bed and snuggled down beneath the thin quilt, sinking deeply into the straw mattress, shivering.

Faylinn closed her eyes tightly. They still burned from the sting of salty seawater. *How we made it here from the island in this weather I'll never know.* She'd had to row the entire way herself.

Will's words repeated in her mind. *It's in God's hands.* She exhaled raggedly, her entire body aching with a bone-weary exhaustion, the likes of which she'd never known. *Maybe if I sleep, the time will pass more quickly and everything will be all right.* Her heart lurched, and she pulled the musty quilt up to her chin, saying a prayer to the God she wasn't sure existed at all. Not for herself, but for someone she loved.

Her last thoughts before she drifted into a deep slumber were of Bridget and the amazing happenings on Cobb Island. *Had it all happened in the past two days?* It seemed like weeks. She drifted back, hazy images running together in her mind.

Banging furiously on the bedroom door. "Judith! Where have they taken Bridget? Where, Judith? Dammit! Open the door! Please!"

The sound of a bolt being thrown, and the door opening slowly. The guilty, frightened eyes of her step-daughter causing her blood to run cold. "She's to be executed as a witch."

Feeling dizzy. Sick. "Wh...What?"

"You've got to hurry. You don't have much time. She's at the cliffs on the other side of the island. Run, Faylinn."

A frantic ride on a high-strung, white stallion, through the pouring rain...thunder booming and the sky opening up all around her.

Seeing her. Shock. They're going to burn you at the stake? *A flash of lightning showing marred, bloody flesh and weary blue eyes, one nearly swollen shut.* My God, Bridget, what have they done to you?

Flying into her arms...

The only kiss that ever mattered.

Pressing a sharp dagger into her hands. "Please live!"

A timeless moment. "I love you!" *being screamed louder than the rolling thunder, without a single word being spoken.*

The cliff? She can't... Not for me. Not for anything! Don't, Bridget. *"No, Bridget. Nooo!"*

Faylinn bolted upright and the quilt and rough linens pooled at her waist. Her heart was pounding. "My God." She lifted a shaky hand to her face and willed herself to start breathing normally.

Once she'd caught her breath, green eyes shifted sideways. The fire was still burning brightly and had managed to knock the chill out of the air. By the looks of the torch on the wall, she couldn't have been asleep for more than an hour or two.

Her head was still throbbing but she wasn't as miserably cold as she'd been earlier. *I just have to be patient,* she chanted inwardly. *I could have stayed and helped...I could do...do...something.* She laid back down in a huff, but soon her eyelids began to grow heavy.

Giving in to the insistent demands of her body, she tightened her grip on the covers, wishing she could disappear beneath their safety. Nothing could touch her there, she knew. Her mother had promised her. *You were right, Mother. The monsters didn't get me.*

Faylinn's hazy mind roamed freely as her grip on the bedding loosened.

Soon she was softly crooning a lullaby to her son, smiling at his sleepy face. Then she was laughing with Bridget on the shore as a large, unexpected wave washed over them as they dug for clams. In the blink of an eye, the surf at Cobb Island was replaced by the rocky beach of the mainland. *"Just a little further. God, won't this rain ever stop? Wait. A farm?"* Squinting through the pouring rain. *"Yes, that's smoke from the house's chimney. Keep walking. Move!"*

"Bridget," she muttered fuzzily, as the spare room that had been built on to the Beynon's barn faded into another room...a secret place hidden deep within the walls of the house on Cobb Island.

Cyril jerked open the door and stared dazedly at his bride, who, after several years of marriage, was still just shy of twenty. "My son is dead," he garbled, his sword clanking against the furniture as he staggered around the room.

"How nice of you to finally notice," Faylinn shot back coldly. She couldn't stand the sight of him, and turned away in disgust.

Cyril laughed without a hint of humor as he drew his blade, the sound of ripping fabric mixing with his words as he wildly slashed apart the bed's expensive canopy. "No longer resigned to your fate, I see. What a pity. I rather preferred you with your mouth closed."

He quickly grew bored and let his sword fall from his hand onto the bed.

"You're drunk."

"How nice of you to finally notice. Now come here," he commanded, his voice dripping with anger.

Faylinn stood her ground, not moving an inch, leveling such a brutally cold stare on the man she'd come to despise that he actually took a step backwards. He cocked his head to the side and regarded her in utter silence, seeing something he hadn't thought the girl capable of—a hatred so pristine in its form that his drunken mind could only marvel at its perfection.

Then the room exploded into shouting.

"Keep away from me," she ground out from between

clenched teeth.

Cyril's face contorted in rage. His eyes bored into Faylinn's and she could see, even beneath the drink, he'd already gone mad. "Shut your mouth, bitch!" He nearly fell when he lunged for her, but she managed to evade his grasp. With effort, he straightened, flinging his long black curls over his shoulder. "I will have a male heir," Cyril slurred harshly.

Faylinn began to laugh, then she couldn't stop. Bridget was dead. Her son was dead. She had nothing to lose. Everything she cared about was gone. Everything.

Cyril took another step towards her and she suddenly quieted. An icy rage filled her, sweeping away her anguish and cutting through her hysterics. "I will die before I sleep with you, you murdering pig! I would sooner lay with Lucifer himself. You can go straight to—" Her words were cut off when a large, cold hand wrapped around her throat and her head was slammed back against the wall. Bright stars invaded her vision and her knees buckled.

Cyril thrust himself against her, pinned her slumping body to the wall with his hips, and grabbed her by her wrists. "I thought I told you to shut up!"

Faylinn closed her eyes and jerked her face away from his harsh breath. Fuzzily, she could feel his excitement growing, pressing into her lower abdomen. She began to fight frantically as her stomach churned.

"Did you fight my sister like this, slut? Did she enjoy it?" Cyril grunted against her neck. His voice dropped to the quietest of whispers and he pressed his mouth to her ear so that his thin mustache tickled her. "The way I've always enjoyed it." Then, on impulse, he dragged his tongue from her ear to the base of her throat, where he placed a sloppy, vicious kiss.

Her vision instantly cleared and she hissed in pure revulsion, her entire body convulsing. "Get...get off me." She brought her knee up hard, slamming it into Cyril's swollen groin and sending him down on one knee, his eyes bulging in agony.

Spittle flew from his mouth and his chest heaved as he fought to stay conscious. A low groan that began in his chest spilled out, making him sound like a wounded beast. He choked back his own vomit.

Faylinn made for the door, but a hand shot out and

grabbed her skirts as she tried to bolt past him. The sudden stop tore the material grasped in his fist and sent her sprawling to the ground. Then she was back in his arms as he yanked her up by her hair and pulled her close. She struggled wildly, pawing and kicking. Faylinn could smell the rancid odor of liquor mixed with stomach acid on his breath, and he forced his mouth onto hers, ramming his hot tongue between her lips and making her gag.

The door flew open and the world stopped as Cyril whirled around to see who had interrupted his pleasure. For several seconds, no one dared even breathe.

"Oh, my God!" Faylinn's eyes went as wide as saucers and she staggered forward several steps. She blinked rapidly, part of her wanting to clear away the beautiful, ghastly vision before her, the other part deathly afraid that if she did, her heart would shatter all over again.

Standing in the doorway, the outline of her tall, imposing form unmistakable even in the dim light, was Bridget Redding. Her thick, drenched hair was matted with mud and blood and hung wildly about her shoulders, several tangles sticking to her blood-streaked cheeks and neck. Filthy clothes hung from her tall frame in tatters, and skin that normally radiated a healthy glow was an eerie, chalky white.

Cyril gaped as his mind reeled. This couldn't be happening. She was already dead*! "Die, bitch!" he howled insanely, his voice unnaturally high as he dove for his sword.*

In a wide arc, Cyril's blade slashed towards Bridget. He was drunk enough to be uncoordinated, but still had the wherewithal to be deadly. His strike missed her by a hairsbreadth when she flung her body sideways. He cried out in frustration, swinging erratically and striking the walls and furniture in his attempts to obliterate his sister.

Bridget ducked the next blow, feeling the quick whoosh of air against her head as the sword whizzed over it. Her jump from the cliff and the days of beatings she'd endured before it had left her body shattered and weak. Every movement caused a fiery bolt of pain in her belly as her guts twisted sharply. Her left arm hung crookedly at her side, useless. And blood still leaked sluggishly from the cuts that peppered her broken body, its salty warmth soaking into her stinking clothes.

It was only a matter of time before Cyril would get in a lucky blow.

Then several things happened at once.

Bridget slipped on the spot where Cyril had spat earlier. She hit the floor with a solid thump, too tired to even cry out.

Her brother smiled wickedly and raised the sword high over head for the killing blow.

Faylinn howled, "Nooo!" and without thought, bolted across the room to put herself between the blade and Bridget.

As the sword sped towards Bridget's head, the tall woman pulled the dagger Faylinn had given her on the cliff from the folds of her cloak. She lunged upward with the last of her energy, thrusting with all her might just as Faylinn's body collided with Cyril's and knocked the blade from his hand, sending it clattering to the floor.

His gray eyes went impossibly wide and he groaned piteously at the sight of his own knife protruding from his chest, a dark stain blossoming on his white shirt. Then he looked down at Bridget and smiled. He opened his mouth to say something...but instead of words came a thin trickle of crimson blood.

He crumbled to the floor.

Bridget shakily stood, falling backwards several steps as spots swam before her eyes. She looked up into Faylinn's fear-filled eyes and slowly extended a trembling hand.

Faylinn felt her heart clench painfully in her chest. She put her hand over her quivering lips as she choked back a sob. But it was no use. There was no stopping the outburst of raw emotion that sprang from her—grief mixed with overwhelming joy and relief. The blonde woman rushed across the room, flying into Bridget's waiting embrace. "You're not a ghost," she cried softly, her words muffled by Bridget's damp cloak. Hot tears coursed down her cheeks as she wept. "You're alive." She clutched at the taller woman helplessly, still unwilling to believe what was before her eyes, in her arms.

"I'm here," Bridget pressed her cheek against Faylinn's fair hair. Her heart threatened to pound out of her chest and she was shaking. I must think, she told herself desperately. I cannot fall apart now or pass out.

A wave of dizziness assaulted her, and Bridget

grabbed Faylinn's hand. She took a moment to press it to her lips, then pulled her out of the room, stumbling a little. She purposely didn't look back at the body lying in the center of the room, its lifeless, gray eyes glittering dully in the candlelight.

There was no time to lose.

They limped down the dark corridor and turned several corners before stopping. "We've got to hurry. Elizabeth..." Bridget paused, a stabbing pain in her belly robbing her of speech.

"What is it?" Faylinn worriedly grabbed Bridget's twisted arm, and the red-haired woman bit her lip and moaned, her eyes widening. Faylinn yanked her hand away as though it had been burned, and took just a second to examine Bridget's arm, then her face. She felt compelled to state the obvious. "You're hurt." Badly hurt, her mind whispered.

Bridget nodded quickly. "I know. There's something wrong..." she laid her good hand across her midsection, "inside."

Panic tinged Faylinn's eyes. "Let's go back. Afia—"

"No," Bridget cut her off. "She can't know what happened. Afia...she must know nothing, or surely that evil brat Elizabeth will read her mind. The less the slaves know the better. For their own safety."

"But—"

"Come away with me," Bridget pleaded, tears forming in her eyes. "Off the island. Away from this place forever...I...I—"

Faylinn placed two fingers gently against Bridget's cracked lips. "Anywhere. Anywhere, as long as we're together."

Bridget swallowed hard. "We won't have money or—"

"I'll have everything I need," Faylinn interrupted seriously. She wrapped Bridget's arm around her shoulder for support again, needing to do something to help. "I can't believe you're here. I must be dreaming," she whispered.

Bridget clenched her teeth at the shift in positions, but was instantly grateful to have something to lean against. She quickly assured Faylinn that her presence was very much real and then warned, "But we need to go. Not in a few days or hours, but now, before everyone *awakens.*"

"*I'll get my cloak.*" While in her room, Faylinn made a quick inventory of the jewelry she could stuff in her pockets. They'd need to sell it.

"*Good idea. I'm afraid it's raining.*" Her words were full of regret. "*I'm sorry you'll get wet.*" Bridget smiled weakly and Faylinn burst into tears again.

"*I don't care about the weather, Bridget!*" she sobbed. "*You're alive.*" But Faylinn knew Bridget's injuries were serious. She could feel the heat pouring off the taller woman's skin, and was unerringly reminded of Henry and the fever that had so recently stolen his life. She closed her eyes tightly, strengthening her hold on Bridget, refusing to let her go.

"*Faylinn.*"

The younger woman's grip grew desperately tight.

"*Faylinn,*" Bridget repeated patiently. "*We have to go, dearest. And it must be now.*"

Faylinn sniffed and wiped the tears from her cheeks with the back of her hand. "*Yes. You need a physician.*"

"*We can't—*"

"*That wasn't a question, Bridget.*" The blonde's tone was unyielding. "*I won't lose you again. We can pay for his silence.*"

Bridget nodded, choosing not to argue with Faylinn at this moment. The nearest physician was a half-day by boat. They would never make that in this weather. She pressed her lips into Faylinn's soft blonde hair. "*I do love you.*"

Faylinn looked up and gave Bridget a hopeful, watery smile. "*And I, you.*" But as confident as the words were, Bridget could hear the fear behind them.

"*It will be all right,*" she cooed, her fingers stroking the soft, damp skin of Faylinn's cheeks.

Faylinn's throat closed tightly and her jaw worked several times before she could speak. She allowed her need to show in her voice. "*It has to be,*" she whispered.

"*Let's go.*"

And the women disappeared into the darkness.

Faylinn began to stir as a faint noise that lingered just outside her consciousness grew louder and louder until finally it was a pounding. Dazedly, she sat up, and glanced at the shaking door.

"Yes?" she called warily, not at all sure that she was ready for the news she would hear.

"Faylinn, are you decent?" It was Will Beynon. The door began to open.

"Wait." Her eyes darted to the pile of soaking, dirty clothes on the floor. "My clothes, they—"

The door creaked open again, but only enough for a hand holding a pair of dark-gray trousers and soft, russet-colored cotton shirt to appear. "You won't be wanting to put back on your wet skirts, I suspect."

A gust of wind rattled the shutters.

Sick with fear, Faylinn rushed across the floor and grabbed the clothes, holding them up to herself to cover her nearly naked body. The door closed, and she spoke through it. "Thank you. Can I see her now? Please, Will!"

"As soon as you're dressed I'll bring her in. I didn't think a small thing like you could wear my Katie's spare dress, so I brought these. They were our son's." Will's tone was nostalgic. "He was tall, but slender as a reed. They should..."

Faylinn didn't even hear the rest of what he was saying. She discarded her shift and quickly tugged on the oft-mended cotton shirt; its long tails hung to her knees. Next were a pair of men's woolen knee-britches that came to her ankles and had thick leather patches sewn on both knees. It took her a moment to push the long shirttail into the waist of the pants.

She'd never worn men's clothing before, except for a wide-brimmed hat that Bridget had loaned her for riding on sunny afternoons. But even then, she'd only dared wear it when she was well away from the house and Cyril's judgmental eyes. She ran her hands down her thighs out of pure habit, the way she always did with her dresses. "Come," she called hastily, stepping away from the door.

Faylinn heard a grunt and the shuffle of feet before the door swung open and in came Will, breathing heavily as he hefted Bridget's limp form. She was naked save for a thick coarse blanket that carried with it the scent of horseflesh.

Faylinn stared at Bridget in shock and her hand froze on the shirtsleeve she was rolling up. The last time she'd seen Bridget, she was conscious and cursing. "No, no, no." Faylinn shook head erratically. *She can't be!* "She's not—" She stopped when her throat closed around the words and the blood drained from her face.

"She's only sleeping," Will assured her. He carefully laid Bridget on the bed, taking great care not to jostle the arm that was sporting a splint made from what looked like two sawed-off floor boards.

Correctly interpreting Faylinn's pasty face he said, "Don't throw up again. I'll not clean it up twice in one night." The words were gruff; he was still a little angry that his wife had refused to help clean up that particular mess.

Faylinn's cheeks colored as she was reminded of exactly why she'd been banished to the back room despite her vehement protests. She'd plainly told Will to go to hell, that she was staying with Bridget. But when Will's wife, Katie, had threatened to turn Bridget out into the rain unless Faylinn let her check her injuries in peace, she'd agreed to go quietly, though the separation, especially now, had torn at her soul. "I'm sorry about before." She couldn't meet his soft, dark eyes. "I...well..."

Will shrugged good-naturedly. "No harm done. If Katie didn't call me a worthless bastard at least once a day, I might think I'd come home to the wrong house." Now it was Will's turn to be embarrassed. "I'm sorry for accusing Bridget of being a ghost. I saw her at an auction last spring, and she's not the sort of woman a man is likely to forget. Yesterday, some sailors in Their Majesties' Royal Navy spoke of her trial for witchcraft, and the sentence, and how before they could execute her, she—" He stopped, sensing the young woman's growing distress.

Jumped, Faylinn's mind supplied sullenly. She wouldn't have believed it herself if she hadn't seen the nightmare come to life before her very eyes. But she couldn't think of Bridget's "death." Not now. Not when that was still so close to being true. "It appears she's not as easy to kill as they'd hoped," Faylinn said quietly. "When I first saw her, I thought she was a ghost, too." *Come to haunt me.*

Will smiled sympathetically at Faylinn and found himself liking her, despite the fact that she'd been married to that slave-running son of a bitch, Cyril Redding. Or maybe it was just the way she looked in his son's clothes.

Glassy green eyes fixed on Bridget's face. "She looks so pale." Will fetched the torch from the wall and brought it closer to the bed so Faylinn could examine her friend. The flickering glow from the flame cast distorted shadows across Bridget's face, deepening the already angular planes and making her appear gaunt. The light highlighted in sickening detail the recent abuse she'd suffered.

Swallowing hard, Faylinn dropped to her knees at the head of the bed and took Bridget's hand in hers. She gently rubbed the small calluses at the base of long fingers. Her frown grew more severe when she noticed a jagged cut just below the dark-haired woman's collarbone. The wound disappeared behind the rough-hewn blanket.

Curious, Faylinn peeled back Bridget's blanket, deciding it was foolish to be modest in front of Will, who, with his wife, had cut away Bridget's clothes and tried to treat her wounds.

"Do you think it would hurt her if I take these off for a moment?" She gave a small tug to the linen bandages that were wrapped loosely around Bridget's upper body. "Just so I can tighten them?"

Will scratched his jaw. The bandages had come loose when he'd carried Bridget in. He wasn't going to fiddle with them until they needed changing, but he found himself unwilling to deny Faylinn's request. "I don't suppose it will do any harm. The bleeding has mostly stopped." He visibly shivered. "But it's not a pretty sight."

"No. I don't suppose it will be," Faylinn agreed grimly. Carefully she slid gentle hands under Bridget's shoulders and undid a small knot.

Will brought the torch closer, and Faylinn gathered up the last of the cloth. Her eyes went round and her hands formed trembling fists as she saw for the first time the brutal price Bridget's body had paid for Cyril's deceit. "Sweet Jesus," she muttered, her stomach clenching painfully despite Will's earlier warning.

Cuts and scratches crisscrossed Bridget's breasts and shoulders, several so deep they'd required sewing. The stitches were crudely done, but Bridget had been wiped clean and even the small wounds showed signs of care. "Thank you," Faylinn said again, wishing there was more she could say that would convey her heartfelt gratitude.

Green eyes were drawn to a small cut in the valley between Bridget's breasts. It had jagged red streaks shooting from it and oozed an unhealthy discharge. Faylinn sighed. *Infected.* But more troubling still, was a black and purple bruise that covered Bridget's entire abdomen. She laid a hand atop the mottled, swollen, flesh, finding it hot to the touch. Her heart sank. Even Faylinn knew enough to know Bridget was bleeding inside. A dark rage grabbed hold of her and shook her to the core. *I should have run you through myself, Cyril, you bastard!*

Faylinn felt more tears coming, and she bit her lip to ward off their flow.

Will felt a stab of pity for this slip of a girl in his son's old clothes and he softened his tone. "Take heart, Faylinn. She's not dead yet. She looks like a strong one. She was heavy as a sow."

Faylinn blinked at Will's choice of words, but chose not to comment. Wordlessly, she re-wrapped the bandages, putting the knot on top this time so Bridget wouldn't be lying on it. She handed Will back what she suspected was a horse blanket and maneuvered the quilt until Bridget was safely underneath. "How could someone do this to you?" She hadn't realized she'd said the words out loud until Will answered her.

"So she would confess to bein' a witch, of course," he supplied conversationally. "Those cuts on her chest and shoulders were no accident. As for the scratches, who knows?" He drew his thick eyebrows together in contemplation. "Looks like she fought with a tree or a bobcat."

"Or a cliff." Her voice was the barest of whispers as she swept a tangle of wine-colored hair off Bridget's forehead. She let her fingers linger in the soft but dirty hair. *How could you have jumped? How could you have lived? How could I have heard your sweet words inside me own head, as though I was saying them? Maybe I'm going mad.*

Will stepped away from the bed, feeling very much like he was intruding upon a private moment between the women. "My wife set the arm as best she could. She's got a talent for doctoring. My Katie gave her a good dose of sleeping tonic for the pain. We couldn't set the arm 'til she was asleep. She kept fighting us." He studied his shoes. "I'm sorry I threw you out. I know you didn't mean to—"

"I'm sorry I got sick. I–I've been under a lot of stress this past week. The sight and smell..."

Will squared his shoulders. "I heard some of what happened on Cobb Island in town yesterday morning as I was passing through."

Faylinn looked at him frankly. "I'm sure it was more than enough."

"It was. We don't believe in witches in this house." The corner of his mouth curved upward. "Or barn."

She managed a tiny smile.

He leaned against the wall by the bed. "She's already got a fever."

"I know. I'll stay with her. We won't be much trouble. And we'll leave as soon as we can. In my dress I have a bracelet—"

Will snorted loudly. "We don't want your baubles or filthy slave-trader money."

Afraid she'd offended him, Faylinn began a rambling apology that was stopped abruptly when he asked, "Can you read?"

She nodded slowly, confused. "Yes, of cour—" Her cheeks

tinted. "Yes, I can."

Her slip of the tongue hadn't gone unnoticed, but Will decided it meant far less than the fact that the young woman was kind enough to try to cover it up. "Then we'll take payment in the form of you reading the Bible to us." He looked a little embarrassed, but pressed on. "Is it a deal?"

"Absolutely." She regarded him curiously. "I wish I could do more."

He kicked at the floor awkwardly and stuffed his hands into his pockets. "That will make Katie happy, so it's enough." When he glanced up, Will was surprised to be looking into green eyes swimming with tears.

In his simple gesture, Faylinn Cobb had just witnessed more love for one spouse by the other than in all her years prior. "Whenever you want me to read, just ask. No matter what it is. No matter when."

"The Bible will be enough. We're not Puritans, mind you, but Katie, at least, is still a good Christian."

Bridget's soft moan interrupted them and Faylinn shifted closer, searching her face for any clue as to how she could make her more comfortable. When her eyes dropped to bruised lips, she had the strongest urge to bend over and softly kiss... *God, what am I going to do?* That she loved Bridget was clear. That she loved her the way a man could love a woman—with a longing and passion that caused her heart to skip frequent beats—was almost as frightening as it was compelling.

Pushing the thought away as unmanageable, Faylinn lifted her hand and tenderly traced the red, angry skin alongside a stitched gash that ran from just above Bridget's eye all the way to her jawbone.

Will sighed. "I'm thinkin' it will scar." He winced inwardly. *More's the pity. She could have had her pick of husbands.* "There was nothing to be done but clean and stitch it. A bandage won't hold on there."

Faylinn took Bridget's limp hand in her own. "Doesn't matter if it scars," she murmured. Her gaze turned fond. "She'll always be beautiful."

A small smile edged its way onto Will's face. "I'll leave you to rest, then." He jerked his chin towards the window. "It's past sunrise, though you wouldn't know it by the looks of it. I'll bring you some food once you've had a chance to rest." He laughed when Faylinn jumped up and began situating herself next to Bridget on the small bed.

The man extinguished the torch in the cool ashes along the

edge of the fireplace, then tossed another round of oak onto the coals. It was going to be cold today. He could feel it in his bones.

Faylinn didn't even realize when he crept out of the room.

Chapter
Four

After sitting for nearly three hours listening to Badger weave the tale, Kayla and Liv decided to have their taxi drop them off at the bottom of the Royal Mile, near the palace of Holyrood House, Queen Elizabeth's official Edinburgh residence. The idea of fresh air and a brisk walk appealed to both of them. The afternoon breeze was still cool: strong enough to tousle their hair and turn their cheeks rosy, but not so cold as to be uncomfortable. It carried with it the scent of wet sidewalks, car exhaust, and the sea.

Kayla had been silent all the way back into town, then a rapid stream of words burst from her. "I can't believe he did that. I can't believe he just stopped!"

Liv was a little startled by her reticent friend's outburst. "What did you expect, Kayla?" she chided gently. "Badger is an old man, and he'd been going non-stop for quite a while. His voice was bound to give out eventually."

"Well, sure. But..." Kayla let out a grumpy breath. "I wanna know what happened, I guess." She threw her hands in the air, not sure how to process things. She was used to having an insatiable curiosity when it came to her work, but never with something personal. "He could have skipped all the melodrama and just cut to the chase, right?"

Liv assumed the question was rhetorical, so she waited.

Kayla began ticking off on her fingers. "We know Bridget killed her brother. But we don't know how she survived her fall from the cliff, or how she and Faylinn made it to the mainland, or whether Bridget ultimately survived her injuries, or—"

"Whether they ended up together," Liv finished. "I'm dying to know that myself."

"Exactly." Kayla gave her an aggrieved look. She was desperate to know that someone in her family was able to make a relationship work in spite of their paranormal abilities. Her father's talents were on the very low end of the scale, and it hadn't ever seemed to be an issue for her parents. But it had always, always been an issue for her.

Liv smiled, thinking that Kayla looked impossibly cute when she pouted. Of course, she wasn't going to share that thought with the nearly six feet of moody baby next to her, but it was true nonetheless.

Kayla stopped walking and turned to face Liv. Her hands flew to her hips and she spoke sharply. "I am not moody! And I'm certainly *not* a baby."

Liv stopped as well, then stepped backwards so that several people who were scurrying up the street could pass between them. She pinned Kayla with a glare. "I didn't *say* you were."

The scowl on Kayla's face was replaced by a tense, worried look. *Oh, shit.* "I...uh...I just—"

"You read my mind," Liv said evenly.

Kayla cringed. "I'm so sorry. I didn't mean to." Her heartbeat sped up. *This is where things go all to hell, and I get accused of spying on her thoughts. I've got to learn better control. I—* "I was just walking along and the thought popped into my head."

Liv chewed the inside of her cheek for a moment, fighting the urge to get good and pissed off. Then her better judgment took over, and she sighed. "Did you do it on purpose?" she asked, already fairly certain of the answer and hating the poorly veiled anxiety she saw in Kayla's eyes.

"No!" Kayla moved forward in reflex, needing to close the gap between her and Liv. She looked around self-consciously to see if anyone was staring. "No," she repeated a little more quietly as her eyes met and held Liv's. "I swear."

There was an intensity to Kayla's answer that made Liv's heart ache, and she gentled her gaze. *Time to start working on this. For both our sakes.* She reached out and took Kayla's hand. "Relax, will ya? I'm not mad."

The dark-haired woman remained warily silent.

Liv sighed again. "You might need to remind me of this every once in a while, but I really shouldn't get mad at you for something you didn't do intentionally. Okay?"

Kayla blinked dumbly at Liv. She couldn't have heard her right. "You...you shouldn't?"

"No," she told her seriously, "I shouldn't." *Who did this to you?* "Honey, I'm not going to blame you for something out of your control." A smile tugged at her lips when she saw Kayla's

face begin to relax. *That's it, love.* "Unless I have PMS." She
grinned recklessly. "Then you're screwed." Liv's words where
greeted with a tiny burst of laughter from Kayla that was equal
parts happiness and relief.

I am so lucky. I'd better not fuck this up. Kayla looked at Liv
with utter affection. "Thank you," she said simply, still a little
dumbfounded, but not about to look a gift horse in the mouth.

"You're welcome." *You're not going to get rid of me that easily. We're going to talk about this... Just not in the middle of the
sidewalk.*

"So," Liv deftly steered the conversation in another direction
as they began walking again, "were you surprised that Bridget was
still alive?"

Kayla willingly allowed herself to be distracted, and her
brows knitted as she thought. "I guess not," she finally decided.
"I know it's all fantastic, nearly too much to believe, but deep
down inside I had this niggling suspicion that their story wasn't
quite over yet."

Liv tucked an errant lock of fair hair behind her ear.
"Mmhm," she acknowledged with a small nod.

Kayla carefully guided them around a tall postcard stand and
a pack of student tourists. "You?"

Liv took several steps before answering. "Oh... Well, the
same as you, I guess." She didn't feel comfortable sharing with
Kayla that her stomach had been in knots until Badger made it
very clear that Bridget had survived the cliff. There was something indefinable about Bridget Redding that reminded her of
Kayla. It went beyond the obvious physical similarities, touching
on subtle, emotional elements that Liv found undeniably interesting as well as attractive. She thought about that for a moment and
Kayla's overreaction a few minutes before. *Maybe there is something about this story that stirs something in us both. Maybe.*

Liv and Kayla turned off the Royal Mile and began winding
their way through the Gothic streets of Old Town. Within a few
moments, they were standing in front of the Keith House, a tall,
narrow three-story structure that had clearly undergone recent
renovations. The centuries of chimney smoke that stained so
many buildings from that time period and added significantly to
their eerie mystique, had been scrubbed clean.

Though Liv would always associate Gothic architecture with
the Addams Family and consider it "classic horror film spooky,"
the Keith House, at least its exterior, already had a less haunting

feel than many others she'd seen. It retained the beauty of the era without the foreboding. Which was odd, Liv considered, since *this* was the house they were about to investigate for... She couldn't remember what Kayla had called it exactly, but it had some long, technical name that had to do with blood and the paranormal. Not that it mattered. Liv's mind had already settled on "some seriously spooky shit."

There was no sign of the press, and so Kayla eagerly trotted up the steps to the front door and inserted the key Glen had given her the day before. "Time to earn some money."

Her excitement was clear and Liv tried to grasp hold of that and make it her own, disregarding some of the nervousness that had been building since they'd turned off the main road onto this lonely street. This was the start of a new career, and she was bound and determined to push past her own silly fears and be of real use to Kayla.

The door to the Keith House was heavy, but it opened without a sound.

They walked inside, into a large foyer with high ceilings and freshly painted walls. Liv spun in a circle, taking in her surroundings openmouthed. "Wow."

Kayla nodded. "Wow. Not exactly what I was expecting."

"Me, neither."

The house was completely empty. No furniture. No rugs. No paintings. Nothing.

Liv carefully crept a few paces deeper into the foyer. "Looks like Mr. Keith is going to do a little...all right, a *lot* of redecorating before his grand opening." Her quiet words sounded unusually loud in the hollow room. She poked her head around a corner, finding nothing but vacuous space. It was only early evening, but the house's interior was already cast in long gray shadows that seemed to move with Liv as she walked. But more than that, it was deathly quiet. Silent as a grave. *Okay, this I don't like.*

"See anything interesting?"

"Yaaaaaaah!" Liv jumped at the low voice right by her ear. "Jesus, Kayla!" She whirled around to face her tormentor, laying her palm across her own chest and feeling the pounding heart. "Are you trying to kill me?"

Kayla bit back a smile and jerked her thumb towards herself. "Who me?" Puppy dog eyes blinked at her.

"Oh, no!" Liv's eyes turned to slits. "Don't give me that 'I'm-too-cute-to-do-something-mean' face."

"Cute?" Kayla managed to sound mildly insulted at the idea,

but her lips continued to twitch.

"You're trying not to laugh, aren't you?"

Think disgusting thoughts. I. Will. Not. Laugh. "Of course not." The words were said soberly, but Kayla's quivering chin betrayed her.

"Liar!"

"I'm...I'm..." Kayla dissolved into laughter.

Liv crossed her arms over her chest and whined, "It's not funny, Kayla! You know I'm not used to this creepy stuff yet."

"Sure it is." Kayla continued to laugh, not stopping when Liv gave her a plastic smile. "Okay, okay," she conceded reluctantly. She grabbed hold of Liv before she could stalk out of the room. "I'm sorry."

Liv arched an eyebrow. "No, you're not."

Kayla crossed her heart and held up three fingers. "I am. Honest."

Now Liv was holding back her own grin, delighted at the appearance of Kayla's more playful side. "You know I'll get you back," she informed her haughtily.

Two slender eyebrows shot skyward. "You can try, Liv."

Liv pinched Kayla's flat stomach. "Ooo, I know when I've been challenged. Don't think I'll forget."

Kayla rolled her eyes, feeling very comfortable in her own environment. She loved her job. "I live in fear."

"Funny." But Liv smiled and stood on tiptoe to give Kayla a quick peck on the lips.

"Liv?"

"Hmm?"

Kayla's face turned serious, and she slowly grasped Liv by the shoulders as though she was going to shake her. She didn't. Instead, she held her firmly. "I need to give you your first lesson in paranormal research." Her voice dropped an octave. "This is *very* important."

Liv's ears perked up, and in the blink of an eye she was mirroring Kayla's serious expression. "Okay, I'm listening."

"This will help you in almost any circumstance, no matter what you're doing. I can't tell you how many times this tip has gotten me out of deep, dark situations that make me shudder just to remember."

Eyes wide, Liv gulped.

"It's something I don't want you to ever forget." Kayla paused meaningfully. "Understand?"

A fiery blue gaze burned into Liv, and the older woman promised solemnly, "I won't forget."

"Good." Unexpectedly, Kayla let go of Liv's shoulders, turned on her heel, and purposefully strode across the floor. When she reached the doorway, her arm shot out and with a tiny "click" the room was cast in a warm, buttery glow. She spoke without turning around, her unseen, crooked grin a mile wide. "Turn on the lights."

Liv blinked. "Son of a—"

Kayla's shoulders started to shake with silent laughter and then she was gone, off to find the equipment that was supposedly waiting for her.

Liv could hear the smug chuckles growing more distant as Kayla padded deeper into the house. *Ooo, I am so going to get her for smokin' my butt that way*, she mused, with more than a hint of admiration. "I hate you, Ghostbuster," she called out.

"No, you don't," came the sure reply.

Liv smiled to herself. "No. I guess I don't," she muttered dreamily. She looked around again, almost casually at first. Then she began to notice that with Kayla's absence, the room's silence had somehow become a little unsettling. Not too much, but enough that Liv's gaze flickered around the room as she sought to reassure herself that everything was all right. That she was, indeed, alone.

She forced herself to relax and take a deep breath, releasing it slowly. "Get a grip, Liv."

Suddenly, she felt a cool rush of air that sent chills skittering across her skin, lifting the hairs on her arms as if a tiny current of electricity had shot through her. Then, as quickly as it had come, it disappeared. "Oh, boy." She shivered in pure reaction and began inching towards the door. "Hey, um...Kayla?" Liv picked up her pace. "Wait up!"

"Okay, another one in that corner." Kayla pointed while Liv fished another infrared motion detector from the metal trunk and headed across the room.

She bit her tongue and her eyes narrowed slightly as she considered its exact placement. *I wonder...* "Kayla?"

"Mmm?" Kayla's eyes remained trained on the detector she held in her hands. She gave it a little shake and the green activation light popped on. "Piece of—"

"What if I put it here, instead?" Liv stepped sideways three long paces and put the small device on the ground, angling it between the doorway and where Kayla was crouched. "Then the beam should not only cross with yours, but also with the one shooting in from the hall. We can avoid that gap you were complaining about before."

Kayla glanced up at the doorway to the hallway. She cocked her head slightly as she gauged the distance and angle. Her face broke into a proud grin. "Yeah, that should work." She gave a satisfied nod. "Great idea. I was just going to lay down another detector. Now we'll have a spare for upstairs." The house had more rooms than Kayla had anticipated, and she wasn't pleased with the spotty coverage she was going to have to settle for in some places.

Liv grinned. "Cool." She stood up and dusted her hands off on her jeans. They'd been placing motion detectors, and video and sound recorders, around the large house for nearly three hours. It was pitch black outside, and Liv could hear Kayla's stomach growling from where she was standing. But they still had one final room to set up in before they were done for the evening, the room where Mr. Keith had awoken to strange noises and a very gruesome sight.

Kayla stretched her arms high over her head. "I need to do some thermal readings next," she began idly. "But I think I'll wait until tomorrow morning and see if we pick up anything strange tonight." She yawned. "This place is huge, and hopefully that will focus us on where we need to test." Kayla grabbed the last three motion detectors and the rest of her video cameras. "Ready?"

Liv gave herself a quick, silent pep talk, then nodded. "Ready."

The Keith House's master bedroom was enormous, taking up a full third of the second floor. The taller woman's nose twitched as she entered the empty room and flicked on the light.

Again Liv was surprised. This room was not just empty, it was antiseptic. "Fresh paint." Even the door appeared new.

Kayla's eyes darkened as she approached the mysterious wall, her sneakers silent on the bare floor. She had expected to see lurid streaks on the walls...not this. "Dammit, Glen!" she exploded. "What the hell am I supposed to do now?"

Liv joined her and laid a calming hand between her shoulder blades. Heat was radiating through her sweater. "How does this change things, Kayla?" Liv slapped away a fly that was buzzing around her head.

"The place has been scoured. Shit," Kayla muttered. She turned towards Liv, consciously tamping down her irritation. "I needed to test to see whether the blood was human, animal, or some other substance altogether."

"And now you can't," Liv surmised.

Kayla sighed and rubbed her temple. "We might still be able to tell whether it was blood or ketchup or something, but not whether it's human. Luminol—"

"That's used by the police on crime scenes, right?"

Kayla looked a little surprised.

Liv shrugged. "I saw it on *America's Most Wanted* the first night I was back from Africa. Sorry. Go on."

"S'okay." Kayla smirked at her lover. "Anyway Luminol, as you may *already* know—"

Green eyes rolled.

"—is a chemical that can show the presence of trace blood evidence, even under paint. But the test to determine whether the substance is human or not requires more than a bare trace. We're limited by our equipment."

Liv nodded her understanding. "You could send it to a big lab someplace..."

"But it would take weeks to get the results," Kayla finished unhappily.

"We can still run the other tests, right?"

"Yeah," Kayla grunted. "We still can." Her face grew pensive. Something didn't feel right about this whole thing. Something was niggling at the back of her mind, just out of reach. Her eyes shifted downward, and she saw Liv studying her intently. Her lover was trying to puzzle out what was going on with her, and it reminded Kayla that she was going to have to voice her thoughts more often, something that had never been a concern in the past. She had been, and to a large extent still was, quite content to live inside her own head. "I have a weird feeling about this job, Liv," she confided uneasily.

Liv's brows drew inward and she snorted softly. "Is there ever something *not* weird about this job?" Kayla's sudden stillness told Liv she'd gone too far. She winced inwardly. *Damn that was stupid. I forgot how sensitive she is about this job and her abilities.* "Hey," Liv curled her fingers around Kayla's wrist, feeling the strong pulse, "I was just teasing. I'm sorry."

"Don't worry about it," Kayla said brusquely, as she moved to set out the video equipment.

But Liv didn't relinquish the hold on her wrist. "Kayla." Her voice was low and apologetic. "Please."

Kayla exhaled loudly. *Stop being so sensitive.* "What?"

"I didn't mean to hurt your feelings."

Kayla gave herself a kick in the ass and purposely lightened her tone. "S'okay. It's not you, it's me."

Liv pursed her lips, but decided not to pursue the issue. They'd barely skirted an argument earlier that afternoon, and now it was happening again. Part of it, she knew, was that they were still tired from their travels. And she knew by her partner's body language that she was hungry. "How about this? How about I let you set up this room, while I go get something to eat and bring it back to our bed and breakfast?" *A little time apart, wouldn't be a bad idea either.* "Then we can chow down there and hit the sack early."

A relieved look washed across Kayla's face. "That's a great idea."

"I thought so." Liv smiled tentatively. "But before I forget, what is it that seems odd about this job? Since I haven't ever been on one before, I don't have anything to compare it to."

"When Glen meets with potential clients, there's a list of information she always gets from them, as well as a set of instructions she gives them if she accepts the case on my behalf." Kayla reached out and drew her finger along the pristine, white walls.

"Kayla?" Liv prompted after a moment.

"Oh, sorry. One of those instructions is to never mess with something the client believes has been in contact with, or has anything to do with, the supernatural."

Liv began to gesture as she worked things through in her head. "Some people don't wait though, they go ahead and clean up if there's been a mess. It probably freaks them out, so they move to fix it right away."

"Sometimes that does happen." *Keep going.*

"And he saw the blood about three weeks ago, when we were on Cobb Island." Glen had phoned Kayla and asked that she cut her vacation short in order to come to Edinburgh. Instead, Kayla had insisted Mr. Keith be put off for a few weeks. She'd surprised Liv by telling Glen that if he couldn't wait, he could find himself another researcher. The women had used the extra precious time to get to know each other, spending part of it at Kayla's grandmother's ranch in West Virginia and the other part in Washington, D.C.

"Yes, again." Kayla grinned. *Now put it together.*

"So he didn't get all creeped out by the blood and hurry up to paint it. He waited until after he was told not to, and then did it right before we arrived in Edinburgh." Liv looked at Kayla for confirmation.

"Exactly."

"Wow, I knew all those Nancy Drew mysteries would pay off someday." Liv stood a little straighter, proud of herself for reasoning that out. "Of course, I was really only thinking about kissing Nancy...but something must have rubbed off."

Kayla groaned dramatically. "Figures."

"I can see why that doesn't seem right. It doesn't fit with the man we met yesterday, who really seemed liked he wanted us to get to the bottom of this."

Kayla set her jaw. "He's going to get his wish."

Liv nodded slowly. "I don't doubt that at all, Kayla." Their eyes met and they shared a moment of profound determination, which was rudely interrupted by the rumbling of Kayla's stomach. Liv laughed. "Okay, okay, I'm going."

Kayla ducked her head sheepishly. "I am hungry. And," her head swayed back and forth for a moment, "I'm sorry about before. I get really moody when I haven't eaten." She glanced up and was met with understanding eyes.

"Me, too." Liv mentally added a grocery store to her stops. *I won't be caught again without some trail mix or something.*

Kayla handed Liv her cell phone. "No walking around at night alone, okay?"

"Noooo problem. I was planning on calling a cab." Liv leaned forward for a little kiss. "Mmm." She smacked her lips happily when they parted. "See you in an hour or two?" She had already learned that Kayla was meticulous about setting up her equipment, and she correctly assumed that once she left the lanky woman alone, Kayla's natural anal retentiveness would take over and she'd feel the need to check everything one more time.

Kayla fondly cupped her cheek. "Two would be great." *You already know me too well, don't you?* Then she found herself unconsciously holding her breath as she watched Liv's eyes flutter closed and a look of concentration overtake her face.

A few heartbeats later and Liv blinked, a little startled, then let out a slightly nervous laugh. She hadn't been expecting that; and though she hadn't exactly heard the words, she somehow *knew* what Kayla had been thinking. She turned and kissed the warm palm still resting on her cheek. Then she winked. "Darn right I do. See you in two."

Kayla's eyebrows lifted as Liv walked happily out of the room. "Oh, boy." She shook her head, but couldn't manage to feel anything other than wonderful. "I am in so much trouble."

Kayla had just locked her equipment trunk when she heard soft footsteps behind her. "Found a take-out place around here, did ya?"

"No. But if you're hungry, I'm sure that something can be arranged."

Startled, she whirled around at the unexpected voice. "Glen." Kayla straightened and took a long look at the petite woman who was, as always, dressed immaculately. She was also carrying an expensive, black leather briefcase. "I thought you were—"

"Liz?"

Pale blue eyes went a little icy. "It's *Liv.*"

Glen cocked her head to the side and spoke casually, completely unfazed by Kayla's stony gaze. "Ah, yes. That's right. She was," the Asian woman stepped closer to Kayla, bringing with her the strong, musky smell of her perfume, "a surprise."

Kayla wrinkled her nose and stuffed her hands into her jean pockets, thinking that couldn't be the same perfume Glen had worn during their brief relationship. "I know. I probably should have said something."

A perfectly manicured, black eyebrow lifted in censure. "Probably?"

"Don't do this, Glen. I'm not in the mood."

"Since when do you need another partner?"

"She's not 'another partner,' she's my *only* partner," Kayla corrected her flatly. "You are paid on commission for your services by me. We're not business partners, or any other type of partner for that matter. And never have been."

Glen's grip on her briefcase tightened convulsively. "You can be a real bitch, Kayla. You know that?"

Kayla chuckled wearily. "Remind me, Glen, why it didn't work out between us. I seem to have forgotten."

That earned her a small smile. "Yes, well, my memory on that subject tends to fade a little when you're this close to me." Glen reached out to touch Kayla's arm.

Kayla stopped her with a quick hand, giving Glen's fingers a friendly squeeze before letting them go. They were soft and warm, and despite herself, Kayla was reminded of at least one thing she'd found attractive in Glen.

"Maybe we weren't partners, but I was still your mentor." Glen could feel herself growing angry, and a slight flush began to work its way up her neck. "It was *me* who showed *you* the ropes in this business. So don't act as though I'm some hired hand."

"And then it was you that decided to only handle the business end of things," Kayla reminded her pointedly. "How many other researchers hire you to do the same thing I do?"

Glen gathered hold of her emotions again and straightened

the corner of her dark silk blazer. "My other business affairs aren't important." She tapped her briefcase impatiently with her index finger. "Do you have some results that I can pass along to Mr. Keith yet?"

"What?" Kayla looked at her as if she was insane. "I haven't even started yet!"

"Jesus Christ, Kayla, what's there to start? This was obviously some ridiculous delusion. Do a quick run through and be done with it." *Why must you always be so difficult?*

"Cut the bullshit and tell me why I'm here, Glen," Kayla ordered unceremoniously.

The angry flush returned to Glen's neck. "You're here because you're a big name in the field." *Because of me.* "And when you say there is nothing out of the ordinary going on, people will believe it, and then Mr. Keith will pay us *very* handsomely."

Kayla looked hard into Glen's eyes. "I want to see the contract."

Glen looked shocked. "What?"

"You heard me, Glen. I want to see the total fee you negotiated, and the terms."

Ruby lips twisted into a snarl. "Are you implying I'll take more than my commission?"

"No. I'm not implying a damn thing, other than I want every scrap of paper having to do with this job, and I want it now."

Glen stiffened. "I see." She closed her eyes briefly, before refocusing on Kayla. There was nothing she could do. If Kayla quit now, Mr. Keith's trust in her would be shattered. She had no choice. "You'll have it tomorrow."

God, I'm already tired of this. "Thank you." Kayla breathed an inward sigh of relief. "And as far as my report for the house, you'll get that as soon as it's finished. Just like always."

Glen swallowed her anger and ducked her head. "Of course."

Kayla made a conscious effort to soften her tone. She gestured towards the briefcase. "Do you have the other files I asked for?"

The small woman held up it up in front of Kayla's face, her brightly painted nails standing out against the dark leather. "The interviews with the housekeeper and her daughter are all here, though I've already briefed you on what you'll find. Time is of the essence. That's why I conducted them while you were off play—" She paused and swallowed. "While you were still in the States."

"Humor me."

"Don't I always?"

Kayla fought the urge to smile. "You've always done right by me, Glen. I don't want you to think I'm hinting otherwise. But there's something odd here..."

Glen's pulse quickened. "Odd? How?"

"I don't know," Kayla replied honestly. "But I do know that we need to talk."

"Sadly, I can't stay." But her coal-black eyes didn't reflect a hint of disappointment. "I have a late dinner appointment."

"You're going to be late, Glen."

Glen could hear the challenge in Kayla's voice and wisely backed off. *For now.* "I guess they'll have to wait." She glanced around the empty room. "I'm hardly dressed to sit on the floor; there's a pub down the street. Okay?"

Kayla glanced at her watch. "Yeah. Let's go."

Liv sat on a soft blanket on the beach, listening to the waves roll in. The lights from the houses lining the sea and the soft twinkle of stars above provided enough light so that she felt safe in her surroundings. When she'd asked Mrs. Thicke, their B&B proprietress, for a blanket she could use, the woman had been only too happy to oblige her. She also gave her a thermos of mulled apple cider to ward off the chill.

The linguist took a long sip of the sweet liquid, letting it slide down her throat and warm her guts. Then two long arms wrapped around her, heating her from within in ways the cider never could. Soft, warm lips landed on her throat and kissed her tenderly before nudging Liv's chin upward for better access. Her skin was slightly salty and cold from ocean spray.

Liv reached up and threaded her hand through thick, red, luxurious hair. "Mmm... That's nice. But you'd better hurry up, my girlfriend was due here an hour ago." The lips stilled for a long, charged second, then dipped playfully, biting Liv's throat. She squealed and laughed, but didn't try to dislodge her phantom attacker.

"Your girlfriend is a very lucky woman." Kayla plopped down alongside Liv so that they were facing each other. "Are you sure I can't convince you to forget about her?"

Liv looked into eyes that shone silver in the moonlight. "What girlfriend?" she mumbled dreamily.

Kayla snorted. "I'll have to remember that." She leaned forward and brushed her lips against Liv's, tasting the spicy tang of the cider. "Mmm. That makes me even more hungry," she growled, moving to deepen the kiss. A hand on her chest stopped her.

"Hold your horses."

Kayla froze immediately, and Liv grinned to let her know this was no rejection. "I'm glad you're hungry," Liv said. "Because I've got tons of food that is getting cold up in our room." She reached up and tugged on a strand of Kayla's gently blowing hair. "I was starting to worry."

"Sorry about that. I had an unexpected visitor about an hour after you left."

Liv's eyebrows disappeared behind wind-blown bangs. "A ghost?"

"Hardly," Kayla scoffed. "Glen."

"Oh." Liv made a face that made Kayla chuckle. "I know she's your friend and all, Kayla, and I'll be nice to her out of respect for that. But I gotta tell you, she didn't impress me too much yesterday."

Kayla let out a long, slow breath. "She didn't impress me too much, either. We went to a pub tonight, and I got a few questions answered about this case."

Liv nodded knowingly and traced the edge of Kayla's wire-rimmed glasses. "You had to read."

"Oh." Kayla quickly pulled them off and clasped them in her hand. "I forgot I was still wearing them." She only needed the glasses when her eyes were strained or she was very tired. "I swear," Kayla said, her Southern accent drawing out the word, "Glen is using smaller print just so I'll have to drag these out and—"

"You look beautiful in them." Liv gazed at her fondly.

Kayla swallowed and her cheeks burned. "I-I do?"

She nodded without hesitation. "Uh huh. You sure do."

Liv's youthful, easy smile made Kayla fall in love with her all over again. "C'mon." She pushed herself to her feet and extended a hand to her lover. "Let's have dinner, and I'll tell you what I found out. I think I'm going to need your help."

Liv gathered up the blanket and thermos, and let Kayla tug her to her feet.

Kayla wrapped her arm around Liv's shoulder as they walked. "Where'd you get this?" She used blunt nails to loudly scratch the thick material beneath her fingertips. "It looks nice."

Over Liv's sweater she wore a dark-navy jacket that fell to mid-thigh. The lining was a tartan print wool, and the shell was an oiled, heavy canvas that was waterproof. "Do you know how many shops I passed on the way from Old Town to Portobello?"

"Hmm. Many." They continued to march through the

packed sand. "I like it."

"Good." Liv gave Kayla self-satisfied smirk. "You have a black one waiting for you in our room."

Bemused, Kayla shook her head. "Nobody has dressed me since I was a child, Liv."

The fair-haired woman stopped and turned so that she was facing Kayla dead on. She wrapped her arms loosely around Kayla's waist and spoke in a low, sure voice that wound its way around her partner's heart. "Maybe nobody has loved you as much as I do." Liv pulled her close and hugged her tightly, burying her face in the crook of Kayla's neck.

Kayla tilted her head back and caught a quick glimpse of the stars before she squeezed her eyes shut. "I love you, Liv," she offered so softly the words were nearly swept away in the breeze.

But Liv didn't really need to hear them to know exactly what had been said. She gently kissed Kayla's throat and removed the remnants of a tiny, hot tear that had made its way down from the cheek above it. Waves of emotion were pouring off Kayla, and Liv simply held on for the ride. "I love you, too."

She allowed Kayla a moment to pull herself together before she backed away slightly and took her hand. "C'mon, let's go eat. We've got mysteries to solve tomorrow."

Kayla twined their fingers together and they resumed their walk. *Yeah, we sure do.*

Chapter
Five

Kayla and Liv had managed to get up in time to enjoy break-fast. Sort of. The night before, Kayla had made arrangements to have a tray set outside their room at 7a.m. sharp, begrudgingly conceding to Mrs. Thicke that they would probably be eating cold food by the time they got to it. But to Kayla's surprise, she had awoken early, refreshed and hungry. So here they were, sitting in bed together, drinking sweet tea and eating buttered toast, hair disheveled, sheets pooled around the waists of buck-naked bodies, with papers scattered all around them.

"Is there any more milk?" Liv mumbled around a big bite. She wiped the crumbs from the corners of her mouth with index finger and thumb, and then reached for the small pitcher that Kayla was absently passing her. "Thanks."

"Hmm?" Kayla didn't look up from what she was reading.

A mischievous smile curled Liv's lips. "I said I'm sleeping with Mrs. Thicke. I hope you don't mind."

"That's nice." Kayla patted Liv's thigh and left her hand there.

"I thought so," the blonde woman agreed cheerfully, taking another sip of tea. "Kayla?"

Nothing.

Liv poked at the hand on her leg. "Earth to Kayla."

"Mmm?"

Liv quirked an eyebrow. "Mrs. Thicke and I roll each other in butter, then sugar and cinnamon, then lick it off. Every day."

Still no reaction.

"On the beach in front of the entire world," she continued blithely. Liv fluffed the pillows behind her back with one hand. "She's a wild woman with amazing stamina. You'd never know that she was a hundred and eleven."

Kayla nodded again. "That's ni—*what?*" Her head snapped up and she tore her glasses from her face. "Mrs. Thicke?"

The combination of shock, bewilderment, and disgust painted so clearly on Kayla's face was priceless, and Liv burst out laughing.

"Eww!"

"Well, hello." Liv grinned impishly. "Nice to have you back."

"Bu–bu–you–but–" Kayla scrubbed her face with her hands, purposely ignoring Liv's saucy wink.

"Heh." Liv was exceedingly pleased with herself. "Now that I've got your attention, care to share what's so interesting in those files? I don't have the mind-reading thing down pat yet, you know."

"Sorry," she grumbled a little sheepishly.

Liv kissed her cheek softly. "S'okay, honey. You just tend to get a little...um..." She quickly searched her mind for a diplomatic way to say anal retentive. "You get so *focused* on one thing, that you tune everything else out." She settled herself back against her pillows again. "So what's up?"

I do not do that. "Sugar and cinnamon, huh?" Kayla grinned. "Can we—"

Liv arched an eyebrow and rattled the file in Kayla's hand. "You're doing it again."

"Oh." The brunette made a face. "Okay. Fine. It seems that Mr. Keith's maid, Mrs. Jane MacPherson, has worked for him since the late 1950s. Her husband also worked for Mr. Keith until 1987, when the husband died of a heart attack. They found his body a few paces from his bedroom in the middle of the night. Jane stated that he had gotten up to investigate a strange noise."

Liv's eyes widened.

Kayla curled her fingers around Liv's and squeezed gently. "He died before he could explain what had happened." She gave her lover a sympathetic look. "He probably just had a nightmare, Liv. There's nothing to show any connection between that and what's going on now."

Liv nodded, not entirely convinced. *Next time we go back we're staying—*

"—together," came the reassuring answer to her unspoken statement.

Liv let out a relieved breath. They locked eyes, and each gave a quick nod of acknowledgement. It was a promise.

Kayla glanced back at the file. "A few months before his

death, the MacPhersons adopted a seven-old-girl they named Mary."

Liv retrieved her plate from the nightstand and slathered some marmalade on her third piece of toast. "That would have made them sort of old parents," she commented conversationally, trying *not* to think of anything frightening enough that it could induce a heart attack.

"Right. In their early fifties."

Liv was a little surprised. "I had assumed Mr. Keith was talking about a child when he mentioned the daughter who lived with his maid at Keith House."

"Me, too." Kayla leaned forward and stole a bit of Liv's toast, her white teeth neatly severing a large piece.

Liv slapped Kayla's bare shoulder. "Hey! You've got your own."

"But yours tastes so good," Kayla said innocently.

Liv snorted at the double entendre but chose not to comment, knowing if she replied they wouldn't be getting any work done for quite some time.

"The daughter still lives with her mom today. Don't you think it's strange that someone would still be living at home at that age?" Kayla poured more tea, then took a deep drink. "Ouch! Shit. Mrs. Thicke was wrong." She peered into her mug, giving it an evil look. "That's still hot as hell."

Liv winced and wordlessly poured a little milk into Kayla's cup to cool the liquid. "I don't think that's so weird. A lot of people are still living at home in their early twenties. That's only a few years older than Dougie and your sister, Marcy," she said wistfully, her thoughts turning to the parents that she'd lost when she was only nineteen. A day didn't go by that she didn't wish they'd had more time to get to know each other as adults. She sighed.

"Maybe," Kayla allowed, wondering at the sad look she saw reflected in her friend's deep green eyes. She herself had moved out of the house at seventeen and, even though she truly loved her parents, couldn't imagine living under their roof any longer than was necessary.

Liv pushed away thoughts of the past and tried to focus on the here and now. "Does the daughter's story match her mom's?"

Kayla shrugged one shoulder. "Pretty much. They both heard Mr. Keith scream. Mrs. MacPherson saw the blood first, and Mary confirmed its existence, though her mother refused to let her into the room at first. Mrs. MacPherson also recalls numerous other unusual happenings in the house that she claimed," Kayla held the file a little farther away as she read the quotation without her glasses, "'chilled my old skin colder than the bottom of a well digger's—'"

"I'm familiar with the phrase," Liv interrupted wryly. "Do we need to talk with either one of them, or will 'jail bait's' interviews be enough?"

Kayla choked on her tea. "Jail—" She continued to cough and laugh, sitting forward as Liv helpfully slapped her back. "Who are you talking about?"

"You know damn well who I'm talking about, Ghostbuster." Liv set her cup and plate on the nightstand and flopped down on the bed, flattening her pillows. "She's twelve years old. You're lucky you're not in prison." *And I should be ashamed at how jealous I'm feeling*, Liv admonished herself privately.

Kayla turned amused eyes on her partner. "The woman has an M.B.A. and a Ph.D. in psychology."

"Great." Liv rolled her eyes dramatically. "Another Doogie Howser."

Kayla laughed as she set the breakfast tray on the floor. She lay back down on her side facing Liv. "She's older than you are, Liv."

"Bullshit."

Kayla feigned insult, pushing the fluffy pillow away from her head so she could see Liv better. "It's true."

"Uh huh."

"Dammit, Liv, she's thirty three."

Liv reached around and gave her a sharp pinch on the ass.

"Ouch!" Kayla squirmed away from Liv's fingers. "I swear," she laughed.

Liv stopped her attack and snuggled into Kayla's embrace, feeling her lover's heart racing. She squealed when Kayla shifted onto her back, taking her with her. "No way, Kayla." Liv lifted her head and eyed her lover speculatively. She blinked at the serious look on Kayla's face. "Really?"

"Mmm hmm..."

The low sound rumbled through Liv, drawing an unconscious smile. She let her head drop against Kayla's shoulder and exhaled contently. "Weird." Liv trailed her fingers along Kayla's hip, enjoying the feel of silky-soft skin. "When is her birthday?" she finally asked quietly.

Kayla's warm breath ruffled Liv's hair. "How the hell should I know?"

"Oooo." Liv chuckled and rewarded Kayla's reply with a kiss to her collarbone. "Good answer."

Kayla suddenly went so quiet that Liv pushed up onto her
elbows and studied her partner's face. "What's the matter?"

Kayla sighed unhappily. "I asked for all the financial records
for this case. Glen usually takes care of all of that. But..."
Another sigh.

"But you don't trust her."

"I did. I want to."

Liv just waited.

Kayla's brows furrowed deeply. "But I don't with this case.
Something is different."

"Mmm." Liv lay back down. "I'm sorry," she murmured,
gently patting Kayla's chest. "Maybe you're wrong, and everything will turn out fine." But even as she said the words, she
didn't believe them to be true. Part of what made Kayla so good
as a paranormal researcher was her sixth sense. If she believed
deep down that something was wrong, it probably was. *Or maybe
it just makes it easier for me to dislike the little bitch if Kayla has
doubts about her, too. Ooo, see? That wasn't nice at all.*

Liv yawned and could feel her eyelids growing heavy again.
She didn't try to fight it as she let herself drift off into a light
sleep.

Kayla, on the other hand, used the time to think, replaying
Glen's reactions to the questions she'd asked her the night before.
The Japanese woman was nervous and slightly evasive, but not
overly so. *And when I asked her about the new equipment she
was supposed to have ordered over two months ago, she changed
the subject or claimed there must have been a mix up in the order
or the shipping.*

When Liv woke up nearly an hour later, she opened her eyes
to Kayla's sleepy smile. The bed was now free of papers, and the
sheet had been pushed down to their feet. The room was cool but
not cold, and Kayla's natural body heat was more than enough to
keep Liv comfortable.

Kayla moved closer, tangling her legs with her partner's and
delighting at the sensation of soft skin sliding between her calves
and thighs. A shiver of desire raced through her. "Morning...
Again."

Liv arched her back and stretched, letting loose a big yawn.
"Morning." She sighed happily. "So, boss, what's on the agenda
for today? I know you said we need the cameras and equipment to
run for twenty-four hours before we disturb them."

Kayla adjusted her head on Liv's pillow, her red hair mixing
with the pale locks that smelled faintly of peppermint. "Don't call
me that," she urged Liv quietly, growing more and more conscious

of the warm skin so close to her with each passing second. "We're...we're partners. I don't wanna be your boss." Her eyes dropped to the pulse point on Liv's throat. Transfixed, she watched the graceful shift of muscles as Liv swallowed. Kayla licked her lips as a low, soft growl erupted from the back of her throat. "At least not for work."

Liv's heart skipped a beat at the timbre of Kayla's voice. "Ooo... I should have guessed you'd be all toppy." Kayla's body shook hers with silent laughter.

"Okay, *partner.*" Liv brought her hand up and caressed Kayla's cheek. "Are we going back to the Keith House this morning or...um..." Hands slid up her bottom and came to rest on the small of her back. "Umm..." *Is Kayla's skin always this hot?* And for the first time, Liv noticed the attractive flush covering the faint freckles on Kayla's chest and shoulders. "Mmm... You feel great," she breathed. Her thoughts began to get away from her as Kayla's body demanded her full attention. Liv's eyes traced the expressive curve of sensuous lips, and she couldn't remember what they were talking about. The look on Kayla's face silently compelled her forward, and she captured the younger woman's lips with quiet, sincere passion. They tasted like tea and honey, and Liv was helpless under their spell, unable to resist their beckoning softness. She hummed at the sensual contact.

When the long kiss ended, Kayla pulled back. "Wow." She laughed a little nervously, slightly startled by the unexpectedly intense exchange.

"Yeah." Liv smiled. "Wow." Then she remembered what she wanted to ask, but her hands refused to remain still and she traced Kayla's eyebrow as she spoke. "Or maybe we could go and talk to Badger?"

Kayla gazed at her lover through half-lidded eyes. "Whatever you want." Then she pinned Liv with an incredulous glare. "You don't mean now, do you?"

She's kidding, right? Just try to get out of this bed! "Well—"

"Liv." The word came out as a beseeching whine that instantly reminded Liv of her younger brother Dougie.

"Awww..." Green eyes twinkled. "You're pouting," Liv exclaimed delightedly, tweaking Kayla's nose.

"I am not," Kayla lied. But her disobedient face creased into a guilty grin. She ducked her head and began to kiss the soft skin behind Liv's ear. "It's too early to go anywhere," she informed her sternly, turning her body and using strong arms to securely tuck Liv neatly beneath her.

Liv closed her eyes and allowed herself to feel the full weight of her attraction and affection for Kayla. It surged through her, making her toes tingle. "You're right. Kayla—" She gasped when Kayla's lips dropped even lower and began painting a trail down her chest. "You should stay... Oh, God..." she gasped, when a hot mouth closed around her nipple, and her voice dropped to a low growl. "Right there."

Glen Fuguchi signaled the waiter by raising her empty glass to eye level and bestowing a charming smile on the young man. He nearly tripped all over himself as he raced over to the bar to fetch her another Bloody Mary. She laughed and shook her head. Eager boys like him were so adorable. Too bad they were of little use. Unless your glass was empty.

She was nursing her third drink when the hostess led a guest over to her table, then quietly disappeared. "It's not like you to keep me waiting." Glen gestured to the empty seat across the table.

Mary MacPherson looked around uncomfortably as she crushed out her cigarette in the ashtray on the table. "It's not like you to stand me up." Her red curls bobbed as she tilted her head downward. She glared at Glen. "Where were you last nicht?"

As always, Glen's manner was detached and in control, despite her slowly building anger at the young woman's impudence. "I don't think I owe you an explanation, Mary. But if you must know, I was unavoidably detained."

"By that psycho woman, no doubt." Mary snorted derisively and waved over a waiter. She ordered an enormous Scottish breakfast and, despite the early hour, a pint of beer.

Glen forced a thin smile. "That's psychic, not psycho. Though she was more than a little angry last night." The Japanese woman leaned forward and lowered her voice. She glanced sideways to make sure no one was nearby before she spoke. "Why didn't the old man listen to me about keeping everything the way it was? You told me he would do exactly as I asked."

Honey-colored eyes dropped to the tablecloth that Mary suddenly found very interesting.

"Mary?" Glen clenched her fists and felt her nails digging into the smooth flesh. "I left Mr. Keith very explicit instructions to leave everything about that damn bloody wall just as he found it for Kayla. Do you have something to tell me?"

Mary bit her bottom lip and braced herself for Glen's reaction. "Don't overreact."

"Oh, God." Glen immediately downed the remainder of her

drink in one big swallow. She pushed the empty glass away with
disgust. She simply wouldn't allow things to fall apart now. She'd
come too far. "Well?"

"I spoke to the old miser a few days ago and convinced him to
repaint the wall and even rip up the floor there."

"You did what?" The volume of Glen's words hadn't changed
one iota, but they were hard and cold as granite.

Mary fought the urge to shiver. "He came over to my aunt's
home, begging my mither to come back to him. Sayin' how much
he needed her on his staff and how important she was, and how he
didn't trust anyone else to run his household." Mary waved her
arms as she spoke, then crossed them over her ample chest. "I
knew the bastard would appreciate her once she was gone. Ha!"
She slapped her palm down on the table, causing Glen to jump.
"It's far too late for that now."

Glen reached under the table and took Mary's freckled hand
in her own. Something was very wrong. "What have you done,
Mary?"

Mary turned away from Glen's coal-black gaze. "Nothing
more than I said I'd do."

Glen's slender brows furrowed. "Then why—"

Mary sighed, but her face brightened when a plate laden with
steaming eggs, fragrant ham, fried bread, sausages and stewed
tomatoes was set in front of her. She let go of Glen's hand and
said to the waiter, "I'll take that." She reached out and took the
pint of beer from the server before he could even set it on the
table. Mary took several long drinks and wiped the thin layer of
foam from her lips with the back of her hand.

The muscles in Glen's cheeks began to twitch, and Mary
could see her lover's patience was at an end. She held up a hand
to forestall Glen's words. "Mr. Keith came asking about Mither.
She was gone to the market, but I talked with him. He said he'd
do anything to get her back and told me all about your lovely para-
psychiatrist."

Glen rolled her eyes, but didn't bother to correct Mary.

"He said the scientist would come and test the house and
prove it wasn't haunted." She stabbed a tomato with her fork and
brought it to her lips. "He told me that the blood on the walls was
likely sheep's blood or some other poor farm animal's, and that
that would prove this whole incident had been nothing more than
a terrible prank. Probably by some rival inn, worried about his
precious Keith House opening up, and trying to scare him away."
She popped the tomato in her mouth. "And the fancy scientists
would run a bunch of other tests to show there was nothing to be

afraid of."

Glen rubbed the bridge of her nose tiredly, wondering how many drinks she'd consumed the night she'd found Mary MacPherson even remotely interesting. She was pretty enough, and lively in bed to be sure; but the time spent the night before with Kayla, despite the fact that they'd argued like bitches in heat for most of it, was a dream compared to this. "So far, that's exactly what we want to have happen," she told Mary carefully.

"Ay. It is." Mary set down her fork, and lifted her warm gaze to meet Glen's. "But I told him that Mither *might* come back to work for him if she didn't have to look at that nasty bloody wall ever again." She waved her hands dismissively. "The bald bastard argued with me, *of course.* But I made sure he'd move quickly by explaining Mither was looking for another job—one that paid far better and wouldn't cause her feet to ache."

Glen's dark eyes narrowed. "And you did all this because..." Her jaw worked silently as Mary hesitated in her answer. "This had better be good, you fool," Glen snapped. "Kayla, who is far smarter than you," she ignored the flash of hurt in Mary's eyes, "is now suspicious."

Mary lifted her chin and glared at the short woman. *Kayla Redding isn't better than me,* she told herself. "I might not be a genius, and I surely haven't gone to any fancy university, but I won't sit here and be insulted either. *You* asked me here this morning." *And you still need me.*

There was a long second of charged silence between them while Glen silently acknowledged that making Mary angry wasn't going to get her the answers she needed. She softened her gaze and reclaimed Mary's hand. "I apologize."

Mary nodded. "I had him paint the walls for one very simple reason. The blood that dripped down them wasn't from some poor bastard dog or chicken."

Glen instantly paled. "You," she paused and swallowed, hoping she had misheard Mary's last words, "you're trying to tell me—"

"The blood was human."

Glen closed her eyes and leaned back bonelessly in her chair. "Oh, my God." She let go of Mary's hand and pinned her with flashing, fearful eyes. "What have you done?" she whispered. *What have I done?*

"Hello, Brody," Liv greeted warmly.

The tall young man's head snapped up from the magazine he

was reading in the booth at the gates of Cobb Manor. "Hello!" His eyes lit up and he tossed his reading aside, stepping outside to join them, and straightening his kilt as he stopped next to Kayla. The breeze blew his shaggy reddish hair into his eyes, and he shook his head a little to dislodge it. "I didn't expect you lassies today." Unconsciously, he reached up and fiercely scratched his lightly stubbled cheeks. When he realized what he was doing, a sheepish grin curled the corners of his mouth. "One day, and I'm already thinking a beard isn't for me."

"Looks good, though," Liv complimented.

Kayla blinked, then her brow furrowed. Her own hand lifted to her smooth cheeks.

"Stop it," Liv laughed, pulling Kayla's hand down from her face and not letting go once it was back at her lover's side. Its natural warmth seeped through her skin, and Liv was hard-pressed not to sigh.

"Your father is going to continue telling us a little family history."

"Ah, excellent!" Brody was never one to pass up a chance at spending some time with the ladies. "Maybe I'll join y— Ouch!" A stinging smack to the back of Brody's head interrupted his words. "Hello, Mither," he said without turning around. "I was just—"

"Haud yer wheesht, you worthless thing! I won't hear any more talk of you leaving your job. Who would take the tickets?"

"Bu—"

Sylla rested her hands on her wide hips. "And didn't you just ask your faither for next Friday off?" she reminded him impatiently.

Brody's eyes went a little round.

Sylla waggled her finger at her only child. "Don't play the innocent with me, young man. And I know you asked for next Monday off, as well."

"To study, so I can take exams to get into the university and learn about gardening," he complained.

"Och!" Sylla swung her large arm towards Brody, but this time he dodged out of the way...and further infuriated his mother by beginning to laugh. She began chasing after him, swatting at his slender bottom with a frustrated hand. "You want to take the day off so you can take out that trashy Englishwoman from that pub that you think I don't know you go to every evening after work! No good, lad!"

"Ouch!" One of Sylla's hands connected with Brody's backside. "Ohh... If...Mither!" He smiled at Liv and Kayla. "If you'll excuse me I should...yeow!...get back to work." Brody jumped back into his booth and shut the half door behind him, effectively placing himself out of his mother's reach. Then Sylla got a good look at the magazine he'd been reading.

"Brody James Cobb!" She began tugging at the door, calling the young man everything short of the Devil himself.

"Now, Mither—" he laughed, holding up his hands to ward off further attack.

"And what is that nasty fuzz on your face?" The booth began to rattle. "Did you lose your razor?"

Kayla and Liv exchanged looks, and both took off towards the house at a near run, eager to escape Sylla "The Sullen," a Cobb family squabble, and the temptation of more shortbread. Liv could swear her jeans were tighter today than they'd been yesterday.

The wind carried Brody's squeals of laughter and Sylla's ranting curses all the way to the manor's front door as they let themselves into the large stone building.

Cobb Manor was far more crowded than it had been the day before, and from the foyer, Liv and Kayla could see a large tour group being led around by a woman wearing a seventeenth century costume that resembled Sylla's. Minus the pink fuzzy slippers.

"Ahh, ladies!" A deep voice boomed from the stairway as Badger nimbly made his way towards them, his stout, bulky body easily traversing the steps. He stopped at the first landing and waved with a powerful hand. "I love lasses who know how to tell the time. Forenoon is what I said, and here you are. I just finished popping in on the tour group you just saw. University lasses, here from Cambridge." He wriggled his thick white eyebrows.

Kayla smirked. Apparently Brody came by his slightly wicked ways quite honestly.

As they drew alongside him, Liv could smell the faint, clean scent of soap mixing with his sweet pipe tobacco. He was wearing the same costume he had the day before, but in deference to the chilly weather, his shirt was heavier, and it looked slightly more worn.

Badger looked up at Kayla as they walked down the long, dimly lit hallway. "I understand from Sylla you were interested in the library."

Kayla's dark head turned towards Badger. "Well—"

"No...um...that was me. I'd love to see it!" A light flush broke out across Liv's cheeks. She hadn't meant to answer for

Kayla. "Please," she finished weakly.

Two sets of slightly different colored blue eyes twinkled at the blonde woman with undisguised affection. And Liv found herself tumbling helplessly under both their spells, though for very different reasons.

Badger's deep laugh shook his chest. "Then the library it shall be."

The library's walls were covered with sturdily built, hardwood bookshelves that ran from floor to ceiling. The musty scent of old paper caused Kayla to sneeze as soon as they walked through the door.

"I do that myself," Badger commented, taking a chair with its back to the window. He handed Kayla a tissue from a box on the table beneath the windowsill. Light spilled in across his broad shoulders, illuminating the swirls of tiny dust motes that danced with his every movement. "The place could use a good airing." He sighed. "But the early rains this autumn have caused Sylla to keep this place shut tight as a drum."

Liv was shifting in her seat next to Kayla, trying to see what was on the shelves in front of her. "Take a look around, lass. That's why we're in this room."

Liv could feel the excitement in her grow as she jumped to her feet. "Thanks. But I don't want to keep you unnecessarily."

Badger blew out a disgusted breath. "Please, if you've seen one tourist, you've seen them all. I'm more than happy to spend some time in your company."

"We appreciate that," Kayla said seriously, surreptitiously glancing at her watch.

Badger chuckled. Kayla's alert eyes and intelligent face couldn't quite manage to veil her natural impatience. "Perhaps I could start while you're still looking?" He shifted his attention to Liv, who was already caught up in a first edition of Robert Tannahill's poetry. "Ahh...I see you've found one of my favorites. Are you familiar with his poems?"

"Not really." Her eyes scanned the verses, and she allowed the words to paint a picture in her heart. "But they're beautiful." She ran her fingers over the worn leather cover wistfully. Her stint in the Peace Corps in some of Africa's most remote villages had made enjoying hidden treasures like this a near impossibility. She'd nearly forgotten how much she loved the written word in all its forms.

"Of course you haven't read him," Badger snorted. "That damn Rabie Burns gets all the attention."

Kayla could feel a sudden flow of wonder and yearning coming from her lover as Liv continued to read and bits and pieces of the words and emotions floating around in the blonde woman's mind made themselves known to her. She narrowed her eyes as she considered what she could do about it. With a slight nod, she silently rose to her feet and stepped over to Badger, bending over to whisper something in his ear.

When she was finished, the old man drew back with his bushy eyebrows nearly on top of his head. Then he nodded and held out his hand. "It's a deal, lass."

Kayla grinned and shook it firmly. A shiver chased up and down her spine and, startled, she looked hard into the man's eyes, searching. Then her gaze flicked to the window over his shoulder.

Badger regarded her kindly and squeezed her hand once more before letting it go. "It's cold in this big place." He patted his woolen kilt. "You get used to it, especially in one of these."

Kayla rubbed the skin on her arms, the hairs still standing on end. "Yeah." The corner of her mouth curved up. "I suppose so." Then she remembered the bargain she'd just struck. "Come sit down by me, Liv," she called out softly." She and Badger exchanged smiles. "And bring *your* book."

Liv sighed and began to slip it back into its spot on the shelf, not understanding the meaning behind Kayla's words. *You'll have time to read and explore later. Don't be a baby, now. They're both waiting.* "One second."

"Bring over *your* book, Liv." Kayla bit her lip, trying to suppress a peal of unexpected laughter that threatened to spill out. Doing something nice for Liv gave her a little thrill that made her feel so good it was almost scary. Then her lover's eyes locked on hers, and what she felt down deep inside was nothing like fear.

"*My* book?" Her fingers instinctively tightened around its worn spine.

Kayla felt heat sting her cheeks and nodded slowly. She swallowed a few times. "Maybe you can read it to me later," she asked hopefully, completely forgetting about the man sitting three paces from her.

"Lord, help me." Badger pinned Liv with a playful glare. "Would you two like to be alone? I can always come back later."

"Oh, God," Liv mumbled, covering her face with her hands.

Heh. I love my life. Badger began to dig his pipe out from his sporran. "Because, although it does my old heart good to see such a happy young couple, a man can only stand so much of the love-sick eyes before he keels over."

Kayla closed her eyes and groaned out her embarrassment. *What on earth is wrong with me today? I'm practically a puddle around her.*

Sensing her friend's embarrassment, Liv crossed the room and put herself between Badger and Kayla, blocking Badger's view of her partner. She leaned over and kissed Kayla's cheek, "Thank you, honey," she whispered softly. "Something this old isn't cheap."

Kayla squirmed uncomfortably. She just knew Badger was sniggering at her behind Liv's back. *Old fart. But I've got Liv, and you've got that battle-ax Sylla. So there!*

Badger began to hack. He pulled his pipe from between his teeth as a cloud of smoke surrounded his head.

"You're worth it, Liv," Kayla said, quietly but honestly.

Liv cupped Kayla's chin and tilted her head up. "Thank you." Then on impulse, she turned around and planted a kiss on Badger's cheek, the bristly hairs of his beard tickling her mouth. "Thank you, Badger. It's a beautiful book."

His face was beet red from his coughing and somehow, after Liv's kiss, it just got worse.

Now it was Kayla's turn to snicker. Loudly.

"Ack." He wiped his cheek with his hand. "You're welcome, lass. Now go sit by that tall friend of yours so I can start up my tale," Badger told her gruffly.

But Liv could see he really wasn't angry. Still smiling, she joined Kayla on a small love seat.

Badger pointed a thick finger to an afghan that hung over the back of the chair. "You might want to cover yersels. With no fireplace, this room is a wee bit colder than where we were yesterday."

Kayla and Liv dutifully complied, snuggling closely together with the warm blanket covering their legs.

"Now, in case you've forgotten..." He knew damn well they hadn't forgotten, but story telling usually is most effective when the storyteller uses some sort of lead-in. "It was the year of our Lord sixteen hundred and ninety, and it was a cold, unforgiving November in the American Colonies..."

Chapter
Six

"No..." Bridget murmured. "I...it...too cold." Her entire body jerked as though she was struggling against some unknown force.

Dazed green eyes slowly fluttered open. "Bridget?" Tiredly, Faylinn lifted her head and peered at Bridget's face, studying it through the shadows.

Rain still pelted the stables, its staccato rhythm magnified by the stillness of the room.

Faylinn's eyes went round, and any trace of sleepiness vanished before her next heartbeat. "God." A small, trembling hand moved to Bridget's forehead, and a tendril of stark terror wound its way around Faylinn's heart...and tightened.

Bridget was on fire.

The tall woman's body convulsed in the throes of her fever and nightmare. Her eyes were screwed tightly shut, and salty sweat poured from her face, pooling in the hollow of her throat and drenching her hair. "C-c-cold."

Faylinn sat up and straightened the quilt that covered Bridget. Then she scrambled off the bed completely and tucked the musty quilt tightly around the shivering woman's body. She could feel herself beginning to panic. Bridget had had a fever when they'd arrived. But not like this. It felt like her wobbly legs might suddenly give way, and Faylinn leaned against the wall with one hand, its cool, rough surface scraping her palm. "Oh, God. Oh, God," she chanted, eyes closed. "It's happening again, and I can't stop it. I don't know what to do."

The blonde bolted for the door. Her hands automatically moved down to lift skirts that weren't there, and her fingertips brushed her heavy woolen trousers instead. She threw open the door, and a blast of cooler air raced over her skin and the scent of clean hay and manure wafted up to greet her. "Will? Are you here?"

Only a gray, hazy light filtered through the cracks around the door, cutting into the darkness. Her eyes scanned the room, darting in and out of the shadows. The workbench where Will and Katie had tended Bridget's wounds had been rinsed clean of blood, and the clothes they'd had to cut off Bridget's brutalized body were no longer strewn carelessly on the dirt floor.

Faylinn squinted as she walked through the stable, which was empty save for a pair of scruffy, gray mules and a sleeping dog, whose light snores could be heard from across the room. She moved towards the light and nervously yanked open the stable door. How long had she and Bridget been asleep? It was impossible to tell.

The rain was cascading down in great sheets, as though she was standing in the center of a roaring waterfall. But if she looked hard enough, she could barely make out the outline of the Beynon farmhouse in the distance.

The mules brayed loudly, stamping their hooves as cold, damp air flooded their stalls and the wind scattered the loose hay against the stable walls.

Faylinn wrung her hands. She didn't care at all about the icy rain; she would walk through the fires of hell if it would help Bridget. But she couldn't leave her alone. Not now. *What if I left her and... No.* She shook her head violently. *I'm not going anywhere.*

An anguished scream from the back room propelled Faylinn's heart into her throat, and she bolted back past the stalls. She entered the small room half-expecting to see Bridget on her feet or on the floor, having fallen. Instead, the dark-haired woman was lying on the bed, eyes closed, the blankets balled in white-knuckled fists.

"Bridget." Faylinn rushed to the bed. "Stop. You're going to tear your stitches. Calm down!"

Faylinn's raised voice caused Bridget's movements to grow wilder, and after staring at her for a second, body frozen in shock, the younger woman forcibly took hold of her scattered emotions. She dropped to her knees and, heedless of Bridget's greasy, sweat-soaked skin, peppered the bruised face with the softest of kisses. "Bridget, calm down," she soothed, pressing her cheek to the brunette's. "It's all right. Go back to sleep."

"Hurry," Bridget hissed, shaking. Scowling, she jerked her face away from Faylinn's. "Cold." The words were as full of fear as impatience.

"I know." Tears stung Faylinn's eyes and she ruthlessly blinked them away. Sitting up, she re-tucked the blankets around her sister-in-law and then threw another log on the fire, stoking it with a long stick that was propped up against the wall. She stripped off her borrowed trousers and climbed back into bed, moving as close as she dared and pressing her legs against Bridget's, trying to share her body heat. "I'm so sorry." She lightly stroked Bridget's face with one hand, her fingers deftly avoiding the many cuts as the room grew brighter from the force of the flames.

"Bridget, you will be fine." She knew the words were as much for herself as her injured companion, but she continued her litany of encouragement anyway. "You must. Do you hear me?"

"No," Bridget said weakly. "You don't understand." She pawed at her blanket. "Hurry."

Faylinn frowned. "You don't have to hurry, Bridget. You're safe here, love." *At least for the time being.*

Bridget began to thrash, grimacing at the pain the action caused her broken arm. "He's in the cold!"

Faylinn shook her head. "No. No one is in the—"

"Henry," Bridget cried softly. "He's still out there."

It was like having a bucket of ice water dumped over her head. Faylinn blinked stupidly for several long seconds until the words penetrated her brain. Instinctively, she covered her ears with her palms and curled up into a tight ball. She couldn't think straight as images assaulted her and recent memories threatened to drown her, dragging her into their madness and despair. But the soft mewing of the woman she loved wouldn't allow her to withdraw completely.

Sky-blue eyes worked furiously beneath closed lids. "I failed. I tried but...my fault." Bridget licked her dry lips. "Sor-sorry."

Faylinn's head snapped up at the words. "Don't say that," she whispered harshly, clinging to Bridget's side. "It's not your fault. By God, none of it was! How can you think that?" she anguished. *You're the only one without blame. And you've suffered so.*

Bridget's hand found Faylinn's and she gripped it tightly. "But he's cold and wet," she breathed raggedly. "I can feel it." Bridget's mind flashed to her toddler nephew huddled in the hollow of a tree, his body shaking from the cold, his laughing gray eyes glazed and unseeing.

Faylinn's breathing hitched, and she had to swallow a few times before she could find her voice. "He's not..." She stopped again, willing herself not fall apart. "He's not outside in the cold, Bridget." Unbidden, the thought of her son in a grave flashed before her eyes, twisting the knife in her gut.

A wretched expression twisted Bridget's beautiful, damaged face. "I can't find him. I'm trying so hard. You have to believe me," she begged, starting to cry. "Please."

"God, forgive me." *This guilt will follow me to the grave. As I deserve.* "I should have believed then, but I was afraid. I *do* believe you now."

"You don't!" The voice was a deep, guttural growl.

"Yes," Faylinn swore fervently. "I will always believe you." *Give me the chance to prove that, Bridget.* "Shh..." she soothed, and carefully pushed clinging bangs from Bridget's forehead. She scooted up to the head of the bed and, through sheer determination alone, managed to get into position so that she was cradling the larger woman with strong, if shaky, arms. Faylinn was panting by the time she was finished, but it seemed to help.

Bridget's breathing began to slow and even out, and her violent thrashing came to an end.

From behind Bridget, Faylinn rested her chin on a broad shoulder as a trickle of perspiration dripped from her own brow onto Bridget's bare skin. She could feel the steady rhythm of Bridget's heart against her own chest, and the wet material of Bridget's shirt stuck to hers. For a moment she became lightheaded, and wished she hadn't stoked the fire, but it passed; and she felt herself growing sleepy. Lazily, she shifted and placed a kiss on the top of Bridget's head.

"Faylinn?"

"I'm here."

"I can't find—"

Please, not again. The blonde woman held her tighter. "You *did* find him, Bridget. You did everything right." She paused. "He's safe now."

Bridget seemed not to want to believe the gentle voice near her ear. The words couldn't be true, could they? She was still looking. And it was so dark. When she was a girl she was afraid of the dark. Henry would be, too. But the calming words were spoken so softly, so lovingly, that she couldn't help but believe them. "He's safe?"

Faylinn voice cracked. "Yes."

Bridget sighed, and her body began to relax. "Warm?" she

questioned finally, the word barely audible.

Hot tears streamed down Faylinn's cheeks and dripped into Bridget's hair. She moved her lips close the darker women's ear. "Yes, love. He's warm." A small bittersweet smile touched quivering lips. "Sleep now. Nothing can hurt him, I promise."

"I'm not a witch."

The unexpected words were said in such a clear, true voice, that, for a moment, Faylinn thought they came from someone else. She gently turned Bridget's face to the side and found a pair of bloodshot, sky-blue eyes peering tiredly back at her. *Awake. Alive.* The strength of her watery smile grew. *Thank you.* "It wouldn't matter if you were a witch," she told her gently, meaning every word. "Not to me."

Bridget sighed and her eyes drifted shut. *I need...I need you so.*

Faylinn heard the words in her own mind and bit back a sob. *Needs me? Oh, God.*

Bridget murmured something unintelligible as her muscles turned to water and she finally succumbed to her need for deep, healing sleep.

"That's right." Faylinn exhaled raggedly, feeling the wracking tension in her body finally begin to ebb. "Rest," she said again, running her fingers through Bridget's thick tresses.

Faylinn began to softly croon a Scottish lullaby. It was one she sang to Henry, that her own mother had sung to her whenever was ill as a child. Even at her tender age, the sunny summers of her past seemed so long ago and far away that her mind could barely grasp them. They vanished like wisps of smoke between her fingers.

A crackling bolt of lightning tore through the sky above the Beynon farm. Exhaustedly, Faylinn clung to Bridget with all her might, refusing to let her go. "You are not a witch, Bridget Redding. But you've enchanted me just the same."

Badger stopped his tale and dug thick fingers into his well-worn tobacco pouch in order to reload his pipe. He glanced up from his task, and what he saw caused his hands to still. "Are you lasses all right?"

Kayla exhaled, feeling a little stunned and lightheaded. *Damn, how long have I been holding my breath?*

Liv could only nod. The telling of young Henry's death and the toll it had taken on his mother had hit her especially hard the first time, dredging up her own insecurities regarding her parents

and the little brother she'd raised herself. Its retelling was having
the same effect, and she was plainly rattled.

Kayla grasped Liv's hand and threaded their fingers together,
giving them a little squeeze. Her forehead creased in thought for a
split second before she pinned Badger with intense blue eyes.
"Does she die?"

The man looked a little surprised. "Faylinn or Bridget?"

Kayla's jaw sagged visibly. "Bu-But... She's not even hurt.
What do you mean, Faylinn?" she demanded. Taking Liv's hand
with her she propped her elbows on her knees and leaned forward
to better hear Badger's answer, despite the fact that the man's
voice rang out clearly in the room. "Just tell us!"

Badger scratched his chin through his thick beard and
addressed Liv. "Is she always so bossy?"

"Hey," Kayla complained loudly, sitting up ramrod straight.

Badger ignored the tall woman completely. "How do you
stand it, Liv?"

"She's not bossy," Liv informed him flatly. Then her eyes
took on a familiar twinkle and she smiled, feeling herself relax a
little. "Just a little...umm...intense. But only sometimes," she
added quickly, already hearing her lover's growl in the back of her
mind.

"Hey!" Kayla repeated, this time shooting a glare at Liv.

Badger grinned unrepentantly, raised a bushy eyebrow, and
said, "Articulate, too, I see."

Liv sighed. *Two peas in a pod.* She slapped Kayla's thigh
playfully and leaned close as she whispered, "You're expressive
and intense in ways Badger can't even imagine. And I love you to
pieces."

Kayla squared her shoulders and grumbled to herself, "That's
a little better." But she was still scowling. "I guess."

Badger regarded both women kindly, his thick Scottish brogue
and deep voice recapturing their attention with ease. "I can see
that neither one of you is going to last for the long...but *highly*
interesting telling. Too bad, too." He shook his head sadly, but
his stare was only mildly reproachful. "So, let me make things
plain for you. Both Faylinn and Bridget died—"

"What?" Liv and Kayla cried in unison.

Badger held up his hands. "Och! If you'd let me finish, you
would not fash yersels so. They both died *eventually*. But not for
many, many years after the terrible events of Cobb Island."

"Oh."

"Thank goodness." Liv closed her eyes.

Badger chuckled. "Feel better now? Or shall I stop?" he

asked innocently, not looking up from his pipe.

"No!" they chorused incredulously.

He bit back a smile. "I'll take that as a 'no.'"

Kayla was tempted to blurt out, "Smart ass," but prudently held her tongue. She was rewarded by a tiny hand squeeze from Liv, who recognized she was making an effort. Which was hard, considering she hadn't missed the gleeful look in Badger's eyes as he teased her. *How does Liv get along with everyone from flirty teenagers to crusty old Scotsmen? And even more bizarre, why would she want to?*

Badger finally pushed a large pinch of tobacco into the bowl of his meerschaum pipe and brushed away a few stray shreds that speckled the rim. "Weel, I've no problem continuing. I'll gab all day if you like." He winked. "Anything to avoid Sylla, ya know." Placing his tobacco pouch back into his sporran he shifted his bulky body in the chair to get more comfortable again. "But seein' as how I let the cat out of the bag about Bridget stayin' alive, how about I skip ahead a wee bit of time...past some of her recovery?"

A dark head nodded. "Absolutely. It's about time to fast forward. I'm especially hoping—"

Badger lifted an eyebrow, and Liv clamped her hand over Bridget's mouth. "She's especially hoping that you'll tell us the story *exactly* as you see fit."

"Oh, I can see that," Badger laughed.

Kayla nipped Liv's palm with sharp teeth, earning a high-pitched yelp.

"Well, at least you're not kissin' each other again," Badger said wryly. Though it always lightened his heart to see people truly in love. He'd seen it with his own parents, enjoyed the blessing himself, but knew it was sadly lacking in today's world.

The stout man cleared his voice. "Here we go then. A thin blanket of snow and ice covered the Virginia coast as a harsh autumn gave way to an equally unforgiving winter..."

Virginia (Mainland)
December, 1690; Christmas Eve

A frigid wind howled outside the small room in the back of the Beynon stable. She paced the room, oblivious to the fireplace she'd let grow cold. She wore a pair of Will's dark-brown, buckskin, hunting trousers and a new navy-blue, woolen shirt that Faylinn had made for her during the past month. The cloth was well worn but clean, having been recycled from several shirts that were too small for even Faylinn. One sleeve had been made extra-wide so it would fit over the splint on Bridget's left arm, and the collar and pocket hung slightly askew.

She smoothed her sleeve fondly and recalled the many nights Faylinn had toiled away with a needle and thread in front of the flickering fire, her pale brows drawn together in utter concentration. Despite her worry, Bridget chuckled. It was truly the ugliest piece of clothing she'd ever owned. And she couldn't have loved it more had it been spun of pure gold.

"Where are you?" Bridget whispered worriedly as she pulled open the rickety shutter and peered out into the cold night. "Faylinn, must you always be late?" They needed a clock, she decided. That way she could stare at it all night and feel justified in worrying over her companion so. *But I must be careful and pay attention, or I'll smother her as my pig brother Cyril did.* But it *was* full dark outside and Liv, Will, and Katie had promised they'd be back from town by late this afternoon, which was now long past.

The trio had left at sunrise the day before, intent on reaching town early enough to shop at the mercantile and locate a reasonably priced inn for the night. Will usually camped in the rough on his monthly trips for basic foodstuffs, tools, and the like, but he'd decided to make this trip a holiday treat for his wife and Faylinn, whom he'd come to think of as a daughter. If this month's shipment of slaves had arrived, the runners would have pumped untold amounts of coin back into the local economy before heading back to sea. If the shipment hadn't arrived, the shops would still be chock-full of wares to catch their attention and tempt the plantation owner, who had come to buy.

Bridget had fought hard to go along, though she was barely healed enough to be out of bed. But Will had told her bluntly that the story of her "suicide" had spread through the Colony like wildfire. And that made her decision for her. At the very least, the Beynons would forfeit their homestead for harboring a fugitive. But for Faylinn, things would be much, much worse.

The Crown recognized no distinction between those in league with a servant of Satan and the servant herself. Methods employed for gaining confessions were often worse than the ultimate punishment itself. *Swinging at the end of a rope would be a kind fate for Faylinn,* Bridget had thought sarcastically.

Then there was Cyril's death, for which Faylinn would surely be blamed. Bridget sighed. In a very real way, Bridget Redding and Faylinn Cobb Redding were, and would forever remain, "dead."

You already knew that, Bridget reminded herself grimly. But she'd never really had time to think about what her life would become. She was too busy trying to save Faylinn...then stay alive. Now she could clearly see what she had really asked of her sister-in-law when she'd begged the younger woman to steal away with her in the night. *God.* Bridget had closed her eyes, feeling the mantle of guilt resting heavily on tired shoulders. *I've stolen a life I fear I can no longer protect.*

Against Faylinn's protests, Bridget had gone for a long, painful walk in the woods...alone. She'd desperately needed some time to process what had happened and would happen now. Her head and arm had throbbed, and she'd felt slightly queasy and winded after the first few paces, but a larger part of her reveled in the freedom of the clean cold that flooded her lungs and the brightness of the newly fallen snow. *Forgive me my ill-tempered words, Faylinn, but if I don't have this time I shall go mad.*

Stress and a nagging flu—no doubt brought on by a horrific boat ride in the pouring rain where Faylinn had rowed for hours to save their lives—had plagued Faylinn for weeks. It was only this week that her body seemed to begin adapting to the shock of what had happened on Cobb Island and the new stresses of frontier life.

It never even occurred to Bridget that though Faylinn still grieved for her son, more often than not, she was happier than she'd ever been. The bright innocence in her emerald eyes had been tempered, but the result was something deeper and infinitely more compelling. Faylinn seemed older and more thoughtful, yet somehow lighter, too. She cried more, but she laughed more as well; and, as always, her gentle touch was a balm to Bridget's soul.

But none of that mattered, because she knew that Faylinn was unselfishly making the best of things for her sake. *It's just like her to suffer in silence. She did it with Cyril, and now she's doing it with me.* In a matter of seconds, Bridget found herself in a full-fledged, self-pitying, foul mood.

Slowly, she'd made her way back to the stables, only to find Faylinn standing outside in the cold, waiting for her.

"I can't leave you here alone," Faylinn had told her, her eyes a little panicky. "You still need help."

But at that moment, Faylinn's pity was more than Bridget could bear. They'd argued bitterly, exchanging harsh, hurtful words as they never had before, until, finally, Bridget had gotten her way. A heavy sensation settled in her chest as the confrontation from the morning before came crashing back.

"Pity? What do you mean pity?" The fair-haired

woman stared at Bridget in disbelief.

Blue eyes flashed angrily even as tears began to well in them. "You heard me, Faylinn. It was, and is, not your place to play nurse-nanny to me every second of every day!"

Faylinn's hand clenched at her sides. "And just who was going to dress and feed you? Keep your wounds clean and your body washed? And yes, by God, even clear away your chamber pot when you could not? Hmm?"

"I don't know!" Bridget shouted back, confused. Suddenly she couldn't meet Faylinn's sharp gaze. Things were spiraling out of control, and she couldn't seem to stop them. "I can manage on my own now." That was a lie, and she knew it.

Faylinn shook her head, fighting the urge to lash back. But Bridget wasn't making it easy. "Be reasonable, Bridget. Even now, you still cannot—"

"I am not an invalid!" Bridget's voice dropped an octave and took on an icy edge that Faylinn had never had directed towards her before. "Though you seem to believe that I am."

Faylinn's cheeks flamed in an angry flush, and she took a step closer to Bridget. "I never said that. I never even thought it!" But then, and at the worst possible moment, her eyes fixed itself on Bridget's splinted arm. How that must hurt. *She blinked as exactly what she was doing hit her. Her eyes snapped upward but it was too late. The raw pain that chased its way across Bridget's face made her gasp.*

"That's right." Bridget's entire body went still. "Set wrong, I suspect. It's basically useless. A burden." She cocked her head slightly to the side, and her dark brows pulled together. "Like me."

"Oh, God, please don't think that's what I believe." Faylinn's eyes went glassy and she wiped at them frantically. "That...that's not..."

Bridget turned her back on her friend and stared at the glowing orange and red coals in the fireplace. In one glance, her faith in herself had been shaken to the very core and her fears confirmed. "No need to fuss, Faylinn. Despite my current condition, I am more than capable of caring for myself."

Faylinn ran a shaky hand through her hair. "As long

*as you don't want to get back up if you fall," she snorted
as the last of her patience vanished. "Or you don't want
to fasten the ties of your clothing. Or—"*

*The older woman's face contorted in rage and she
whirled around, ignoring a wave of dizziness. "I will be
fine. Go!" She pointed to the door with a trembling
hand. "Get out of this wretched, smelly room. I don't
need you at all!"*

*It felt like a stinging slap to the face, but Faylinn
didn't recoil. Instead of fleeing the room, as Bridget
knew she would, she marched up to the redhead, seeth-
ing. She grabbed two large fists full of Bridget's shirt and
yanked her down towards her. They were nose to nose,
feeling hot, labored breaths against her lips. Her heart
began to pound out of her chest, and for a split second
Faylinn had the strongest urge to barely tilt her chin and
brush her lips...*

"Faylinn?"

*Bridget's voice startled her, forcing her back to the
moment. She shook her head. "You, Bridget Redding,
are the most idiotic woman on God's earth." Heedless of
Bridget's arm, she shook her roughly, feeling the muffled
groans of pain as though they were her very own. But
she didn't stop. "What you see in my eyes when they
look at you is not pity, you imbecile!" Her gaze found
her hands, and she stared at them as though they
belonged to someone else. She uncoiled her trembling
fists and let them fall to her sides.*

*Their eyes met and Bridget found herself holding her
breath.*

"It's love."

*Dumbstruck, Bridget watched as Faylinn turned on
her heels, grabbed her cloak from the peg near the door
and marched out of the room, grumbling loudly all the
while. She should, she knew, go after Faylinn, drop to
her knees and beg her forgiveness. Instead, she watched
in pained silence as the other woman trudged angrily
towards the Beynon house...and away from her.*

"Bloody hell!" Bridget cradled her left arm, and tapped
impatiently on the splint. Violently, she tore it off her arm, nearly
biting her lip through in agony. "That," she hissed through
clenched teeth, "was not smart." She could feel some sensation in
her hand and fingers, but couldn't make a fist or even bend it at

the elbow. For all intents and purposes, it hung limply at her side like a piece of meat. *Useless.*

Her cuts and bruises had faded, and she'd been making slow but steady progress in gaining back most of the weight, but only some of the stamina, that she'd lost over the past six weeks. But in Bridget's mind, it wasn't nearly enough. Faylinn needed her now more than ever.

She rested her forehead in her hand and sighed raggedly. How had things gotten so out of control and changed so quickly. While she had always spent a fair amount of her time on the mainland, Cobb Island was still her home. Judith and Afia and even Elizabeth were her family. Now she was as unsure of her own place as she was Faylinn's.

Will snapped the reins of his cart sharply and the mule dutifully complied, picking up his sluggish pace. Lifting the tricorn hat from his head, he gazed up at the blanket of twinkling stars and scowled. "Lazy beast. We should have been home hours ago." He replaced his hat. "Snow's not that deep."

"Mmhm." Katie agreed softly as she patted Will's leg. She shifted on the seat next to him, tilting her head closer to his. "I've no doubt Bridget is at this very moment climbing the walls, blaspheming all the while."

Will snorted. "It wouldn't surprise me one bit to see her on the road up ahead, waiting." They weren't but a mile or so from home, and Will guided his cart off the path that ran along the coast and over a grassy, snow-covered hill.

"She certainly cares for her sister-in-law." Katie's tone was full of honest admiration. "God bless them, they are the picture of sisterly devotion."

"Sisterly?" Will's eyebrows crawled up his forehead and stayed. He turned to his wife and opened his mouth.

"Yes?"

The air was silent except for the dull thudding of the mule's hooves and the creaking of the wheels. "Umm..." He quickly thought of the young woman huddled in the back of his cart and gave his head a little shake. "Not a blessed thing, sweet Katie." *Lord above, what was I thinkin'?* He had nearly violated one of life's sacred rules; and he repeated it over in his head, lest he forget again sometime soon. *What Katie doesn't know can't hurt* me. *What Katie doesn't know can't hurt* me.

The cart lurched heavily to one side, and Faylinn's head jerked up...and right into a small keg of beer. "Oww." She rubbed the spot just above her ear.

"Serves you right for falling asleep back there," Will said gruffly.

"That means: 'I'm sorry for steering the cart right into that big hole and I'll try to be more careful in the future,'" Katie explained to Faylinn, who chuckled quietly.

Faylinn rubbed the sleep from her eyes. "Apology accepted, Will."

The man didn't answer verbally, but his face creased into a happy smile.

Faylinn pulled her cloak tighter around her shoulders and tilted her head towards the sky. It was a moonless, cloudless night, and it looked as though God had scattered a handful of glittering diamonds into a great black sea. "We're late," she commented absently.

Will snapped the reins again in response.

Katie heard Faylinn's sigh and reached back to squeeze the young woman's shoulder. "She'll be fine."

Faylinn swallowed and nodded. "I know she will. I'm just being silly, I suppose. But... Do you think she'll have eaten?" Bridget hated to cook, and Faylinn pictured her having had nothing but jerky and stale bread over the past two days.

Will burst out laughing. "If she hasn't eaten in the past two days, she'll either be dead or weaker than gnat's piss by the time we get home."

"Will!" Katie scolded. "Watch your language."

The man smiled sheepishly and leaned backwards over his seat, making a great show of tipping his hat to Faylinn. Any sense of class-consciousness had long since disappeared between them, . but it was still worth teasing over. "My apologies, Mistress Redding."

Katie narrowed her hazel eyes at her husband. "I said hush. No more teasin' the girl. It's right for her to be concerned about her own kinfolk. It wasn't so many days ago that we were thinking we'd be buryin' Bridget before the first hard freeze."

"What?" Faylinn gasped.

"Big mouth," Will grumbled to Katie. Then he moved to reassure Faylinn. "Bridget is a strong woman, and she's well enough to be left alone or we wouldn't have left her in the first place." *And she needs some space to breathe.* Though Will prudently kept that thought to himself.

Faylinn fingered the small bundle tucked beneath her cloak. "I...I suppose she is." But their parting argument had left her feeling unsettled and shaky. In the months since they'd met, she and Bridget had rarely exchanged a cross word. Until now. Part of her was petrified that they'd return to the homestead to find Bridget gone.

"Wilfred is right. Concern is fine, worry will only give you gray hairs." Katie pointed to her own salt-and-peppered head. "If this isn't proof, I don't know what is!"

"Be quiet, woman," Will admonished.

Katie blithely ignored him. "Faylinn, how are you feeling?"

"Fine." A pause. "I think."

"You're still tired." It wasn't a question.

Faylinn's eyes slid shut and she shivered. "A little, I guess." She'd had a comfortable bed with a feather-filled mattress all to herself the night before, but still hadn't slept a wink. She'd missed the warm body she curled up against each night. "Though I did fall asleep back here."

"Only the good Lord above will ever know how, with the way my Will drives."

Will turned to his wife and frowned. "Next time I'm leavin' you at home, nag!"

"You are not," Katie informed him bluntly.

"If you sass me like that again, I most certainly will!" He puffed up his chest, daring her to say differently. Which, of course, she immediately did.

"Ha! You will..."

Faylinn shook her head as the couple bickered. She'd never seen two people who loved each other so, argue so bitterly. And strangely, that made her feel a little bit better about her and Bridget. *You're every bit as stubborn as Will, Bridget. And I love you every bit as much as Katie does him.* They hadn't so much as shared a kiss since that single, desperate time, the night Bridget was to be executed. Still, she knew she held Bridget's heart; she only hoped that after they spoke this night, Bridget would still want hers. The mere thought of another confrontation caused Faylinn's stomach to churn mercilessly, and she wrapped her arms around herself in mute comfort.

Then the arguing and the wagon came to an abrupt halt.

"Here we are."

Faylinn looked up in surprise. They were parked right out-side the stable.

Will jumped down from his seat and stretched with a loud groan. He quickly unhooked the mule and led her inside, telling her how, come next spring, she was going to be turned into several new pair of boots and a set of tack.

The blood drained from Faylinn's face when she looked at the door. She should see a trail of smoke coming from the chimney above, but not a single sliver of light shone through the shutters.

"Thank you for the beautiful cloth and keg of beer for Will." Katie's exhale sent a cloud of fog spiraling upward. "We didn't expect any Christmas gifts."

Faylinn pushed away thoughts of Bridget for just a moment and smiled weakly at Katie. "Then why I am wearing a new dress?" It was as simple and shapeless as a dress could be, but it was made by Katie's own hand; and Faylinn had come to realize just how precious a commodity cloth was. The gift was yet another kindness from a couple whose generosity already astounded her.

Katie's blush was evident even in the starlight. "Well, it would hardly be proper for you to go walking about town dressed as a man."

Unlike Bridget, who frequently wore trousers, they had taken some getting used to for Faylinn. Though she had to admit they seemed far more practical now that she'd actually tried them out.

"Did you enjoy town? A far cry from London, I suspect."

Faylinn smiled gently. "It wasn't London, Katie. And it didn't need to be. I had a grand time. Thank you for the invitation."

Unlike Bridget, Faylinn had spent her entire time in the Colonies on Cobb Island. On the mainland, she was just another young woman, completely anonymous unless she happened to run into one of the naval officers with whom Cyril had done business. But Will had assured her that if she steered clear of the local docks, taverns, and brothel, she would have nothing to fear. However, just in case, the young woman never lowered the hood of her cloak.

In town, Will had helped her pawn a necklace Cyril had given Faylinn as a wedding gift. The amount she received for it was a paltry sum for a piece of jewelry of passable quality, but it allowed her to buy gifts for the Beynons and still have plenty left over to purchase a few food items and sneak them into Katie's crate. Her favorite gift, however, she had yet to give.

Faylinn grinned. "I felt much more comfortable in town with this on than I would have wearing trousers. Thank you again." The grin slipped as Faylinn eased herself out the back of the small cart.

"Don't fret so much." Katie pulled the smaller woman into a tight hug and pressed her lips to Faylinn's cold ear. "She will understand."

Faylinn nodded. "Merry...Merry Christmas, Kat—" Her throat closed tightly and she bolted past Will, who was exiting the stable.

"Whoa." He turned worried eyes on his wife as he hefted the small keg of beer onto one shoulder and Katie helped him lay a fifty-pound sack of flour on the other. "Is she all right?"

Katie filled her arms with the bolt of cloth and a wooden crate full of cooking supplies—she'd have to make another trip for the rest. "If she's not, you'll be diggin' that grave for Bridget Redding you were so worried about before."

Will's wide eyes followed his wife's portly form as it plowed through the snow towards their house. "Uh oh."

Chapter
Seven

Virginia (Mainland)
December, 1690; Christmas Eve

The dog ran up to Faylinn as soon as she entered the stable. He howled his greeting, his shaggy body shaking wildly as he rubbed himself against her skirt. "Hello, boy. Yeah," she cooed fondly, "I missed you, too." She sighed. "And someone else who lives here." She gave him a gentle pat on the head and straightened, exhaling with exaggerated slowness. Her eyes were riveted to the door to the back room. From inside of the stables, she now could see the tiniest slice of golden light coming from beneath the doorway and spilling out onto the fragrant hay that lined the floor. *Thank God. No matter what, at least she's here. Asleep, I'll hazard.*

"I'm going to go in there now," Faylinn told herself firmly, setting her resolve. But her feet didn't move. She looked down in disgust. "All right, *this* time I mean it." And with gritted teeth, she forced herself across the room. She felt as if she was wading through a thick molasses swamp. Every step was a colossal effort, as her disobedient legs were doing their best to ignore her brain's command to hurry up and get this over with.

When she finally reached the door, she groaned and let her forehead rest against the cool wood as she closed her eyes. *Go on, Faylinn. You cannot avoid her forever.* Pushing away from the door, she pulled the edges of her cloak together and dropped her hood, her golden hair spilling out over her shoulders. She swallowed and reached out for the door handle, but before she could open it, it flew open. "Whoa!" She stumbled backwards to avoid being struck.

When she found her legs, she glanced up. Breathless, she

drank in the sight before her. Bridget stood tall and proud in the bedroom doorway, backlit by a small flickering candle that cast long shadows across the walls. Her long hair was slightly disheveled, as if she'd been sleeping or out in the wind.

Even through the near darkness, Faylinn could see the keen awareness in her features. The familiar thought that Bridget looked larger than life raced through Faylinn's mind and, despite her concern, she was hard-pressed not to swoon. "Umm..." Bridget was staring at her, and she found herself slightly tongue-tied. A little self-consciously, she squared her own shoulders. *She can see right through me. I know she can.* "Hello."

She's all right. "Faylinn," Bridget acknowledged quietly. She stared down at her own boots for a moment before her eyes lifted. "You're...umm...you're late." *Dammit, that is not what I wanted to say.*

Faylinn nodded slowly. *At least she's still talking to me.* She starting moving forward, and Bridget backed into the room and allowed her to pass.

Faylinn immediately noticed the cold fireplace, but decided not to comment. She tucked her hands inside her cloak. "We got more snow last night, and the road was slow traveling."

"It's all right." Bridget shrugged one shoulder with forced casualness. "I wasn't really worried."

A tiny smile twitched at Faylinn's lips. "You weren't, huh?" she challenged quietly.

Bridget's eyes softened in response to Faylinn's smile and a tentative grin eased over worried features. "No. Not at all. Though I did miss you." After a second's debate, she held one arm out in invitation.

Faylinn couldn't close the distance between them fast enough. Her shoes scraped loudly on the rough wooden floors, and before she knew it she was wrapped tightly in Bridget's embrace. Her pulse was pounding so loudly she could barely hear anything else, and she felt Bridget's thumping wildly against her chest in return. She wrapped her arms as tightly around the other woman as she dared, her relief so staggering she thought her knees would give way. "I'm sor—"

"I apologi—"

They both stopped and laughed in simple relief, though there was still a very faint, underlying tension between them.

"God, Bridget," Faylinn drew in a greedy breath of the darker woman's scent, allowing it to flood her senses and calm her, "I wasn't..." She stopped and swallowed past the lump in her throat, startled at how much just saying the words hurt. "I wasn't sure if you'd be here when I got back. I know you've been going mad under my constant care. It's just...just—" The words came out in a jumbled rush. "But...I...you were hurt. And I couldn't make you... I just needed to help you."

Bridget pressed her nose in Faylinn's hair and mumbled against the silken strands. "I know. It really is all right, Faylinn." She soaked in the sensation of Faylinn in her arms and faced up to a very basic truth about herself. "I'll *never* leave you. I know I'm quite impossible sometimes." She licked her lips nervously, but was determined to press on. "I love you far too much to even consider living without you, whether it is best for you in the long run or not." She placed a tender kiss on Faylinn's head. "To my great shame, I am doubtlessly the most selfish bitch alive."

"You are not!" Faylinn shouted. "How can you question this? I know you feel it, too. You *are* best for me in the long and short run. Don't you dare say any different, Bridget," she warned her seriously. "I mean it. I have the Devil's own temper when pushed." She stamped her foot for emphasis. "Hearing you talk like that taxes me beyond all reason. And if you do it again, I'll... Well, I'll... I don't know! But it will be fearsome, I guarantee that!"

A small, unexpected laugh bubbled up from within Bridget. "Fearsome?"

"Don't you dare laugh at me!" But Faylinn couldn't help but crack a smile herself. "You are quite stuck with me, whether you want to be or not." The curve of sensual lips, flash of white teeth, and eyes suddenly brimming with glittering tears let Faylinn know just how Bridget felt about that. Faylinn let out another more relaxed laugh.

Bridget drew in a deep breath, and for a second Faylinn worried she would have another fight on her hands. But instead, to her delight, Bridget only nodded. " *We* are stuck with each other," she corrected warmly. Low and sweet, her voiced wrapped itself around Faylinn's heart.

In the decades that still stretched before them, each would talk of many things, argue over countless subjects, and evoke tears of pain and laughter from the other. This question, however, was settled firmly on that cold Christmas Eve night...for all time.

Faylinn reluctantly loosened her death grip on Bridget, already missing the comforting warmth she'd been deprived of the past two days. Feeling drained, but knowing they still had several important things to discuss, she curled her fingers around Bridget's and led her to the bed where they both sat down.

"Just a moment." Bridget gently pushed Faylinn's cloak from

her shoulders. The cloth was cold and damp, and she got up to hang it near the fireplace.

She could feel something in the inside pocket and caught sight of the very tip of a bright red ribbon. She opened the cloak a little more for a better view and smiled to herself, knowing she had a gift for Faylinn hidden away as well. She wondered idly if the younger woman would make her wait until Christmas morning for her booty.

"No peeking," Faylinn called to her sternly.

Bridget jumped a little, and her cheeks colored as though she were a child caught stealing sweets from her mother's pantry. "That was not nice, Faylinn."

"It was so. Not nice would be making you wait 'til New Years just for peeking."

Bridget arched an eyebrow at her companion's wicked streak and padded back to the bed. She sat down and kicked her feet up onto the soft surface. The silence between them lingered, and after the high emotions surrounding Faylinn's homecoming, for once it was Bridget who found herself wanting to break it. Relentlessly, she picked at a loose thread in the quilt. *Since this appears to be a night for confessions and brutal honesty...* "Faylinn?"

"Hmm?" Faylinn answered absently. She was twirling a lock of glossy, wine-colored hair between her fingers, enjoying its coarse but silky texture and the way the candlelight seemed to make it shimmer.

"It is..." Bridget stopped and kicked herself for not knowing where to start. But this was so hard.

"Yes?" Faylinn smoothed back Bridget's unruly tresses and did her best to sit and wait patiently. The confused, stressed look on Bridget's face, however, was enough to make her anxiety mount.

"My foul temper since coming to the mainland has not solely been because I needed to get out of this God be damned room for a while." Bridget gathered her courage and forced herself to tell Faylinn everything. "I've *needed* you these past weeks. I still do." Bridget looked away, and therefore completely missed Faylinn's heartfelt smile. "More than I've ever needed anyone or anything in my life."

"I need you too, Bridget. You—"

"Let me finish." She pressed two fingers against Faylinn's lips and continued despite the interruption. "And I'm afraid I haven't handled it very well. On Cobb Island, I felt that it was *you* who needed *me*. You needed to be rescued from Cyril. But now—" She gave her head a little shake and removed her fingers from Faylinn's lips, very aware of their softness as she pulled away. Her voice dropped to the barest of whispers. "Everything has changed. I've never been so afraid."

When Faylinn sensed that Bridget wasn't going to continue, she reminded her simply, "The most important things, Bridget, have not changed at all." She cupped Bridget's cheeks with sure hands and stroked high cheekbones with her thumbs. Her gaze softened as she looked deeply into frightened pale eyes. "What is it that frightens you so?"

An embarrassed look chased across Bridget's face and focused on the bedspread, falling silent once again.

Blonde brows knit tightly together. "Certainly not me."

Bridget sighed. "You don't understand."

"Then help me," Faylinn whispered, clearly deeply adrift.

A sudden storm erupted in Bridget's eyes. "That's just it!" She tried to jerk her head from Faylinn's hands, but the younger woman seemed to know what she was going to do before she did it, and held her firm.

"No you don't, Bridget." Then she tried another tack. "I'm mortally tired from our trip, and I haven't the energy to chase you all around this room. Please." Faylinn relaxed her hands again and her touch shifted into a tender caress.

As fast as it came, Bridget's anger melted away under the soothing touch. She sighed.

"Please, love."

Bridget swallowed hard at the endearment, and her breathing came a little faster.

"Tell me."

Bridget's jaw worked for a moment, then she blurted out, "Don't you see? I *cannot* help you!" She looked at Faylinn as though that explained everything.

Faylinn blinked as she searched Bridget's face for any clue. "I'm sorry, I still don't understand. I—"

"Look at me!" Bridget jerked away and swung her limp, slightly twisted arm towards the shorter woman, stifling a cry as a searing bolt of pain shot from her shoulder to the tips of her fingers. With her other hand, she pushed up her sleeve, exposing most of the damaged limb.

Faylinn did her best not to let her face show just how upset she really was. "Oh, Bridget." The full shirtsleeve had hidden the fact that the splint was gone from Bridget's arm, and before today it had always been heavily bandaged. Faylinn closed her eyes.

"Look," Bridget repeated roughly, shaking her arm until Faylinn complied. *Now you'll understand why I cannot be what you need.*

"Bridget, you must give it time. It's only been—" Faylinn paused and did the math, realizing grimly that the bone would have knitted together by now and that something must have gone terribly wrong. She'd replaced the splints many times, though it was always Will, who, at Bridget's insistence, had changed the bandages.

The arm was crooked and, even with the splint on it, Faylinn had known that. But she'd always looked past its misshapen bones, assuming it would heal and somehow right itself with time. *Or maybe I just didn't want to see the truth,* she admitted shamefully. She gently reached out and took the cool, relaxed hand in hers, feeling it twitch slightly at the unexpected contact. Its palm was soft and smooth, free from the small calluses that had characterized it before. She stroked the skin gently.

Bridget closed her eyes at Faylinn's touch. "It's not a matter of time anymore, Faylinn."

"It's not your sword hand, Bridget."

Bridget's eyes snapped open. "Bu—"

Faylinn silenced the protest with a look. "You've had your say, Bridget Redding, and now I shall have mine." She waited for the grumpy frown to leave Bridget's face and for her to nod before she went on. "So stubborn," she mumbled. But her reassuring smile took the sting out of the words. "I want you to really listen to what I'm saying, not just hear it. You *need* to believe this as I do." *For both our sakes.*

Warily, Bridget nodded. There was nothing she would deny Faylinn.

"Even if you could no longer lift a sword at all, it wouldn't matter." Faylinn sharply raised an eyebrow at Bridget and her gaping mouth, daring her to interrupt again. "I do not require a bodyguard. And despite your chivalrous inclinations, I never have." With great care she lifted Bridget's injured hand, watching the larger woman's face for the slightest flinch. Seeing none, she placed it on her own chest, directly over her heart. She held it there until she was certain Bridget could feel its strong beat. "I want *more* than that. I *need* more than that." *As you have always given me, from the very start.*

"Anything within my power, Faylinn. Anything I have is yours," Bridget swore fervently.

"I'm glad you said that." Faylinn smiled and gently removed Bridget's hand from her chest, allowing it to rest in her lap. She shifted closer still, ignoring any sense of propriety and the butterflies in her stomach as she brought her face to within inches of

Bridget's.

She could see the rapid rise and fall of Bridget's chest as she breathed, and the flare of her nostrils as she reacted to Faylinn's close proximity. Experimentally, and with all the tenderness she felt inside, she leaned in and placed a tiny, feather-light kiss at the very top of the jagged scar that ran from just outside Bridget's eye to her jaw.

Bridget forgot how to breathe as tiny kisses worked their way down her face. *Oh, God.*

Faylinn heard a faint whimper, and it increased her desire tenfold. Her stomach clenched, and when she reached the end of the scar, the very tip of her tongue flicked out and licked it. She felt as much as she heard Bridget's low growl of arousal. She pulled back and regarded the hooded eyes she felt certain she could lose herself in. Swallowing roughly Faylinn husked, "I cannot understand this, Bridget. If I am damned to hell for something that feels this right—"

"Then I am damned as well," Bridget whispered, each word sending a warm puff of air against Faylinn's face. "Either way, we will be together."

Faylinn's gaze dropped to Bridget's mouth, and this time her heart refused to be denied. "So be it." She fully intended to move forward and capture what she'd desired for so long, but Bridget beat her to it.

Their lips met in gentle, consuming passion, and both women hummed into the sweet contact. Small hands naturally found their way into thick tresses, and Faylinn felt an answering arm wrap tightly around her waist and draw her to Bridget's body.

It was like no kiss she'd ever experienced, and Faylinn felt it all the way to her toes. Without effort, it chased away the room's chill, though she still found herself shivering, helpless under Bridget's spell.

Faylinn's lips were soft and yielding and everything Bridget had dreamt they'd be. She moaned throatily when Faylinn gently parted her own lips with an inquisitive tongue and pushed softly forward into her mouth. She was enveloped in a blissful, staggering heat that robbed her of all reason. Bridget eagerly deepened the kiss, desperate to taste everything Faylinn was offering and more. Hot tongues swirled against each other, sliding together effortlessly but with mounting desire. With each passing second, Bridget's blood pulsed hotter in her veins.

Unconsciously, Faylinn's hands clenched tighter in Bridget's hair and she used them as an anchor against the maelstrom of sensation. Her whole universe narrowed to the mouth loving hers so perfectly. There was a dull roaring in her ears, and she realized in a far off way that it wasn't the wind outside, but the frantic beating of her heart.

Shadows danced on the walls as the candle began to gutter. The wick neared its end, then fell sideways into the hot pool of aromatic beeswax, darkening the room further until it gave off only the barest flicker of light.

The kiss ended naturally, but not without several parting nibbles and whimpers from each woman.

Bridget pressed her forehead to Faylinn's and let out a shuddering breath, her chest heaving. "Oh," she breathed, "that was..." Her words trailed off as she fought for some way to articulate the wash of bright emotion still swamping her senses.

"Mmm hmm." Faylinn agreed, too stunned to actually form a coherent sentence. She licked her moist lips, remembering the taste and exquisite feeling of Bridget's tongue sliding against them. She groaned quietly as the mere thought sent a bolt of heat careening between her legs. Her groan gave way to a nervous gasp when the unfamiliar sensation caused a blossoming warmth deep in her belly to spread outward.

"We should have done that much sooner," Bridget finally said.

"God, yes," Faylinn breathed. She looked up into eyes gone nearly silver in the dim light, and a shyness that Bridget hadn't seen on Faylinn's face since her earliest days on Cobb Island shone plainly through. "We...um..." *God, why am I blushing now?* "We will do that again, won't we?" *If she says no, I shall drop dead on the spot. I know it.*

Twin eyebrows disappeared behind dark bangs and Bridget laughed. "I certainly hope so." She gazed at Faylinn fondly and trailed a fingertip down the younger woman's slightly upturned nose. "Merry Christmas, dearest. It must be well past midnight."

Faylinn's expressive face was suddenly transformed into that of an excited adolescent. "Merry Christmas, love. It always was my favorite holiday." She paused, and the face that was the very picture of youthful innocence only seconds before creased into a sexy grin. "I just never knew why until now."

Bridget scooted up to the head of the bed and patted the spot next to her, sparing a look at the candle that was threatening to die, but far too content to care. "You look lovely, by the way." She gestured with her chin at Faylinn's new dark-brown dress. "Though I must admit, I find you adorable in trousers."

Faylinn laughed. "That's doubly good then," she tugged at her collar, "because, and don't you dare tell Katie, this itches like the Devil's own backside."

"I won't," Bridget chuckled and shook her head indulgently. Her gaze moved from Faylinn's eyes to her golden hair, and she admired it openly. After the kiss they'd shared, she felt somewhat more comfortable showing and voicing her appreciation. Gone were the days of stealing jealous glances at her sister-in-law. She hoped. Bridget gently tugged on a strand of pale hair. "You should wear it down more often. It is too beautiful to hide."

Faylinn joined Bridget at the head of the bed, then reached up self-consciously and felt her head. Her braids and pins had worked themselves free, but since she'd worn her hood all day, she hadn't bothered bringing it back to order. Now it hung loosely across her shoulders and down to the center of her back. "Thank you." She took the opportunity to examine Bridget's attire, and made a face. "You are the most beautiful creature I have ever laid eyes on, Bridget." She grinned broadly. It felt so good to be able to say that out loud without fear of censure, reproach, or even damnation. "However, you look as though you have a blind seamstress."

Bridget bit her bottom lip in an attempt to ward off her laughter. "It's not that bad," she offered diplomatically, still struggling to keep a straight face.

Faylinn sighed and pinned Bridget with a knowing look. "You're right. It's worse. Your seamstress was not only blind, but daft as well." She tugged on Bridget's sleeve and snorted. "This is pitiful."

"Tch." But this time Bridget couldn't suppress her laughter. "I, for one, think precise measurements are highly over-rated. I'll have you know this is my favorite piece of clothing."

Faylinn's eyes narrowed playfully. "You only have one other shirt, Bridget."

An elegant eyebrow arched. "Yes, but I like this one more, therefore it is my favorite." She artfully changed the subject. "How was your first experience in a Colonial town? Did you find what you expected?"

The blood suddenly drained from Faylinn's face. *Sweet Mother, how could I have forgotten?* "I...I—"

"Hey," Bridget frowned. "What's the matter?" She turned sideways so she was fully facing the younger woman. "Faylinn?"

"No." Faylinn licked her lips. "I didn't expect to find..." The blonde woman swallowed hard. So much had happened tonight, she had intended on telling Bridget sooner, but... Her face dropped into her hands. *Where is my mind? When she said she'd never leave me, she didn't know. What if...*

Bridget gently pulled Faylinn's hands away from her face and ducked her head so that she could look directly at her. "You're frightening me, Faylinn. Did you run into someone who knew who you were?" Her eyes widened. "God, why didn't you say something sooner?" Bridget fairly flew off the bed, cursing roundly as she lost her balance and stumbled a step sideways. "We need—"

Faylinn grabbed her by the shirt to steady her. When the tall woman had found her legs, Faylinn tried to haul her back onto the bed. "That's not—"

Bridget slapped away her hands. "Faylinn! We must hurry! You—"

Faylinn sighed and grabbed for her shirt again, getting a better hold this time and tugging firmly. "Bridget, please—"

"Faylinn, I mean it! There's no time to—"

"Stop! By God, Bridget will you calm down and get back onto this bed? The Crown is *not* hunting me down. I'm pregnant!"

Bridget's jaw hit the floor.

Faylinn cringed. *Lord, help me.* "I didn't mean to tell you like that."

Bridget blinked stupidly.

"Since coming to the mainland I haven't...I mean, I never got my..." Faylinn just shook her head. "At Katie's insistence I visited a mid-wife in town." The older woman's stunned silence sent Faylinn's mind racing, and her speech grew faster. "Please understand, Bridget. Cyril expected, no, *demanded* more heirs." She sighed and rubbed her temples with trembling hands, not wanting to think about the wretched nights her husband would visit her bedchamber and forcibly remind her of her wifely duties. Her stomach twisted into a solid knot. "By my heart, it was *never* my choice."

The room was as quiet as a grave, and Faylinn was seconds away from an all out panic. Then she squinted through the near darkness and took in her companion's ghostly pallor. "Sit down, love. Before you pass out." She gave Bridget's sleeve another tiny tug and it tore away from the rest of the shirt, ending up a rag in her hands. She rolled her eyes. "Why am I not surprised?"

The candle hissed and released a tiny plume of inky smoke before the room went black.

Bridget dropped limply back onto the bed. She looked to where she knew Faylinn was sitting, and with eyes as round as saucers exclaimed—

"Pregnant?" Kayla and Liv chorused.

Badger burst into laughter and slapped his kilt-covered knee. "Oh, lasses, that's just what Bridget said."

"Wow," Liv said. She blinked a few times, trying to absorb the news. "I didn't see that coming at all."

Badger nodded. "And according to family legend, neither did Bridget."

"Cyril was a first class asshole," Kayla muttered darkly, her thoughts still swimming in the past. "How could he do that? He raped her."

Badger and Liv's expressions both went very serious. "Ay, that's what people would say today."

Kayla glanced up at him, a storm brewing behind her eyes. Faylinn reminded her so much of Liv that she couldn't stop herself before the words were out. "Are you saying differently?" she challenged.

"Kayla," Liv warned softly. She could feel the upset in her partner, and wondered if perhaps it wasn't time to leave Cobb Manor and come back another day. The restless waves of dark, edgy energy flowing from her lover were causing an unsettling feeling in the pit of her stomach. "He didn't say that."

The white-haired man met Kayla's level gaze, his own every bit as steely. "No, lass. She was taken against her will, and that the man was her husband doesn't change that. Although at the time, I don't believe that Faylinn herself would have called it rape, it was that. What I was laughing at before was the surprised expression on both your faces when I told you she was with child. Not at how she got that way."

Kayla suddenly felt ashamed and she glanced down at her hands, threading her fingers together nervously. She twiddled her thumbs a few times. *I need to get a grip. It's over and done with. I can't change it or help. It's not Liv. She's right here, looking at me as though I've lost my ever-lovin' mind.* "Of course. I uh..." She paused and chewed the inside of her cheek. "I just said the first thing that popped into my head. And I shouldn't have. I'm sorry."

"Well." Awkwardly, Badger stood and cleared his throat. "No harm done. As I said before, some of the tale is dark in the tellin'." He tried to smile at Kayla and let her know that he wasn't angry, but she refused to meet his eyes. *Lord knows the first time I heard the tale I was fit to be tied myself.* "Do you lassies have to be getting back to town? There's more to tell if you're willing and have the time."

Liv's worried eyes shifted from her lover to Badger. "I'm not sure." She turned back to Kayla and moved aside a heavy shock of hair so she could rest a reassuring palm on the back of Kayla's neck. "Maybe we could just take a break?"

"Aye. Of course." Badger stretched his thick arms above his head. "Let me get some blood moving around in these old legs. I think the last tour for the day should be coming through the parlor soon." He looked at Liv, his eyebrows raised in question. "I'll drop in on them and say hello, then stop back?"

Liv smiled kindly and mouthed a thank-you to their host.

Badger gave her a ghost of a wink and left the room without a sound.

As soon as he cleared the doorway, Liv focused on Kayla. "You wanna tell me what just happened?"

Kayla's eyebrows pulled tightly together as she thought.

The silence went on so long that Liv was sure she wasn't going to answer. Then, seemingly out of the blue she said, "This is why I spend my time alone. I don't know how to do this."

Liv hadn't been expecting such a serious, general answer. *Oh, boy.* "Do what, honey?"

Kayla gestured aimlessly. "This. Talk. Chat. Be nice."

"You *are* nice," Liv insisted, stroking Kayla's neck.

"Uh huh. That's why after one evening together on vacation, you knew more about my own sister than I did. That's why your brother Dougie looks at me like he's afraid I'm just going to lose it any second. That's why, when we go someplace together, taxi drivers, waitresses, hotel stewards, all of them, talk to you and not me and look grateful that they have a choice."

Liv's mouth went a little slack at the steady stream of words coming from her normally quiet partner.

"That's why Glen deals with all clients unless they insist otherwise. My telling them to 'go to hell' or walking out in the middle of a meeting if I don't think they're sincere in their claims is always a great way to win friends and succeed in business." Her eyes begged Liv to understand. "I'm just not good at this."

For a second, Liv was stunned. She let her hand drop from the warm neck she was stroking, wrapping her fingers around Kayla's instead. "The way you're good at everything else?"

Their eyes met and Kayla felt as though Liv was looking right through her. As much as she didn't want to admit it, that was a little part of it, too. Her eyes darted back to her hands. "I suppose."

"It's really okay, Kayla." Liv softened her voice and that did the trick as Kayla's head lifted, and once again they were looking eye to eye. "Badger wasn't angry, and I do understand." And she did. Being a genius gave Kayla obvious advantages in almost everything she tackled. She'd succeeded most of the time—so long as intellect was the key. But when it came to the highly illogical and volatile things like emotions, Kayla was truly a babe in the woods. At heart she was a loner, and many social situations were trying at best.

"You do?" Kayla eyed the blonde woman warily.

"I think so. You're a natural introvert, and no amount of socializing is ever really going to change that. As a teen you were taller than everyone else, gangly," she paused and smiled affectionately, "probably clumsy and definitely impossibly beautiful—"

Kayla opened her mouth, but Liv silenced her with a raised finger. She wasn't finished yet.

"You liked girls not boys, and were so smart that nobody knew what to do with you."

A startled look planted itself on Kayla's face.

"As if all that wasn't enough, you had special telepathic abilities that set you apart from everyone else, and even you couldn't fully understand and appreciate them. People hurt you because of it, and you moved deeper inside yourself where you felt safe and comfortable." She leaned forward and kissed Kayla's forehead. Her lips lingered on the spot. "And you've been living in there as much as possible, ever since." She sighed and backed away. "I know that interacting with people is hard for you and doesn't always work out the way you want, but *that* will change with practice," she assured. "I promise."

The painfully open expression on Kayla's face made Liv's heart clench.

"You think?"

Liv nodded. "I know so. I'm not shocked in the least that you're a quiet person who is more comfortable in her own head than anywhere else. After everything you've been through, I'm actually surprised you don't stay there more often."

The younger woman's face relaxed into a smile. She was utterly charmed by Liv's keen insight and the fact that she'd obviously taken the time to understand her on a level that no one else had cared enough to even consider. "The answer to that's easy, Liv." She knocked on her own head. "It's lonely up here."

As quickly as the words were out, Kayla watched in fascination as tears welled up in her partner's eyes. She cupped Liv's chin tenderly. "You're out here." She gestured to the room. "And now I'm not lonely anymore."

Liv sniffed, and despite herself, a tear splashed onto her cheek. Her smile was full of affection. "I'm not lonely anymore, either." Her voice cracked and she sniffed again.

Kayla carefully wiped the salty tear away with her thumb.

They neither one quite remembered how it happened, but somehow their lips met, and what started out as a kiss of comfort and affection sparked into something much deeper and infinitely more passionate.

"Well, now," Badger boomed from only a few feet away, his hands on his hips. He grinned. "I can see that everything is back to normal. If I came into the room and you two weren't kissing, I'd think something was wrong."

Liv and Kayla separated and looked up at Badger with twin guilty grins and flaming cheeks. They'd been so absorbed in each other, they hadn't even heard him come in.

The old man scratched his white whiskers and shook his head. "Shall we give it another go?"

Kayla rubbed her red cheeks furiously, trying to remove the blush. How many times was she going to let Badger catch her making out with Liv like some horny teenager? Just then Liv scooted a little closer and the smell of her lover's shampoo and skin gently flooded her senses, surrounding her in a sensual fog. She knew that as many times as Badger left her alone with this enticing woman was as many times as he'd catch them kissing when he came back.

Kayla smiled to herself and glanced at her watch. "We can stay for a while longer, but not too long." She nudged Liv. "Our readings from the Keith House should be ready to go within the hour."

Liv nodded and resettled the blanket that had fallen to the floor during her groping of Kayla back on their knees. "Anything you can start and finish in an hour, Badger?" she asked the old Scot, seeing an immediate spark of competitiveness flare in wise eyes.

"Aye." He puffed up his barrel-chest a bit. "I am the family storyteller, you know. I think I can manage."

Kayla and Liv both nodded gravely and Kayla bit back a smile. If she sat back and was quiet long enough, she figured she was sure to learn a lot about handling people from Liv. "We know," Kayla said as she finally let go of her impatience at Badger's insistence on spinning his tale according to his own time line and not hers. "We'd love to hear more."

He sensed Kayla's quiet surrender and gave her a respectful nod as he moved back to his seat. "Very well." Badger tugged at his belt and shifted back and forth in the seat until he groaned happily.

Liv figured that meant he'd finally found a comfortable spot.

Badger smoothed his kilt with one hand, tempted to take out his pipe. But his audience was ready, and so he would have to wait for a soothing smoke until later, when he could annoy Sylla with the stench. "Faylinn was with child; and though Bridget cursed her brother's name for the way he'd treated his bride, she loved Faylinn no less for it. She vowed to take care of both mother and child as best she could, loving them with all her heart and protecting them with her dying breath. But no matter how Faylinn reassured her, she knew that having only one good arm would be a constant source of worry and self-doubt. So, she set about fixing that problem the only way she knew how. And in doing so, she got back two pieces of her life that she thought she'd left behind on Cobb Island forever..."

Chapter
Eight

Virginia (Mainland)
January, 1691; New Year's Day

Bridget sat comfortably on a large driftwood log on the beach. She watched the short, foamy waves crash rhythmically against the shore, sending up a spray of salty mist as water met land. A strong, cold breeze blew her hair from her eyes and caused her cloak to billow and flutter. She'd taken the long walk here every day for a week. And waited.

Cobb Island loomed dark and barren in the distance, and she was bound and determined that no ship would dock there without her knowledge. It was, she knew, almost time for the Royal Navy to return. They would have undoubtedly heard of Cyril's death by now and would ferry her nieces, and whatever slaves that hadn't already escaped, to a larger port in South Carolina or perhaps New York, where they would book passage on a ship returning to England. The girls' tender ages and the lack of a male guardian in the house would insure they would not be permitted to stay on the Island.

Bridget wondered if Judith would have the wherewithal to keep control of the family property and not allow it to fall wholly into the hands of her father's slave trader business partners or the male cousins in England who would use this chance to try and increase their own holdings. She smiled to herself. Her niece was a smart, sensitive girl whose gentle demeanor went a long way towards hiding her strong will. Though it wouldn't come easily, Bridget was confident that Judith would grow into her role as family matriarch and would be a force to be reckoned with. Bridget tried not to think of Judith's twin, Elizabeth. The girl's betrayal had cut Bridget to the bone and was still a source of shame and sorrow.

"You're looking awfully serious," came the soft voice. Faylinn sat down beside her, and the brittle wood shifted and creaked under the added weight.

"Faylinn! What are you doing here?" Bridget instantly scooted closer to the younger woman. She pulled the edges of Faylinn's cloak tightly together and frowned at her pink, windburned cheeks. "You're cold."

Faylinn laughed. "I am fine, truly." She shrugged one shoulder and looked a little embarrassed. "I just wanted to be with you."

In mild exasperation, Bridget lifted one of Faylinn's legs and dusted her calf free of snow.

Faylinn grinned indulgently and held her tongue as Bridget fussed.

She repeated the process with Faylinn's other leg and set it down gently. "So you tramped several miles through the snow to find me?"

"I knew where you were," Faylinn answered reasonably. She stretched her legs, and kicked her feet out in a mixture of snow and sand. "You told me yourself."

Bridget slid her hand out of one of the warm leather gloves Faylinn had given her for Christmas. She parted Faylinn's cloak carefully and laid her palm on the still flat belly she found there. "How are you feeling?" Her eyes narrowed slightly as she considered collecting some wood for a fire. "Still nauseous?"

Faylinn laughed, absorbing the warmth of Bridget's hand and her concern with almost giddy pleasure. "No," she replied dreamily. "I feel absolutely wonderful. But I do love you so for asking." For the millionth time she counted herself lucky that Bridget had been so accepting of her pregnancy. It had, she knew, complicated things to no end, but she couldn't really bring herself to think of it as a bad thing. She firmly believed in her heart what Bridget had assured her of on Christmas Eve: a child is a blessing to be treasured and cherished, a gift whose value cannot be measured, and that any future trials they would face would be handled together.

Bridget leaned forward and gently brushed her lips against Faylinn's, drawing a soft sigh of pleasure from her friend. Then she wrapped her arm around Faylinn's shoulder and they both looked out at the sea, content to share the gray afternoon together in comfortable silence.

Their physical relationship had not progressed past kissing, and though Faylinn wasn't sure *what* they could even do past that, Bridget most certainly was. She'd been courted by several young men during her teenage years, all of whom would have been suitable mates and potential business partners for her brother and father. But even then, she'd already decided that marriage was not for her. Her mind, her will, and most certainly her body were hers alone; and to her parents' great distress and her brother's endless censure, she'd outright refused to surrender them to anyone. Little did she know, a pair of soulful green eyes and a young woman's fiery spirit would capture her so completely. Whether or not to surrender every part of herself was never a really a question at all.

Bridget's male suitors had been turned away without so much as a peck on the cheek. That did not, however, keep her from engaging in several brief but pleasurable liaisons with some of the Court's most eligible young women. She snorted softly at the hypocrisy of these girls, who had privately been eager to taste the forbidden, but in public were among the first to vigorously scorn such disgusting, sinful behavior.

The noise drew Faylinn's attention from the water and she turned to Bridget, bestowing on her a lovely, youthful smile that made Bridget's heart beat faster. *Yes, dearest, we do need to have an intimate conversion.*

Faylinn turned back to the water, enjoying the salty mist on her face and the warm body nestled close to hers.

The small hand on Bridget's knee slid innocently up her thigh, stopping just short of the crease between her hip and leg. She swallowed hard. That talk would have to be soon.

"Bridget!"

The taller woman jumped and pushed Faylinn's hand off her thigh, instantly feeling guilty for her lascivious thoughts. "What?"

"Look." Faylinn pointed to Cobb Island.

Approaching from the northwest was a large ship, sails of all three masts flying high.

"At last." Bridget sighed.

Faylinn looked at her curiously. Her memories of the island were a mixture of joy and stark misery; and while the many good times with Henry and Bridget went a long way towards canceling out some of the horror she'd experienced, she shuddered at the thought of going back. "Why should it matter when the girls leave the island?"

"Because I intend to go back there, and they must be gone before that can happen." Bridget looked at her companion compassionately. "I don't expect you to join me, Faylinn. Though maybe someday you'll feel differently. There is a beauty even in the harshness of Cobb Island."

"But—"

"You've been vomiting for weeks. Do you really want to embark on even a short trip across rough waters?"

Faylinn turned a peculiar shade of green at the mere idea. Bridget did have a point. "Can I ask why *you* feel the need to go back then? Surely, the house will be empty and your possessions gone?"

Bridget stood and brushed off her cloak. She offered her hand to Faylinn. "Because there is something important there that I want to reclaim. And if I know Judith the way I think I do, it will be waiting for me when I return."

Cobb Island
Mid-January, 1691

Will threw his back into the job and, with a great grunt and as much assistance as Bridget could manage, he heaved the rowboat up onto the shore. The dock in front of the house was only moments away, but Will was worried about the gloomy skies and had decided it was safer to walk the rest of the way to the house than it was to row there.

He and Bridget both dropped onto their backs on the island's dark-soiled beach, panting from their exertions. They had each taken an oar, Bridget one-handed, and made good time from the mainland.

Faylinn and Katie had flatly refused to allow them to make the trip earlier in the month, insisting instead that they wait until the waters had calmed. Initially both Bridget and Will had refused, but then Faylinn had made it clear to Bridget that if she was going to risk her life, it wouldn't be without her. And *that* threat was one Bridget took seriously. This particular trip was no place for Faylinn.

Nearly two weeks of solid rain mixed with high winds had delayed the trip far longer than Bridget would have liked. She had, however, ultimately found herself begrudgingly agreeing with the blonde woman's sharp words: coming home *alive* took precedence over her natural impatience. And so they had waited.

The skies were overcast and restless, and even though it was still early afternoon, the island was cast in long, ominous shadows. Will took off his hat and wiped his sweaty brow with the back of his arm.

His muddy brown eyes surveyed the land curiously and with more than a touch of apprehension. Even with the leaves gone and most of the plant-life dry or dead, a dense, impenetrable curtain of vegetation surrounded the island, making it look like a fortress. He scowled. "The view of this island up from its own shores is even more harsh and ugly than from the mainland. The entire place looks damned to me. I can't believe your brother chose to put a house here."

Bridget snorted harshly. "He chose to put a house here because it is the perfect port for slave trading. Large slave hulls can anchor in the deep waters off this island and avoid the reef closer to shore. Here, they transfer the slaves onto smaller, waiting boats that will carry them to the mainland and the auction block."

"Ah." Will nodded cautiously. That was a good idea. Many a ship had run aground on the reef that lined the shore for many miles. "Too bad the peddling of human flesh is such a nasty trade." Out of the corner of his eye, he watched Bridget, wondering if she would agree, despite the fact that selling slaves had no doubt added to the Redding family fortune.

Her face was grim. "I know." She pushed awkwardly to her feet. "Let's go."

Will called after her, "Where exactly are we goin'?" When Bridget announced she was planning a trip to the Island, Faylinn had begged him to go along so she wouldn't be alone. To his surprise, Bridget had instantly agreed. She never would tell him exactly why. "Hey! Wait for me." He resettled his hat and sped up his pace as Bridget disappeared into the dry forest ahead of him.

After a half-hour of climbing over brittle vines and weaving between endless dead branches, they rounded a corner and the landscape seemed to open up, bringing the house into view.

"Gadzooks!" Will's mouth dropped open. He couldn't get over how quickly the look of the Island had changed, and the amazing, undeniably beautiful house he was now face to face with. "It's...why it's enormous!" he sputtered, craning his neck to get a better view of the third floor.

A bored expression crossed Bridget face. "Cyril's architectural masterpiece." She snorted. "If it were up to me, I'd burn the place down." Then she remembered the history that Afia had sworn to compile and hide someplace deep within the bowels of the house. God willing, it would be discovered by future generations. "But I cannot."

Will's eyes darted from side to side, then he rocked back on his heels and grinned engagingly. "I don't see anyone here to stop us."

Bridget smiled. *Will Beynon, a rebel at heart? Who'd have guessed?* Despite his grumpy, usually gruff manner, she truly liked Will. And he adored Faylinn. In Bridget's estimation, anyone who felt that way had exemplary taste and was obviously a person of keen insight. "It's not my place to decide what happens to the house. My niece is the head of the household now."

They walked up the winding path that led to the front door, but instead of going inside as Will had expected, Bridget detoured around the side of the house, her boots crunching loudly in the shallow snow.

When she reached the back, she lifted her fingers to her mouth and gave a shrill whistle. "Apollo! Show yourself! Apollo!"

Will's eyes widened. "You're..." He swallowed. "You're calling to a pagan god?" He looked around nervously, half-afraid of what would happen next. Perhaps she was a witch after all.

Bridget's face was a cross between compassion and impatience. "You needn't fear me, Will. Apollo is my steed. And I've sorely missed him."

"Ahh... Whew." Relief flooded through him. "Now that, I can understand." He tugged up on his waist of his trousers, a little ashamed at his sudden fear. "Back home, when I was a lad in Wales, I had a brown filly that ran like the wind." He smiled wistfully. "Since coming to the Colonies I haven't been able to afford another. Mules are cheaper and better suited to frontier life anyway." His voice was somber and tinged with regret.

He scratched his bristly, square jaw. "Wouldn't the Navy have taken the horse with them?" That was his nice way of saying that no officer of the Crown would have allowed a beast of quality to be set free in the wild, not if there was profit to be made by its sale. Transporting horses from England to the Colonies was an expensive and risky proposition at best. Their price at market reflected that fact.

Bridget frowned. "Perhaps. But I won't know for certain until I look, now will I?" She strode towards the stable calling out "Apollo" the entire way. When she reached her destination, she stopped dead in her tracks. The stable door had been propped wide open by a bale of hay. A bolt of fear lanced through her. "Apollo?" Carefully, and with Will trailing curiously behind her, she poked her head inside the doorway. It was dark, and the building had lost most of its familiar scent. Patches of dirty snow covered the ground and the bales of dried grass near the door.

Bridget's gaze narrowed as she peeked into the darkness and stepped inside. Her heart began to pound wildly, and she told herself she had to be strong no matter what she found. She hadn't shared with Will her deepest fear, that Apollo had been killed. Animals were often believed to be in league with their witch masters, and it wouldn't be unheard of for a horse to be hung by the neck or burnt at the stake exactly as his master had been. *Exactly as they* tried *to do to me.*

Just then her gaze lit upon a dark, still shadow in the corner stall, and her face went ashen. *No,* she anguished silently. Her breath exploded from her chest in harsh pants as she tried to make out what she was seeing. Her feet refused to take her any closer.

Then...she heard it. Something in the corner. Her eyes darted back and forth wildly but she couldn't see what was producing the noise, she only knew it was coming closer and closer.

"Buh!" Bridget jumped backwards as family of raccoons darted out from beneath a pile of hay and made for the door. Her presence has scared them nearly as badly as they had frightened her, and they ran in panicked circles until finally skittering over her boots and escaping out the door.

Bridget's yell startled Will so badly that he lost his balance and stumbled over his own two feet, ending up on his butt in the snow. "Ouch," he complained belatedly, in a flat voice.

"Damn." Bridget's covered her face with her hand and laughed mirthlessly. After a moment, she took a deep breath and walked to the side wall, where she violently tore open a shutter, tearing it off the wall in the process. Gray light poured into the room and with her heart in her throat, she stared at the last stall, seeing clearly what had only been outlined in shadows before.

A saddle and set of tack hanging from a hook on the wall.

"Sweet Mother." She nearly sank to her knees in relief.

Will looked on in wonder, having no earthly idea what had just happened. He stood up and rubbed his backside, his eyes following Bridget as she crossed the room. "I can't believe they'd leave valuable goods like that."

"I can," Bridget answered absently as she plucked a note from between the leather folds of the saddle and began to read.

> *Dearest Aunt Bridget,*
>
> *After the shock wore off, I realized that you are far too stubborn to ever truly give up on anything. Especially yourself. As surely as my own heart beats, however, I know that you are alive but that I shall never lay eyes upon you again. Of Faylinn's ultimate fate, I am less certain. If God is truly merciful and good, then Faylinn is*

with you, wherever that may be.

I pray that someday you are able to forgive Elizabeth the darkness that dwells within her. It is a part of her as surely as good was, is, a part of you. She cannot change that. Yet I have faith that in time, and with love, she will learn to temper it. There IS good inside her.

No doubt you are here for Apollo. Rest assured that he lives and that I refused to surrender him to the Royal Navy. He could only ever have one master. He has been set free.

As you have.

The ship and my twin await, so I must close. Be well, Auntie.

In love and eternal respect,

Judith Redding
January 2, 1691

Bridget neatly folded the note and slid it into a pocket of her trousers. "Stubborn?" She laughed weakly and closed her eyes. *Thank you, Judith. Goodbye and be well.*

"Bridget?"

Her back to Will, Bridget opened her eyes as she straightened, resettling her cloak on her shoulders. "He's here." She turned and smiled. "We need only find him."

Will smiled back, responding instinctively to the enthusiasm on Bridget's face. "Where do we start?"

Bridget walked past him and back outside. She thought of her long time confidant, who, for most of her time here, was her only real friend. "C'mon. It's a fair walk, but I have an idea."

She began leading Will to the far side of the island and as they progressed, the man decided to ask something he'd been wondering about for weeks. "Bridget?"

"Hmm?" She carefully stepped around a jagged stump.

"How is it you survived execution?"

Her step faltered, but she got hold of herself quickly and kept going. "Why haven't you asked me sooner, Will?" She had seen the question on his face many times, heard his thoughts as he debated whether or not to voice them.

He let out a long breath, sending a pillar of fog from his mouth. "Because of Faylinn. Katie asked her once and she burst into tears." His heavy brow furrowed. "I thought it a subject best saved for when I was away from her company."

"Thank you," Bridget said softly, well aware that the subject of her execution was still too raw for Faylinn to speak about.

"Does she know?"

Bridget slowed her pace until Will was walking directly alongside her. "Does she know what?"

"How you survived."

"Ahh..." Bridget's face grew serious. "Yes, she knows. We spoke of it once, when we first came to stay with you. It..." She paused, trying to find the right words. "It's...hard for her, I suppose. She was there that night and truly believed, like everyone else, that I was dead."

"If you don't want to—"

Bridget shook her head. "No, Will, I'll tell you." She cracked a smile. "Though the simple truth is probably less dramatic than you've imagined." To Bridget's surprise, Will burst out laughing. In all the time she'd known him, it was something she'd only seen once or twice.

"You don't *want* to know what I've imagined."

Bridget smiled wryly and pointed to the left. "Pretty ridiculous, huh?"

Will filed in behind her as she began walking in the direction she'd pointed. "Tell me what happened, and I'll be the judge of whether or not it was ridiculous."

"Fair enough." Their trek began slanting upward and Bridget picked up a long stick as she walked, swinging it aimlessly as she recounted the events of that night.

"It was raining. No," she shook her head, "that's not quite right. It wasn't *just* raining. It was storming as though the heavens themselves were falling down around us. Lightning pierced the sky and thunder shook the entire island. Waves broke against the shore like great walls crashing down, and hail pounded us when the rain finally gave way to the cold."

"I remember that night. We were holed up at home, afraid the world was coming to an end. I've never seen a storm like that."

"I was taken to the cliffs to be burned at the stake."

"In the pouring rain?"

Bridget and Will both snorted and indulged in a bit of gallows humor. "I never claimed my brother was clever."

"Poor Faylinn."

"Indeed. Anyway, the men of the Royal Navy, who were there to perform the execution, couldn't even keep their torches lit; they decided that hanging would suit their purpose just as well. What they didn't plan on was Faylinn. Cyril hadn't told her what was to take place, but somehow she found out. She arrived at my execution scene atop Apollo, amid the flashes of lightning.

It was like something from a book; I had never seen her look so magnificent. She tried to reason with my brother.

"Stop this madness before it's too late. She is your sister for God's sake. This will be an error you can never undo!"

Bridget's lips formed a thin line. "But he would not be dissuaded, and became hysterical with jealously. 'Hang the witch!' he shouted as he glared at me with eyes as cold and stony as a tomb." Now Bridget smiled. "He and I both got the surprise of our lives when Faylinn turned on her heels and flew into my arms with such force she nearly knocked me over." Bridget stopped her story and glanced back at Will uncertainly. "Will," she began hesitantly, "before I go on, I need to make certain that you understand—"

"That Faylinn loves you? And you, her?" he answered casually.

Bridget blinked. *Was it that obvious? Neither he nor Katie, who talked incessantly, had ever said a word!*

His dark eyes twinkled. "I knew that the first day, when Faylinn came pounding on my door and begged us to help you. That girl's emotions were written all over her face. If you had died, I feel certain we would have ended up burying you both. I wasn't sure you felt the same way until the day I saw you together in the yard and she had her hands on her hips in that scolding way I've seen Katie use a million times, insisting it was time for your bandages to be changed and a bath. I heard you mumbling and cursing, but when she held out her hand, you stepped forward and grasped it instantly." He winked. "A lamb led to the slaughter, you were."

Bridget felt her cheeks grow hot, chasing away the chill of the wind.

"I suppose that's about as good a showing of true love as I've ever seen." Will leaned against a tree with one hand. "But we can never speak of it, Bridget." He slipped off his hat and ran his hands through his sweaty hair before replacing it firmly. "My Katie is a devout woman, and as much as she cares for you and Faylinn, this is something her faith would never allow her to accept. If it comes down to it, though it would sadden me greatly, I would not ask her to compromise that. I cannot."

Though it wasn't what Bridget wanted to hear about Katie, she couldn't help but respect Will's decision. "You have my word, Will Beynon. The tender feelings Faylinn and I share will never be made clear to your wife."

Will grinned wryly. "I don't think you'll have too many problems. She has come to accept even the most...er...'intense' displays of affection between you as the new standard for sisterhood everywhere. I only thank God that Katie has no such sisters, or I would be as useful as tits on a boar."

Bridget couldn't help but chuckle. She slapped Will on the shoulder and grinned broadly, relieved that at least he was willing to take her love for Faylinn in his stride. It was more than she had any right to expect. She made a mental note to explain the situation to Faylinn that evening when she returned.

Their climb grew steeper and she could hear Will's breathing pick up. "I'll continue with the tale, then."

> *The younger woman crushed her lips against Bridget's in unrestrained passion, pressing a small, hidden dagger in her love's hands. "I love you," she whispered fiercely against Bridget's mouth as she kissed her thoroughly, smiling through the kisses when she heard her words echoed. "Please live," she whispered again, as Cyril tore her away from Bridget and the tall woman tucked the dagger underneath her cloak, out of view.*

"Then Cyril began babbling about me enchanting his wife, and the soldiers began to circle me, intent on carrying out the execution, even if it meant simply running me through with their blades."

Will shivered, more from the coldness in Bridget's voice than the chill in the air.

"I fixed my eyes on the first man I would kill, determined not to meet my Maker alone, when I saw..." Her jaw worked for a moment, and she swallowed a few times before she could continue. "I saw my pig-assed brother with his sword at Faylinn's throat, ready to murder her before my eyes." She heard Will's angry growl behind her and grinned savagely in concert.

"Bastard!" Will spat.

"I've always suspected."

Tiny snowflakes began to fall.

"Cyril's eyes locked with mine, and I knew he would kill her if I continued to struggle. I had no choice." Bridget couldn't tell Will about the look in Faylinn's eyes when her decision became clear, or the young woman's desperate cries. They still tore at her soul and haunted her nightmares. Discussing them, even with Will, was out of the question. "So then, I did it," she said simply.

Did it? "Did what?"

The smell of the sea was getting stronger now, and Bridget could hear the waves beating against the rocks. Tiny snowflakes landed on her hair and on her face, disappearing as quickly as they touched warm skin. "I jumped."

"Jumped?"

"You'll see." Her words were prophetic, because at that very moment they stepped onto a small, barren plateau. At its edge was a 40-foot high jagged cliff that led to nothing but the sea. Near the edge a wooden post still stood, marking the spot where Bridget was to be burned at the stake.

Will eyes went round as he recognized the post for what it was and took in its location. "You jumped off that?" He edged his way over to the post and beyond, but refused to get too close to the edge. "That...that's impossible!" he murmured, shocked. He turned disbelieving eyes on Bridget. "You would have hit the rocks below; the water isn't deep enough to save you. You should be dead!"

"I should," Bridget agreed. "But Faylinn saved my life. The long ropes for my execution were still tied around my neck when I leapt." She pointed to the wooden post. "The other ends were tied to that." Bridget tried to block out the sound of Faylinn's screams as she recalled the feeling of weightlessness as she plunged through the air. "I grabbed the ropes with one hand as I fell, and with a quick turn looped them around my wrist and fore-arm." She held up her good arm and imitated the motion.

Will nodded quickly.

"I had only one chance, and I knew it. If I failed, I would either crash to my death on the rocks below, or my neck would be snapped like a chicken being readied for Sunday dinner.

Will gulped.

She joined Will near but not too close to the edge. "From my cloak, I pulled the knife Faylinn had pressed into my hands, and the very second the ropes were taut I slashed them with all my might, and to my amazement they fell away." Bridget unconsciously cradled her disfigured arm. "My timing was far from perfect; and while I managed not get my neck broken, for a split second my arm bore the full burden of my fall." Bridget licked her lips. "It snapped in two places so quickly that I didn't really know what had happened. I thought I'd simply torn it from my body." She walked closer to the ledge and gestured Will over.

His pride was the only thing that kept him from refusing out-right.

"My angle of descent changed, and I slammed into the side of the cliff. I continued to fall until, tearing through those branches," she pointed, "and those rocks," her finger shifted, "I came to rest in a crevice near the bottom."

"By God, you fell almost the entire way?"

Bridget nodded and moved away from the edge. It was making her sick to her stomach.

Will gratefully followed.

"I woke up the next day: cut, bloodied, broken, the knife still gripped in my useless hand, and freezing; but quite alive."

"Bridget?"

"Yes?"

"Don't tell anyone else that story."

Bridget's forehead creased. "Well, considering my current circumstances I hadn't planned on it. But for curiosity's sake, why not?"

Will looked at her frankly. "Because they won't believe a blessed word."

They smiled at each other until it became awkward and Will looked away. "I appreciate seeing the spot you spoke about, but did you drag me all the way across the island to show me the cliffs?"

"Hardly. We came because—" Bridget's ears perked up and she grinned wildly, looking at something over Will's shoulder. "We came because of him."

Then Will heard the furious pounding of hooves. He turned around and a great white beast bolted passed him, stopping just in time to keep from running into Bridget and sending her over the cliff again.

The stallion thrust his hooves out in front of him as he came to a stop directly in front of his mistress, spraying her legs with snow and dirt. She let out a happy laugh and the animal nuzzled her chest, whinnying loudly as she hugged him tightly.

"Apollo?"

"The one and only. Hello, boy. I've missed you!" she cooed, forgetting to be self-conscious about the lavish attention she was paying the animal.

Will admired him openly. "He's a fine piece of horseflesh, Bridget." Hoping not to get kicked in the head, he approached them both cautiously, stopping to give the steed's strong neck a pat only when Bridget nodded her consent. "I can see now why you'd hate to give him up. I thought that only dogs stayed in the last place they'd seen their owners, waiting for their return."

Bridget lovingly stroked the soft wet skin of Apollo's head. "You don't know my horse." She tangled her good hand in her horse's thick mane and threw her leg over his back, groaning slightly as she hauled her body on top.

Will scrambled back a step when the large stallion reared.

Bridget only laughed and held on tightly with one hand. "Apollo!" But her voice was more delighted than scolding. "I think he'd like to burn off some energy. I...well..."

"Go on, Bridget. I'll be here when you get back."

Bridget's eyes showed her gratitude. "Thank you, my friend. I'll be back in a few moments and give you a ride back to the house." She smacked Apollo's rump lightly with a gloved hand. "He's a big boy and won't mind riding double." And with a happy yell, Bridget lifted her thighs slightly and tightened their grip on his muscled body. Then she kicked her steed into motion, and with a spray of snow and dirt they were off.

Will sighed longingly and tucked his hands under his armpits, unable to keep the smile off his face as Bridget flew across the snowy plateau, red hair and cloak billowing wildly as she rode.

Bridget straightened and let out a tired breath, stretching her sore back. Then she bent again and shifted the wooden crate a little closer to the boat's side, trying to balance it against the other items she'd stowed in the rowboat's bottom. The weather hadn't worsened as Will had feared, and they'd rowed the boat from their original landing spot to the small dock directly in front of the house. The light snow had stopped falling and the sun was trying to peek out from behind the late afternoon clouds.

"Are you sure this is all right?" Will asked as he pulled a tarp over two crates in the back of the boat. "I know these things were left behind, but it still feels like stealing."

A slender brow arched. "You were ready to burn the place down with me a few hours ago."

"That's different," Will answered moodily.

"How so?"

Will rubbed a callused palm on the back of his neck as he thought. "Because burning the place down would have felt like a blow against your slave-trading brother."

"God rest his black, putrid soul."

"But this makes us plain old thieves, doesn't it?" he finished, balancing carefully as he made his way out of the boat and climbed onto the dock where Bridget was now standing.

"Don't worry so much, Will." She laid her hand on his forearm and squeezed gently. "These belong to the Redding family. Of which, I am still member. Albeit a dead one."

"That's not funny."

"That depends entirely on your point of view," she replied drolly. "Besides, some of these items are Faylinn's. Surely you wouldn't begrudge her the comfort of her own possessions?"

Will blinked indignantly. "Of course not!"

"Then it's settled."

"It was settled before I busted my arse towing these crates to the boat, I'll have ya know."

"Oh." Bridget smiled. "Well, it might make you feel a little better to know that I believe Judith intentionally left behind a few items of value for me...just in case."

"Like Apollo?" Will's gaze drifted out to the salty sea. His throat was as dry as the desert, and he wished he'd thought to bring a canteen of drinking water.

Bridget's lips shaped into a fond smile just thinking of the horse she'd had to say goodbye to again already. "Just like Apollo." She shot Will a determined look. "But I have a plan in that regard, too. We can sell the items in the boat, and buy or rent a raft. In the springtime we shall come back for Apollo and ferry him to the mainland. He should have plenty of grass and hay in the stable until then, and the island has several natural springs that never freeze over."

Will nodded approvingly. It was an outright sin to waste such exquisite horseflesh.

Bridget's eyes suddenly took on a sparkle that made Will nervous. "I was also thinking," she began casually, "that we could take the rest of the money and purchase a brood mare or two."

The man's ears perked up. "A mare, you say?"

"I seriously doubt that Apollo would mind the company, and a fine colt is the least I can offer you in payment for your kindness to Faylinn and me."

Will blushed a bright scarlet. "I cannot accept that," he mumbled half-heartedly.

"Don't be ridiculous," Bridget scoffed, touched by her friend's humility. "You deserve far more. You saved both our lives, Will." Her gaze softened. "That is a debt I can never repay."

"As I told Faylinn that very first night, I'll not be taking a red cent of slaver money. "However," his smile removed most of the word's sting, "something to drink would go a long way. Where's your well?"

"I've got a better idea. Cyril had a stash of brandy hidden in a wall panel. There is no way the girls would have known to empty it." She extended her arm towards the house.

"Mmm." Will licked his lips. "I haven't had brandy in years, and then only a sip or two. I wonder if it tastes as good as I remember."

"May it match your memory, then." The pair made their way up the steep stairs that led to the front door. Bridget gathered her courage and commented, "That reminds me, Will. I have a small favor I'd like to ask you."

"You want me to what?" Will glared at Bridget as though she'd grown a third eye.

"Calm down, Will."

"I will not." He threw his hands in the air. "You're mad."

Bridget's expression darkened. "I've seen madness; I'm not. Here." Bridget took a swig directly out of the bottle and passed it to him. "Have another drink. Mmm...burns." She hissed as her throat tingled from the strength of the liquor. They were sitting on the dock in front of the house, cloaks wrapped tightly around their shoulders, their legs dangling off the dock's end.

"If you're not insane, then you're drunk," he accused, but he took the bottle and downed a healthy gulp himself.

A lock of dark hair blew across Bridget's face. Exasperated, she pushed it back. "Not quite yet. But I am trying."

Will narrowed his eyes and let out a grumpy breath. "I knew there was a reason you didn't pitch a hellcat's fit when Faylinn begged me to come along."

Bridget grinned knowingly. "Well, then you're a wise man, just as I've always suspected." She took back the bottle, and brought it to her lips. The fumes tickled her nose and she closed her eyes this time as she tilted it back for long, deep drink. "Ahh..." She wiped an errant drop of liquor off her chin with the back of her hand. "Smooth." Unseeing eyes shifted out to the churning waves. "It has to be done, Will. Please."

Will sighed. "Katie and I set your arm the first time, Bridget. What makes you think if we break it again and reset it that you'll be any better off?"

Bridget was silent for a long time. Finally, she took two large gulps of brandy in rapid succession and passed the bottle back to Will. "Because it can't be any worse." Weakly she held out her damaged, twisted arm, grimacing at the pain the action still caused. "It's all but useless. I can never give Faylinn a life of propriety or even of comfort, but I can give her the best of myself. I won't lose my arm forever without a fight." Will remained unmoved and Bridget felt herself growing angry. *This is not your choice, Will Beynon!* "Either you help me do it right, or by God I'll just do it myself!" She moved to stand, but Will stopped her with a firm hand on her shoulder.

"Bridget." His voice was low and controlled.

She turned flashing, slightly bleary eyes on him. "Make your choice, Will. If you haven't the stomach for it, you need only say the word." She snorted derisively. "Next time I'll bring Katie along with me." *Damn.* Bridget regretted the harsh words the second they escaped her lips.

Will stiffened, and his grip on her shoulder tightened convulsively.

"I'm sorry," she muttered quickly, looking away. "That was quite uncalled for." She peeled his hand off her shoulder and pushed to her feet. Reaching down, she quickly snatched the bottle from his hands and downed half of it in one endless chug.

Will's eyes widened and he began to sputter as he also stood. "Je-Je-Jesus Almighty!"

Bridget grinned rakishly. "No, the name's Bridget Redding," she slurred. "But there've been women in my past who've made that same mistake. Why, one time—"

Will clamped his hand over her mouth. He pushed his hat further back on his head with one finger and lifted a bushy eyebrow. "I won't have you sending me straight to hell with your sinful confessions, Bridget."

Bridget blinked slowly. "Huh?" *Hell could kiss her arse!*

With a roguish expression of his own, Will threw back, "Because then I'd feel compelled to tell you how Katie screams her fool head off when I—"

"Ewwww!" she interrupted, her face twisting into an expression of pure disgust. "Ewww. Ewww. Ewww. I don't want to hear that!"

"It's not that bad," he complained with mock indignation.

"Say you." Then, abruptly, she held her injured arm straight out, this time not flinching a bit. With her fist she gave it a jab or two. "See?"

Will blinked in amazement. "It doesn't hurt anymore?" *This is some liquor.*

"No. It still hurts like the Devil." She burst out laughing. "I'm just too drunk to care."

Will joined her in a hearty chuckle, feeling the alcohol seep into his bloodstream and envelop him in comforting, buzzing warmth. Any hint of stress between them bled away and they continued to pass the bottle, with Bridget doing most of the drinking.

"Are you going to help me?" she asked after a few moments, needing to steady herself with a hand on his arm.

Will looked her dead in the eye. He didn't want to, but... "I am."

She went a little pale at his words, but still felt relieved. "Let's do it, then. It won't fix itself."

Will let out a shuddering breath, unhooked the clasp at his neck and slipped his cloak from his shoulders. He rolled it until it was long and cylindrical in shape and then handed it to Bridget. "Think happy thoughts. I'll be right back."

"Happy thoughts." She nodded a little. "Right." Bridget steeled her nerves, which threatened to make her teeth chatter. *This is my only chance, and I'm going to take it no matter how bloody much it hurts!* Then, as though unconsciously following Will's directive, her mind drifted to her favorite subject and she smiled. She thought about Faylinn's gentle kisses every morning as she awoke, and the sweet, lingering scent of the soap that clung to her skin. It never smelled quite the same on her or Will or especially Katie. *Thank goodness my Faylinn is not here to witness this now. I'll have hell to pay as it is. Oh, wait. Hell is busy kissing my arse.* She dissolved into laughter again.

Bridget took another drink, noting absently that the liquid didn't burn on the way down anymore. Instead, it seemed to pool in her guts and send a tingling warmth out to her extremities. Warm. That's how she felt for the first time all day.

"Are you all right?"

Bridget's head snapped up, and she realized she'd almost fallen asleep. Disobediently, her gaze drifted from Will's face to the stick in his hand. It was at least two feet long and as thick as her forearm. She looked back up, feeling a little dizzy. "I have not passed out from fear or drink, so I would say I am quite fine, though highly unlucky."

Will could only nod.

Bridget pushed her sleeve up to her shoulder, exposing the crooked lay of her arm. "Here and here, I think." She pointed to the two places her bone had been broken before. One was only a few inches from her wrist, the other directly above her elbow.

Will's belly clenched. He hadn't really thought about having to break it twice. He ran his fingers lightly over the two spots. He didn't have to memorize their exact locations. The skin around the bone was still a light shade of purple and it was obviously swollen. He settled his cloak over the higher spot first so that the wood wouldn't damage the skin any more than necessary. Then he held on to her left hand so that her arm was outstretched. "Ready then?" The man searched Bridget's eyes for any chance she'd spare herself this. He saw only grim determination.

"Ready." She hiccupped, then her brow furrowed. "Wait." She took one last drink and set the bottle back on the dock as she padded unsteadily over to one of the wooden support posts. The post was about shoulder high, and she stretched her bad arm out as best she could and placed her hand, palm down, on the post. When he joined her, she grabbed his shirt with her other hand and focused her eyes on his. "One strike each time, Will. Hard and fast. Make them count."

"I will, Bridget." It was a promise.

"Will?"

A little of Bridget's fear showed through in her expression and Will felt a heavy sensation creep into his chest. "Yes?"

"I don't know if I'll be able to stand for the second blow."

Will set his jaw. "It will be done. Never fear." His fist tightened around the rough length of maple in his hand until his knuckles shone white.

"Thank you," Bridget whispered, and allowed her eyes to flutter closed. Her heart began to pound. *I can do this. I must.*

For a moment Will stood looking at this woman in utter amazement. She wasn't shaking or crying; instead, she was standing perfectly calm with her arm outstretched, ready for him to shatter it to pieces. The only visible sign of strain was a fine sheen of sweat that glistened on her face and the working of her neck muscles as she occasionally swallowed hard. Then he reminded himself that Bridget had endured the tortures of being an accused witch and still not buckled. She was no stranger to pain. He wondered if he would be so brave.

Setting his feet shoulder-width apart, he bent his knees a little and raised the piece of wood high overhead. *God, help me to help her.* Putting all of his considerable muscle into the motion, he began the swing.

Bridget heard a soft grunt and the whooshing sound of the club as it approached her arm with startling speed. Time seem to slow just before she felt the impact. She felt the air shift around her elbow and goosebumps break out across the exposed skin, making tiny hairs stand on end. Then the piece of wood exploded against her body with a pain so great it was more than she could truly comprehend all at once. The stunning blow snapped the bone cleanly in half, sending it tearing through muscle and sinew until it ripped through the skin at her elbow in a jagged mess of blood and flesh.

In less than a heartbeat, her knees violently hit the dock and she tasted the metallic tang of blood where she'd bitten the edge of her tongue clean through. Her eyes bulged and she gasped, as the agony that had failed to fully register a second before came roaring to the forefront of her consciousness with savage intensity.

Arghh!! Saliva mixed with blood dribbled from the corners of her mouth as she panted harshly. She instinctively gripped her dangling arm closer to her body as she began to shake. Her eyes were screwed tightly shut, and hot, salty blood dripped from her elbow to her hand, trickling from her fingertips in a steady stream onto the sun-bleached dock. A light fog lifted from the crimson liquid as it pooled on the ground.

Virginia (Mainland)
That same day in January, 1691

"Do you think they'll make it back before dark?" Katie asked, holding her mending up to the light coming in the window so she could examine her handiwork.

Faylinn sat in front of the fireplace and next to Katie so she could learn the new stitch the husky woman was trying to teach her. She brought a cup of tea to her lips and took a sip, enjoying its warm, sweet flavor on this cold winter's day. "Bridget assured me they would. She—" The blonde woman stopped abruptly as every ounce of air was crushed from her chest in a violent spasm. In a panic, she tried to stand, but before she could find her feet, her legs buckled and she dropped to the floor with a solid thud. Her hands flew to her ears as a mind-numbing scream ripped through her consciousness and sent her heart into her throat.

"Faylinn?" Petrified, Katie jumped up, knocking over her sewing in the process. "Are you—" Her eyes automatically shifted to Faylinn's belly. "The baby?"

Faylinn shook her head vigorously, still trying to process what had just happened. She was trembling and felt as though she was going into shock. *That scream could have only come from one source.* "It—" She paused as Katie helped her back to her seat and pushed the cup of tea back into her hands, placing her own hands around Faylinn's shaking ones. "It's Bridget." Terrified green eyes met Katie's. "Something's happened."

Katie's face showed her confusion. "Something? Bridget's not here, girl." Her eyes darted back and forth nervously as she responded to the horror in Faylinn's eyes. "What are you talking about?"

Haphazardly, Faylinn set down her cup and stumbled to the door. She grabbed her cloak from a peg on the wall as she went. "Something bad," she said tightly as she disappeared into the cold.

Will's eyes were so round it would have been comical had Bridget not been writhing around on the dock in pure agony. "Oh, God. I think I hit you too hard." The stick fell from his limp hand, and he sank to his knees alongside Bridget, afraid to even touch her. "I-I-I..."

"S'fine," Bridget hissed from between clenched teeth as she rocked back and forth, one arm wrapped around herself in mute, pitiful comfort.

"Sweet Mother Mary, I can't believe you're still conscious!" he screeched. "What in the hell is wrong with you?"

Bridget sneered at him, though she herself had wondered the same thing.

Will had thought for certain the shock of the strike in combination with the amount of alcohol she'd consumed would have knocked her out instantly.

For a moment, Bridget thought the normally stolid man might actually burst into tears. "T-time for hit number two, eh?" she joked faintly. She wasn't sure at all if she'd live through another strike, but it was too late to turn back now. She tried to smile to remove the stricken look from Will's face, but her mouth refused to cooperate. Instead, it shaped an "O" as her stomach lurched and she began to retch painfully. Her breakfast made an unwelcome reappearance.

When she was finished, Will took one look into vivid, bloodshot eyes and knew what he had to do. "Let me help you, Bridget." It wasn't a question it was a command.

"What?" She coughed weakly at the acrid taste in her mouth and tried to focus her fuzzy mind on anything besides the millions of knives that were stabbing her arm.

"Sit up a little." He guided her with gentle hands. "There."

"Wh—" The last thing Bridget remembered was the sight of a meaty fist hurling directly towards her jaw.

Virginia (Mainland)
That same day in January, 1691

"Jesus protect and keep me," Will said to himself as two figures appeared on shore like apparitions emerging from the evening fog.

It was Faylinn and Katie, hands on hips, feet tapping impatiently.

His rowing suddenly slowed and he turned to a very drunk Bridget, who had regained consciousness on the open sea, halfway to shore. "I'm about to be the victim of a bloody murder. I just thought you'd like the opportunity to thank me for torturing you today before I die."

Bridget sniggered. Her lower lip was twice its normal size and a lurid purple bruise covered most of her jaw. Her left arm, now broken in two places, was splinted and tied to her body so tightly she couldn't move it even an inch. "Feckless coward!" she snorted, pointing at her friend and laughing some more.

"I only thank God that I didn't knock out any teeth."

Bridget reached up and stuck her fingers in Will's mouth. She felt around curiously. "Why would you knock out your own teeth?"

"Phft. Blah." Will glared, then slapped her hand away, snapping a long string of spit that ran from his lips to her fingers in the process. "Ewwww. Keep your filthy hands to yourself, Bridget. I already feel sick to my stomach as it is. You've no need to gag me, too."

"I do beg your pardon," she giggled unrepentantly.

As they approached the shore, her laughter, however, died down. She took another drink of brandy then tossed the empty bottle into the floor of the boat. "Dammit!" Tears welled up in her eyes. "Why didn't I take two bottles?"

The boat creaked loudly as Will put his back into the last several strokes, and they caught a small wave, gliding them safely onto the sandy beach. Now Bridget got a good look at the worried, furious gleam in Faylinn's eyes. "Goodbye, Will," she said.

Will couldn't speak. He could only close his eyes and whimper. Katie had a rolling pin in her hands.

"Well, it's truly been a pleasure." Badger stood up and smiled at Kayla and Liv. "Will you ladies be stopping by another day?"

"Wh-wh—" Liv and Kayla exchanged startled glances.

"You can't just leave us here in the story," Kayla complained, yanking the blanket off her legs as she stood up.

"Leave you where, lass?" Badger's eyes opened a touch wider, and he regarded her with his normal mixture of mirth and curiosity. "You don't really think that that slip of a girl, Faylinn, killed Will Beynon, do you?"

Kayla scowled. Now that she thought of it, it did seem pretty ridiculous. "No." She shoved her hands into the pockets of her well-worn Levis. "I mean, well, how do I know? But, I guess not."

"Good."

Green eyes twinkled as Badger offered Liv a hand up. "Thank you, Badger."

He bowed gallantly at the waist, just as Brody had done earlier in the week, causing Kayla to roll her eyes dramatically. Being with Liv was like walking around with a life-sized sample of catnip.

Liv folded up the blanket Kayla had tossed aside and set it down on the cushion. When she was finished, she dusted off her hands, wondering what she'd do if someone hurt Kayla like that. Even if her lover had stupidly been the one to ask for it. "So, how many teeth did Will lose, Badger?"

Badger chuckled and winked at Liv. "Only one. But it was Katie and her rolling pin that were responsible for the concussion."

Chapter
Nine

Liv peered over Kayla's shoulder at the laptop that was perched on the darker woman's knees. She rested her chin on a broad shoulder and yawned. It was almost 10 p.m. "Ever notice how tired you can get from sitting around doing nothing like we did this afternoon? That's so weird."

Kayla was too absorbed in what she was doing to do more than grunt.

Liv rolled her eyes.

An intense blue gaze flickered from place to place on the screen as Kayla watched over twenty-four hours worth of surveillance recordings taken in Mr. Keith's bedroom. *No blood gushing out of the walls, big surprise.* She was sitting uncomfortably on the hard wood floor of the bedroom in question, watching studiously as the laptop's digital recording whizzed by at a startling rate. To her left was a small stack of DVDs. The women's damp coats had been laid out in the corner of the room next to a pile of take-out cartons, empty soda cans, and Styrofoam cups that had once held hot, black coffee. And as per Liv's doing, every light in the house was shining brightly.

"How can you watch that so fast?"

"Whaddya mean?" Kayla answered absently, pausing the picture for a split second before clicking a button and starting it up again.

"Won't you miss something with it playing that fast?" she asked patiently, waiting for Kayla to come out of her trance. The only indication that time was passing on the screen was the eerie movement of shadows as they progressed across the room's floors and walls, and a digital time display in the lower left hand corner.

"Nah." Kayla paused the display again, then frowned and

pressed play. "I know what I'm looking for."

"Carrie in her prom dress?"

Kayla smiled wryly. "That would make for a nice change of pace. Actually, I'm looking for anything out of the ordinary, and especially for light balls." She looked at the screen as she spoke. "There seems to be an association between light balls and hauntings."

"Light balls?" Liv rubbed her cheek affectionately against Kayla's before dropping down alongside her on the floor.

Kayla paused her computer. "Tiny focal points of radiant energy." She cocked her head to the side. "That's what I hypothesize they are, anyway." The tall woman paused the playback and set the machine on the floor next to her. Then she went over to her equipment trunk and dug down to the bottom, not stopping until her hands hit something smooth that felt like paper. "Ah. Here we go." She padded back over to her lover. As she sat down, she handed Liv a ragged manila envelope that contained a single photograph. "They sort of look like little stars, or like those penlight pointers people use for presentations."

Liv opened the folder and examined the photograph. It was of Kayla and an old woman sitting at a small kitchen table. Kayla looked a little younger, and her hair was several inches shorter. The old woman was clutching a crucifix with one hand and gesturing wildly with the other. Tiny pinpoints of light dotted the space around her. "Did you see these at the time?" Liv pointed at the picture where Kayla appeared to be looking directly at the other woman.

She shook her head. "Nope. It wasn't until I looked at the recording the next day that I caught a glimpse of them." With her index finger she traced the dots. "Those are yellow. I've seen pictures of green, white, and red, too." A buzzing fly circled her head, and she shooed it away with a few swats of her hand.

"Wow." Liv set the photograph down and looked at the computer screen with renewed interest. "So, have you seen any yet on this recording?"

"Not yet. But that's why I've got the speed cranked up. They're actually easier to spot in fast-forward mode. Sometimes the balls appear and disappear all in the same spot. Those are called stationary light balls. But more often, they dart around objects or people like fireflies and leave a light trail the way a shooting star does. There's almost no research on them, though, because the only evidence they exist at all is photographic. They're not visible to the naked eye in real time, and no 'normal' or at least plausible environmental cause can explain their presence in most cases." Kayla turned her head and regarded Liv seriously for a moment. Then she smiled. "I like this." She wrapped her fingers around Liv's and squeezed gently.

"Holding my hand?" Liv asked impishly.

"Yes," Kayla admitted with an arched brow. "But I meant working with you." Her smile widened until it shaped such a contented, happy grin that Liv found herself mirroring it without thought.

"Me too, Kayla. I feel like I'm learning a lot."

"You are. And you're doing great." As abruptly as it came, however, the tender moment passed and Kayla was all business again. She pulled her reading glasses out of the front pocket of her denim shirt and tucked her hair behind her ears before starting up the recording again. "This is murder on my eyes," she complained with a trace of petulance. "No wonder I need these damn things."

They were sitting shoulder to shoulder, and Liv whispered her thanks when Kayla tilted the screen a little so they both had a good view. The picture suddenly went black, and Kayla took a moment to replace the DVD. "Nothing for the kitchen. First floor hallway's next." The scene changed to the narrow passage that led to the first cluster of guest rooms.

"So, do you think this place is haunted?" Liv asked curiously, her eyes glued to the screen. She wasn't sure she wanted to hear the answer, but if she was going to get serious about this job, she was going have to accept that it was at least a possibility.

"The feelings you described to me earlier...the ones you had last night, downstairs?"

Liv nodded, remembering the icy chill that had chased down her spine and how the hair on her arms had stood on end as though being subjected to static electricity. "How could I forget?"

"Those are very consistent with reported hauntings." Kayla frowned. "Though the whole blood-on-the-wall thing is really more in line with demonic possession or some sort of cult ritual than it is ghostly. The profiles of those events are very distinct. And if I do say so myself," she shrugged self-deprecatingly, "I have a pretty good sense about these things; and this seems like a haunting of some sort to me." Kayla surprised herself a little by how sure she was. She tried not to form any sort of opinion until she'd analyzed all the hard data, but something about this job was different.

Liv swallowed hard. "Demonic? As in: Linda Blair, crosses, and spewing green pea soup?"

"Don't be ridiculous," Kayla laughed. "Besides, I'd spew too if I ate pea soup." She mock-shivered. "Yuck."

"Thank God." Liv breathed a sigh of relief. "I knew that had
to be fake."

"Oh, it wasn't fake," Kayla corrected her conversationally.
"The film just combined several well-documented accounts of
Satanic possession into one single incident for dramatic effect."
She snorted in disgust. "So unrealistic. Speaking in tongues, the
Stigmata, *and* levitation? I mean, come on!" She looked at Liv as
though her conclusion was completely obvious. "You might get
two of those—tops."

The smile vanished from Liv's face. "I feel so much better
now," she said flatly. "Thank you."

"No problem. But we don't deal with those intentionally, Liv.
There are specialists who do, just like I specialize in—"

"Ghosts?"

"You could say that." Kayla stopped the recording again and
jumped to her feet. She handed the machine to Liv. "Bathroom
break for me and those six cups of coffee you bought." She
glanced at the computer, then back at Liv. "Can you keep going
on your own?"

"Sure," Liv answered excitedly. Another fly buzzed around
her face, and she batted it away, smiling diabolically when she hit
it and sent it sprawling to the wood floor.

"Great. I'll be back in a few. If you spot anything out of the
ordinary, just pause the recording, okay?" She left the room,
chuckling to herself when she heard Liv cursing as the dazed
insect flew up from the floor and began annoying her again.

"Go 'way!" Liv's hand darted out and, in an impressive display of coordination, she snatched the fly out of mid-air and threw
it hard against the floor, ending its tiny existence instantly. She
stared at its lifeless, black body for a few seconds. "Don't look at
me that way," she warned. "You made me do it. It's not like I
wanted to."

Free from distraction, the blonde woman turned her attention
back to the laptop screen. After a few moments, she felt her attention begin to wane. She rubbed her eyes and when she glanced
back at the screen, she saw it. "Whoa!" She hit 'pause,' then
'rewind,' and 'play.' It was so fast that she nearly missed it, but if
she was careful, she could pause it at just the right frame and see a
fluorescent blue light ball. It looked just like the ones from the
picture Kayla had showed her, and when she allowed the recording to play she could see it begin at one end of the hallway and
race erratically to the other end, where it disappeared. "Oh,
wow." Liv paused the recording again and pushed to her feet. "I

can't wait to show Kayla this. She's going to freak."

She looked towards the door, feeling for the first time since coming to Edinburgh that she'd actually made a contribution towards this case. Sure, Kayla would have probably found it herself. But the point was, it wasn't Kayla, it was her. It wasn't obvious, either; it had been a good catch. "Where are you, Ghostbuster? You didn't drink *that* much coffee."

Another fly landed on the tip of Liv's nose. "God dammit!" She knocked it away and glared down at her previous victim, which was still lying on the floor, quite dead. Liv carefully set down the laptop, her eyes scanning the large room. In the very upper corner she spied several more buzzing flies. "Where are you little nasties coming from?" she wondered aloud. Moving closer, she peered at the white wall, the same wall that had supposedly been drenched in blood only weeks before. Would bugs still be attracted to it? Probably, she decided, though surely the painters would have scrubbed it clean before painting, right?

She lifted her eyes up to the corner again. Several more flies had mysteriously joined the first few. She walked a few steps to the window and gave it a firm tug. It was closed tight. When she looked back the number of bugs had decreased. "What the— Ah. Ha." The flies were moving into the corner of the room and disappearing into the wall. *There must be a crack.* She took a step closer and heard a tiny crunch under her foot. Liv lifted her shoe and noticed a few crushed paint chips stuck to its sole. She brushed them off. "Hmm..."

Doing something she'd only seen in the movies, she made a fist and knocked on the wall. *Okay, that would have been more enlightening if it hadn't sounded exactly like a wall.* But gamely she walked over to another wall and repeated the process. The resultant noise sounded firmer, and definitely less hollow.

Twin eyebrows jumped. *Something behind the other wall perhaps?* Liv spun around at a faint noise. "Kayla," she called out loudly, straining to listen. "Are you there?"

Silence.

"Okay, don't be such a chicken," Liv said on a shaky exhale. "The only working bathroom is downstairs." She cringed because she'd found that out the hard way yesterday. "Kayla just can't hear you." Liv put her hands on her hips and returned her attention to the wall, puzzling out how she could see what was behind it without tearing a hole in it. Next door, she remembered, was a small sitting room. "Well," she sighed, "might as well see what it sounds like from that side. It's probably best that I'm alone anyway, considering I'm already talking to myself like a crazy person."

Like the rest of the house, the study sat empty. Except for the wall that it shared with Mr. Keith's bedroom, which was covered with built-in, ornate, oak cabinets. Liv drew her fingers across the dust-free surface. The craftsmanship was truly beautiful. And they also meant that she wasn't any closer to figuring if there was something behind the wall. She opened one of the tall cabinet doors, which creaked quietly. The empty space was almost big enough for her to stand in, so she did just that. Deciding this was as close as she was likely to get to the actual wall, she knocked on the cabinet back, giving it several solid thumps. On the third hit, the wooden back gave way, swinging away from Liv and sending out a wave of warm, stagnant air.

A horribly putrid smelled assaulted her, and Liv covered her mouth and nose and stumbled back out of the cabinet. "Jesus," she coughed, trying to keep from gagging as a small swarm of flies flew out, some hitting her in their confusion before darting away. "Eww." Safely out of the cabinet, she glanced back at the study door. "Kayla," she called again, growing more alarmed with every passing second. Her partner had been gone for nearly twenty minutes, and she was torn between going downstairs to look for her and continuing her exploration of the secret she'd just discovered.

With a sigh, she schooled herself in patience. *She's still busy, Liv. Get a grip. You can't go charging downstairs for no good reason and start banging on the bathroom door like some psycho. She'll think you're ridiculous. Part of her taking on a partner should be that she can have a few minutes to pee in peace if she wants to. But how friggin' long does it take to use the bathroom? Tomorrow, dammit, we're going to the grocery store for some prunes or bran muffins or something. I don't care what she says.*

"Okay." Liv shooed away several more flies. "Let's see what we have in there. Please, God, don't let it be a body." She froze, not having really considered the possibility until the words tumbled out. "Oh, shit." She searched her mind, but neither the files nor Glen or Mr. Keith had mentioned that someone was missing. *Okay, it's probably not a body. Maybe it's a dead mouse or something. Yeah.* She suddenly felt a little better. *That's disgusting, but I can live with that.*

Liv pinched her nostrils shut and moved back to the cabinet, ducking her head into the space between the walls. It wasn't, she discovered, really a hidden room like the ones they'd found in the house on Cobb Island. Rather, it appeared to be nothing more than an extra-large space between the walls. *That's how all these old houses are, for all I know.* The space was no more than three feet wide and traveled the full length of the wall. The light that spilled in from the study wasn't strong enough to reach the corners of the hidden space, but Liv's eyes were already beginning to adjust to the shadowy interior.

A folding metal chair came into view, and a tiny table that was, upon closer examination, a TV tray. On the tray was a pair of sewing scissors, a roll of masking tape, and a small pad of paper covered with doodles and phrases that were scribbled unevenly across its surface. *I can read that later, when I'm not in here.* She stuffed the pad in her back pocket and picked up an empty pack of cigarettes and a matchbook. *Ah. Some light.*

She let go of her nose and lit a match and moved a few steps deeper into the space between the walls. The smell was filtering through her pinched fingers, bringing with it a disturbingly familiar odor.

Blood.

She closed her eyes. *Don't freak. Don't freak.* "Ouch!" The match burnt out against her fingertips. Wincing, Liv popped her fingers into her mouth then lit another match. Several more flies buzzed around her head, but she didn't try to knock them away for fear of extinguishing the tiny flame with her movement. The pack only had three left.

A few feet more and her eyes widened at the sight of what the flies were so attracted to. She stared in horror. "Oh, my God."

Liv felt a sudden rush of cool air behind her. The match blew out and the hidden door behind her slammed shut, plunging her into inky darkness.

Liv's heart began to pound so hard she truly feared it would explode out of her chest, and her fingers were trembling so hard she could barely light another match. But finally it did light, illuminating the space in a hazy, golden glow. She let out a slightly hysterical laugh, relieved beyond measure that, other than the flies, she was still alone. She moved to the hidden door, and with a gentle tug on a rope that had been nailed to the wood as a makeshift door handle, she pulled it open. "S'okay," she told herself, laying a palm on her heaving chest. "Everything is okay. It was nothing."

Grabbing the folding chair, she placed it in front of the wood panel that served as a door, making sure that it couldn't somehow blow closed again.

The match went out with a gentle *poof,* sending a spiraling trail of dark smoke into the air. Liv lit the last match and quickly turned back to Mr. Keith's bedroom wall, taking in the sight for the second time.

Lines of IV tubing had been strung from mid-wall to ceiling at two-foot intervals all along the wall. At the bottom of these lines hung collapsed, mostly empty, IV bags of blood. They all had at least an inch or more of the thick substance still pooled at their bases and several of the bags had split down the sides. Inside the bags were dozens of dead flies that had crawled in too far while feasting on the rich blood and become trapped. The floor below these bags was sticky, buzzing with live flies, and utterly rank.

Green eyes lifted to the top corner of the space and Liv saw the tiniest shred of light piercing the shadows. It was a crack in the wall into Mr. Keith's bedroom and the passageway to the outside world for the flies.

The final match burnt out and Liv ran from the room into the study, taking deep breaths of the fresher air. "Kayla was right. Ghosts sure as hell weren't responsible for that." Shutting everything up tight, she stalked into the hall and stuck her head into Mr. Keith's room. It was empty. *Where are you, Kayla?* "Okay, Ghostbuster. Ready or not, here I come."

Liv was just about to step onto the first stair that would lead her to where she thought Kayla was, when she felt it. A sense of foreboding crept over her senses, and before she could even process it, a dark wave of misery washed over. So strong was the emotion that she cried out softly. *Kayla!* her mind called frantically. Her chest tightened until it became nearly impossible to breathe, and she felt a rush of cool air that made her shiver. She would have gasped if it hadn't felt like an elephant was sitting on her chest. But the physical pain couldn't touch the emotional anguish she was feeling. *God.* Her hand shot out and gripped the banister so she wouldn't topple down the steps.

Then the pressure on her chest eased, and the air around her seemed to warm. She straightened, and looked around with dazed eyes as she sucked in an enormous breath. It was over, and the whole thing hadn't taken more than five seconds. "Holy Christ."

Her mind reeled. *What is going on?* The blood on the walls had clearly been a set up. She'd found proof of that. Yet something *was* happening here. The light balls had shown up on the recording. And this was the second time that she'd experienced feelings that made no sense. *Kayla's?* She thought about that for a second. *No.* This wasn't even the telepathic or emotional connection she shared with Kayla. *Thank God.* This was something altogether different.

"Liv!"

Now I'm hearing things? But now there was the sound of footsteps. "Kayla?"

"Liv?" Kayla's voice boomed again from near the house's entrance.

Liv pushed her hair from her face with a trembling hand and looked up to see Kayla bounding up the steps. Her voice caught as she said, "Thank goodness it's you." Her knees nearly gave way with relief when the younger woman wrapped long arms around her in an embrace so comforting it was nearly painful.

"What happened? Christ, you scared the shit out of me."

"Where were you? I—" A noise at the bottom of the stairs caused green eyes to dart sideways.

Standing at the bottom of the steps, wearing a pair of black slacks, matching blazer, and a canary-yellow silk blouse was Glen Fuguchi. She looked up at Liv curiously but didn't say a word.

Liv's eyes narrowed, and Kayla could feel the body in her arms stiffen. "Are you all right?" Kayla repeated, concern coloring her words.

Liv tuned out Glen's presence and burrowed closer to Kayla. She dropped her voice to a whisper. "I think so. How...I mean how did you—"

Kayla's brow furrowed. "I heard you scream my name."

Liv nodded and rested her forehead on Kayla's collarbone, knowing she hadn't called to Kayla out loud. The telepathic link was growing stronger between them every day, and right now she couldn't help but believe that was a good thing. "I should have thought to do that before," she commented softly against Kayla's shirt.

"Do what, honey?"

"Never mind." She tilted her head back and regarded her partner with a mixture of worry and consternation. Liv gestured with her chin. "Is she the reason you've been gone so long?"

Kayla closed her eyes for a minute. *Uh oh.* She'd totally forgotten that Liv would be waiting for her. Glen had shown up when Kayla was on her way back from the bathroom. The Japanese woman had let herself in with her key, and they'd literally bumped into each other. They'd been having a discussion that was, in actuality, an argument, ever since.

Glen chose that moment to clear her throat. Loudly.

"Are you going to tell me why you turned as white as a sheet and headed for the steps like the hounds of hell were chasing you, Kayla? Or will I be left to wonder?" Glen smiled sarcastically, and Liv found herself with the urge to bitch-slap her into next week. The bad feeling she had about this woman intensified every time she saw her. How much was simple jealousy and how much was, well, *more* simple jealousy, Liv wasn't sure.

"I'm sorry about running out on you in mid-sentence, Glen," Kayla piped up, releasing Liv from their embrace only to wrap a casual arm over the other woman's shoulder. "But I just had a bad feeling."

Glen arched a disbelieving eyebrow. "Ahh, more of your paranormal feelings." She emphasized the last word by drawing it out.

Liv's nostrils flared. "What the hell is that supposed to mean?"

Kayla blinked at her partner and then turned the same stunned expression on Glen.

"I didn't mean anything at all, I assure you. I should be used to them by now. At one time we did spend a lot of," she paused and smiled again, "*quality* time together." Glen's eyes locked on Liv's and the look she threw her clearly said, "Kayla was mine, and you only have her now because *I* don't want her."

Liv's skin flushed as her hackles rose. *You little twelve-year-old bitch, I need to wring your scrawny neck.*

"As I was saying to Kayla before she...well, before. I spoke with Mr. Keith on the phone this afternoon. He'd like to have the furniture delivered tomorrow, and is hoping to start showing the house to groups of travel agents by the end of the week. He was able to book a group from France earlier than he expected and wants this mess behind him first. I assured him you'd have a full report by tomorrow, explaining that there is nothing haunted about this property. We'll be holding a press conference the next day."

Two mouths dropped open.

Liv turned to Kayla, unsure whether this was how things always worked. One look at the dark-haired woman's face, however, and she was sure her original reaction had been right on the money. This was bullshit. "Kayla," she said, taking this opportunity to let Glen know that she wasn't only around Kayla because she had the hots for her. *Okay, I do have the hots for her, but that doesn't mean I'm going to be dead weight in this partnership.* "Light balls did appear in the recording from the hall, just like the ones you showed me in the photograph. I paused the computer on the exact spot so you could take a look at them."

Kayla smiled proudly. "Great work, Liv."

Liv blushed a little under not just the praise but the undisguised adoration in Kayla's eyes. *I am so lucky.* But her expression changed when she remembered the reason Kayla had come flying up the stairs. "Just a minute ago, something happened here. I got this weird sense of—" Liv shook her head, not sure how exactly to articulate what had happened. It was similar to what she'd felt before, only far more intense. "It was an overwhelming feeling of—"

Kayla's hand dropped from Liv's shoulder. "Sadness? Like something terrible had happened, or was about to happen, but you were powerless to stop it?"

"Yes!" Liv exclaimed, her eyes widening. "That's exactly it. It was a horrible feeling of longing."

Kayla nodded gravely. "Yes, it was. I felt it, too. On the way down the stairs when I was heading for the bathroom."

Glen couldn't believe what she was hearing. This was impossible. She marched halfway up the stairs then stopped and blurted out, "What *are* you talking about?" She wasn't going to lose a top-paying client over Kayla and most *especially* over Liv's *feelings*.

"The same thing I was trying to explain to you five minutes ago. Only now Liv's found something on the recording to back it up," Kayla answered impatiently.

"That doesn't prove anything and you know it."

Kayla looked at Glen as though she was staring at a stranger. Any other time she'd been able to capture light balls on film, the woman had nearly done handstands. While they weren't definitive proof, even within the scientific community, they were something that always made Kayla dig deeper, and nearly every researcher she knew felt the same way. But more than that, and why Glen had always cared before, they were something, on film, that you could show a client. "There is something happening in this house, Glen. I don't know what that something is, but my gut, my equipment, and now my partner are all agreeing with me. You can't—"

"Please," Glen interrupted hotly. "Now you're basing your research on your girlfriend's impressions? I don't care *what* she says! You don't expect me to believe that blood was dripping down the walls, do you? That's the most ridiculous thing I've ever heard."

Kayla's face became more animated with her exasperation. "But it wasn't so ridiculous that you insisted I fly half way around the world to come and check it out?"

Liv drew in a breath and opened her mouth ready to blurt out what she'd seen upstairs.

Kayla and Glen looked at her anxiously as they waited for

whatever it she was going to say. "Liv?" Kayla prompted after a few seconds. "Were umm..." She rolled her hand in the motion for her to continue.

Liv licked her lips and focused on Kayla, turning her back on Glen, who was still standing in the middle of the stairway. Something told her to wait until she was alone with Kayla before talking about what she'd discovered behind the wall in Mr. Keith's room. "No, I wasn't going to say anything," she said evenly, and in a slightly raised voice for Glen's benefit. For Kayla's eyes only, she mouthed, "Later."

Except for a tiny jump in dark eyebrows, Kayla's face remained passably neutral. "Okay." Kayla's eyes pinned Glen. She wanted there to be no debate about this. "Whether or not you care what my new research partner thinks is immaterial. I *do* care. She's already proven to me not only her intelligence, but that she has a natural gift for this work. You know how important my work is to me, Glen. Don't belittle it by assuming I'd compromise my integrity for a quick fuck."

Glen mentally blanched as the words unknowingly hit too close to home.

Liv's head whipped around and she stared at Kayla in disbelief. She wasn't sure whether to hug her or slap her senseless. "Quick fuck?"

Kayla winced and lowered her voice. "That didn't come out right, Liv."

Liv pursed her lips. "Uh huh."

Glen glared at Liv evilly then, and pinched the bridge of her nose to ward off her impending headache. It had to be the linguist's fault that Kayla was being so obstinate about this case. Though in all honesty, Glen couldn't recall Kayla being anything *other* than difficult. In the past, however, she'd always been able to work around it. *And I will again. Olivia Hazelwood is nothing more than a new obstacle on a very well-worn path.* But even as she thought the words, she couldn't make herself believe them totally. "I want that report tomorrow, Kayla." Her voice was unyielding. Kayla's gaze went so cold Glen could have sworn the temperature in the room dropped ten degrees.

Kayla pointed an angry finger at Glen. "Since when is my research dictated by what you want?" She allowed her hand to return to her side. "But if Mr. Keith wants a report tomorrow, I'll be happy to give him one," Kayla answered amiably, surprising both Liv and Glen again.

Glen let out a deep breath. *Yes. She's finally seeing reason.* "Thank you."

"The report will say that at this point in my research I suspect paranormal activity."

"Kayla!" Glen stamped her foot in a frantic gesture of juvenile frustration that made Liv smile.

"I'm sorry, Glen." But Kayla's tone made it very clear she wasn't in the least bit sorry. She crossed her arms over her chest. "He's paying for my opinion, and so far that's what it is. After a few more days," she shrugged, "who knows? I need time to take more readings and see if I can get some base numbers to work with. Then I want to research the house itself. I should also interview Mr. Keith, the maid, and her daughter. I want to hear for myself what they've seen and heard over the years, not just about the incident with the wall."

Glen's hands shaped fists as she felt her temper rising to the surface. This job was supposed to be simple and clean! Kayla was supposed to confirm that there was nothing otherworldly going on in the house, and then everyone would be happy. Didn't the woman care how hard she worked to get clients? "We don't have a few more days. Mr. Keith wants the report by tomorrow night, and the client is always right."

"Not this time," Kayla shot back stubbornly.

Glen marched up the steps. "At lunch the other day, you practically accused him of being a doddering old man or a drug addict! And now suddenly you believe him?"

Kayla's jaw worked. "It's not suddenly. It's..."

But Glen wasn't really interested in Kayla's answer, and the taller woman's unusually reasoned response floated right over her as she stewed malevolently. *Does she really believe the huge fees I negotiate are because people actually want real scientific answers? Is she that naïve?*

Glen's thoughts began to filter into Kayla's consciousness, but she pushed them away without examining them as she continued with what was fast turning into a tirade.

Glen knew all too well what their clients wanted. They wanted peace of mind, sleep without nightmares, and a rational explanation for the irrational from someone with lots of letters after her last name. So what if every once in a while she "created" a little business? She gave them what they wanted, they paid her well for it, and nobody got hurt.

Kayla clapped her hands together loudly, causing Glen's eyes to snap up. "Are you even listening to me, Glen?"

Glen nodded as she broke out into a nervous sweat. *This cannot be happening. I will not lose this client. His fees are already spent.* With Mr. Keith she'd gone further than she ever had before, guaranteeing not only Kayla's final results, but a time-frame for those results. After all, she and that cute, curly-haired simpleton, Mary MacPherson, had created this little "haunting." It *couldn't* be real.

"Glen!" Kayla's hands twitched with the need to reach out and shake the small woman until she was sure she had her full attention. "Dammit, are you paying attention, or am I talking to thin air?"

Glen shook her head a little as she snapped out of her own thoughts. "I heard you, Kayla. I'll be back here tomorrow evening for your report. Unless you've got something tangible to show me, I expect that your research will reflect the *truth.*

Kayla's body went ramrod straight. "Are you saying I'm lying?"

Glen turned around and began trotting down the steps. She had to get away from Kayla's prying mind and think. She needed a contingency plan. "I'm saying that your reputation and mine are nothing to trifle with." When she reached the bottom, she glanced over her shoulder at Kayla. "There is nothing going on here other than the overactive imagination of an old man. There will be a press conference the day after tomorrow, whether you're finished poking around here or not. If you want to make a fool of yourself by announcing there is a ghost, or Big Foot, or the Loch Ness monster himself living in the mud puddle on the front side-walk, then be my guest! But you won't be taking me down with you." Her dark eyes flicked to Liv and she all but sneered. "This could ruin her career. If you care for her at all, you won't allow that to happen."

Glen slammed the door on the way out, leaving the old house silent except for the ragged sounds of Kayla's breathing.

Liv was too stunned to breathe at all.

Eyes closed and alone in bed, Liv heard the clock in their room at the bed and breakfast chime three times. She turned on her side and reached out with one hand, feeling the cool empty space next to her where Kayla should be. She sighed and opened her eyes, finding no peace even in the warm bed and cozy room.

Liv stood and wrapped the blanket from the bed around her shoulders. Slipping a hand out, she pulled back the thin curtains and looked down to the beach below. She could see Kayla still sit-ting there on a blanket, bathed in moonlight, hair blowing gently as she silently stared into the night. Alone.

"Kayla," Liv sighed, her heart urging her to go out to the

beach, but her head reminding her that Kayla had asked for this time alone. When she'd shared with Kayla her discovery of the IV bags and the hidden space between the walls, where someone had waited to frighten Mr. Keith, her partner hadn't been at all surprised. To the contrary, the blood on the wall had never impressed Kayla as a true paranormal event. The fact that she could now be certain of that allowed her to shift her focus to the areas that were truly intriguing to her.

They'd spent nearly an hour studying the light balls that had shown so clearly in the recording of the Keith House's hallway. Those, and the feelings both she and Kayla had experienced in the house, were more than enough to whet Kayla's appetite for discovery. Kayla had expressed, with typical enthusiasm for her job, that she was certain the house had more to reveal. Just because part of the mystery had turned out to be a hoax, it didn't mean that the rest of it was.

It wasn't until Liv remembered the pad of paper in her pocket that the evening came to an abrupt and painful end. She and Kayla had flipped through the book and with every turning page exactly what had happened to Mr. Keith that night became crystal clear. They learned the who, how, and why, as though the entire thing was a cheesy, scripted story and now was the time for the ' answers to be revealed to them before the final act.

The first page, with the name printed in bold letters in the upper right hand corner, had identified the notebook's owner: Mary MacPherson, daughter of former Keith House maid Mrs. MacPherson. And Liv and Kayla both admitted that at least part of that made perfect sense. Of all people, she would have had total access to the house. She'd grown up there and had likely explored every nook and cranny of the old place. Who better to ferret out a secret hiding place than a child?

Page two yielded the "how." Mary had written down step-by-step instructions for herself.

```
Call blood bank and make sure Tracy is working.
Remember to pay her with cash.
Meazure wall for tubing—ask Tracy about size.
```

And on and on it had read. Liv and Kayla had actually burst out laughing. Mary was either several fries short of a Happy Meal, or the most helpful criminal on the planet. Her entire plan was laid out in great detail, and in hideous spelling, right there in black and white. Liv wouldn't have believed someone could be so careless if she hadn't seen that "stupid criminal" special on cable

television just before leaving for Edinburgh. The bad guy had
written a ransom demand to a bank teller on the back on an envelope addressed to him, and then forgotten to gas up his getaway
car, which ended up puttering to a pathetic stop right in front of a
local police station. Actually, compared to that guy, Mary looked
like a mastermind.

On the next page, Mary reminded herself to buy more cigarettes, a book on hauntings, and to call about her mother's doctor
appointment. And she drew a picture of a tree that wasn't half
bad.

When they flipped to page four, the smile fell from Kayla's
face and landed with an unceremonious thud. Things didn't seem
quite so funny anymore. This page was spotted with lovely three-
dimensional hearts containing the initials G.F. + M.M. Below the
hearts was a phone number. When Kayla saw the phone number,
she jerked the pad from Liv's hands and stared at it hard, her lips
forming a tight, thin line, the hearts reflecting dully in Kayla's
glasses.

"Kayla?" Liv had inquired, wondering what was wrong and
feeling an unexpected panic well up so quickly from inside her
that she'd literally grabbed hold of Kayla and held on tight. "Hey,
are you okay?" She'd searched her face. "You don't look so
good."

Without a word, Kayla had gently removed Liv's hands and
pulled her cell phone from her bag. She handed it to Liv. "Go
ahead. See for yourself." The words were bitter, and Liv found
herself caring nothing about the Keith House and everything
about the well-being of her partner.

"Kayla, you're scaring me. What's wrong?"

The tall woman had wrapped her arm around Liv's slim waist
and squeezed gently. "Call the number, Liv," she'd repeated. "Do
it."

And Liv had, her eyes flicking back and forth between the
phone's number pad and Kayla's face. When she'd finished dial-
ing, she brought the phone to her ear and heard the person on the
other end of the line answer, "Glen Fuguchi."

At the sight of Liv's mouth hanging wide open, Kayla sighed
and flopped down on the floor, her head in her hands. "Dammit,"
she'd cursed, in a low voice that sounded every bit as hurt and
bewildered as it did angry. "I can't believe it. She set me up."

After that, they'd locked up the Keith House and come
straight home to sit on the windswept beach and talk for several
hours. Kayla's emotions were as raw as Liv had ever seen them,
and she felt powerless to help her. It didn't matter that Kayla had

suspected that Glen was up to something with this job. The bottom line was, Kayla considered Glen a friend, and her friend has used her. Badly.

With tears in her eyes, she'd explained to Liv that she could count on one hand the number of people she considered more than mere acquaintances, and that Glen was the only ex-lover who'd ever shown even the slightest bit of interest in remaining friends after the affair had ended. Trust was something Kayla placed a high premium on, and she rarely felt it in others. This was a painful reminder of why that was.

Liv pressed her forehead against the cool glass as she sleepily regarded the way her lover's strong profile was outlined by silvery moonlight. *I've got to do something. I can't stand watching her brood out there all alone anymore.* She tossed the blanket off her shoulders and sat at the foot of the bed as she slipped on her sneakers and tied the laces.

Glen, Liv believed, had been right about one thing. Kayla's reputation was on the line. They could take the information they'd found to the local police, but what then? All they could really prove was that Mary thought Glen was worthy of sharing several neatly drawn hearts with her. Even though Kayla was now certain Glen had been behind the whole thing, they still couldn't prove that. And what if they could? Who would want to hire Kayla then?

Liv stood and grabbed her jacket, shrugged it on. Taking the blanket in one hand, she quietly crept out of her room and through the house, not wanting to wake any of the other guests or Mrs. Thicke, who—she was sure—would go to the trouble of fixing them some tea no matter what time it was.

The air was brisk and fresh, and any vestiges of sleepiness disappeared with the ocean breeze as she strode across the quiet beach.

Kayla turned her head when Liv was still several paces behind her. "Why aren't you sleeping?" she scolded gently.

"Because you aren't," Liv answered, dropping down onto the blanket in front of Kayla.

"That's not a good reason."

Liv took the blanket she'd brought out with her and wrapped it first around Kayla then herself, as she sat down between Kayla's legs and leaned back against her chest. She sighed as long arms closed around her, pulling her closer. Kayla's chin came to rest on her shoulder. "I don't need a good or rational reason for anything I do when it concerns you, Kayla." Liv smiled. "I'm in love."

As Liv had hoped it would, that drew a tiny laugh from

Kayla, who turned her head and kissed a pink, chilled cheek. "I know exactly how you feel."

Liv patted Kayla's arm, and her eyes turned out to the black ocean. Like the night itself, it was beautiful and scary at the same time.

They sat there for two more hours, sometimes talking, sometimes quiet, and, for Liv at least, sometimes sleeping. Just before dawn, when Liv was feeling utterly safe and content, wrapped tightly in Kayla's arms, a wicked idea came to her. Lips more often used for smiles of delight and laughter curled into a predatory grin. Tomorrow they would set a trap for Mary MacPherson and Glen Fuguchi. "Only this time, *I'm* the spider."

Kayla's heavy eyelids opened a crack, and she searched the soft blanket for an eight-legged arachnid. "Huh?" Her eyes moved to the sand. "Where?"

"Never mind, Ghostbuster. Morning will be soon enough to explain."

"Sometimes I have no idea what you're talking about," Kayla muttered, giving up, at least for the moment, on trying to understand Liv.

Liv chuckled softly. "I know." She pushed to her feet, her butt feeling numb and her muscles sore from the long period of inactivity. "Uff." She extended a hand to Kayla. "C'mon, let's go crawl into that nice warm bed with our names on it." Liv looked up into a spectacular blanket of twinkling stars. The cold night air burned deep in her chest as Kayla's lanky body popped up alongside her.

They walked in comfortable silence until Kayla turned and said, "Liv?"

"Hmm?"

"Tonight...I mean, I know you were in bed...and...I want to thank you—"

"Kayla," this time Liv's smile was full of love, "you don't have to thank me, honey. That's what friends do."

Kayla didn't even try to talk past the lump in her throat. She just squeezed Liv's hand and continued her trek up the beach, knowing deep in her soul that in a world where it wasn't really safe to count on much of anything, a few things were written in the stars. Her heart filled with quiet wonder at the sure, solid knowledge that she and Liv were one of them.

Chapter
Ten

"I dunno, Liv." Kayla pulled a thin, gray, v-neck sweater over her head. "That's a long shot with Glen." *And I don't know if I'm that good.* She felt Liv, who was clad only in a pair of faded jeans, step up behind her and tug her hair free from her sweater, her small hands lingering there and running lovingly through her hair.

Liv heard Kayla's comment but didn't really have an answer, so she stayed quiet. If a long shot was all they had, she'd gladly take it. "Can I braid it today?" she whispered softly in Kayla's ear, giving the strands of long, thick hair in her hand a tiny tug and smiling when she felt Kayla shiver a little as her breath caressed sensitive skin.

"Sure." Kayla's voice was dreamy. "You can do whatever you want."

"Wow, a blank check. I've always wanted one of those." Liv laughed, and guided Kayla to a stool that stood in front of a small table and mirror. With a gentle push on her shoulders, she directed her to sit. She picked up a large, soft-bristled brush from the table and ran it carefully through still damp tresses, stopping every so often to delicately undo a tangle.

Kayla closed her eyes and only barely stopped herself from purring. Despite what she'd learned about Glen yesterday, at this very moment she was far too happy not to share it. *Open your mind to me, Liv.*

Liv's mouth shaped a delighted grin as, silently, Kayla's thoughts eased their way to the forefront of her brain. She consciously relaxed, taking deep slow breaths and continuing the soothing stroking of the brush. One by one, she separated her thoughts from Kayla's, until, as she'd been recently taught, she could properly focus on them alone. She let out a happy sigh. "Oooo, I love you too, Kayla."

Kayla's eyes popped open and her eyebrows disappeared behind damp bangs. "You've been practicing the relaxation techniques on your own," she accused, privately pleased that Liv had taken the initiative in an area where she knew her partner was leery and perhaps even a little frightened.

"Uh huh." The admission came with another grin. "But I think I would have heard the words anyway, they were so clear."

Kayla shook her head in amazement. "You're years ahead of where I was when I first started to figure out my abilities." She had no doubt that, while she had always struggled to pick out individual words from general impressions, someday Liv would be able to do that with little effort. The blonde woman was truly gifted, though so far she had only been able to experience a telepathic connection with Kayla. Just the way that Kayla had only experienced emotions, along with the typical mental impressions that were part and parcel of her telepathy, when she was with Liv. She wondered idly if, in time, that would change.

"I'm working with a good teacher."

"True," Kayla quipped without a trace of modesty. "Ouch!" Her hand flew to her shoulder where she'd just received a light swat the brush. She glared playfully into the mirror, trying not to smile at Liv's look of faux-innocence. "You're lucky I don't mind frisky women."

"I'll show you frisky..." Liv's hand flew to her belly, when a loud grumbling sound interrupted her. *I should be embarrassed. But it's so cool that I'm not.*

Turning her head to the side, Kayla reached behind her, and drew Liv to her ear, pressing her cheek against the soft warm skin just above breasts. "I think I've discovered what's haunting the Keith House." She dropped her already deep voice an octave. Sounding like a television announcer, she said, "'Revenge of the Killer Tapeworm—If She'd Had Ketchup The Entire City Would Have Perished.'" Her head moved up and down as Liv laughed.

"Very funny, Kayla. Just feed me soon, or I'll be forced to become a Twinkie ho and sell my body in front of convenience stores."

"A Twinkie ho?"

"I'm sorry, but I just can't hide it from you any longer. I'm addicted. I'm a slave to the tasty lard-and-sugar filling. I used to have Dougie mail them to me in Africa. I wouldn't ho myself for vegetables or anything, Kayla," she told her haughtily. "I have my standards."

Kayla nodded. "I can see that." While not as ravenous as her partner, she was pretty hungry herself. They'd stayed up until nearly dawn and then slept later than they'd intended. It was nearly 11 a.m. "I think we can do a little better than Twinkies, though." She smiled at Liv's indignant gasp. "Okay, maybe not *much* better. But a little."

The women had missed breakfast *again*, but today they'd found a note from Mrs. Thicke on a tray outside their bedroom door, saying she'd made egg sandwiches out of their breakfast, and that they were waiting for them in paper bags in the refrigerator downstairs. Mrs. Thicke's note had also reminded Liv about stopping at a grocery store before they left Portobello. Liv had then said something mysterious to Kayla about "not taking any chances" and "roughage."

Bewildered, Kayla had just nodded amiably, correctly figuring that sometimes in a relationship she was expected to just shut up and go along with whatever Liv asked. Were men ever this confused? She suspected so. And *now* she understood. But if the price for being in love was broccoli or an oat bran muffin, well, she would deal with it somehow. Slathering enough peanut butter onto something generally covered up most of the taste.

"Kayla?"

"Yeah?"

Their eyes met in the mirror's reflection.

"What we're going to do tonight is really rotten, isn't it?"

Kayla nodded very slowly. "Oh, yeah."

A pale eyebrow quirked along with the corner of Liv's mouth. "Good."

A gusty wind blew outside the Keith House and fat raindrops pelted it, the sound amplified because the house sat empty and quiet. Kayla peered out at the front sidewalk from a small window near the entryway. Lightning pierced the sky in jagged streaks, and thunder boomed sporadically overhead. *Oh, yeah.* She smiled.

A key slid into the lock and turned, but the door wouldn't open. *Ding Dong. Ding Dong. Dingdongdingdongding-dongdingdong.*

Kayla padded over to the front door and called out in an amused voice, "Who iiiiiiis it?"

Bang. Bang. Bang. The door shook in its frame. "God dammit, Kayla! I'm getting soaked. You know who it is!"

Kayla leaned against the back of the door and crossed her

long legs at the ankle. "Did you lose your key or something?"

"*Let me in!*"

"Get a grip. It's only water," Kayla mumbled. With exaggerated slowness, she pushed off of the door and turned to throw open the deadbolt. She stumbled backwards as the door flew open, nearly hitting her. "Why, hello, Glen. I didn't know it was you."

Glen smoothed back her wet hair and shook the lapels of her black London Fog raincoat as Kayla pushed the door closed. She didn't like looking foolish, and right now she knew that's exactly how she looked. The storm outside was worsening, and her taxi had already driven away. She was just glad to be in out of the pouring rain. "Of course you didn't know it was me." She set her briefcase down near the wall. "You only called me and told me to get down here right this very second! I hope it's because you're ready with your report. I'm supposed to meet with Mr. Keith later tonight." She made a face as she scanned the foyer. "God, I hate Gothic. So depressing." She peered around Kayla. "Where is—" Glen made a vague gesture with her hand. "You know."

"Shut the fuck up," Kayla snapped, all traces of her former good humor gone. "I'm not in the mood to deal with you being a bitch tonight."

"I could say the same thing about you." Glen ran her hand down the front of her suit, indicating how soaked she was. "Don't tell me your linguist dumped you already? Whatever will you do without a cute All-American girl to hold your equipment for you?" Glen sighed dramatically. "It must be difficult finding someone who appreciates your...*unique* talents and your penchant for drafty old houses." She kept her voice light, but knew the stinging words had hit their mark by the subtle shifting of Kayla's jaw muscles and cooling of sky-blue eyes.

"That's enough."

"Does she know about your trust fund, Kayla?" She smiled when suddenly Kayla couldn't meet her gaze. "Ah, I can see that she doesn't. Whyever not? That is something a girl likes to know. It can make up for a lot." *Too bad I'm not willing to wait five years for you to get it.* "It will soften all the times you won't call because you're too wrapped up in work to bother." She began ticking points off on her fingers. "Or when you'll forget to eat or sleep, and become a total grouch because of it. Or—"

"Enough!" Kayla's temper snapped as Glen skillfully pushed all her buttons, making her feel raw and exposed. "She didn't dump me," she ground out. "We had a little..." Her dark head shook as she searched for the right words. "A difference of opinion is all. If you must know, she went back to the bed and breakfast. Which is fine with me, because I still have some work to do."

"Pity," Glen said tonelessly, holding out her hand.

A loud boom of thunder shook the house, and Kayla felt a nervous ball of fear form in the pit of her stomach. She recognized its source immediately. *It'll be okay, Liv.* She projected the words with all her might, completely tuning out Glen. *Hang in there. It's just a storm, nothing to be frightened of.*

"Do you have my report or not?"

Kayla's whole demeanor changed as she looked down at Glen seriously. "That's what I wanted to talk to you about."

When Kayla paused and glance around, Glen couldn't help but notice the unsettled look that flitted across her face. *The fight with the girlfriend?* She studied her carefully, using the many years she'd known Kayla as her frame of reference. *No, it's something else.* What she saw was a good dose of nervousness and...fear? Whatever was going on with her had to be serious. It was more than Kayla being angry with her for pushing this case through. Maybe she'd gone too far with the comment about her trust fund.

"There's something you should know, and you're not going to like it."

Now Glen was worried. She laid a hand on Kayla's arm, truly concerned. "What's wrong?"

Kayla bit her lip and fought hard not to jerk her arm away. She could feel the coolness of Glen's hands through her thin sweater, and her touch, knowing about her betrayal as a friend, repulsed her. "I... Well, I think it's better if you see this for yourself."

An earsplitting clap of thunder boomed and Glen looked longingly towards the door. "No, thank you. I'm in a hurry, Kayla." *I need to be out of here. A lovely bar maybe, with lots of laughing people and strong drinks.* Not that she planned on talking to a soul. She craved the comforting sound of people chattering away and not the thunder and pouring rain. Glen lifted her chin a little, determined not to show her discomfort.

She doesn't like storms any more than Liv does. How come I never noticed that before?

"Just say whatever it is you have to say, and give me my report so I can be on my way. Your fee will be deposited in your account by noon tomorrow. Consider this job over. I'll contact you again soon for more work."

Kayla shook her head slowly. "You don't understand, Glen. There is something wrong with this house. Very wrong."

Glen put her hands on her hips. "The only thing wrong with this house is that I'm still in it."

A crackling bolt of lightning shot across the sky, followed instantly by a tremendous boom.

The house went black.

"And the lights don't work," Glen continued, trying unsuccessfully to defuse the tension that now filled the air.

Kayla didn't laugh.

It was so dark that Glen could only see Kayla in the occasional flash of lightning. She heard soft footsteps. *Why is she way over there?* Kayla was now standing across the room in the doorway of the foyer with a grim look marring her beautiful face.

The tall woman glanced at Glen, her eyes shining silver in a bright burst of light. "Don't you feel it?" The room went black again and Kayla disappeared back into the inky darkness. She traveled out of the foyer and into another room.

Glen moved closer to Kayla's voice, telling herself that that was her shadow she could see moving. "F-feel what?" the Japanese woman groaned in frustration.

"How cold it is," Kayla answered quietly. "I have goosebumps, don't you?"

Glen shivered and unconsciously dropped her tone to match Kayla's. "I'm soaked to the bone, of course I'm cold!"

Kayla didn't answer and Glen felt another, stronger chill chase down her spine. *This is preposterous,* she told herself disgustedly. *I'm scaring myself. I will not be frightened of an empty old house.*

"It's not your wet clothes. I've felt it, and so has Liv," Kayla finally said. "It's a...a presence. It feels like something brushing lightly over your skin, doesn't it? Not like wind, but like fingers or a cool breath from lips barely touching you."

Unseen in the darkness, Glen's eyes widened.

"I think it has something to do with the blood that Mr. Keith saw pouring down the wall." Silently Kayla moved right alongside Glen and whispered in her ear, "What if it's dangerous?"

Glen snorted incredulously but felt her unease growing with every passing second. She couldn't see the other woman, and the words seem to come from thin air. "You've finally lost your mind, Kayla." But her voice betrayed her doubt.

"You know I know what I'm talking about, Glen. You've always been a skeptic, I know that; but you *know* me, know how rarely I've been wrong about these things. You trust and believe me, don't you?" The words left a bitter taste in Kayla's mouth. She found small comfort in the fact that she really did believe there was a supernatural presence in this house.

Glen didn't know what to say. She did know Kayla. Part of her was absolutely certain that Kayla was a perfectionist and was, admittedly, an expert in her field. But no matter what she said, the blood on the walls was nothing more than a trick. She *knew* that with even more certainty.

Then she felt it again, as tangible as her own heartbeat. Light as a feather, a touch traveled from her jaw to her throat to her arm. She slapped at her arm. "That's it. I'm leaving! You can drop the report at my hotel when you come to your senses." She turned around and marched over to what she thought was the door, then adjusted her path when a flash of lighting outlined the dark wooden panel. She reached for the knob and pulled, but the door wouldn't open. "Kayla, is this some sort of joke?" She pulled harder on the door, shaking it. Her hand shot up to the deadbolt and she turned it, checking to see that it was open. It was. "Shit!"

"Glen?"

An eerie voice called her name from the stairway. It was not Kayla. The low whisper repeated, drawing out the word. "Gleeennnnn."

Glen swallowed hard. "Kayla?" Her eyes darted wildly as she strained to see through the darkness. "Kayla, where are you?"

She was greeted with a stone-cold silence.

"That's it. This isn't funny. I'm calling the police, and they can break down this door." Glen reached for her briefcase to retrieve her cell phone, but it was gone.

"Glen." The whisper had moved across the room. "Gleeennnn."

"Who are you?" Glen cried, dropping to her knees to search for her briefcase. The wooden floor was cold and hard against her skin, and she knew she'd torn her pantyhose. A hand squeezed her shoulder and Glen screamed.

"Glen! What the hell is wrong with you?" This time it was Kayla.

"Kayla?" Glen could hardly hear her over the pounding of her heart.

Kayla helped her to her feet. "Of course it's me. You took off and I couldn't see you. I thought you'd left until I heard you call my name."

"I-I am leaving." *I am.* Glen rubbed her temples, pushing hard. "Why were you whispering to me? That wasn't funny."

"Whispering?" Kayla's brow creased. "Why would I be whispering to you? I thought you'd gone, remember?"

"I can't get out." Glen's emotions were starting to get the better of her and her panic was rising fast, calmed only by Kayla's presence. "The door's locked. Try it."

Kayla did. "Is this locked from the outside? How did—"

"My briefcase," Glen interrupted anxiously. "What did you do with it?"

"I never touched it. I saw you set it down when you came in. It's on the floor." But when Kayla began feeling around, she couldn't find it. "It was right here. I—" She stopped talking and the silence between them grew thunderous. "I think we should call the police, Glen."

The new urgency in Kayla's voice sent Glen's pulse racing again. "Yes. Yes. Okay," she babbled. "Oh, no. My phone is in the briefcase!"

"Gleeennnn." The whisper had returned.

Glen's eyes went round as twin moons. "Don't you hear that?"

"You need to calm down." Kayla reached for Glen again, and the smaller woman nearly jumped out of her skin at the unexpected contact. Kayla had barely touched her when they were lovers and never since. "Relax."

"Don't touch me!" Glen could taste salt on her lips from a cold sweat.

"Gleeennnnn."

"You can't tell me you don't you hear that. It's clear as day." She moved closer to Kayla, wanting some sort of contact so long as *she* was the one initiating it. That was safe.

"Hear what?"

"My name!" Her breath was coming in short pants. "Listen for Christ's sake!"

The whisper had changed locations again. "Gleeennnn."

"Oh, God. Oh, God, there it is again. See?" She whirled around and began tugging violently on the doorknob. "The voice is moving. I think it's coming closer. Why can't you hear it?" Tears welled in her eyes and she started to shake.

Kayla grabbed Glen by the shoulders and spun her back around so that they were facing each other again. "I don't know what you're talking about or what's happening to you, but we need to call the police so we can get out of this house. My phone is in my backpack upstairs. I'll go get it and be right back. You can wait—"

A loud boom of thunder interrupted Kayla, cutting through the sound of the pouring rain and howling wind like a knife through hot butter.

Glen shook her head, causing her black, wet hair to stick to her cheeks and neck. "You're not leaving me alone, Kayla Redding. Not for one second!"

"But—"

"No buts. Let's go now."

"All right."

Glen reached out to take Kayla's hand, but she was already several steps in front of her. "Dammit! Wait!" She could hear Kayla's footsteps, but she couldn't seem to catch up to her and make physical contact. "Kayla? Kayla!"

"Yes?" Kayla said softly, feeling for the banister railing as she quietly ascended the stairs.

"I-I-I..." Glen didn't really have anything to say. She'd only wanted to hear Kayla's voice and reassure herself that she wasn't alone. "What room are we going to?"

Glen reached the top of the stairs. Somehow the rain seemed louder there, and she squinted as she turned a corner to a long hallway and tried to catch sight of the other woman. "Kayla?"

Silence.

"Not again!" Glen brought shaking hands to her face. "Calm down." *You're just being silly and imagining things. There's nothing haunted about this place. You know that, even if she doesn't. Kayla is just being dramatic.* But that thought stopped her dead in her tracks. Kayla dramatic? That would require creativity and imagination, and Glen was certain those were two qualities that Kayla didn't possess at all. Hesitantly, she began walking forward, running her fingertips along the wall to help guide her as she moved. Rooms lined both sides of the passage and she listened carefully at each open doorway, hoping to find which one Kayla had stepped inside. She flipped another light switch, but nothing happened.

"Glennnn."

"Is that you, Kayla?" Glen whispered harshly. She knew deep down it wasn't, and her stomach twisted painfully.

"Glennnn," the whisper persisted.

"Shut up! Shut up! Leave me alone!" The small woman sped up her pace.

A bedroom door behind her slammed shut and she jumped. She whirled around and tried to see what had happened, but it was too dark.

"Glennnn. Glennnn." The whisper was growing louder and angrier and another door slammed, then another, with the sounds coming closer and closer.

It's coming for me! Glen let out a bloodcurdling scream and her hands flew to her ears to block out the loud sounds.

A pair of hands reached out of the darkness and snatched her out of the hallway into one of the rooms.

Glen screamed so loudly her throat felt like it was on fire, and she began thrashing wildly.

"Glen! Stop!" Kayla wrestled with the distraught woman, working to calm her. "It's me! It's Kayla."

Glen's frantic movements slowed, and she grasped hold of Kayla's sweater, clinging to her. "Kayla?" She began to cry.

"Yes," she said softly. "It's me, and I have something to show you. Proof of what I was saying."

"I don't need proof. We need to get out of here! Something is coming."

"Something is already here," Kayla said gravely. She pulled Glen over to the wall. "Look."

"It's too dark. I—"

Kayla's grabbed Glen's hand and pressed it against the wall.

Glen's heart stopped when she felt thick, sticky liquid flow hotly over her fingers. "No. It can't be."

"Glennnn." The whisper was now in doorway of the room.

"It's blood," Kayla told her right in her ear. "Blood." Just then a flash of lightning illuminated the Keith House's master bedroom and the wall where Glen's hand was pressed. It was awash with dark, crimson blood.

"No!" Glen screamed, wrenching her hand away from Kayla's grasp. She ran to the corner of the room and slid down the wall to the floor, sobbing hysterically. She wrapped her arms around herself and the blood on them dripped into her coat sleeve and trickled down her forearm.

"Glennnn."

"Shut up! You can't be real." She began rocking back and forth.

"It is real!" Kayla shouted.

"It's not!"

"It is!"

"*No!* Don't you see, it can't be! I made it all up." Glen's sobbing intensified. "It's a trick. I hired Mary to do it. It's a trick. It's not real!" Her face crumpled. "It's not! It's not!"

A bright light suddenly flared in the doorway.

Glen screamed and covered her eyes with one hand, temporarily blinded. A few seconds later, when she removed her hand, her red-rimmed eyes flicked past Kayla, who was looking down at her boots, to find a dripping wet, young man wearing a kilt and overcoat and a very self-satisfied smile. Next to him stood Mr.

Keith with a mini tape recorder in one hand and his cane in the other. Finally, there was Liv, holding a large flashlight with the beam pointed at the ceiling, her white-socked feet drawing Glen's attention.

Liv padded over to Kayla and wrapped her in a big hug, lingering there long enough to whisper something in her ear. Glen watched dazedly as Kayla nodded, whispered something back to Liv, and returned the embrace. A few heartbeats, then Kayla pulled away, but not before tenderly kissing Liv's cheek.

With a gentle pat to Kayla's side, Liv shifted her focus to Glen and slowly crossed the room.

Glen was still shaky and confused, trying to process what had happened, when Liv crouched down in front of her and waited until frightened eyes lifted to hers and held her steely gaze. She spoke in a gentle but firm voice. "Your briefcase is in the study next door, and I think you owe Kayla an apology."

Glen's mouth dropped open.

Liv leaned a little closer and whispered, "Kayla cared about you, and your little scheme really hurt her." She let the words sink in for a moment before the Southerner in her took over and her light Virginia accent unconsciously intensified, becoming nearly as pronounced as Kayla's. "You should really thank her after you apologize." She felt a rush of protectiveness for her lover and she narrowed her eyes at Glen, barely resisting lashing out at her for hurting Kayla. "It was because of her that I went to all this trouble." Then Liv's expression cleared and her lips curled into a deceptively sweet smile. She put her hand on her knees and pushed to her feet, holding her hand out to Glen. "*I* would have just kicked your lyin' ass."

Kayla sat up in bed, her back against the headboard, as she watched Liv getting ready for bed. As a little girl she'd seen her mother go through the same routine and she smiled, wondering idly why it wasn't one she shared.

Liv was sitting on the stool in front of the mirror, wearing a pair of flannel pajama bottoms and an old t-shirt. She'd bought the pajama pants here in Edinburgh, declaring it too cold to be running around in shorts—her usual sleep attire, or her birthday suit—which was fast becoming the norm with Kayla. She ran the brush through her hair for the final time and set it down on the small table in front of her. By rote, she removed the studs from her ears and unclasped a small gold chain she wore around her wrist. Then she picked up a tube of fragrant lotion and applied it liberally to her cheeks and neck, softly rubbing it in until it disappeared against smooth skin. She repeated the process with her elbows and hands, finally catching a glimpse of a smiling Kayla in the mirror. Liv smiled back. "What?"

"Nothing."

"Uh huh. It doesn't look like nothing. It looks like you were thinking about something pretty hard."

"I wasn't." Kayla shrugged one shoulder. "I was just watching you is all."

"Oh," Liv replied, suddenly a little shy. "I like watching you, too." She set the lotion down on the table and clicked off the small Tiffany lamp below the mirror, casting the room in long shadow. The storm had moved out over the sea, and the sky was only occasionally lit with a flash of lightning and the gentle rumble of far off thunder. She slipped into bed alongside Kayla, joining her against the headboard and pulling the sheet and comforter up to her waist.

"Mmm." Kayla sighed. "You smell like flowers and sunshine."

Liv laughed delightedly. "I didn't know sunshine had a smell."

"Oh, it does," Kayla drawled emphatically, leaning closer to Liv and kissing the top of her head. "Because I said so."

Liv wrapped her fingers around Kayla's hand and cradled it in her lap. "Can you believe the timing of that storm tonight?" She shook her head. "Perfect. It was perfect. I think it's the only time in my life I was happy to see one."

"Mmm hmm... Nothing like a little thunder and lightning, and a torrential downpour to make a place look spooky."

"True." Liv scooted down the bed and adjusted her pillow so that she was lying flat and it was cushioning her head, as Kayla did the same thing next to her. "I heard you, you know."

Kayla let her eyelids drift shut. "Heard me?" she murmured.

"Telling me that everything would be okay, during the storm."

Kayla's eyebrows jumped, but somehow her eyes remained closed. "Wow. All the way upstairs?"

"Yeah." She giggled quietly. "Having you pop into my head when I wasn't expecting it nearly caused me to wet my pants."

The brunette chuckled softly and rolled onto her side so she could see her partner's face. She traced Liv's cheek with her fingertips. "I'm sorry."

"Don't be." Liv smiled at her fondly. "It helped. That thunder was starting to freak me out again."

Kayla was silent for so long that Liv wondered if she'd fallen asleep. "Kayla," she whispered. "Are you okay?"

The tall woman had to swallow a few times before answering. This was the first time in her entire life her ability had helped someone she loved. She'd helped the scientists in college—who'd treated her like a lab rat—with their own research. Unwittingly, she'd allowed her ability to feed Glen's greed. She'd even helped total strangers a time or two. But this made her heart hurt with pleasure. She was truly speechless. "Yeah," she finally croaked softly, deciding not to try and explain her feelings right now. "I'm fantastic."

Liv blinked. "Well, okay," she answered slowly, not sure why Kayla was suddenly so chipper. "I'm glad you're happy."

Kayla chuckled softly. "God, that horrible voice calling Glen's name was awesome."

"That was me sneaking around in my socks, using my hangover voice."

"Remind me not to let you drink too much."

"I will."

"The locked door?"

"Brody standing out in the pouring rain. I knew she'd bolt eventually."

"Mmm."

Liv yawned. "But you slamming those doors, one after the other. That was the best. That scared *me.* I wasn't expecting it at all. How did you manage to get behind Glen in the hallway?" she asked interestedly.

Dark brows drew together. "I didn't, Liv."

"Kayla?"

"Yeah?"

"Don't say shit like that." Liv began smacking the darker woman, who burst out laughing.

"Ouch! Ouch!" She tried to defend herself against Liv's vicious attack with little success.

"I mean it!" Smack. Smack. "That's creepy!"

"Okay, okay. I was just joking, I did manage to get around behind her." *Not.*

Liv's hands stilled. "You're lying aren't you?"

"Yes."

"Well, don't start telling the truth now!" She began hitting her again.

Kayla tried to grab Liv's flying hands, but they were too quick. "All right, I'm not lying!" She dissolved into laughter again.

"Thank you. Jeez, keep your freakin' stories straight. How can I believe you when you're lying for my own good if you confess immediately?"

"You won't?"

"Exactly."

"Liv?"

"Don't talk about it."

"Bu—"

"Not a damn word, Kayla."

"Fine," Kayla groused.

A light rain still pelted the window but its rhythm was soothing and constant, and both women felt their eyelids growing heavier as the gentle patter cast a lethargic spell over them.

"I'm sorry I couldn't get Mr. Keith to let you continue researching the house." Liv's voice was so hushed Kayla almost missed it. "I tried my best."

Kayla lazily slid her hand beneath Liv's t-shirt and let it rest against the warm soft skin just below her partner's ribs. "Your best was more than good enough. He was a lot nicer about the whole thing than I would have been. I don't know how you managed it, but somehow I think everything is going to work out."

After a long, very private conversation with Liv, where Glen and Mary's actions had been explained to the old Scot, Robert Keith had agreed not to file charges against Kayla or go to the press about what had happened. But no amount of cajoling could convince the man to let Kayla continue studying the house. He'd informed the women blithely that whatever restless spirit dwelled there now had likely been there for hundreds of years, and as long as he, she, or it wasn't the cause of the blood on the wall, his guests could live with getting an unexpected chill every now and again. This was, after all, Edinburgh.

Refusing any payment, Brody had agreed to watch Glen until morning, when he and Mr. Keith could accompany her to the First Bank of Scotland where she would execute an intrabank transfer of every red cent she had. Mr. Keith would be refunded Kayla's fee plus interest, and the remaining funds would be deposited into a new account in Kayla's name, where they would stay until Glen's books could be fully audited. Not that it mattered. Kayla had already decided to use that account to simply refund every client she'd had in the past two years.

When Kayla had told Glen what was going to happen, the Japanese woman had nearly had a stroke. Liv had come to the rescue again, gleefully explaining that if Glen didn't agree to the money transfer, Mr. Keith would be more than happy to contact the authorities, and not only would she end up penniless, but she would also be afraid to bend over and pick up a bar of soap for the next three to five years.

Kayla had burst out laughing, but Glen had had no earthly idea what Liv was talking about and the blonde woman had taken great pleasure explaining it. In detail. Twice. Kayla smiled just remembering it. *God, even Brody blushed!*

As for Mary MacPherson, Mr. Keith assured Kayla that simply telling her mother would be more than enough punishment. The old man had literally shivered at the prospect of what his former maid would do to her wayward daughter. Kayla suspected that he had just enough of a soft spot for Mary not to want to see her in jail, but not so much that he was going to let her off the hook completely, which was fine by her. Kayla found herself wanting to go home to Virginia in the worst way. She could visit her sister Marcy again, and she knew Liv would love to spend more time with Doug. She could also give the history they'd found on Cobb Island the study it deserved, but mostly she needed to regroup.

"Liv, I know we talked about this already, but—"

A sigh. *Not again.*

"But don't you think it's wrong that Glen won't be punished." Mary was one thing, but Glen had been the brains behind the whole thing.

"Yes and no." Liv rolled to over face Kayla. She propped herself up on one elbow and rested her head on her hand. "If she gets exposed, your career could be over."

Kayla's brow furrowed. "But—" Her speech was cut off as two fingers landed on her lips, and stayed there.

"It's not worth it, Kayla. People will get their money back, and you won't get hurt." Even in the shadows, she could see Kayla's eyes flash. "Please," she said quickly. *God, we've been over this a hundred times already.* She tried another tack. "If not for you, how about for me? I just started down this particular path with you. I'm not ready to get off it so quickly."

Kayla let out an explosive breath, and Liv knew she'd won. She removed her fingers from Kayla's soft lips and replaced them with her mouth.

The kiss went on for long, charged moments, neither woman wanting to stop. Finally, breathing raggedly, Liv pulled away just enough to glance down at herself. Kayla had slid one hand inside her pajama pants, and it was firmly kneading her bottom while Kayla's other hand was under her shirt caressing a very grateful breast. *No wonder I'm having so much fun.* "God, wouldn't this be better without all these clothes?" Liv said thickly, already working her way out of her t-shirt.

"Well, yes," Kayla, who was blissfully nude, agreed, "but you're the one who—"

"What do I know?" Liv's pajamas sailed across the room.

"You do get cold in the mor—"

Liv pushed Kayla onto her back and laid fully atop her, their legs easily tangling together.

The younger woman moaned softly at the sensual contact, her previous thoughts whisked away by the erotic onslaught of soft breasts pressing snugly against hers. Moist golden curls tickled her lower abdomen, and the musky scent of Liv's arousal called to her with a song so powerful it put the Sirens to shame.

Liv looked down into Kayla's eyes and innocently asked, "Do you think you'll have trouble keeping me warm? Do you think you can handle that, Ghostbuster? Do you?" she taunted with nearly diabolical glee.

A low rumbling growl was her answer, and she half-gasped, half-squealed as Kayla picked up the gauntlet and their positions were reversed before she could blink.

"I can handle it, Olivia." Kayla's husky voice sent a thrill through Liv, and her mouth went as dry as cotton candy. "The question is..." A flash of white teeth. "Can you?"

Liv's heart hammered in her chest. "I-I'm not sure, Kayla," she answered honestly, seeing the passionate glint in her lover's eyes. She smiled. "But I'm willing to die trying."

The sheets and blankets lay cold and forgotten for most of the night.

Chapter
Eleven

The morning found Kayla and Liv resting lazily in bed and hoping to spend some more time with Badger before heading back to the States. Kayla was able to book a plane out of Edinburgh the next day, so this looked like it would be their last chance. Though she usually ended up doing some work in this city at least once or twice a year.

"So call him and see if he's around today." Liv stifled a yawn with the back of her hand.

Kayla lifted her disheveled head from the bare belly on which it was resting. "He said we didn't need to call. Just to come by."

"Okay." Liv closed her eyes and sighed. "It's early, right? We don't have to get up yet." She felt Kayla chuckle against her stomach.

An eyelid opened and a blue eyeball rolled sideways to get a good look at the clock. She blinked tiredly, trying to focus on the numbers. "We missed breakfast."

"What a surprise," Liv mumbled wryly. She laid her hand on the warm skin between Kayla's shoulder blades. "You okay this morning?"

"You mean, am I sorry about what we did to Glen?"

Liv opened her eyes as Kayla sat up. "Yeah, I guess so. And everything that's happened." *I'm worried about you.*

Kayla smiled affectionately at her partner and lifted her hand to cup Liv's cheek. "You don't have to worry about me. I'm disappointed in Glen, and my business is going to be...well, things are going to be different now. I've never had to try to get clients. Glen sort of just said 'be here' or 'go there,' and there would be a ticket for me at the airport, and my bank account would get a boost after every job."

Liv's eyes widened with alarm.

"Yeah, I know." Kayla's gaze dropped from Liv's. "I made it pretty easy for her to use me."

"Mmm." Liv agreed wholeheartedly but she didn't think Kayla needed her to rub it in. "You can always get another agent."

Kayla just snorted.

"Or, we could do it ourselves. I can do scheduling and basic accounting," Liv offered. "I think."

Kayla looked up hopefully. "Really?"

"Sure." Liv turned her face and kissed Kayla's palm before she set it on the bed. "How hard can it be? You had a twelve-year-old doing it before," she laughed. "I don't know how we'll find clients yet, but we'll figure it out."

Kayla gave her partner a brilliant smile. "All right then. It's a done deal. Come on." She sprang out of bed and ambled over to the dresser where Liv had unpacked her clothes. "Looks like it's going to be warmer today," she said conversationally as she opened a drawer. She picked up a heavyweight, long sleeved, white cotton blouse and shook her head slightly. *I've never even used a dresser when I travel. Always just lived out of my suitcase. From now on things are sure gonna be...* Two warm arms wrapped around her middle and squeezed gently.

"Will you hand me my blue sweater, hon?"

Yeah, she sighed inwardly. *Things are going to be great.*

They dressed in companionable silence, comfortable in the unknown future that stretched out before them because the most important thing was settled: they were together.

It was such a beautiful, crisp autumn day that Kayla and Liv had the cab driver drop them at the end of the long, winding dirt road that lead to Cobb Manor. Their boots splashed happily through the shallow puddles caused by last night's storm, and pebbles crunched under their feet. The sky was dotted with white, fluffy clouds that floated amiably on a background of dazzling blue.

"Huh." Kayla pointed to the quiet booth by the front gate. A sign reading "Closed" was neatly taped to the booth's door. "Brody didn't mention they wouldn't be open today. He should have been back from dealing with Glen hours ago." She turned to Liv. "Let's just knock."

"Do you think we're being pests?"

"Probably. So?" Kayla draped her arm over Liv's shoulder, admiring the way the sunshine reflected off Liv's golden hair.

Liv tilted her head up and brushed her lips against Kayla's. "You're so much trouble," she said against Kayla's soft mouth.

"Isn't she though?" Badger boomed loudly, appearing from behind the gate and taking a good five years off Liv's life.

"Jesus Christ, Badger!" Liv laid her hand on her pounding heart.

Kayla narrowed her eyes. "You wait until you can do that to us, don't you?"

Badger jerked a thumb towards his barrel chest, his light eyes going round and conveying a devastating innocence. "Who me?"

The gesture was achingly familiar, even to Kayla, who blushed at the man's dead-on imitation. "Very funny," she grumbled petulantly.

Liv couldn't help but join in Badger's laughter. She liked Badger more every time she saw him, and was already feeling a sense of loss over their upcoming departure.

Badger's gaze softened as it landed on Liv. *I'll miss you too, lass.* "We're closed to the public because we have a large private tour going on today. At this very moment, Sylla is trying to convince twenty-five Norwegian housewives that they are in dire need of pounds and pounds of shortbread."

"Ooo." Liv's eyes glazed over with hedonistic desire, and Kayla stepped between the smaller woman and Badger before the blonde woman could bankrupt them both by ordering another huge quantity of the tasty dessert.

"Are you free today?" Kayla inquired, an eyebrow lifting slightly.

"I just might be." Badger crossed his arms over his chest. "But it would take the right offer to keep me from spending my afternoon sneaking up behind Viking tourists and scaring them as they walk through the halls of Cobb Manor."

Liv scratched her jaw as she recalled the night before. "That sort of thing *can* be...err...interesting."

Badger laughed, low and deep, his entire body shaking with delight. "Indeed it can, girl. So," he refocused on Kayla, "back to hear more of Faylinn and Bridget, I take it?"

"We are."

"You ride?"

"We do."

Badger nodded. "Good."

Liv watched them both in wonder, amazed that they'd planned their entire afternoon in less than twenty words between them.

The trio strode around the manor towards the stables. Badger pointed towards the door with a thick finger. "Pick your mounts, ladies. They're all bonny boys with lovely spirits. I'll be right back."

The stable smelled of fresh hay and rain, and Kayla greedily drew in a deep breath of the comforting scent, deciding on the spot that the best place to hole up and study the history they'd found on Cobb Island would be her grandmother's ranch in West Virginia. "Liv?"

"Absolutely."

Kayla grinned. "I'll call Granny tonight."

Liv selected a ginger gelding, whose long mane was a shiny coal-black. She led him over to Kayla, who had just settled a saddle blanket on a muddy-colored stallion with gray socks. She scratched her horse's nose. "Aren't you pretty?" The animal whinnied loudly.

"Thanks." Kayla smirked. "You smell great."

"I was talking to the horse, Ghostbuster."

"So was I. Ouch. Ouch." Kayla started laughing as she ducked Liv's hands.

"Oh, I see I got here just in time." Badger walked in leading a white mare speckled with black spots.

Liv's hands froze.

Kayla smiled, assuming Badger was going to help her with her feisty partner, and breathed a sigh of relief.

Badger plopped down on a bale of hay. "Now I've got a better view. Carry on, lass."

Kayla sneered at him. "Thanks, a lot, you old f— Ouch!"

When Liv was finished, she made a show of dusting off her hands. "We're just about ready here, Badger. As soon as Kayla stops dawdling, we'll be good to go."

Kayla's mouth dropped open. "Bu—"

"Hurry up, Kayla. There's rain coming in again tonight, and I don't want to be caught in it." Letting go of the reins in his hand, he marched over to where several saddles were hung on the wall and hefted one. When he got close to Liv and Kayla's horses, however, they began to dance nervously and snort.

"Wow." Liv got a good hold of her mount, afraid he'd rear. "They don't like you much, do they?"

"I suppose not." Badger narrowed his eyes at the beasts, ignoring Kayla's very interested stare. "Snobby things. Think they're better bred than my own bonny girl." He handed the saddle to Kayla, and their eyes met and held for a long moment. He quirked an eyebrow at her, but she held her tongue as he padded back to his waiting horse. The mare pressed her nose to his chest affectionately. "I don't keep her inside with the others; I let her graze wild out back."

"Kayla?" Liv couldn't help but notice the curious look on her friend's face.

The tall woman snapped out of her trance and smiled at Liv. "Ready?"

They all led the animals outside, and Badger stuck his foot in the stirrup. "You might want to turn your heads, lasses."

"So we don't see you tumble off into that puddle there?" Kayla chuckled and pointed to the ground.

"Suit yourself." Badger flipped his muscular leg over the powerful animal's back and the gusty breeze caught his kilt, flipping it up against his back.

"Oh, good Lord." Liv covered her eyes with both hands, feeling almost lightheaded as blood rushed to her head. She opened her fingers to find Kayla staring. "Kayla!" she admonished, horrified.

Kayla turned her head slowly. "What?"

"Give the man some privacy!"

"What are you talking about? I'm blind! I'll never see another damn thing as long as I live!"

Liv dissolved into laughter at the indignant look that swept across Badger's creased face, glad that her lover had finally scored a point. But Kayla was right. That *was* the whitest ass Liv had ever seen. "Full moon over Scotland."

"You should have warned us to bring sunglasses," Kayla continued blithely.

"I've had no complaints before!" He snorted grumpily and gave his mare a swift kick, sending her galloping across the grass.

Laughing so hard they had trouble getting into their saddles, Liv and Kayla headed out in chase of a very crabby, white-haired storyteller.

It took them a while to catch Badger, who'd galloped over the closest hill, but soon they were riding slowly through the tall, blowing grass.

"What else is it you'd like to know of the story? There's a lifetime to tell, and if I know it, I'll share it with you freely."

"Bridget's arm," Liv began. "Did it ever heal right?"

Badger blew out a breath. "Ay. It healed. I don't believe it was ever like it was before she tangled with the cliff on Cobb

Island, but she could use it well enough. And that was more than she'd had a right to hope for."

Liv said a little prayer of thanks. *Good for you, Bridget.*

"The baby?" Kayla asked, shielding her eyes from the sun as she glanced sideways at her companions.

"I was planning on spinnin' that particular yarn, as it's one of my favorites. Nothin' else?" Badger shifted in his saddle and smiled at Liv.

Liv cleared her throat softly. There was just one more little thing. "Did they ever...um...you know?"

Kayla's eyes widened. "Liv!"

"Well, I wanna know."

Badger chuckled softly and pulled out his pipe, letting his horse wander where she would. "So you want to hear *that* tale, do you?"

"Yup. And so does she." Liv gestured towards Kayla with her chin. "Don't you dare say differently, Kayla Redding. You were talking about that very thing just the other night."

Kayla bit her lip and shot Liv a withering glare. "Big mouth."

Badger grinned inwardly. These two were simply perfect together. "Well, as you can imagine, it's not a story that I would normally pass along. Though I do know it, mainly because Faylinn and Bridget are sort of...well, they were very colorful characters in a very conventional family. Among their own kin, they weren't shy about the love they shared. And because they were both women, how it was that they came together was something asked over the years and answered with surprising candor or a smack in the back of the head..." Badger's blue eyes twinkled. "Depending, of course, on whether you asked Bridget or Faylinn."

Kayla lifted a sardonic eyebrow. "Would the one who couldn't keep her smacking hands to herself happen to be...oh, I don't know..." She tapped her chin with her index finger and pretended to ponder. "Blonde?"

Liv stuck out her tongue.

Virginia (Mainland)
March, 1691

It was an early spring and wildflowers covered the hilly Virginia countryside, filling the air with the fragrant scent of azaleas, snapdragons, and oxeye daisies.

Will and Bridget had retrieved Apollo from Cobb Island

nearly a month before, and the two mares they'd purchased several weeks back were happily munching on the thick, damp carpet of spring grass behind the stable. The mares had both been the recipients of Apollo's romantic attentions, though the stallion appeared to have a preference for the butter-colored mare over her chestnut cousin. It was, however, too soon to know if they would be expecting foals next February.

Faylinn paused in her work in the garden to stretch her tired back. She leaned her hoe against the wheelbarrow and sighed, blocking the sun with the back of her hand and looking towards the west, the direction she expected to see Will and Bridget coming from.

"Don't worry so much, Faylinn," Katie admonished, walking over to the well and lowering the bucket into the cold water at the bottom. "They'll be back today."

Faylinn sighed and ambled over to Katie, who looked down at her belly and smiled.

"Your little one is growing."

Faylinn followed Katie's gaze to her belly, and she laughed. "He's going to be a big one, I'm afraid."

"Please," Katie scoffed. "I was twice your size with my boy Richard." Will and Katie's only child had taken ill as a teenager and died the previous summer, just before his seventeenth birthday, and the Beynons spoke of the lad often. "You're barely showing at all."

"You're not a very good liar, Katie," Faylinn grinned, unconsciously rubbing her rounded belly as she spoke. "No matter how big I am, it'll only get worse. I still have two months to go."

The bucket splashed into the water. "True." Katie made a face. "You've got the hardest months yet to come."

Faylinn groaned in remembrance as she thought of her previous pregnancy.

The heavy-set woman finished reeling up the water bucket and shoved a tin dipper into it. "Here." She passed the overflowing dipper to Faylinn. "It's cool, but the sun is bright. You can't forget to drink in *your condition*," she teased.

Mossy-green eyes rolled, their gold flecks glinting in the midday sun. "Not you, too! Bridget talked to you before they left, didn't she?" Faylinn accused with a mock-glare.

"Oh, that she did." Katie took back the dipper and took a long, satisfying drink. Breaking up the soil each spring was always the hardest part of gardening. "There's a long list of things that you're not supposed to be doing in your delicate state, and they include most everything except sitting on your arse and drinking lemonade."

Both women burst out laughing. They were used to Bridget and Will's tendency to hover over the blonde to make sure that she wasn't taxing herself, but it was still a source of amusement between them.

"I see." Faylinn sighed. "And am I allowed to continue with your reading lessons?"

Katie nodded gravely. "Only if I hold the Bible. It might be too heavy for one such as yourself."

Faylinn gestured wildly as she spoke. "Did you finally set her straight and tell her that I don't need to be pampered like a newborn?"

"And take away your chance to be doted on like a queen? I most certainly did not," Katie huffed. "I just shook my head and smiled." She demonstrated a completely insincere smile that caused Faylinn to be glad she hadn't lost any teeth.

Faylinn cocked her head to the side and listened. "Katie, do you—"

Just then, Will and Bridget appeared at the top of the hill, riding in the Beynon's small, mule-drawn cart.

"Bridget!" Faylinn waved.

Bridget's smile was visible from the garden as she waved back. She jumped out of the moving, rickety cart and walked beside it, rooting through the tools in the back until she came up with a large leather saddlebag, which she threw over one shoulder.

"Why don't you—" Katie stopped when she realized she was talking to thin air. Faylinn was already making her way across the homestead as quickly as her blossoming belly would allow. "Why don't you meet them and say hello?" she finished wryly, and leaned the dipper against the well.

Faylinn's grin grew larger and larger the closer she got to Bridget, who looked fit and nearly back to normal. The tall woman had, by any measure, had a terrible winter. The re-breaking of her arm had led to a blood infection that had lasted for more than six weeks and had Faylinn at her wits' end. Bridget had lost a shocking amount of weight, and her skin looked pale compared to the rich, exotic color it had been when Faylinn first came to Cobb Island. But all that seemed to be in the past now, as several weeks of good food and mild exercise had done Bridget a world of good. Faylinn couldn't help but admire her lean, muscular build as she watched Bridget's powerful gait speed her through the tall grass.

Panting slightly, Faylinn launched herself at Bridget, laughing when Bridget staggered a bit but still caught her easily. "I missed you!"

"Hello, dearest," Bridget greeted her joyfully, tipping back her broad-brimmed black hat and opening her arms just in time to catch Faylinn. "Whoa! I missed you, too." Bridget hugged her tightly, closing her eyes and pressing her nose into soft hair, before setting her bundle down gently. She laid a palm on Faylinn's protruding stomach and smiled broadly when she felt the baby kick hard enough to make her hand jump.

"Uff!" Faylinn's eyes widened a little at the sudden jolt. "Why must you make him do that? He's a baby, not a kicking mule," she complained, secretly pleased that Bridget continued to treat her pregnancy as though it were a cherished blessing. She rested her hand atop of Bridget's and stroked it gently.

Bridget cleared her throat and proceeded with her familiar correction. "*She* was just glad to see me and wanted to show it." Blue eyes twinkled. "Like her mama."

Faylinn nodded and locked eyes with Bridget. "Like me," she agreed softly.

Will rode by the women, intentionally making as much noise as possible by snapping the reins and stamping his feet against the buckboards. "Don't pay any mind to me, Faylinn. That's fine." He stroked his newly grown whiskers. "I don't mind a bit. I'm just passing through on the way to my lovely wife, who is likely to make me shave before I even get a kiss hello. But that's all right," he called over his shoulder. "Don't mind me."

Faylinn waved absently at Will, her eyes never leaving Bridget. "Hi, Will."

The man just shook his head. Those two only had eyes for each other. When Katie caught sight of Will's new beard, she turned on her heels and stamped into the house. He let loose a string of curse words that made even Bridget blush.

"Are you hungry?" Faylinn asked, wrapping her arm around Bridget's and guiding her towards the stables.

"Starving." Bridget slowed her step so that her stride would match Faylinn's. "We didn't take time to hunt while we were there, and I detest Katie's jerky, which is more fat than meat."

"Eww. And to think that I was eating fresh venison that someone, who shall remain nameless, killed, dressed and left hanging in the kitchen before she left."

"Sounds like you're a very lucky woman."

Faylinn stuck her nose in the air in a snooty gesture that unerringly drew both women's mind back to the life they'd left behind in London. "I think so."

"Except for one thing."

"Which is?"

"You're standing next to someone who smells worse than Will's mules," Bridget replied flatly. "I need a bath before anything else. Though you've been nice enough not to comment so far, I know that I stink."

Faylinn stopped and pressed herself up against Bridget. She made a show of sniffing the other woman's neck, then pressed the tip of her nose into the skin exposed by the V of her linen shirt. "You smell good to me," she growled, surprising herself with the sexy timbre of her own voice.

Bridget felt a bright flash of desire and swallowed hard. "I-um... You can kiss me there again," she squeaked as Faylinn's lips grazed her pulse point.

"All right," Faylinn answered happily, dropping another tender kiss on the spot. "But let's go inside first. I think Will is going to fall out of his cart if he leans over any further to watch us."

"Bloody pervert!" Bridget called out, drawing only a wave from an unrepentant Will. She chuckled, then drew a playful fingertip down Faylinn's nose. It came back sweaty. Now that she took time to look, the younger woman looked flushed. She pressed her palm against Faylinn's forehead as she checked for fever, not that she would know anything but the most extreme of fevers if she felt it. She did feel warm, and her hands and trousers were stained with dirt. She scowled and shot Faylinn a stern look. "You need a bath as badly as I do. You mustn't overdo it, love. I've asked you countless times to—"

"Don't you dare start that again. I was *not* overdoing, Bridget," Faylinn snapped crossly. "The garden won't plant itself, you know. With Will gone, Katie needed my help."

Sensing Faylinn's temper beginning to rear its ugly head, Bridget backed off. She wasn't about to risk not getting a good night kiss from her beloved. "Fine." But her tone made it clear she still wasn't happy.

Time to change the subject. She's barely home, and I don't want to argue. "Was the spot for the cabin as you remembered it?" Bridget and Will had gone in search of a meadow at the end of valley near a small lake that Bridget had come across while exploring the mainland the previous summer. It was two days' ride from the coast, beautiful, teeming with game and fish, and most importantly, it was very private.

Several times over the winter, men from neighboring farms had shown up unannounced, needing something or other and sending Bridget into hiding. After a difficult conversation with

Will, Katie, and Faylinn, they'd all decided that it was simply too dangerous to remain this close to town and Cobb Island. Katie forced Bridget to swear on her mother's grave that they'd come to visit often, and Bridget had easily made the solemn promise.

"The spot was just as I remembered it." Bridget smiled and draped her arm around Faylinn's shoulders as they continued to walk. "I was sure of its location, but I needed Will's help with digging the well since my arm hasn't regained all its strength. We won't need to live in such isolation forever, Faylinn. Just until people forget about Cyril's death, his sister the witch, and his wife's disappearance." They could never return to England, but just maybe... "Perhaps if we can raise enough horses to book passage to Scotland in a year or two..."

Faylinn smiled wistfully, remembering her family's beautiful ancestral home just outside Edinburgh. It was surrounded by fields of tall grass, and an enchanting forest lay just to the south. The estate held fond memories for her, despite the fact that, because she was born in London, even her own kin called her Sassenach when riled. "Maybe someday, when the baby wants to see where his people come from."

"Someday, *she* will like that," Bridget corrected with a chuckle. They entered the stables and her eyes automatically began scanning the stalls. "Apollo?"

"Out back, with the mares. I think it was a very good thing that you decided not to take him this week. He's gotten quite close with one of the mares, though he's mounted them both. He's—"

"Oooo, the randy slut!" Bridget's face lit up. "Excellent."

Faylinn's eyebrows lifted. "I can see I'll need to guard your honor with a sword should any eligible bachelor come our way."

"Hardly," Bridget snorted. "My heart is quite spoken for."

A tiny smile curled Faylinn's lips. "It is?"

"Of course! You know how I feel about Will," Bridget said with a straight face.

Faylinn bumped hips with her companion and ignored Bridget's burst of raucous laughter. "Aren't you clever?" But she was smiling herself.

Once inside their room, Bridget tossed the saddlebag on the straw-filled mattress with a great sigh of relief. A large, split barrel, whose sides had been lined with pitch and that served as a tub, was already sitting in front of the fireplace, three-quarters full of water.

Bridget groaned in rapture just looking at it. The lake she'd bathed in three days before had been just this side of freezing.

"I've died and gone to heaven, and we *know* that can't be right."

Faylinn giggled. "You said you'd be back by this afternoon. The water will only be room temperature, but—"

"It will be perfect," Bridget interrupted. She pulled Faylinn close again. "Just perfect. Thank you."

Faylinn's eyes fluttered shut as she reveled in the comforting feel of Bridget's warm embrace. She'd done a lot of thinking over the past week, and she'd made some frightening but necessary decisions that had her pulse racing. She was tired of being afraid, and determined to move forward in her relationship with her former sister-in-law.

Faylinn had craved Bridget's touch since she'd first seen her on the dock at Cobb Island, dressed all in buckskin atop a prancing Apollo. Since then her feelings had grown more and more intense, and she'd found herself wanting...something. Something more. Though she wasn't exactly sure what that could be.

They'd shared tender kisses and snuggled together nightly, but between Bridget's injuries, the resulting infection, and the nausea that had accompanied the early months of her pregnancy, things hadn't gone any further. To make matters worse, since Bridget had found out she was pregnant, the older woman treated her as if she was made of spun glass and would break under the slightest handling.

If I have to continue to wait for you to start...whatever it is two women can start, I'll go stark, raving mad! I've seen the way you look at me, Bridget. The way you react to my touch...my kiss. The way you watch me from the corner of your eye when you think I'm not looking. This, she decided, was something they both wanted. Now she just had to summon the courage to make it happen.

"Why don't we bathe together?" Faylinn suggested innocently. She fixed her eyes on the laces of Bridget's rough-spun shirt and gave them a gentle tug, holding her breath as she waited for an answer.

"Uh... Bu-bu..." Bridget mumbled stupidly, clearly startled. "Together?" *Since when do we bathe together? By God, that would involve being naked with her. I might die just thinking about it.*

"That way we won't have to empty the water after you're finished," Faylinn countered sensibly. "You did say we both needed a bath, if I recall."

Bridget tried to keep her voice even. "All right." She looked at the barrel. "It will be a tight fit."

"I don't mind being close to you."

Faylinn looked up into Bridget's eyes and the darker woman knew that all was lost. She would do anything Faylinn asked. She couldn't help herself. Bridget swallowed again, afraid that if she actually tried to speak she would ramble on like a dullard who'd never laid eyes on a pretty girl before, which was exactly how she felt at this very moment. *Get hold of yourself. You've seen her undressed before. Mostly.* "I don't mind that either, Faylinn." She smiled affectionately. "Though if you're going to join me, then perhaps I should heat the water."

Faylinn just shook her head. "I warrant our joined body heat will warm the water up nicely. I'm not worried." She bent over and stuck her fingers into the tub, then brought her hand back to Bridget's lips and painted them with the cool water. "It's not that bad, is it?"

Bridget's knees turned to jelly and she shook her head. "Not at all." Her voice cracked on the last word.

"It's settled then." Faylinn moved to a small trunk at the foot of their bed, praying her legs didn't appear as wobbly as they felt. Opening the trunk, she removed a large bar of soap and a scrap of linen. She could hear Bridget undressing behind her and felt her pulse quicken, but decided not to turn around. *Let her get into the tub. I don't want her to think that I... Well, I do want her to think that... Oh, God, I don't know what I want her to think!* She let out a frustrated breath and calmed her shaking hands.

"You were right," Bridget sighed, as she lowered herself into the tub. She could just barely stretch out her long legs, and she wiggled her toes in pleasure. Faylinn seemed to be taking her time at the trunk, so she dunked her head underwater and came up after several seconds, smoothing her hair back with both hands.

Faylinn took a deep breath and turned around just in time to see Bridget re-emerging from the water. "Oh, my." She nearly dropped the soap.

Bridget wiped the water from her eyes but didn't open them. "Aren't you coming in?" she murmured. "It's divine."

Unabashed, Faylinn stared at Bridget's wet, naked body. Firm breasts were half submerged in the cool water, and the room's partially open shutters allowed in just enough sunlight to paint golden stripes across glistening skin. *Divine is an understatement.*

Transfixed, she crossed the few steps to the tub and moved behind Bridget, bending to dunk the linen into the water. She settled on her knees, idly musing that men's trousers were more convenient for just about everything. Looking appreciatively at the expanse of naked skin before her, Faylinn soaped the wet cloth, then gently rubbed it over broad shoulders, dipping down for more water and repeating the process tenderly. This intimate act had become routine between them and neither woman wanted to stop it, even when Bridget's arm was healed enough so that she could easily take over the job.

Bridget forgot to censor herself, and a deep, lusty moan escaped her throat as nerve-endings all over her body flared to life under Faylinn's gentle touch.

The unexpected sound caused a flood of moisture between Faylinn's thighs and she shifted uncomfortably, recognizing these first strains of arousal as the familiar signals her body sent her whenever they kissed. Losing herself in the moment, she groaned quietly in response, then blushed when she heard herself.

Bridget completely misinterpreted the sound, and her eyes popped open. She realized the shorter woman's hands had stilled and felt a pang of guilt over taking advantage of Faylinn's kind-ness for her own pleasure. She reached up and grasped Faylinn's hand. "Thank you, dearest. But my arm is healed now." She hes-itated only briefly before forcing herself on. "I can do this from now on. You needn't trouble yourself."

"Trouble?" Faylinn's forehead creased. "But I like it."

"I like it, too." *More than you can imagine.* "You're not my slave. Come join me, instead, and have your own bath."

Faylinn frowned. She wasn't nearly ready to be done touch-ing Bridget. She leaned forward and placed her lips directly on a wet, pink ear and whispered, "Let me do your hair, Bridget. Please. I enjoy it so."

Bridget was glad she was already sitting down. The mael-strom of sensation caused by the warm breath in her ear was more than enough to set her blood aflame.

Faylinn didn't wait for an answer; instead, she lathered her hands and sank them into Bridget's hair, pressing firmly. Her ears were treated to the most delicious, subvocal sounds of pleasure from Bridget, and she wasn't sure which one of them was enjoying this more.

"Oh, Faylinn," Bridget sighed. "I'm leaving more often if this is how I'm treated when I return."

Faylinn laughed and tugged playfully on a strand of hair. "Don't you dare. I missed you far too much for that. Besides," she reminded, "I always wash your hair. I love how it looks when you wear it down. It's so...so..." She couldn't think of a word to adequately describe the wild, free look it gave Bridget that was so different from the elaborate, uncomfortable style fashion dictated, so she gave up trying entirely. "Rinse."

Dutifully, Bridget dunked her head. When she came back up for the third time, Faylinn laid warm, lathered hands on her shoulders and set to work on several stubborn knots.

"I do love you," Bridget said blissfully, letting her eyes slide closed again, and floating in that magical place where she was both aroused and relaxed at the same time. She'd done as much digging as her arm would allow, and now her body was paying the price.

"And I, you," came the familiar reply. Faylinn concentrated on relaxing Bridget, not speaking again until she'd given sore muscles her full attention. "Bridget?"

"Hmm?"

Her voice was barely a whisper, and she still spoke directly in Bridget's ear. "Did you think of me while you were gone?"

"Uh huh." Bridget nodded, her mind drifting. "Constantly."

"Does constantly include at night?"

A puzzled scowl chased lazily across Bridget's face. "Of course."

"Mmm." Faylinn worked her way lower, pressing her thumbs firmly into Bridget's spine, and earning another languid groan. "That's good. Because that's *especially* when I thought of you."

Blue eyes blinked open, and Bridget suddenly found herself very awake as welcome warning bells went off in her head. "Really?" she inquired gently.

"Oh, yes." It took all of Faylinn's willpower not to kiss the throat that was so cruelly tempting her with its softness. *Not yet.* "Katie is a sweet woman, but she doesn't come close to replacing you for companionship. Still, we did spend our days together, and that made them bearable. The nights were different. I was here all alone, with nothing more to do than think of you."

Bridget sat up a little more, leaning into Faylinn's expert touch, and exposing her nipples to the air. Faylinn's words and the drafty room caused them to grow painfully hard, and she felt her breathing quicken.

Gathering her courage, Faylinn ventured into uncharted territory, subtly shifting her massage to a lighter more sensual touch—a caress.

Bridget's nostrils flared as fingertips floated down her arms and then back up. *Yes, Faylinn. Do that.*

"I missed your body lying next to mine. The feel of your hair," for emphasis Faylinn ran her fingers through the soft wet strands, "your skin." She ducked her head and dropped a feather-light kiss on Bridget's shoulder, sighing softly at the taste and silken texture that made her want to devour this woman completely.

Bridget's belly clenched, and with dripping hands she reached up and grasped both sides of the tub. "Fay-Faylinn?"

The smaller woman didn't feel like talking anymore. She swept a tangle of dark, wet hair from Bridget's shoulder and began feasting on her neck.

"God!" Bridget's entire body jumped, and her chest heaved as Faylinn's lips wreaked havoc on her senses. She had never been kissed like that before. Not with such devastating sensuality, love, and affection, all at the same time. Who was this woman who had replaced the shy, mostly innocent creature she lived with, and how long could she stay? "Are... I-I can't believe I'm going to say this." *Please don't let me be wrong.* She let her head fall back, giving Faylinn more room to explore, which she did eagerly. "Are you t-trying to seduce me?"

Faylinn brought her lips back to Bridget's ear, letting any remaining inhibitions fall by the wayside and doing what came naturally. "Yes." She let her hands glide down strong arms and into the water, only to bring them up in front of Bridget. Faylinn ran them up a lean stomach to cup Bridget's breasts tenderly, feeling their weight lovingly as she firmly ran her thumbs over erect, sensitive nipples. "Mmm."

Bridget bit her lip in a vain attempt to keep from crying out as she arched towards Faylinn's hands. But the erotic touch proved too powerful and she let out a tiny whimper, praying fervently that Faylinn's newfound courage wouldn't desert her now.

"Is this all right?" Faylinn asked softly, the brazen seductress suddenly replaced by the gentle young woman who was still painfully unsure of herself in this arena.

"God, yes, Faylinn," Bridget breathed. Her hands moved to cover Faylinn's hand on her breasts. "That feels wonderful. Don't stop."

"I-I..." As though Faylinn suddenly realized exactly what she was doing, her eyes widened. She tried to pull her hands away, but Bridget held them firm.

"Stay, love. It's all right."

Faylinn stopped trying to escape and felt tears sting her eyes. "I don't know what to do," she whispered in anguish. "I only know that I want to touch you. I *need* to."

"Oh, Faylinn," Bridget's heart went out to her companion, and she cursed herself for leaving Faylinn to make the first move. She had meant to do it months ago. "You must know I want this, too. I want *you*."

"Have you ever—"

"Yes."

Faylinn's head sagged with relief.

Bridget blinked. That wasn't quite the reaction she had been expecting.

"Then you'll show me?"

Bridget felt her heart start beating again. "Yes. I'll show you." She turned around in the tub until she was facing Faylinn, then she tenderly cupped the younger woman's cheeks. She graced her with a smile full of heartfelt compassion and undying love. "You can touch me anywhere you like. *Anywhere*," she purred, her lips forming a hopeful, sexy smile.

Faylinn's eyes dropped, but her mouth shaped a small grin. She felt herself begin to relax as she grew more and more confident that Bridget wanted this as badly as she did. And that she wouldn't be left to fumble aimlessly in her ignorance. "Anywhere?"

"Absolutely anywhere," Bridget swore, lifting Faylinn's chin and forcing eye contact.

"Now?" Faylinn whispered, her eyes conveying her need.

Bridget closed her eyes. She wanted to scream, "Hell yes!" and simply ravish the pretty woman, but thoughts of her brother and his appalling actions held her back. *Patience.* "I pray so, dearheart."

Faylinn nodded, resolute. "Now."

Both women let out relieved breaths and leaned forward to share a deep, probing kiss that seemed to go on forever. When it ended, Bridget stood, sending a cascade of sudsy water down her body.

Faylinn dragged her gaze past well-shaped calves on her way up Bridget's body, taking in every inch of the lanky woman with sensual delight. When she finally reached Bridget's head, she allowed herself to be pulled to her feet.

The dark-haired woman looked down at the bath, then back at Faylinn. Raising her eyebrows in entreaty, she said, "Join me?"

Faylinn nodded shyly, already aroused beyond words. She lifted trembling hands to her shirt, only to have them replaced by steady ones.

"Let me," Bridget said huskily. Skipping Faylinn's shirt for the moment, she bent down and quickly removed her boots, stockings, and the pair of borrowed and patched men's trousers. The younger woman's shirttails hung to her knees, and Bridget suppressed a smile at how cute she looked as she carefully guided Faylinn into the tepid water.

The cool liquid soothed Faylinn's overheated skin, but any

pretense of rational thought was whisked away when Bridget began to remove her shirt.

Bridget took her time, her knuckles gently brushing over the lush curve of Faylinn's breasts and her fingertips moving purposely lower to stroke a round belly through the linen.

Suddenly the loose shirt seemed rough and hot against her skin, and was too much for Faylinn to bear. "Hurry, Bridget!" she insisted, her voice hoarse with desire. "Please."

Bridget smiled and pushed the thin material from Faylinn's shoulders. It pooled below her breasts, Bridget openly admired every inch of exposed skin in a way she hadn't permitted herself before, her eyes darkening at the arousing sight.

Faylinn held the material around her middle and looked up at Bridget nervously. "My stomach—"

"Is beautiful. Just as you are," Bridget assured her seriously. To prove her point, she dropped to her knees, sending a wave of water over the edge of the tub. Leaning forward, she lifted the tails of Faylinn's shirt, kissing every new inch of exposed skin, humming with undisguised delight and desire as she went.

Faylinn felt as though she was on sensory overload as wet lips traveled up her thighs. Her breasts ached, and her center throbbed in time with her heartbeat. This new, unknown level of arousal would have been frightening if it were not for the loving woman who had one arm wrapped tightly around her waist, grounding her.

By the time Bridget's mouth reached the apex of Faylinn's thighs, the blonde woman was whimpering softly, sure that her legs wouldn't hold her weight. She grasped Bridget's shoulders for support, moaning when lips softer than any she'd ever known skimmed quickly over damp, blonde curls, to lay a series of sweet kisses on the underside of her belly.

Never stopping her kisses, Bridget swept the shirt down over the flare of Faylinn's hips instead of lifting it over her hips, removing the garment completely.

With a tug of Faylinn's hand, Bridget guided her into the water until she was straddling her. Their combined mass sent more water sloshing over the edge of the tub, though neither gave it a second thought.

Warm thighs slid around Bridget's hips and she sighed at the contact, a wave of heated blood pooling in her belly. She picked up the linen rag from the edge of the tub and ran it over Faylinn's face and neck and shoulders, enjoying returning the gentle attention she'd so lovingly received all these months. Finally, she dropped the cloth and repeated the gentle motion with her fingertips, causing Faylinn to whimper at the sensation.

"Don't be afraid," Bridget whispered, leaning forward to kiss the tip of Faylinn's nose, her cheeks, and finally her closed eyelids. "I would never hurt you." She dropped her hands to Faylinn's waist, feeling the ribs expand and contract quickly at her touch.

"I know." Faylinn's eyes opened slowly and she gasped at the look of breathless desire on Bridget's face, knowing herself captured in the smoldering sea of vibrant blue. She loosely wrapped her arms around Bridget's neck, bringing their bodies closer together and feeling a tuft of dark, coarse hairs tickle her inner thighs and bottom as she moved.

They both smiled, feeling the importance of the moment but relaxing under each other's loving gaze.

Bridget sank her fingers into Faylinn's pale hair and drew their lips together, kissing her teasingly. She nipped first at her bottom lip, then her top, not stopping until Faylinn used the hands at the nape of Bridget's neck to crush their mouths together in a passionate frenzy. Hot tongues collided, tasting and stroking, each woman's urgent moans fueling the other's actions.

Remembering the feeling of soft, firm breasts in her hands, Faylinn sought to repeat the experience. She reached between them and rubbed her palms over erect nipples.

Bridget hissed as though she'd been burned.

Overcome with curiosity, Faylinn broke their torrid kiss and stared at the aroused flesh beneath her hand. Unconsciously, she licked her lips as a crazy thought entered her mind. She felt compelled to move forward, wanting to drop her lips...

"Do it," Bridget whispered hotly, Faylinn's thoughts merging with her own.

Faylinn glanced up quickly, blushing despite her wanton position, and understanding at once that Bridget had read her mind. The Redding family's abilities had been explained to her more than once over the past few months, and she'd accepted what it meant for her and for her unborn child with a measure of grace, courage, and inquisitiveness that stole Bridget's heart all over again. Faylinn had never imagined, however, how such a skill might come in handy in situations like this, and she found herself wondering how long Bridget had known that she desperately wanted her as a lover. "Can I?" she questioned for the second time that afternoon, needing to be reassured.

Bridget nodded, her heavy-lidded heated gaze burning a hole through Faylinn. Her nostrils flared gently. "Do it, before I do it to you."

Faylinn felt the words like fire racing over skin. She let out a primal growl and descended upon Bridget's breasts, fondling with both hands and kissing them from the outside in. She thrilled at how Bridget writhed under her lips and tongue, and at the feeling of skin so silky it melted in her mouth. When she reached a dusky nipple, there was no hesitation; she enveloped it in her hot mouth, rolling her tongue around it and purring against the exquisite flesh.

Bridget moaned loudly, her hips thrusting upward of their own volition as Faylinn continued to suckle her. The younger woman's teeth grazed the sensitive tip and she cried out again, wondering if she might come from this alone. When she could take no more, she put her hands on both sides of Faylinn's face and brought their mouths together for another incendiary kiss.

The last remaining vestiges of their inhibitions were washed away when Faylinn's thoughts made themselves clear in Bridget's mind once again. They mirrored her own needs, and there was never a question that Bridget would do everything within her power to fulfill her lover's deepest desires. Wasting no more time, she leaned forward taking Faylinn with her. "God, I want to make you explode," Bridget murmured.

The words barely penetrated the hedonistic haze that Faylinn was drowning in, but insistent hands broke her suction on Bridget's nipples. Her face was flushed and she shook her head in frustration. *Can women... I don't...* "I-I don't understand."

"You will," Bridget vowed, leaning forward and kissing the valley between Faylinn's breasts. Her other hand snaked down between their bodies and began stroking the silky skin of Faylinn's inner thigh.

Faylinn screwed her eyes tightly shut and braced herself by grabbing the side of the tub. A pressure was building deep within her so fast and strong she didn't know what else to do. "Oh, God."

Bridget turned her head and brushed her cheek against Faylinn's hypersensitive nipple before taking it into her mouth. She groaned against the luscious flesh, sucking greedily.

"Jesus!" Faylinn nearly spasmed out of the tub, but a long arm held her securely in place.

"Let me touch you," Bridget drew her fingertip over Faylinn's swollen lower lips, "here."

Faylinn swallowed hard and nodded. "Yes! Please," she begged shamelessly, her heart threatening to beat out of control.

Bridget stroked her relentlessly, feeling Faylinn's body begin to quake. The motion of her fingers never wavered as she kissed her way up from heavy breasts. She took her time when she reached Faylinn's slender neck, dipping her tongue in the hollow of her throat and kissing her pulse point gently, feeling the pounding of the younger woman's heart and the rushing of her blood against her lips. By the time her lips found a delicate ear, Faylinn's arms were shaking and their bodies were slick with sweat.

Breathing heavily, Bridget pressed her lips to Faylinn's ear and said the words she knew her lover needed to hear. "I love you. And it's all right, dearest."

Faylinn whimpered and let her forehead drop Bridget's shoulder as her hips took on a life of their own, moving against Bridget's hand.

"I've got you," Bridget promised. "Relax and let it happen."

Faylinn shook her head wildly. "I-I don't—"

"You do," she assured her, dropping a heated kiss on the delicate skin below Faylinn's ear. "Let me love you," she whispered. "Let me have all of you." Bridget moved her fingers slightly and began a massage of Faylinn's most sensitive spot.

Lips parted, Faylinn's eyes flew open and her entire body stilled, her white-knuckled grip causing the wooden slats in the tub to creak in protest. The pressure from within her built to the breaking point and beyond until, in one furious instant, the dam was shattered and her body began to quake. Her eyes clamped shut and she threw her head back, screaming as a powerful orgasm swept through her, threatening to tear her in two. She convulsed again and again, groaning loudly and sending more water cascading to the floor.

Faylinn's heart began to calm and she fell bonelessly against Bridget, still panting.

Bridget wrapped her in a tight embrace, thrilled to the core by her lover's response. She pushed pale, damp hair from Faylinn's eyes and kissed her forehead, quietly murmuring words of heartfelt devotion and love.

"Oh, my God," Faylinn whispered when enough blood had finally made it to her brain so that she could actually think. "We could have been doing *that* every night and you've allowed me to get by with only a kiss goodnight? What is *wrong* with you, Bridget Redding?"

Bridget let loose a rarely heard, full-fledged laugh. "I love you madly, Faylinn."

Faylinn found the strength to lift her head and look at Bridget. She quirked an eyebrow, then she kissed her soundly. "I love you, too."

"Faylinn?"

"Mmm?"

"You...um...   Well, you still want me to show you some things, don't you? *Now,* remember?"

Faylinn smiled at the hint of desperation that colored Bridget's words, well imagining the state she was in. She brought both her hands to her lover's flushed face and stroked her cheeks tenderly, giving her a dazzling smile that managed to show every ounce of the love she held in her heart. "Yes, Bridget. *Now.*"

Chapter
Twelve

Kayla and Liv blinked dazedly as Badger stopped talking, turned over his pipe, and tapped out the few shards of remaining tobacco.

Liv closed her sagging jaw and shook her head as she gave her horse a quick kick, sending him galloping away from the old man and Kayla.

"What in the—" Kayla turned in the saddle and watched Liv's flight across the grassy meadow.

"Better go after her, lass. I've got to get some water anyway." Badger lifted an old-fashioned leather bladder whose handle was made from woven strips of leather and dyed in the same colors as his kilt. He held it up and sucked down the last few sips of water, wiping a few errant drops from his beard. "My throat couldn't be drier."

"Wouldn't a regular canteen be easier?"

Their eyes locked and a wordless understanding passed between them. Badger bowed his head slightly, then winked. "Now you ken as well as I do, Kayla Redding, one of those shiny metal canteens, or worse yet, an awful plastic one, would ruin my lovely costume. What would the tourists think?" He reached down and absently stroked his mare's snowy mane. "Go on now. Find out what sent your lady tearing out of here like the Devil was on her heels. Or maybe you're just trying to stay around long enough to watch me climb down off this horse?"

Kayla paled. "No!"

"Your loss, lass." Badger grinned roguishly. "There's a clean stream at the bottom of the brae, just on the other side of the tree line. I'll see you there in a few moments." He reached back and patted his horse's rump, sending her cantering towards the trees.

Kayla rode over to Liv, who was talking to herself. Loudly. "What's up?"

Liv looked at Kayla as if the answer was obvious. "I can't believe it."

Kayla waited for Liv to continue, but the older woman simply crossed her arms over her chest. Kayla sighed. "Believe what, Liv?"

"Badger and that freakin' story! I was...you know." She emphasized the last word.

Kayla wriggled her eyebrows. "Well, you *did* ask. But even if their story is family lore, I have a hard time believing that they would ever tell anyone something so person—"

"That's not the point," Liv snapped.

"Are you expecting me to read your mind here?" Kayla put her hands on her hips, her patience quickly slipping away. "Because if you just tell me what has your panties in such a wad, it would really make things easier."

"The point is, I was riding along, listening to a man old enough to be my grandfather and who looks like Santa, talk about two dead chicks getting it on, and I was getting *hot!* I'm worse than Dougie, who is a walking breathing hormone. I'm sick," she exclaimed, thoroughly appalled.

Kayla bit her bottom lip.

"Don't you dare laugh, Kayla." Liv narrowed her eyes. "It's not funny. It's...it's yucky! I just ran the speeding chariot to hell right off the road so I could get there first. And now Christmas is ruined, too!"

Kayla couldn't take it anymore and dissolved into laughter. "Why did you ask, then? It's not like he offered to tell you out of the blue, you know."

Ignoring what she considered a rhetorical question, Liv shot Kayla a disgusted look, then noticed for the first time that they were alone. She glanced around. "Where's Badger?"

"He went to get some water from a stream over there." Kayla pointed to the spot in the heavy tree line where the sturdy man had disappeared.

"Why didn't you say so?" With a tug of the reins, Liv turned her horse around. "You know sex makes me thirsty." She guided her horse closer to Kayla until their thighs were touching but they were facing in opposite directions.

Kayla's eyebrows shot skyward. "But we didn't have sex."

"That's only because Badger is waving at us." Liv smiled at the man, who was sitting on his horse at the edge of the woods, patiently waiting. She waved back, then reached out with one hand and grabbed the front of Kayla's sweater, pulling them nose-to-nose. "We don't want to disappoint him, Kayla. He's used to catching us kissing. Plus," she shrugged one shoulder, "I'm horny anyway." She tugged hard on the sweater in her hand, stifling a surprised gasp, then a languid moan, with a deep, passionate kiss.

At Badger's urging, they all continued their ride, but in the woods. It was warmer and darker there, sheltered from the gusty afternoon breeze and protected from the bright sun, which was now mostly hidden behind gray clouds. The earthy smell of wet leaves and rich soil wafted up from their horses' hooves as they slowly navigated the large tree trunks and the jagged rocks that peeked up from the lush forest floor.

"There's someplace I want to show you, lasses. But first, I believe there was one last auld tale I promised to tell."

Kayla and Liv listened carefully as a strong, clear voice floated over them, taking them back in time...

Virginia (Mainland)
May, 1691

"How are you feeling?" Bridget dropped down onto the ground next to Faylinn and draped her arm over the smaller woman's shoulders. "Tired?" she asked sympathetically.

Faylinn let out an exhausted breath and looked up into the clear spring sky, wiping a trickle of sweat from her brow. "How much farther, Bridget?"

"Not far, love. A few more hours at the most."

"Thank God," Faylinn sighed. "Wait." She pinned Bridget with a withering glare. "Didn't you say that a few hours ago?"

"Yes. But this time it's really true."

They'd been riding for two and half days, on their way to the partially completed cabin Will and Bridget had been working on since March. The week before, Katie Beynon had walked in on the women unannounced, and the passionate kiss she'd witnessed could not be explained away. Days of confusion, arguments, frustration, and tears had led to the result that Will had foretold months earlier. Katie had searched her soul and, with watery eyes, came to the only conclusion she could live with. A physical relationship between Bridget and Faylinn was an affront to God, a sin that was to be repented of, not accepted. Even Will couldn't convince his wife to the contrary, though to his credit, he argued diligently on his friends' behalf.

Katie had offered to allow Faylinn to stay on alone so she could help with the birthing of her baby, but the blonde woman had refused without thought. Nothing in this life would separate her from Bridget. Not again. And so it was time to leave the coast, and the tiny haven they'd known since the fall.

"Can you ride some more? It will make the trip faster." They'd already added a day and a half to the trip, mainly because Faylinn had to stop and use the bushes every hour or so.

"If I must," Faylinn growled.

Bridget's eyebrows disappeared behind windblown bangs, her eyes going round. *Uh oh.*

"Please, Bridget, not that wounded look. I can't take that." She pinched the bridge of her nose and closed her eyes. "I have a headache, and my back has been killing me all day. I know I'm tired and grumpy."

Bridget's face took on a shocked expression. "You?"

Faylinn's eyes popped open and she sneered. "Yes, me. I know it's hard to believe." She let out an aggrieved sigh. "I'm sorry."

"I know. I'm sorr—" Bridget's words were cut off by an impudent hand.

"Don't say it," Faylinn warned her dangerously. "Don't say you're sorry. Not one bit of this is your fault, and if I have to say that *ever again* as long as I live, I'll scream. Besides," she managed a small smile, "except for feeling as if I swallowed an elephant, I'm truly happy." There was no comparing the love she shared with Bridget with her marriage to Cyril. So she didn't try to. "Even if I am acting like an ornery shrew."

Bridget saw Faylinn struggling to get up and jumped to her feet to lend a hand. "You're not acting like anything of the sort," she lied kindly.

Faylinn stood up straight and awkwardly reached behind her to brush off her trousers. Even Will's pants were now too small, and these were a pair Katie had made by cutting apart a pair of Will's old trousers and adding the material to the ones she'd already been wearing.

"Even if you were a shrew, I'd still have to say you were a cute one."

Tenderly, Faylinn reached up and gently traced the scar that ran from Bridget's eye down to her jaw. The thin, jagged line was the only visible reminder of her love's ordeal on Cobb Island. "You are a sweet woman, Bridget Redding. I selfishly thank God every day that you spurned the attention of Court's eligible bachelors, and that you came into my life. I love you."

That earned Faylinn a sunny grin that caused her heart to skip a beat. "Well," Bridget cleared her throat, a little taken aback by Faylinn's heartfelt declaration. "I love you, too. Now that's all settled," she teased, "are you ready to go? We're nearly there, I swear it."

Faylinn nodded, and the women spent the next five minutes settling her on the back of her gentle butter-colored mare, who was aptly named Jezebel. They'd left the second mare, who was pregnant, at the Beynon's homestead as a small token of gratitude for the kindness they'd been shown. Even now, Bridget and Faylinn harbored hopes that in time Katie would change her mind, and that someday they would be able to resume their friendship.

Will had seen them off and, as he gave her a parting hug, whispered into Bridget's ear that she should have in faith in the future. Faith that some day Katie would come around. Faith in their friendship. And so she did.

They rode in companionable silence for the next three hours until the sun hung low in the sky, a wash of crimson, gold, and pale purple. Faylinn turned her head to see an enormous smile on Bridget's face. "What is it?"

"You'll see."

Their horses climbed the last few steps to the top of a small hill and stopped.

Faylinn could only stare in awe as Bridget watched her nervously. "By God," she whispered.

"Well?" the red-haired woman finally prompted.

Faylinn shook her head a little. "It's-it's incredible."

Bridget let out a relieved breath. *Thank you.* "I hoped you'd like it. C'mon." She slid off Apollo's back and yanked off the rough wool blanket on which she'd been sitting. They only had one saddle and Faylinn was using it. She gave him a loving smack on the shoulders. "Go on, boy. Run around and get used your new home."

Not one to give up a chance to run unhindered, Apollo raced across the meadow, kicking up his heels wildly and swaying his head in delight. Bridget smiled at the beautiful beast. She turned to Faylinn's horse and lifted a dark eyebrow at her. "See how magnificent he is? Why aren't you pregnant yet?"

"Because she's smart!" Faylinn laughed. She bent down and petted her mount approvingly. "She's been carrying me and our saddle bags these past few days. She knows what extra weight really means. In fact..." With great effort, Faylinn threw one leg over the saddle.

"But—"

"She must be tired, Bridget. Let her play with Apollo for a while." Faylinn fell into Bridget's arms as the tall woman tried to help her down. "Uff!" She pushed a hand against her lower back and groaned at a spasm of pain. "One cannot go from no riding at all to days in the saddle without paying a horrible price."

Bridget chuckled, knowing all too well what Faylinn meant.

Verdant eyes flicked to the partially completed cabin in the distance. It sat on a clearing's edge, under a large, shady tree. *Too far? Nah.* "I can walk the rest of the way. I've been sitting far too long anyway, and it'll do me good," she pronounced, unwilling to hear any protests.

Faylinn drew in a deep breath of fresh air and nodded approvingly. She would, she admitted privately, miss the salty smell of the sea, but the scent of fresh blossoms, sweet grass, and the tiny lake she could barely see in the distance more than made up for it. Not that any of that really mattered in the end. She turned her head and watched fondly as Bridget stripped off Jezebel's saddle, blanket, tack and heavy saddlebags. She set them on the carpet of soft grass at her feet.

The mare whinnied in appreciation, then darted towards Apollo. When she reached the young stallion, her gait changed and she strutted past him proudly, earning his full attention. Then she bolted across the field at a full gallop, with the steed hot on her heels.

"Hussy!" Faylinn called as she felt Bridget's warm fingers wrap around hers.

"C'mon. Let me show you the cabin. The inside and outside are finished. Only the roof remains to be done. I'm not sure what we'll do for furniture."

"Are you as good a carpenter as I am?"

"Every bit," Bridget replied wryly.

"Uh oh." Faylinn covered her face with her hands and mumbled as she shook her head. "We're in deep trouble."

"But at least you won't be sleeping on the ground tonight. The last time Will and I were here we did some trapping, and I've some beautiful furs stored inside to keep you nice and warm." Bridget shortened her step to accommodate her lover's humorous waddle.

Faylinn stopped walking and stretched her back. "Soft furs sound wonderful. I—" Her eyes went round as twin moons, then her face twisted in disgust.

"What?" Bridget searched Faylinn's eyes nervously and clutched her shoulders.

"Eww! That was more disgusting than I remembered!" she complained loudly. Her fists clenched and unclenched rhythmically.

"What?" Bridget was at a loss until her gaze tracked Faylinn's. "You wet yourself?" Her voice conveyed her surprise, and her brows drew together in puzzlement. "You've gone to the bushes every ten minutes. How is that even possible? Even with as much as you drink, you should be empty."

Faylinn rolled her eyes and squirmed wildly at the nasty feeling of drenched legs and boots full of warm, sticky liquid. "By God, have you lost your mind? I didn't wet my pants!"

Bridget snorted rudely. "You don't have to be embarrassed, but it's clear—" Her jaw dropped and the blood drained from her face. "You're having the baby? Now?"

"Not at this *very* moment," Faylinn assured her, but she could see by the look on Bridget's face that her words weren't registering.

"Your water's broke," Bridget told her needlessly.

"Really? And to think I thought I'd merely wet myself like a one-year-old."

"This is no time for jokes!" Bridget spun in a circle and with outstretched arms, indicated her surroundings. "You're having it here? In the middle of a field?" *With no physician or mid-wife. No one to help. No medicines. Nothing!*

"How thoughtless of me," Faylinn deadpanned, an eyebrow lifting sassily.

"Faylinn," Bridget warned in a deep voice. "I'm serious."

"So am I, honey."

"But it's not time! Katie said we have at least two weeks, maybe three"

Faylinn rolled her eyes again. "Katie is not the one having... Ooooo," she hissed as a contraction rolled through her.

Bridget's hands shot out to steady her. "Are you all right?" She pushed down her impending panic. *Judith and Elizabeth's mother died in childbirth. And her screams... God.* She swallowed back the taste of bile, her body trembling.

"Bridget? Sweetheart?"

Faylinn's low, concerned voice and a warm palm cupping her cheeks cut through her mounting dread.

"Yes?" Bridget replied quickly. "We've got to get you to the cabin. We—"

"We do need that. But I need you to be with me, not passed out." Faylinn grabbed Bridget's hands and gripped them tightly. "Breathe," she reminded her. "Now, Henry was born fairly quickly. Or so that hag mid-wife kept telling me," she remembered wryly. "But it still took hours." She was about to tell Bridget to relax, when another contraction tightened her belly, causing her eyes to widen in surprise then pain. "Yeow!"

"Oh, God. Oh, God." Bridget's eyes darted around wildly, looking for the horses. The cabin was at the opposite end of the long, sloping clearing and she decided instantly that it was too far for Faylinn to walk. "Let me fetch a horse."

Faylinn nodded and awkwardly sat down. "You'd better make it Apollo. Jezebel will follow him anywhere, but doesn't listen well on her own yet."

"Apollo!" Bridget gave a sharp whistle, and across the field, the steed's snowy white head popped up. She turned back to Faylinn, expecting her horse to join her at her side. A few moments passed, while she continually asked how Faylinn was and her friend continually assured her she was fine, before Bridget impatiently glanced over to find Apollo. When she spied her horse, her eyes narrowed to slits.

The smitten steed was still at the opposite end of the clearing, rubbing his nose against Jezebel's shoulder, his mistress' command completely forgotten.

"Dammit, Apollo." She whistled again, and once again his head popped up and he slowly turned to find Bridget. "Leave that mare alone and get over here!" she called angrily.

"Oh." Faylinn's eyes clamped shut and she hissed loudly as another contraction with even more force worked its way through her, the pain beginning in her lower back and settling tightly in her lower belly. "Damn." Her hands automatically went to her back, and she realized with a start that what she had thought were aches and pains caused by riding for days were actually labor pains. And she'd been having those for hours. "Bridget?" She glanced up at her warily. "I think perhaps we should hurry."

Bridget paled and stood stock-still, staring at Faylinn.

Faylinn shook her head, suddenly glad that Cyril had gone to a local pub with his business partners and gotten drunk while she was in labor with Henry. He would have undoubtedly annoyed her even more than Bridget was doing right now, and she was considering killing her just because she could. She started to get up.

"Wh–what are you doing?" Bridget screeched, easing Faylinn back onto the grass.

"What does it look like? I don't want to have this child in the middle of a field, Bridget; I'm going to the cabin."

"You can't walk that far." Bridget's face suddenly reddened. "And I don't think I can carry you with my arm. Let me get

Apollo."

"I can—"

"No."

Faylinn sighed. *Be patient. Bridget's only trying to help. She's just afraid.* The blonde woman was well aware of how dangerous childbirth was, and she felt a pang deep in her chest at the possibility of leaving Bridget and the life they'd barely started together. *I won't.*

The muscles in Faylinn's abdomen tensed to what felt like breaking point, and she moaned long and hard. "Ugh!" When the contraction was over, she was seeing tiny stars; and she reminded herself to breathe or she'd be the one passing out.

The two horses were speeding through the grass, playing and stamping their hooves. Knowing she'd never catch him if he didn't want to be caught, Bridget didn't bother trying to chase him down. She took several long strides away from Faylinn, then stopped and roared at the top of her lungs, "Apollo, get over here now! Or I will run you through and turn you into a saddle for that slut Jezebel!"

Faylinn stifled a slightly hysterical giggle with the back of her hand.

Bridget whirled around and narrowed her eyes at the now openly laughing Faylinn. "You are not helping! He was trained by my own hand and has never done this before," she insisted indignantly.

"I think at the moment Jezebel can offer him something you can't, Bridget."

Bridget turned back around. Her voice was every bit as loud as before, but this time it held a note of menace that made even Faylinn blink. "Don't make me call you again, horse!"

Hearing the unmistakable threat in his mistress' voice, Apollo regretfully moved away from Jezebel and began trotting over.

"About time," Bridget mumbled as she bent to retrieve the saddle. Long fingers and strong hands got a good grip on the well cared for leather, and she hefted it, deciding it would be a good idea to give Faylinn something to hold on to as she led the horse to the cabin. Or maybe they'd go bareback. It would be quicker. She was spared the burden of deciding when Apollo galloped right by her at full speed, following Jezebel, who had decided she wasn't done with her play.

Violently Bridget threw down the heavy saddle and it made a loud thumping sound at her feet. "I'm going to kill you, horse!" She took off running after them, leaving Faylinn to stare in wonder at her lover, who had clearly snapped.

Faylinn leaned forward onto all fours then pushed herself to her feet, determined not to have the child right there in the grass when the cabin was close enough that she could see it. Her legs felt a little wobbly and when she straightened, she could feel that the baby had dropped, its weight pressing down between her legs.

The horses darted sideways and thundered past Faylinn at a dead run.

Bridget, who had nearly caught up to them, wasn't quite as adept at changing directions while running at full speed, and her feet flew out from under her. But that was all Faylinn saw as her eyes clamped shut with the force of her next contraction. They were coming quicker now, and her breathing was growing faster as she had less and less time to recover between pains. When she opened her eyes again, Bridget was at her side, covered in dirt, and grass stains. Faylinn reached out and plucked a twig off Bridget's shirt. "Are you all right?"

"Never mind about me," came the terse answer.

Bridget's breathing was rough and Faylinn caught a whiff of skin, rich soil, and perspiration, and for a long moment she drank it in with idle pleasure, forgetting about the pain.

"Faylinn?" Bridget's eyes flicked to her partner's bulging belly. "The baby?"

"We're fine." Faylinn's eyes tracked Bridget's, and she grabbed Bridget's hand and pressed it to her own stomach. "It's getting close." Her body instinctively bent over as another contraction tore through her, making her knees shake. "Argh...hurts."

Bridget let out a surprised breath at the feeling of Faylinn's stomach growing as tight as a drum under her palm. "Hang on, love." She felt useless and scared and wanted to kill her horse and...

Faylinn released a shaky breath as the contraction came to an end, and the long arm that had wrapped around her to help her maintain her balance gave her a gentle squeeze. "God," she hissed, sweat dripping down her throat and disappearing behind her shirt. *That hurts!*

Bridget heard the words in her own head. "I know," she soothed, pulling Faylinn close and saying a little prayer as she tried to calm her racing mind. *She has to be fine. She just has to. She deserves nothing less, and I can't...I won't live without her.*

Apollo came within twenty yards of the women before Jezebel stepped in front of him. They both stood motionless for several seconds before the white horse trotted up to his companion and rubbed his nose against her rear flanks. Jezebel moved forward a step or two and Apollo, like a lamb led to slaughter, was helpless to do anything but follow. He began sniffing her again, this time managing to do a much more thorough job.

"Uh oh."   Faylinn   recognized   the   foreplay   instantly. "Bridget, I think we can forget the horses for a—

"Bloody hell! Not now!" Bridget's shocked and disgusted voice rang out so loudly it stopped the noisy chatter of nearby birds and buzzing of countless insects, bringing a blanket of utter silence over the clearing. All except for the grunting and snorting coming from the horses.

"Ewww." Faylinn turned away from the scene, the absurdity of this entire situation causing her to burst into unrestrained laughter. "It's not as though you can compete with that for his attentions, love."

"I don't believe this," Bridget ranted. Part of her wanted to go over and pull Apollo from Jezebel, another bigger part of her knew that now would be a dangerous time to interrupt them. Her eyes dropped back to Faylinn, and she was unable to stop her smile. The younger woman was nearly hysterical with laughter.

Faylinn's laughter stopped as another contraction hit, and she tried to focus on Bridget's voice as she rode out the pain in the safety of her arms.

"At least Apollo chose well for his final activity before I kill him," Bridget said quietly into Faylinn's hair, feeling the smaller woman's body tense against hers.

Faylinn groaned as she was torn between laughing and crying out. "Do-don't make me laugh now," she said through gritted teeth.

"I'm sorry, love." But Bridget wasn't in the least.

When the contraction finally passed, Faylinn looked up to see Apollo sliding off Jezebel's back and stumbling away drunkenly. "God!"

Startled, Bridget jumped. "What? What is it?" Her eyes ran over every inch of Faylinn, searching desperately to see what was wrong.

"Already? I'm so glad I'm not a horse."

Bridget let out an unsteady breath, feeling lightheaded. "You are going to be the death of me, Faylinn. I swear you are." But now it was Bridget that couldn't help but laugh at her lover's exclamation. "C'mon, let me be your horse."

Faylinn put her hands on her hips. "What?" *You'd better not be suggesting what I think you are, Bridget Redding!*

Bridget rolled her eyes. "Climb on my back, love." Her gaze shifted upwards. The sun had fully set, its last golden rays streaking across the horizon. "It'll be harder for me to see where I'm going in the dark."

"I— Owww!" Another pain gripped her. "I don't know if I can."

Bridget nodded, and when Faylinn's wild panting began to subside, she knelt down in front of her. "Here. Just lean across me... That's it." She tightly grasped Faylinn's wrists, and stood slowly with the pregnant woman draped over her back. "Good Lord," she grunted under the shorter woman's weight as she began to walk. "Ouch!" Faylinn's knee somehow bumped her kidney.

"Don't make me kill you now, Bridget. I was just starting to think you might live through this."

Bridget didn't answer, instead she concentrated on taking slow steady steps and avoiding any potholes in the waning light. The sounds of the field seemed to intensify as she walked, Faylinn's heavy breathing blending with the chirping crickets and the thumping her own labored footsteps.

Faylinn laid her face against dark hair and tried her best to wrap her legs around Bridget's waist to make it easier. She could feel another contraction coming and tried to hang on through it, but it was too strong. "Stop, Bridget," she gasped. "Stop!"

Bridget immediately dropped to her knees, wincing as they hit the ground.

Faylinn pushed off her back and doubled over, almost managing to stifle a cry of pain as another contraction seized her, making her feel as though her body was being torn in two. Her face was flushed and her skin was covered in a fine sheen of sweat. Bridget laid a comforting hand on her back and the blonde woman reached for it blindly, threading their fingers together and gripping tightly as the pain swept over her. She could feel herself opening up, and the pressure mounting between her legs.

They repeated this procedure again and again until it was fully dark and Bridget stumbled the last few steps to the sturdy-looking cabin. Its two rooms, a bedroom and slightly larger common room, shared a stone fireplace. The only thing not completed was the roof, which consisted of a crisscross of wooden rafters. With an enormous breath, Bridget lowered herself to the ground. Both women rolled on to their backs panting, but for different reasons. The dark-haired woman caught her breath long before Faylinn did and stumbled tiredly to her feet. "I'll go back for our gear."

"No!" Faylinn shook her head wildly, feeling a sudden surge of panic. "Don't leave me." She could hear Bridget swallow loudly and felt herself being pulled to her feet. This time she was cradled in Bridget's warm arms like a baby, and carried into the cabin. It was empty, except for a large bird's nest sitting in the middle of the floor and a partially constructed door for the bedroom that had been left leaning against the common room wall.

Bridget's boots sounded loud against the wooden slats, and she tightened her arms around Faylinn when another contraction wracked her small form. "Here we are. Welcome home," she joked faintly, worry coloring her words. She shifted Faylinn until her feet hit the ground. "Wait here."

Faylinn wrapped her arms around herself. It had gotten cooler with the disappearance of the sun, and goosebumps broke out all over her body even though she was sweating. She closed her eyes and rocked back and forth, hearing Bridget stalk across the room followed by the rustling of cloth. Then a hand was grasping hers and leading her over to a pile of soft furs that had been spread out on the floor.

"I need to get these trousers off!" Her voice held a note of rising panic. "The baby— Oh, God!" She clutched her stomach.

"I know. I know. I'm trying." Frantic hands pulled off Faylinn's boots and stockings. Bridget tossed them aside and set to work peeling off her wet trousers, trying her best not to think about why they were wet so she wouldn't be sick on their bedroom floor. "Okay, there," Bridget mumbled to herself, but Faylinn was already sinking into the furs.

Faylinn was panting and Bridget pushed sweaty bangs from her forehead. "I'm thirsty," she said softly and the older woman cursed herself for not thinking to bring the water bladder.

Bridget stroked Faylinn's eyebrows tenderly. "Let me go get it. I can run and will only be gone a minute. All right?"

Faylinn's face was still for a moment as she considered telling Bridget not to go, but her dry throat got the best of her and she gave her a short nod. "Hurry."

"I'll be right back," Bridget whispered, fervently. "I swear."

"I know—" Bridget surprised her by kissing her firmly on the mouth before bolting from the bedroom.

Outside the cabin stood Jezebel and Apollo, contentedly chewing at the thick carpet of early summer grass. "There you are, my soon-to-be-dead horse!" Bridget grabbed Apollo's mane roughly and pulled herself up onto his back. A swift kick sent him galloping up the hill towards the saddlebags. "Faster," she urged him and the horse responded instantly, his powerful legs touching the ground so briefly that for a moment Bridget felt as though she was flying.

Panting, Faylinn tried to relax as the pain of another contraction subsided. She tilted her head back and looked up between the rafters into a blanket of twinkling stars. A tiny white light shot across the sky, leaving a trail behind it that sparkled like diamonds for just an instant before it was gone. She closed her eyes in wonderment, a smile tugging at her lips as she made a wish. The confusion and near desperation she'd felt during Bridget's long walk to the cabin began to ease, and she found herself better able to focus. "You've done this before, Faylinn. You can do it again," she told herself.

Knowing it was nearly time, she spread and hitched up pale legs, the soft fur tickling the bottoms of her bare feet. The urge to push was growing stronger, and just as she felt another contraction, Bridget burst into the room and set the saddlebags behind her back, giving her something to lean against.

Blue eyes gone silver in the moonlight dropped to the spot between Faylinn's legs. She let out an explosive breath. *I'm not too late. Thank God.* "Are you doing all right?" Bridget brought the water bladder to Faylinn's parched lips and the younger woman sucked greedily, having to stop when another contraction assaulted her.

"Oh," Faylinn murmured in pure relief when the contraction ended. "I am now." She took another drink, then passed the bladder back to Bridget. "I missed you."

Bridget drank deeply, then set the bladder down within reach before scooting next to Faylinn on the edge of the pile of furs. Then she reached back into their bags and pulled out a candle and flints. After a few tries, the candle lit, and she placed it just out of Faylinn's reach so she wouldn't accidentally burn herself. It cast the room in long shadows and illuminated Faylinn's tired face. "I missed you, too." When she looked back at Faylinn, their eyes met and the exchange of emotion was palpable. They each held the other's gaze and traded nervous but loving smiles.

"You look worse than I do," Faylinn said softly, her palm cupping Bridget's dirty cheek.

Bridget leaned into the touch and laughed quietly, knowing she was drenched in sweat and filthy from chasing Apollo. "Then I'm in luck. Because you look beautiful," she answered sincerely, running her fingers through Faylinn's damp hair.

Pale brows creased for just a second, then Faylinn brought Bridget's hand to her lips and kissed it softly. Her eyes never left Bridget's, and her voice was the barest of whispers. *"Tha mise Faylinn a-nis 'gad ghabhail-sa Bridget gu bhith 'nam chéile phòsda."* Faylinn's grandfather had taught her the language of her people as a child, and she smiled at the bewildered look on

Bridget's face.

Bridget shook her head. "I-I don't know more than a few words of Gaelic, Faylinn."

"Shh..." Faylinn kissed her hand again. "I know." Then she softly repeated the words in English. "I, Faylinn, take you, Bridget, to be my wife." Bridget's eyes went wide as saucers, but before she could say a word, Faylinn explained, "I won't have this baby born a bastard, Bridget."

Bridget opened her mouth a second time, but again Faylinn beat her to the punch. "I know, technically that wouldn't be true. But you'll help me raise this child, not Cyril." Heart thumping, she searched Bridget's eyes. "It's your words I want to hear. I know it won't be legal and is probably a sacrilege unto itself, but I want it anyway. I want you." *Please.*

Bridget swallowed past the lump in her throat and her eyes grew moist. "I want you, too," she said hoarsely. "You know that."

Faylinn nodded, feeling the ragged edges of another contraction, and she spoke quickly but with such astounding conviction that Bridget held her breath as she listened. *"Cho fad's a bhios an dithis againn beò."* She repeated it in English. "For as long as we both shall live."

Bridget wasn't sure she could speak, so she nodded.

"I wo-won't say *'gus an dèan Dia leis a' bhàs ar dealachadh'*, Bridget." She closed her eyes as the contraction hit her full force. "Because I won't agree to be separated from you, even in death." She whipped her head back and her hands shaped white-knuckled fists. "I need to push!"

Bridget's mind was awhirl, but she positioned herself between Faylinn's legs, seeing the crown of the baby's head through a thin layer of mucus. "The baby's coming!"

"You're telling me this?" Faylinn shouted angrily, as she began pushing, grunting with the force of her efforts. Her thighs quivered helplessly, and she couldn't stop it now even if she'd wanted to. Which she certainly didn't.

"That's it, Faylinn," Bridget encouraged, her face showing her wonder. "She's almost here."

With a mighty yell, Faylinn gave a final push and tiny shoulders slipped free, sending the squirming baby into Bridget's waiting hands. She gasped at the searing pain, and then at its almost magical absence as soon as the baby left her body.

"Good Lord!" Bridget fumbled the slippery infant, speechless as she looked at its wrinkled, red body.

"Bridget?" Faylinn said nervously, leaning forward to see.

"What's—"

The tall woman smacked the baby soundly on its bottom, earning a faint, choking cough and then a loud, lusty cry.

"Thank God." Faylinn nearly cried in relief, dropping back against the saddlebags so she wouldn't pass out.

"She is a he. It's a boy," Bridget laughed, not even noticing the tears on her cheeks that glistened in the candlelight. She looked at Faylinn and grinned stupidly. "He's beautiful."

"Toldja," Faylinn said smugly, knowing her own cheeks were wet. She sniffed, and wiped her eyes with the back of her hands when Bridget's face went blurry.

Bridget leaned down and kissed Faylinn's knee. "So you did." She reached over and grabbed one of the smaller pelts that Faylinn wasn't lying on and carefully wrapped the crying baby in it, taking time to cut the cord with the knife she wore at her waist. A final push by Faylinn, and there was nothing left to be done.

Faylinn ran her hands over the cap of blonde hair when Bridget laid the infant in his mother's arms. He looked very different from her dark-haired son, Henry, and tears filled her eyes again when she spared a long, loving thought for the sweet little boy she'd lost. "He's beautiful," she whispered, holding him close and kissing the top of his head, smiling when he immediately quieted.

"Toldja," Bridget repeated happily, pulling the soiled fur out from under Faylinn's lower body and replacing it with a clean one. Using the water from the bladder and a small cloth from their bags she cleaned up Faylinn the best she could.

Faylinn laughed and nodded as she repeated her lover's words. "So you did."

As soon as she was assured that Faylinn was as comfortable as she could be under the circumstances, Bridget moved so she could get a better look at the baby. She wrapped an arm around Faylinn and the baby. Both women watched in fascination as Bridget caught a tiny waving fist and allowed the baby to grab hold of her finger. "Hello, little one," she cooed, missing the beaming look of happiness and devotion Faylinn turned on her.

Faylinn reached up and with her fingers lifted Bridget's chin so their lips could meet in a slow kiss. "Thank you," she said softly, backing away from Bridget's mouth only a fraction of an inch. She said the words in her mind, knowing that her companion would hear them, and believing just as surely, she would repeat them for a lifetime.

Bridget's answering smile told Faylinn she was right, and the older woman whispered back the phrase she'd heard Faylinn use in passion and laughter, and through tears of joy and sorrow. She would never tire of it, and they were the only words of Gaelic she knew. *"Tha gaol agam ort-fhèin,"* Bridget said softly, her voice cracking with emotion.

Through a watery smile, Faylinn translated for the newest member of their family, who was cradled safely in both their arms. "I love you, too."

Kayla let out a long breath as she guided her horse around a tree. "That was some story," she admitted, not quite knowing what to say but finding herself in the uncharacteristic position of wanting to break the silence that had enveloped them after Badger had stopped speaking. They were riding single file now, with Badger leading her and Faylinn through the trees. A heavy fog had settled over the forest, and it was far denser at ground level. She couldn't see the lower half of Badger's horse's legs, though it was only a few paces in front of her.

Liv wiped her eyes and looked over her shoulder to smile at Kayla. She mouthed the words "Thank you," then turned back towards Badger. "I can tell you like that one." Several times during the tale, and especially when Bridget was chasing after her wayward horse, the old man had shook his head and burst out laughing.

"I must admit that I do, lass." He shifted in the saddle and stretched stout arms over his head, causing the leather to creak under his weight as he moved. "But there's no crime in a man having a favorite." He gestured to the left with his chin. "We're almost there now. Follow me closely because it's a tricky ride in this damnable fog."

Both women leaned forward a little in their saddles and their hands tightened around their reins as they rode down a small ravine, the horses' breath coming short and quick as they navigated the steep terrain. Several minutes more and they could hear hooves splashing through a stream beneath them, though they couldn't see the water.

"Ah. Just up ahead now." They came up on the far bank of the stream and rode into an area where the trees didn't seem quite so dense and the ground was flat. It was quieter here, too. Even the wind didn't seem to rustle the branches or the dead leaves.

"Whoa," Badger commanded under his breath, bringing his mount to a halt. He looked back at Kayla and Bridget, and they both dutifully covered their eyes as he jumped down off his horse and smoothed his kilt into place. "All right, ladies. I think Kayla is free from the risk of blindness now."

Liv laughed and climbed down off her horse, keeping a firm hold of the reins in her hand. "Should we tie them up?"

Badger shook his head. "No. They won't go far, and they know this land. Let them get a drink in the stream. It's been a long ride."

Kayla eased off her gelding's back and watched her horse trot after Liv's, back towards the stream. Badger's mare stayed right alongside him as he walked, his feet crunching loudly on the sticks and rocks that were scattered on the ground.

Near a tall oak tree, Badger stopped and peered down at the forest floor through the heavy fog. "I thought you'd like to see this." He looked around and drew in a deep, satisfied breath. It was good to be back, and he made a mental note to ride this way more often. "I haven't been here in a while myself." He turned inside himself for a moment, thinking hard before he gently cleared his throat. "C'mon girls, don't let the nostalgia of an old man scare you off and keep you waiting back there." He motioned them forward, and Liv and Kayla joined him. "We can't stay long, mind you. If you don't head back suin, you'll be riding in the dark."

"I don't see anything," Liv commented. She noticed Kayla was looking down. Her forehead creased and, curious, she followed Kayla's gaze.

A lone gravestone, about two feet high and carved from a thick slab of gray rock, poked crookedly out of the damp soil.

Liv and Kayla exchanged glances, and Badger moved away a few paces to let them look and discover for themselves. A hazy mist rolled along the ground, obscuring the words that were neatly carved into the stone in bold letters. But several seconds more, and the air around them cleared slightly on the heels of a breeze that smelled of earth and sodden leaves.

The stone read simply:

Bridget and Faylinn
1732

The elements had worn most of the face of the stone away, and the few words below the date looked indecipherable.

Liv crouched down and traced the words with a reverent fingertip, her mind easily filling in the missing Gaelic letters that time had erased. "Together They Found Peace."

Kayla knelt next to Liv and brushed a few leaves away from the stone's crumbling base. Her heart clenched as she felt an overwhelming sense of loss. By the death grip Liv had on her hand, she knew her partner felt the same way. They turned questioning glances on Badger, who was waiting quietly, idly stroking his horse's mane.

It was Liv who found her voice first. "Here?" she asked needlessly. "Not Virginia?"

"Ay." Badger gave his mare a good pat, then dropped his hand. "When their laddie was eight years old and big enough to travel, they booked passage back across the sea." His eyes softened in sympathy as he read the sorrow in Kayla and Liv's faces. "There's no need for that. No need at all. They died after a life well lived and well loved. And in the end, that's a far greater accomplishment than most souls can claim."

"They died together?" Kayla asked, noting the single year that marked both deaths.

"They did." Badger unconsciously looked towards an opening in the trees. Small bushes and trees grew there, but none of the towering oaks that they were under now. It was obvious that at some point, that spot had been cleared. "Even here they couldn't prance about as though they were free. Bridget was, after all, supposed to be dead and was branded a witch. And a letter from Judith Redding to Faylinn's family claimed that young Faylinn had disappeared in the colonies and was presumed dead as well."

He tucked his hands into his belt. "A small house stood there, but only the stone foundation remains today. The walls crumbled away over time. Behind it was a small stable." Now he smiled. "Bridget never did kill Apollo, and he and Jezebel came to stay there, and over time, so did their offspring, and so on.

"In the autumn of 1732, a thunderstorm ravaged the land and lightning struck the stable. Faylinn and Bridget were mostly past riding by that age, but Bridget, the stubborn thing, still kept a single horse to carry them back to Cobb Manor to visit their family and the servants of the house, who over the years became trusted friends. Or they'd ride back to fetch a grandchild or two they had a hankering to visit. You see, after he'd finally had a good taste of the wanderlust, their son and his family came to settle at the manor alongside Faylinn's kin. Of course, the entire family told Bridget and Faylinn they'd bring a wagon out here to get them whenever they desired, but the women wanted the freedom to come and go as they pleased, and you can't truly begrudge them that."

He sighed and looked down at the ground. "Anyhow... When lightning struck the barn, it went up in flames, and Bridget went

in to try and save her horse." His white head shook. Despite himself, his voice had taken on a hint of melancholy and he laughed
softly, thinking he was truly getting sentimental in his old age.

"And Faylinn went into the stable after Bridget," Liv said
bleakly, knowing in her heart she'd do the exact same thing.

"Ay. That she did, and neither one came out, which is exactly
as they'd have wanted it." He cocked his head to the side and
regarded the women seriously. "Kayla Redding, how long have
you been in Liv's company?"

Kayla's eyebrows jumped. "Not long."

"But long enough that you should've explained to her what I
know you know," the man admonished. He glanced back at Liv.
"The graves only hold their bones, lass, not their spirits or souls.
If that weren't true, then Kayla wouldn't be traipsing around the
world and encountering spirits herself now, would she? They
would all be trapped in their cold graves." He reached up and
took his horse's reins in his hand. "So, there is no earthly reason
for sadness. Faylinn and Bridget are every bit as much together
today as they were three hundred years ago."

Faylinn smiled, believing his words without question and
feeling a weight lift from her chest. "I suppose you're right."

Kayla and Liv examined the old gravestone one last time,
then headed back towards Badger, hand in hand. "What did they
name the baby?" Kayla asked, keeping her gaze on the ground and
hoping she wouldn't step someplace she'd regret.

"They named him Roderick."

She looked up and two sets of blue eyes met and twinkled.
"And what was the pelt they wrapped him in when he was born?"

The husky man threw his head back and let out a hearty laugh
as Liv looked back and forth between them, wondering what was
going on. "There's a reason you're so good at your job, isn't there,
lass?" This was, he decided, a very good day. "You already know
the answer to your question."

Kayla nodded slowly, a tiny smirk appearing.

Baffled, Liv gave her head a little shake. "Well, I don't!"

Kayla draped her arm over Liv's shoulders. "It was a badger
pelt, Liv."

Badger scratched his thick white beard and shrugged. "The
name stuck. Though both my mithers did tend to call me Roderick when they were comin' after me with a switch."

Liv's eyes widened and she began to stutter. "You-you're
him? You can't be him... You're Sylla's husband!" *And how
about the fact that Roderick would have to be dead? That's a
pretty damn good reason!* But one look into his honest blue eyes

told her he was telling the truth. She turned an accusing glare on Kayla. "You knew?"

"Not for long," Kayla assured her, squirming under Liv's stare. "I wasn't really sure until today."

"I never exactly said I was Sylla's husband. You just assumed that, and I let you," he admitted, an apologetic look on his face. "A little trickery on my part kept sending the poor man to the wrong place at the wrong time, so you wouldn't meet."

Badger fell silent, and turned his head away from the women as though he was listening to something.

Liv and Kayla went quiet as a slow grin spread across his face. He began to walk in the direction he'd been listening, talking as he went, and moving deeper into the fog. His horse followed closely behind him. "If you close your eyes," he told them, "and listen with more than just your ears, sometimes you can hear echoes from the mist around you. It's where all manner of things from the past live and breathe as though they'd never died at all." He drew his hand through the fog, and it swirled around his thick fingers. "Most people just don't bother to stop and listen." He paused in his trek and another smile touched his lips as he faced them.

Kayla and Liv were helpless to do anything other than smile back, as his words wrapped around their hearts.

"Can you lasses find your way back to the manor?"

"I-I think so," Kayla answered, wanting to ask him to stay but somehow feeling it wouldn't be the right thing to do.

"Good." He smoothed his woolen kilt with one hand and his eyes strayed back to the direction he'd been walking. "Because right now, those echoes are calling me home."

"You're leaving?" Liv looked around in confusion, searching for something to say.

Without another word, Badger and his horse took a few steps forward and disappeared into the hazy autumn air.

The women's horses trotted over to them and the sounds of the forest came gently floating back, leaving them to wonder if they'd ever really gone in the first place.

Kayla reached over and with a single finger clicked Liv's mouth shut. She smiled weakly at the other woman, hoping she wouldn't be too upset. "Surprise?"

Liv's eyebrows crawled up her forehead and stayed there. For a moment, she was truly speechless. She felt Kayla wrap her in a bear hug and eagerly returned the embrace.

"Are you okay?" Kayla whispered into fair hair.

Liv sighed and burrowed closer to Kayla, the warmth chasing

away her chill. She took a deep breath and closed her eyes, listening with her entire being as she opened her heart and mind.

Kayla's ability flared, and she could literally feel what Liv was doing. Her eyes slid closed too and she extended her senses beyond the here and now to what *could* be.

In the far off distance they both heard the faint echo of laughter. Badger's robust, lively chuckle was impossible to miss, but along with it was mixed two women's voices: one slightly lighter and gentle, and the other deep and true. They'd never heard them before, but somehow they were as familiar as their own reflections. A peace stole over them, filling them completely.

Liv looked up into Kayla's eyes and the voices faded away, leaving them alone together in the woods. "Yeah. I think I am okay," she said, meaning every word.

The breeze picked up a lock of blonde hair and Kayla tucked it behind Liv's ear, smiling the entire time. She knew that Edinburgh and the secrets it held would surely call them back again someday.

But for today, it was time to go home.

Don't miss the spellbinding

Cobb Island

Cobb Island offers not one but three romances in this novel set off the coast of Virginia. Marcy and Doug have had only sporadic contact since Marcy's family moved away a year ago. Their older sisters agree to supervise the lovesick teens during a week-long stay in an eerie island house that has been in Marcy's family since the late 1600s. But who will chaperone the chaperones? Sparks fly between them almost from the beginning, growing into lightning-size bolts when Liv notices that Kayla is answering her questions before she has even voiced them. It is Liv's training in translating foreign languages, however that proves to be the key that unlocks the house's secret history—and the story of a tragic love begun and ended four centuries earlier.

ISBN: 1-930928-39-4
Available at booksellers everywhere.

Be sure to read these other RAP books by
Blayne Cooper:

Madam President

By Blayne Cooper and T. Novan

It's the year 2020 and history has been made by Dev-lyn Marlowe—the first woman to win the U.S. Presidency. When it comes time to select a biographer to chronicle her historic term in office, Devlyn breaks with tradition and choses a writer based on very personal reasons. She wants Lauren Strayer, a young author whose writing has always captivated her. There's only one problem—Lauren isn't interested in the job.

Despite Lauren's reservations, the persuasive Commander-in-Chief is able to sway the author's opinion with the promise of true editorial freedom—a biographer's dream come true. Realizing that the opportunity of a lifetime awaits her, Lauren reluctantly accepts the position and soon finds herself residing at 1600 Pennsylvania Avenue alongside the First Family.

Caught up in the frenzy of life at the White House, Lauren begins to unravel the complex woman that is the President and finds herself more intrigued by Devlyn with each passing day.

Painfully realistic at times, funny, romantic, and endearing, Madam President is a drama set against one of the most dynamic backdrops imaginable and follows two lives destined to be entwined.

ISBN: 1-930928-69-6
Available at booksellers everywhere.

The Road To Glory

By Blayne Cooper and T. Novan

When Leigh Matthews finds herself lost due to an unexpected detour in her normal trucking route, she ends up in the middle of nowhere. As soon as she lays eyes on RJ Fitzgerald, however, a beautiful and intriguing handyman for a lonely country diner, she realizes that nowhere can be a very interesting place.

The Road to Glory is a story of two women and the bumpy road from *lust* to *love* and the multitude of varied turns along the way.

ISBN: 1-930928-27-0

Available at booksellers everywhere.

Also Available
By Blayne Cooper

The Story of Me
(written under the penname Advocate)

If you enjoyed the mad-cap antics of male and female squirrel in *The Road to Glory* then you'll want to read the crazy romantic-comedy that introduced the characters and started it all.

In *The Story of Me* Randi is just trying to make sense of it all as she sits in the park, pouring out her woes to a pair of squirrels. The first thing she determines is that she sucks at thinking up snappy titles. Hence, the prosaic name for this classic farce that is described as a free fall into insanity. In truth, it would be hard to find something better to call this screwball comedy, featuring the misadventures of a tall, dark driving instructor and the blonde nurse who is stalking her. Mac is intent on drawing Randi into a madcap plot to exact revenge upon a common enemy; the two-timing wench who dumped Mac for her brother, the doctor—and who, years earlier, deprived Randi of academic fame and a college scholarship. The ill-conceived plan takes them across America to Las Vegas. It's a 'road trip from Hell' that features a wild array of occurrences, ranging from mere mishap to outright disaster. Inexorably—delightfully—the women slide into an endearing, nutty relationship that was simply meant to be.

ISBN 059513744X

Other Books from
RAP

Darkness Before the Dawn
By Belle Reilly
ISBN 1-930928-06-8

Chasing Shadows
By C. Paradee
ISBN 0-9674196-8-9

Forces of Evil
By Trish Kocialski
ISBN 1-930928-07-6

Out of Darkness
By Mary D. Brooks
ISBN 1-930928-15-7

Glass Houses
By Ciarán Llachlan Leavitt
ISBN 1-930928-23-8

Storm Front
By Belle Reilly
ISBN 1-930928-19-X

Retribution
By Susanne Beck
ISBN 1-930928-24-6

Coming Home
By Lois Cloarec Hart
ISBN 1-930928-50-5

And Those Who Trespass Against Us
By H. M. Macpherson
ISBN 1-930928-21-1

Restitution
By Susanne Beck
ISBN 1-930928-65-3

You Must Remember This
By Mary D. Brooks
ISBN 1-930928-57-2

Bleeding Hearts
By Josh Aterovis
ISBN 1-930928-68-8

Jacob's Fire
By Nan DeVincent Hayes
ISBN 1-930928-11-4

Full Circle
By Mary D. Brooks
ISBN 1-930928-25-4

A Sacrifice For Friendship
By DS Bauden
ISBN 1-930928-30-0

These and other
Renaissance Alliance titles
available now at your favorite booksellers.

Printed in the United States
1156000004B/298-303